THE PERFECT GUEST

Ruth Irons grew up in South Wales before studying music at Exeter University, and then musical theatre at Central School of Speech and Drama. She worked as an actor, musician, and music teacher for many years before turning to writing as a creative outlet, completing courses with Curtis Brown Creative and The Writers Bureau. Ruth lives in Kingston-Upon-Thames with her husband and two daughters. *The Perfect Guest* is her debut novel.

THE PERFECT GUEST

Ruth Irons

Black&White

Black&White

First published in the UK in 2024 by Black & White Publishing
An imprint of Black & White Publishing Group

A Bonnier Books UK Company
4th Floor, Victoria House, Bloomsbury Square, London, WC1B 4DA
Owned by Bonnier Books, Sveavägen 56, Stockholm, Sweden

Paperback ISBN: 978-1-7853-0678-5
eBook ISBN: 978-1-7853-0677-8

A CIP catalogue record for this book is available from the British Library.

Typeset by IDSUK (Data Connection) Ltd
Printed and bound in Great Britain by Clays Ltd, Elcograf S.p.A

1 3 5 7 9 10 8 6 4 2

Every reasonable effort has been made to trace copyright-holders of material reproduced in this book. If any have been inadvertently overlooked, the publisher would be glad to hear from them.

Black & White Publishing is an imprint of Bonnier Books UK
www.bonnierbooks.co.uk

To Ollie, Heidi and Maeve.

Cambridge Dictionary

belonging
noun
UK /bɪˈlɒŋ.ɪŋ/ **US** /bɪˈlɑː.ŋ.ɪŋ/
a feeling of being happy or comfortable as part of a particular group and having a good relationship with the other members of the group because they welcome you and accept you.
A sense of belonging is one of humanity's most basic needs.

Chapter One

I sat in my car on the driveway, staring at the blinding white façade of the house that had sucked up the last of my overdraft. Once again, the words played in my head. *Why am I doing this?* And once again, the answer came back. *Because this is what normal people do. They go on nice weekend breaks and enjoy themselves with friends.*

My gaze remained on the house while my fingers picked at a spot of dried food on the thigh of my jeans. I should have found something clean to wear. This was the type of house where clean people stayed, not grubby, sleep-deprived, skint café workers. *Why am I doing this?*

'Oh, for fuck's sake,' I muttered to myself, flinging open the car door before the same words repeated and repeated again and again.

There were three other cars parked on the gravel driveway and now I noticed they were lined up in a neat curve that carefully mirrored the curve of a central, sand-stone fountain. I glanced back at my red Nissan Micra and its rebelliously perpendicular position, and squeezed the keys in my hand, about to head back and re-park it in line with the others. But before I could take a step, the front door of the house burst open and Megs appeared.

'Dinny! Oh my God, it's so good to see you!' She beamed, her lipsticked mouth showing large, bright teeth, and her caramel hair flicking around her shoulders in soft curls. I hadn't seen her in a couple of years and there were new lines around her eyes, but her forehead was smooth and I wondered if she'd had fillers, or whatever they were called. She pulled me into a hug and I smelt Chanel and Prosecco.

'Hi, Megs, great to see you too.' My voice sounded forced, and something sank inside me. I'd forgotten how tiring it was trying to match Megs' undiluted, relentless energy.

'Come in and check this place OUT.' She grabbed my hand, which still held the car keys. I balled it into an awkward fist, wondering if I should move the keys to my other hand or whether she'd let go of me soon.

She swung open a door to our left and I caught a glimpse of a large, plush living room with dark walls and coral curtains. 'Isn't it GORGEOUS?'

I didn't have time to take it in before she swept me towards an opposite door, and what appeared to be a sort of cloakroom.

'Not that we'll be needing that with this glorious weather! We've totally lucked out. I mean, I know it's June and it bloody well SHOULD be sunny but you just never know, do you?'

The wide, white corridor ended, and the space opened out. I felt my eyes blinking to adjust to the light and the beauty in front of me. Chevron oak floors stretched towards a glass-box extension at the back. To my right, oversized cream sofas faced a square cut-out fireplace that sat on top of a wide, sandstone ledge along which plants and cream candles were dotted. Above the fireplace hung a huge abstract oil painting of dark swirls and pin-pricks of light, like stars viewed from under a stormy sea.

'Dinny, my lovely.' Priya appeared from a door on my left that I assumed was the kitchen. She handed me a glass of bubbles and chinked her own against mine before leaning in to kiss my cheek. 'So pleased you could make it.' Her glossy black hair was pulled over one shoulder and she wore fashionable, thick-rimmed glasses. Her dress was pale-blue linen, and impossibly uncrumpled for a garment that had either been worn in a car or packed in a suitcase. But then Priya was the sort of person who hung clothes in plastic covers from the hooks in the back of her car – something I'd never done in my life.

'This place is just stunning,' I said, still gazing about, taking in the high lantern ceiling, and the wooden lintels driven into the wall to make up the floating staircase.

'Hats off to Megs for finding it and arranging the whole thing,' Priya said, raising her glass towards Megs.

'I do have an eye for these properties, don't I?' Megs said, with a smug grin. 'Remember that place in Greece?'

'Oh my God, that infinity pool,' said Priya. I didn't say anything, having not been invited to Greece.

'It's just such a shame Neve couldn't make it,' added Megs, marching into the kitchen. Priya and I glanced at each other and my insides clenched. I sipped my Prosecco and looked down. Megs reappeared with her own glass of bubbles. 'She would have gone crazy for this place.' She wrinkled her nose and took a large swig.

Priya stared meaningfully at Megs, who gave a sud-den flash of embarrassment. We all knew I was Neve's last-minute replacement, and that if her father hadn't been taken ill last week, she would have been here instead of me.

'Where's Rachel?' I said, trying to change the subject.

Priya nodded towards a set of metal-framed seats arranged in a corner near the wall of glass. Rachel was hunched over, clenching a phone to her ear and staring with a serious expression at a small metal sculpture that sat on the glass coffee table in front of her.

'So she won't take the bottle at all? Has Mum tried?' Her voice bounced off the hard surfaces and came to us in tense bursts. 'No, of course I'm not saying that; it's just perhaps if you let Mum try . . .'

'Longest she's been away from Phoebe,' said Megs, leaning towards me with a conspiratorial wink. 'I reckon she won't last the two nights and will be off home later. Priya reckons tomorrow. We've got twenty quid on it.'

'Shhh,' said Priya. 'Dinny's going to think we're awful. Stop it.' She nudged Megs but couldn't stop the sly smile spreading across her face.

'Oh, Din, if you reckon she'll stay till Sunday you can get in on it too – what do you think? Twenty quid?'

I felt a spike of panic. Twenty pounds. God, that was a lot of money. Well, to me it was. The idea of casually betting it away, as a joke, made me feel sick. But then the amount of money I'd spent to be here also made me feel sick. And then another thought occurred . . . I could win forty pounds.

'OK,' I found myself saying. 'Sure.' I gave what I hoped was a nonchalant shrug and Megs laughed and squeezed my arm.

Priya gave me an uncertain look. 'It's just a silly thing, Dinny, you don't have to . . .'

'No, I want to,' I said, my smile feeling forced and somehow manic on my face.

Priya gave a small nod and looked down into her bubbles. She knew I didn't have the bank balance the rest of them did. It wasn't like they were trust-fund babies – they didn't waltz around Oxford brandishing Daddy's credit card or anything like that. But they had extra funds that I didn't. They'd come to Oxford through private school, plus years of after-school tutoring and carefully chosen extra-curricular activities that looked fabulous on application forms. They also had that natural confidence born of charismatic parents and expensive education. That ability to tap a spoon against a champagne flute then deliver a perfectly charming, off-the-cuff speech to a room full of people without so much as a flushed cheek or a sweaty palm. That ability to tell a joke with the casual smirk of someone who knows it's going to bring the house down. I, however, was not one of them. I'd been coerced into Oxbridge meetings when I'd arrived at sixth form after comp and my teachers had realised I'd probably get straight As. There were no tutors, and no strategic extra-curricular activities – just a love of reading and a talent for analysing texts in a way English Literature examiners seemed to like. I also played piano reasonably well, but that wasn't because my parents wanted me to be a virtuoso; it was because I liked Elton John.

No one was more surprised than I was when I got the acceptance letter in the post. I remember the tears in my father's eyes, him squeezing my shoulder and sniffing. 'Oxford,' he'd whispered, almost to himself. 'Oxford.' My mother had made little squeaking sounds and fumbled for her reading glasses so she could read the letter again 'properly' with shaking hands. I see that moment in my mind's eye almost daily. Probably because it's the only time I've ever seen my parents look proud of me.

'God, someone get me a drink,' Rachel said, dropping her phone onto the coffee table and burying her face in her hands, her platinum bob falling forwards across her face.

'On it!' said Megs, dashing to the kitchen.

Priya walked over to Rachel and laid a hand on her back. 'What's the deal? Richard not coping?'

'Honestly, you'd think with my mum there too they'd be able to sort it out between them.' She shook her head and reached for the glass Megs produced, before taking a long sip of Prosecco. 'Perhaps it's still too soon. Perhaps I shouldn't have left them.'

'Look, Rach.' Megs perched on the arm of an orange chair next to Rachel. 'You deserve a break. This is a tough phase. I mean . . . obviously it was a while ago for me, but I can still remember it like it was yesterday. The sleepless nights, the bleeding nipples . . .' Rachel visibly flinched and I watched her hand move almost involuntarily towards her left breast. 'You need to let your hair down.'

Rachel nodded uncertainly, and looked up at Priya as she spoke. 'It's true. These first few months are tough – you've got to make a concerted effort to make time for yourself.' She rubbed Rachel's back as if soothing a child.

'The first time away is always really stressful. But it gets easier, I promise. I mean, these days I can just stock up the fridge for Doug and he's pretty good at getting them up and dressed and fed.'

'Great . . . so how many years have I got until that happens?'

'Oo, I'd say only about four or five?'

Rachel groaned.

'But if you wait even longer, they bugger off to university and you don't have to think about them at all!' Megs beamed. She always relished an opportunity to make light of her parenting journey. In truth, getting pregnant straight out of uni then raising a child on her own must have been hideous. But Megs was never the sort to dwell on trauma – she took her role as life and soul of the party very seriously, and the toils of single motherhood did not fit her chosen narrative. Of course, having parents with serious means who gave her a flat to live in had no doubt blunted the struggles most women would have experienced in her position. Part of me wondered if she recognised this, and if it was the reason she steered well clear of the 'woe-is-me' narrative.

Rachel, by contrast, was very good at woe-is-me. 'It's just so draining. It's constant, you know?' She sipped her Prosecco, a frown knitted across her pale face.

Megs and Priya nodded and murmured sympathetically. I experienced a familiar awareness that I had nothing to offer this conversation. Even an attempt at an understanding noise or comment would have felt insincere. At forty-two I had no children, and no partner with whom I was about to even consider them. I had left no nervous husband behind when I'd closed my door this morning, nor any instructions or lists or food for child-care providers. There was no one missing me, or waiting for a text to find out I'd arrived safely, or wondering what I'd instruct them to do if I were there. Tomorrow morning, there would be no beep from my mobile with *how did you sleep, sweetheart?*

I stood by the floating staircase, watching the montage of motherhood in front of me, bathed in white sunlight that flooded the glass-box conservatory, and I felt the usual othering of myself.

'Oh God, Dinah doesn't want to hear all this boring bloody mumsy stuff!' Megs came to my rescue with perfect timing. 'Let's get your bags in and show you your room. You're going to love it!'

Once I'd fetched my rucksack from the car, Megs whisked me upstairs, which was decorated in the same understated way as the living area. Large skylights illuminated pale walls that were dotted with paintings and various wooden items that looked as if they'd been brought back from exotic countries. The landing led to a square gallery surrounded by an oak bannister. Luscious plants hung from corners in macramé baskets, and sunlight from the glass ceiling shone down on a Moroccan-tiled area below.

'Games room and sauna down those stairs,' Megs said, giving me a wink.

'Wow,' I said, unable to grasp the sheer size and extravagance of the place.

She led me to a corner of the gallery, and a door next to a rattan chair that was draped with a white fur throw.

She swung the door open to reveal the most beautiful bed-room I'd ever seen. The light poured in through double casement windows and a glass door that appeared to lead out onto a wrought-iron balcony. A pale rug covered most of the floor, artfully distressed grey floorboards peeping out at the edges, and the huge bed was draped with a yel-low, tasselled throw. A modern, cut-out fireplace sported unburnt logs, entwined with fairy lights – a touch that seemed somehow childlike in this sophisticated environ-ment. An oak chest of drawers sat along one wall, a pale-pink dressing table along the opposite. To my left a pale wood door stood ajar, and I suspected from the white floor tiles I could see that this must be the en-suite bathroom.

'*Voilà!*' said Megs. 'What do you think?'

'It's gorgeous,' I said, still absorbing the artful seren-ity of the place.

'This is the smallest bedroom, I hope you don't mind?'

I let out an involuntary snort. 'I don't mind at all – it's about the size of my entire flat.'

Megs' phone beeped and she stabbed at the screen. 'Fuck's sake. Can't I go away for a couple of nights with-out work falling apart?' I watched her type furiously. 'Honestly, these bloody new graduates. Can't do any-thing without you holding their hand.' She looked up. 'Sorry, I'll leave you to it and deal with this downstairs.' She swept out of the room and I was left in silence.

One of the windows was open wide and a warm breeze washed into the room, trembling the leaves of the fern that sat by the door to the balcony. I closed my eyes and could hear the shush of trees outside, sprinkled with birdsong.

I dropped my rucksack onto the bed, wary of disturbing it, anxious not to imprint myself too heavily upon this perfect place, and spoil it with my imperfection. I trod lightly towards the balcony door and opened it. The structure was more of a fire escape than a balcony, only really big enough for two or three people. Tight, spiral steps led down to a patch of gravel below.

I dug into my jeans pocket and brought out a crumpled pack of cigarettes, closing the bedroom door before lighting up and leaning against the warm, black metal of the balustrade. Inhaling deeply, I felt the tingle of nicotine stretch through me. I leaned over the railing and looked to the right. The pale sapphire ripples of a swimming pool peeped from behind the corner of the house, and I heard a faint slosh of water, as if someone was dangling their legs in, just out of sight. Straight ahead of me was a boundary wall and, beyond, a deep gully with thick trees on the opposite side.

My phone beeped and I delved into my back pocket to retrieve it. It was Hen: *Dinah, where are you? Kate called saying you'd taken time off work. Let me know what's going on. Xx*

I took a long drag and exhaled slowly, trying to think what to type back. Perhaps *I'm 42, I can take time off work without my big sister's permission.* Or *you live in Aberdeen, why do you care about your sister in London taking a couple of days off work?* But I knew why she cared and why she was asking. Just as I knew why Kate and Hen had each other's numbers and texted behind my back to keep tabs on me. I tried to think of the most grown-up, least passive-aggressive thing to say. As I did,

I realised I was searching for the words a non-fucked-up person would say to a concerned sibling. It frustrated me how hard that was.

I'm fine, Hen. Just taking a mini-break with the uni girls! Gorgeous place. I'll be back on Sunday. Hope you're well. Love to George and the girls. Xx

Never mind un-fucked-up, that message sounded like someone else entirely had sent it. Hen was probably reading it, thinking I'd been taken hostage and someone had control of my messages. Sure enough, *beep*.

What do you mean 'mini-break'? You're completely skint and Kate said you were on your last warning at the café. Apparently you've used all your holiday up so what do you mean you've taken time off? Unpaid??!!

I didn't think so hard about the next message: *Fuck off Hen.*

I dropped my cigarette stub onto the floor and stamped on it before scuffing it over the edge of the balcony with my shoe. I told myself I'd collect all the stubs on Sunday and put them in the bin.

Back in the room I tipped my measly belongings onto the bed. I imagined Megs, Priya and Rachel lounging by the pool in their designer swimsuits with sheer cover-ups and oversized sunglasses. I held up my black swimming costume with the patches of brown where the elastic had perished. Kicking off my trainers, I wriggled out of my jeans and into the swimsuit, grabbing a pair of denim

11

shorts and scrambling into them. I looked at myself in the mirror of the pink dressing table, trying to remember the last time I'd worn either of these items. The swimsuit was basic with no support for my breasts or stomach, and the shorts were definitely tighter than they'd once been. A roll of fat bulged over the top, and I hoisted them up further so they sat higher around my waist, marginally improving my silhouette.

I pulled out a pink stool from under the dressing table and sat down, staring at my blotchy complexion in the mirror. My hair was a straggled mane, dark at the top and then bleached from about halfway down where it corkscrewed into unruly spirals. I crammed my fingers into my pockets, already knowing I hadn't brought any hair ties with me.

I scanned the table top, eyes going to a small box encrusted with shells and plastic jewels. It was a strange object for this tranquil room, just like the pink dressing table and the fairy lights in the fireplace. But then I remembered what Megs had said when she'd emailed me the details of the weekend. The house belonged to a family who rented it out when they were on holiday. It blew my mind that somewhere this pristine could be someone's normal, everyday home. But at least it made sense of the objects in here: this was probably a little girl's room. I imagined a bedspread with pink and yellow unicorns, and toys scattered on the floor. That made sense. They'd done the best they could to make it adult-friendly before they went away, but there were still signs of the owners' lives left like fingerprints. I stood and crossed to an oak wardrobe that stood in the corner next to the window, but when I pulled the handle, it was locked.

Infused with a vague disappointment, I sat back down at the dressing table, turned to the jewellery box and flipped open the lid. It could have been mine from my own childhood. Inside were tangled chains, a purple heart keyring, and a minuscule peach lip gloss that looked as if it had come with a magazine. I found what I was looking for at the bottom. A hair tie. It was orange, with a chunky plastic rainbow attached to it, but it was the only option, so I scraped my hair back and secured it into a bun. I stood up then, as an afterthought, and opened the top drawer of the dresser. There was a bottle of Body Shop Citrus Breeze spray, which I pumped liberally over myself before throwing the bottle back and heading downstairs to the others.

Chapter Two

When I emerged from the glass conservatory, I could hear voices from behind a long privet hedge. Through a gap, I spied a glimmer of blue and headed towards the pool. As I crossed the grass, I took a moment to look back at the house, the resplendence of the white walls and gleaming glass forcing me to squint. To the left I noticed a balcony, fronted by more glass and sporting ferns and snake plants in large terracotta pots, but I couldn't see into the room beyond.

At the poolside, Megs was reclining on a sun lounger, one leg bent and an arm shielding her eyes in a theatrical pose I didn't think could be sustainable for any length of time. Priya was doing lengths in the pool, her slender brown limbs slicing the water in practised strokes. She was someone who always did things properly. If she wanted to swim regularly then she'd have lessons. She'd never skip a lecture at uni. She ground her own coffee. I'd only seen glimpses of her as a mother, but I imagined she baked from scratch for every school cake sale and sewed name labels into every sock.

Rachel paced along the length of the opposite side of the pool, her phone pressed to her ear, still wearing the cropped trousers and denim shirt she arrived in. 'It's in the top drawer of the changing table . . . no, not that one, the one upstairs . . . yes . . . but make sure she's properly dry first or it won't sink in . . .'

I tried to imagine it but couldn't. Someone calling me from miles away because I had some expertise or knowledge they didn't, and they required my help. Someone needing me to tell them where to find the cream to soothe a baby's skin. Or some underling at work calling to pick my brains because they had an important meeting and wanted my advice. The only person who called me was Hen, and that was to check up on me, or to tell me I'd fucked up again.

'God, Dinny, your LEGS. I can't cope. Put them away and stop making us all jealous.'

I smiled at Megs and pointed a toe. 'What, these old things?'

She laughed and I felt a swell of gratitude. Megs always had a way of making you feel better by picking out positives. In my darker moments, I wondered why these women still bothered with me. When we were young and fresh from school, living in Oxford and preening at the power of our own potential, it seemed our trajectories might be similar. And for the others, they were. But while their stars rose, mine fizzled out. I discovered I wasn't a shooting star, after all; I was a wet firework, destined to lie in the damp grass and stare up at my twinkling friends.

But for some reason these bright, shining beings still tolerated me. We weren't as close as we once were – hence my being a last-minute replacement for a *properly* close friend – but I was still there, clinging to their tails. Sometimes I worried they laughed at me behind my back.

And maybe I *was* more of a source of gossip and entertainment than a real friend, but sometimes I didn't care. I mean, it's not as if I had a choice of friends. It's not like I would have had other offers if I hadn't taken them up on this holiday. I'd be back in Hounslow in my mouldy, rented flat above the electrical shop, weighing up whether to shut the cracked window to muffle some noise from the traffic and the pub opposite, or to keep it open to get some fresh air into the place. I'd be eating unsellable, stale muffins from the café for dinner, and drinking the cheapest thing available – tap water.

I sat on a grey wicker sun lounger and Megs sprang up from hers. 'Priya made a margarita mix, and God it's good!' She retrieved a large frosted jug from the shade under her lounger and a huge, plastic martini glass, pouring me a measure up to the brim then bringing it to me.

I took a sip and it was bitter and salty and so, so strong. 'That's delicious,' I said, taking another sip, the lime and ice cubes bumping against my lips and the salt stinging my tongue.

Megs grinned at me with mischief in her eyes. 'Told you.'

Rachel finished on the phone and Megs swooped towards her with another newly filled glass, squeezing her shoulder sympathetically as Rachel recounted the details of the phone call and the ineptitude of the people she'd entrusted her daughter to.

Priya swam to the side of the pool and rested her elbows there, looking up at the other two to listen to what was being said. Once again, I stayed put, knowing I had nothing to contribute.

I took another swig of my drink, then remembered I'd brought two bottles of cheap wine and scavenged a random assortment of pastries from the café by way of a contribution.

I got up and walked back inside, setting my drink down on a long, Scandinavian-style trestle table in the conservatory. The air in the house was cool, and my bare feet felt clammy against the hardwood floor. I retrieved the warm wine and sticky pastries from my stifling car, hoping they'd be acceptable if we ate them later today.

I set the bottles and box of pastries down on the kitchen island and surveyed the room. The window above the sink looked out towards the pool, but the view of the water was obscured by the hedge. The island was made of pale granite or marble, and silver threads ran through it like veins through sickly skin. A large, oval table dominated the floor space, but I wondered why anyone would eat in this room when they had the space and light of the conservatory. Perhaps they used this dining area for the bustle of the everyday routine. I thought of my bedroom upstairs, and imagined a small, pigtailed girl in school uniform crunching cornflakes at this table, her mother making sure her school bag was ready.

Instead of heading back the way I came, I walked towards an opposite door that led to a dark corridor. In a few steps the space lightened and I was standing on pebble-grey Moroccan tiles, looking up to see the huge skylight and balustrade above – the gallery where my bedroom was. I continued across the square hallway and opened a door that revealed a spacious games room with a pool table, dart board and table football. Another door concealed the steam room – a dark space with slatted wooden seats and an electric control panel near the door.

Under an archway was a long utility room with wooden shelves and a large chrome draining board. The tumble drier door was open but the appliances looked empty. Hanging from a wall hook were two men's shirts, and I approached, running my fingers along the stiff collar of the teal one. I don't know why, but I leaned in close and smelt the fabric. It smelt like any clean garment would – of detergent. I was hoping for more. A clue as to what the father of the little girl in the bedroom upstairs smelt like. I knew the girl smelt of Body Shop Citrus Breeze, as I did right now.

I retreated into the hallway and towards the final door. As I'd expected, it was a toilet. The walls were sage green, and trailing plants sat in front of a small, frosted window. But what caught my attention more than anything were the pictures. From waist height to the ceiling, the area was crammed with framed photos. My gaze darted about the room like a mosquito, unsure where to settle first, until at last it came to rest on a large photo directly opposite where I stood. The photo showed two adults and a toddler on a beach, wet sand underfoot and the tickle of a wave almost reaching their feet. The sky behind was grey but the family beamed at the camera, the mother holding the child, and the father resting his arm around the mother's shoulders. The woman's expression was serene and self-assured, her smile one of complete contentment. Her hair was a natural gold, and her prominent cheek

THE PERFECT GUEST

bones burnished by the sun. The father was cartoon-like in his good-looks – a kind of action man, Ken and Prince Charming all rolled into one. The chiselled jaw-line, the strong, slightly raised eyebrow, and the black hair, wet and swept back but falling into tousled per-fection, even down to the one stray lock that fell across his brow. I remembered the teal shirt in the utility room and imagined him wearing it.

Next to this photo was a black-and-white one of four women, cheeks pressed together, surrounded by fur and each with reflective ski goggles perched on their fore-heads. A framed poster above this read 'Sarah's 40th Bash!' in psychedelic seventies font, and next to it a photo of people in multi-coloured fancy dress, holding their glasses up in a toast towards the photographer. I realised the group was gathered around the swimming pool and the photo taken from one of the upstairs bed-rooms, or perhaps the balcony.

'Dinny, you in here?' Rachel's voice echoed from the hallway and I startled as if caught doing something I shouldn't.

I stepped out. 'I'm here. Just been to the loo.'

'Oh, sorry. I just came to find you and give you a hug! I've been so antisocial since you arrived.' She wrapped her arms around me and pulled me into her soft body. Rachel's hugs were never throwaway – they always felt sincere and meaningful. At the same time, they were entirely choreo-graphed by her, the end signalled by a painful clench of her fingertips into your flesh, which I'm sure was intended to be affectionate, but I invariably winced, unsure if she knew how uncomfortable her embraces were.

'So great to see you,' I said now, as she pulled away. How would she respond, I wondered, if I said *fuck, that really hurt!*

'You too, it's been too long.' We stared at each other then, and I looked down, clearing my throat. Rachel and I weren't particularly close. We wouldn't be friends if it weren't for Megs. Rachel had always idolised Megs, hanging on her every word, following her around like a lost puppy. I'd watched her earlier when she'd come off the phone to Richard: Megs imparting her nonchalant parental insights with a casual flick of her wrist; Rachel looking up at her adoringly, as if some of Megs' carefree wisdom might fall from her fingertips like fairy dust and be absorbed into her skin.

'Anyway, I think Priya's making dinner tonight so there might be some nibbles on their way.'

'Great,' I said, my stomach gurgling with hunger at the idea of 'nibbles'.

As we walked back into the main living area, I found myself glancing at the walls and shelves, scouring the place for more photos or family trinkets. I wanted to go back into the toilet to finish looking at the pictures, but as Rachel was effectively escorting me towards the others, I would have to wait until later.

Sure enough, Priya was in the kitchen. We both made offers of help but were firmly told no. 'I just need to get my head around things by myself when I'm cooking, you know?'

I didn't know. But then my idea of cooking was scattering chicken nuggets onto a baking tray and waiting fifteen minutes. Rachel's phone beeped and she wandered off, frowning at the screen.

I was about to leave too when I noticed something. 'Oh, I left some wine here . . .' I said, realising it was gone, and keen to let Priya know I'd actually contributed something to the weekend.

'Yes, I've put it in the fridge, looks lovely!' said Priya, with rather more enthusiasm than I felt Co-op Sauvignon blanc deserved.

'And these are some sweet things I bought from Covent Garden . . .' I placed my hand on the white box. I hadn't intended to lie, but 'bought from Covent Garden' sounded better than 'brought from the café in Covent Garden where I work' . . .

'Gosh, that's brave, bringing pastries all that way in a hot car.'

I felt a familiar stab of annoyance in my chest. I'd forgotten that phrase of Priya's. *That's brave*, meaning *what a stupid thing to do; I'd never have done that.*

I withdrew my hand from the box. I think she expected me to make a joke or something because she was still looking at me, smiling, but I didn't. I just turned and walked towards the door.

Her voice stopped me. 'I've got some cream we can have with them later . . . they'll be delicious.' The annoyance squirmed again, and I made myself smile, unable to say anything, but wondering what she'd do if I said *don't be so fucking patronising*.

I headed back towards the living room. Finding my now warm margarita, I downed the sharp liquid and

21

walked out to the pool. Megs and Rachel were lying next to each other on sun loungers, the jug of margarita mix between them.

'Mind if I top myself up?' I said, crouching to grab the jug.

'Not at all, that's the spirit!' chirped Megs, extending her own glass for more. I topped it up.

'Rachel?' I said.

'Gosh, no. I'll be on the floor if I have another one of those.'

I filled my own glass to the brim, quickly slurping at it so I could carry it without spilling, then setting the jug back down. Megs and Rachel were in deep conversation about maternity leave so I backed away and walked through the gap in the hedge, over the grass towards a copse of trees. The afternoon sun was still beating down and the heat combined with the alcohol gave me a hazy, distant feeling.

It was cool under the cover of trees, and the twigs and leaves were rough under my bare feet. There was a vague path forged through the undergrowth and I wondered how far the grounds of the house extended. But just as the thought occurred to me, the trees ended and the space opened up. In front of me was a flat expanse of green water. A huge pond, or a small lake, I wasn't sure which. A wooden jetty stretched from my bare feet out over the water, like an invitation.

I stepped out of the shade onto the warm, gnarled planks, noticing a battered boat resting in the reeds below where I stood. There was water in the weather-beaten hull, an old oar resting across the two benches.

The boat didn't look particularly watertight, and I wondered when it had last been used. I walked to the end of the jetty, sitting and slipping my feet into the frigid water, scattering diamonds of light across its surface. Dense trees encircled me, and I heard their whispering along with a sprinkling of birdsong. I sipped my drink and closed my eyes, trying to imagine that I had this sprawling house and garden to myself. That I lived here, and wanted for nothing, and could make myself a margarita and wander down to this jetty at any time I liked, to dip my feet in the water and think about nothing.

My phone beeped and I opened my eyes to retrieve it from my pocket. Hen.

Call me as soon as you can. We need to talk. You can't just disappear like this.

I clicked out of the message without replying and went into my contacts, finding the one I needed.

Hi Dad, how are you? I just wanted to say please don't worry about me. I know Hen's going mental, but honestly, I'm fine. I'm on holiday with some friends, and I'll speak to you soon. Lots of love, Dxx

I didn't text Mum. Her attitude to me over the years had settled into disappointed resignation, so I doubted she was clucking about like Hen, worrying where I was. I could see her in my mind, rolling her eyes with a 'what's she done now?' sort of expression, then shrugging and saying, *Hen, sweetheart, it's just Dinah's way. Leave her to it.*

Shaking off these thoughts, I swigged back the rest of my drink in three large gulps, placed my plastic glass down and stood up, wriggling out of my shorts and stepping towards the edge. My toes curled over the rough plank ends and I stared at the glistening surface, swaying as the alcohol hit my bloodstream. The water looked clean. Near the edges, reeds poked through the surface, and I wondered how deep it was. Did the reeds tangle and stretch towards the centre, awaiting the flailing limbs of swimmers? Was the bed soft soil, or strewn with jagged rocks? The light on the water twinkled at me, as if the ripples were winking, beckoning me. Swinging my arms over my head, I bent my knees and sprung forwards, diving into the icy water and feeling the coldness consume every thought in my head, obliterating everything in one blissful surge.

Chapter Three

'Dinny!'

The words were muffled by the water, distant but frantic. I opened my eyes and they burned against the cold, the surface above me distorting the cornflower sky. I pushed with my arms and broke through, treading water and wiping my face with my hands. A blurry figure was standing on the jetty, leaning forwards as if about to dive in too.

'What are you *doing*?' Rachel's voice was shrill and angry, and I imagined her in the school where she was Deputy Head, scolding a disruptive child.

'I'm . . . swimming,' I said, wondering if it was a trick question.

'You can't swim here! Didn't you see the danger sign?' She gestured towards a red metal circle on a pole at the base of the jetty.

'No, I didn't. But it's fine.'

'You don't know what's down there!'

'I think we can rule out alligators or sharks.'

She sighed, and I watched her jaw clench in exasperation. 'The sign is obviously there for a reason – it might be too shallow, or there might be sharp rocks, or reeds you could get tangled in.'

I swam towards the jetty and hoisted myself out. 'Well, I'm fine. Water's lovely.'

'I think in future we should all just stick to swimming in the pool.'

I looked at her furiously crumpled face and felt the full force of the passive-aggressive *in future*.

I shrugged. 'Sure,' I said, grabbing up my shorts and empty glass and walking back towards the house, Rachel scurrying behind.

There was no margarita mix left, so I opened one of the cheap bottles of white I'd brought. I offered it round but only Megs joined me, both Priya and Rachel saying they needed to 'go easy' for a bit. Megs and Rachel perched on bar stools at the kitchen island, watching Priya preparing three different types of salad in enormous bowls. There were only four of us and I wondered why she was making so much. I nearly made a joke about her thinking we were vitamin deficient, but they were speaking about Priya's dad's cancer op, so I kept quiet. Besides, I was still stinging from Rachel's reprimand. How dare she make me feel like a naughty child? We were all in our forties, for fuck's sake; who did she think she was, speaking to me like that?

I topped up my wine and slipped out of the room unnoticed by the others, and made my way into the living area. It seemed wrong to call it a 'living room' or 'lounge' because it was so vast and open, and yet somehow it had been made to feel homely and comfortable. Not like those awful billionaires' mansions you see on TV that look like hotel lobbies with glittering marble floors and chrome chairs that could be art installations. No, this was spacious but serene. The sofas looked soft and the cushions plump. A multi-coloured batik hung on one wall, and the chimney breast was flanked by bookshelves.

A brass-framed mirror hung on the wall next to where I stood, and next to that I noticed three photos hanging like a ladder from a piece of driftwood. It looked like a souvenir you might pick up at a seaside giftshop, with the wood and strands of knotted rope. A wall recess held a candle and an ornament of a bird, so I set my glass of wine down in order to inspect the photographs properly. The top one showed the ridiculously handsome man grinning into the camera with a young girl of about six sitting on his lap eating a pink ice cream. This must be the baby from the photo in the downstairs loo . . . the girl whose bedroom I was staying in . . . whose rainbow hair tie was holding back my damp hair.

The photo below showed the man and the golden-haired woman looking like a Hollywood couple, her in a long red dress and him in a tuxedo, his arm around her waist, fingers crinkling the fabric as he pulled her towards him. The bottom photo showed the three of them standing on the deck of a gleaming yacht, all wearing T-shirts that read *Turkey 2011*.

I felt my gaze penetrating the photo as if trying to project myself into the scene. As if trying to feel the heat of the Turkish sun on my skin and hear the lap of the salty water against the hull of the boat. The sway of the waves under my feet. I tried to imagine what it would be like to have been a child that got taken to exotic places for sailing holidays, or to be the parent of a child I could afford to whisk away to foreign countries, and share experiences like that with.

I heard a sharp crack and watched the glass splinter across the picture, slicing a diagonal line across the child's body, the mother's neck, and obliterating the father's face with a blood-streaked star.

I looked at the photo, uncomprehending. How had this happened? But then I realised the picture was no longer resting against the wall, and was instead clutched in my hands. I must have picked it up to get a closer look and somehow pressed too hard on the glass. The teardrop of blood that trickled down the father's body was mine, and I looked at the cut in my thumb before sucking it to stem the bleeding.

'Shit,' I whispered, looking towards the kitchen, hoping the others wouldn't come and find me like this. I set the photo back against the wall then grabbed my denim shorts, which I'd flung over the arm of the sofa when I'd come in from the lake. I wrapped the fabric around my bleeding thumb, gripping it hard. When the bleeding subsided, I dropped the shorts on the floor then picked up the photo again, twisting it around on its ropes and prising up the metal prongs that held the back in place. It popped out into my hand, and I pressed lightly with the other so the shards of glass slid out too. I carefully separated the broken pieces, laying them on top of each other on the shelf next to my wine, then blew on the photo to make sure no glass dust remained. I brushed the family's faces with my fingers, eyes searching their skin for any sign of damage, or blood. Thankfully there was none, so I pressed the photo and the wooden backing into the frame, bending the metal prongs into place once more. I set it against the wall again, comparing it to the photos above. Unless someone looked up close, I didn't think they'd notice the glass was gone.

Then I carried the slivers of glass out onto the patio, into the warm evening sun. I knew I couldn't get rid of them in the kitchen with the others there, and risk them asking what I was doing, so I slunk around to the side of the house, to the fire escape under my window. I deposited them deep in the greenery of a hedge, telling myself I'd retrieve them, along with my cigarette butts, before I left on Sunday. Then I walked back inside, grabbed my wine from the recess, cast one last glance at the photo, then slumped down on the cream sofa, feeling the cushions give beneath me as I sank into their soft embrace.

'There you are!' Priya said, emerging from the kitchen with a large bowl of salad and carrying it to the long table in the conservatory. She turned back towards me. 'Are those your shorts on the floor?'

'Oh, yeah. Sorry.'

'No problem.' Her steps faltered as she crossed back to the kitchen door. 'Just . . . are you in your swimsuit? Be careful on the sofas if you're wet . . .' Her mouth moved as if she wanted to continue but didn't know quite what to say.

'OK, Mum,' I said before I could stop myself, raising my wine glass in a salute. She cast her eyes down and scurried back into the kitchen.

I took a large gulp, wondering if she was at this very moment telling the others about my shorts on the floor, and my wet arse staining the precious sofas. And I wondered if Rachel would then reciprocate with a whispered account of what had happened at the lake, and whether the three of them would huddle around the kitchen island, rolling their eyes and shaking their heads. But why did I care? Why was I sat here with something akin to teenage fury broiling inside me when I should be past all this?

Because I *wasn't* past it. It was the same as it had been more than twenty years ago. That feeling of being talked about and looked down upon. The conversations that stopped when I walked into a room. The forced, overdone smiles when I spoke. The insufferable advice. That intolerable way girls have of swooping around the wounded sparrow and gleefully squeezing tears from it with heartfelt words and stroked backs and understanding nods. I didn't want any of that. I knew I'd made mistakes and I knew what needed to happen – I didn't need a sobbing fanfare of patronising friends to hold my hand.

I'd fucked up. It really was that simple.

When you start shagging a university professor, it's supposed to improve your marks, isn't it? That's what happens in the films. What's not supposed to happen is that the professor confesses to his wife, resulting in said wife persuading him to take out a restraining order against you when you turn up at his house to talk things through. But in the end, even without the restraining order or the letter from the university chancellor explaining I was suspended, I wouldn't have been able to carry on at Oxford. I wouldn't have been able to bear any more sideways glances or whispered remarks. And I wouldn't have been able to walk past him every day, or sit in lectures listening to him droning on, knowing he'd told his wife everything, and that everyone thought I was just another slutty student who'd slept with a member of staff. Because, make no mistake, he was still a member of staff. I'd been cast out of the 'Oxford club', but he'd been allowed to stay once a few fingers had been wagged in his general direction.

The look on my father's face when I told him what had happened, and that I wouldn't be completing my degree, is scorched into my memory as deeply as the image of him reading my acceptance letter. The proudest moment and the most ashamed. The polar emotions his younger daughter brought out in him.

I grabbed my phone from the oversized coffee table and looked at the notifications. Three missed calls from Hen, and another WhatsApp from her simply saying *Call me!* I clicked into the message I'd sent Dad earlier and stared for a while at the grey ticks. Unread.

My eyes began their familiar, unwelcome stinging and I gulped at my wine to push down the knot forming in my throat.

'Dinner's ready!' announced Priya, marching into the room with yet another salad bowl. I noticed she'd changed into a floaty, orange maxi dress with gold bangles at her wrist, her long hair up in a graceful chignon, and wondered when she'd had time to do that. When Megs and Rachel emerged from the kitchen, I saw they'd changed too, Rachel into cropped white jeans and a sheer, lime-green shirt, and Megs into a red halter neck top that made her golden shoulders look like something from an advert for tanning lotion.

I walked over to the dining table, still wearing my saggy black swimming costume, adjusting the material around my bottom and casting a glance at my discarded shorts before realising I couldn't put them on because they were stained with blood. None of the girls mentioned what I was wearing as I lowered my damp backside onto my wooden chair.

Megs took a selfie of the four of us, grinning, wine glasses aloft. When it beeped onto my phone, I opened it up and it really did look like we were all having the time of our lives. Old friends, reunited, rediscovering common ground. But the conversation around the dinner table was more of the same. Newborn rashes, breastfeeding, maternity leave, teenagers, incompetent husbands. I made sporadic comments like, *Wow*, and *Gosh, that sounds hard*, but there wasn't much room for me within their words. They barely acknowledged I was there.

I made a vague attempt to reminisce. 'Remember smuggling a bottle of rum into that Modernist Fiction seminar, Megs?'

To my relief, the three of them burst out laughing.

'Oh my God, did you?' said Rachel, holding an awe-struck palm to her chest.

'Well, it was so bloody boring, we had to do something!' said Megs, wafting her wine glass around in her coral-manicured hands.

But the raucous laughter ebbed away, and The Mothers resurged. 'Gosh, can you imagine drinking rum at 10 a.m. nowadays? I'd be asleep by lunchtime,' said Priya.

We ate the three salads, which I begrudgingly admitted to myself were bloody delicious, along with homemade falafels and brown rice. Priya then rose and went into the kitchen, returning with my pastries on a navy-blue plate, and a small jug of cream. She'd cut the larger pastries into several portions, presumably so no one felt obliged to eat a whole one.

'Hmmm, delicious, Dinny,' Megs mumbled through a mouthful of profiterole. I felt like a child who'd cooked for the first time, created an inedible mess, only to be humoured by well-intentioned parents. I don't know why I felt like this – I hadn't made the pastries myself. But they were my responsibility . . . my contribution . . . so I suppose I felt a certain ownership of them.

I loaded four of Priya's portions onto my plate and covered them with cream, suddenly desperate that there should be no leftovers, and that we should have to neither face them down again, nor have a discussion about whether to throw them out or keep them in the fridge for another night.

The surface of the choux still glistened, the cherries still looked succulent, and the pastry had held its form, but they were clearly not fresh fare. The textures were cardboard and the pecans soft. It became clear to me the further I chomped through my overloaded plate that I would not be able to finish what was there, let alone the remaining pastries. Megs had made a good attempt at her profiterole but it had clearly defeated her. Rachel had cleared her plate, but she'd only eaten a quarter of a chocolate torte, and Priya had waved her tiny fork around to demonstrate her eating of a pecan slice, but there appeared to be the same amount on her plate now as when she'd started.

I waited until everyone had set their forks down then sprang to my feet. 'I'll clear these and wash up, you guys relax.' No one objected. I piled up the dessert plates and cutlery, balancing the pastry plate on top of the teetering stack and marching with it into the kitchen.

I scraped all remnants of the disastrous pastries into the bin then fetched the second bottle of wine I'd brought with me and opened it. I was sure the others wouldn't want any, so I decided to drop the pretence that I'd brought anything they'd consider worth consuming with me, and just drink it myself. I poured a generous measure into a bulbous glass from a tastefully downlit display cupboard, only briefly wondering if one of the girls would appear and tell me I was using a glass I wasn't supposed to, from a forbidden cupboard. But then I heard Ed Sheeran drifting from the Bluetooth speakers in the conservatory and Megs' voice saying 'Come on, Rachel, don't be so lame – *dance!*'

I filled the sink with warm, bubbly water and began washing the dinner dishes. There was an empty dishwasher next to me but I wanted a reason to stay in here. I didn't want to be with them. I thought about university and how close we'd all been at the beginning of that first year, as bright-eyed freshers. Admittedly, Megs and I had always been more the hell-raisers, but I think we both used to play off the gleeful disapproval of Rachel and Priya. But perhaps Megs was ultimately more of a crowd-pleaser than I was. She'd rally everyone, buy a round of drinks, persuade us to carry on the party back at halls, that sort of thing. Whereas I'd more likely be found leaning over the bar when the staff weren't looking, trying to nick a bottle of tequila. I didn't do things like that hoping the others would notice and be impressed, but I couldn't help feeling proud when they told me I was *so naughty*, delight glittering in their drunken eyes.

But the delight wasn't there any more. I wondered if they'd invited me out of pity, knowing I had no money, no partner, no kids. But they knew this place was ludicrously expensive, so why would they ask me to come along if they suspected I didn't have the money? I wondered if they'd expected me to say no.

Placing the last plate on the rack and drying my hands, I contemplated going into the living area to retrieve my shorts, but I couldn't risk Megs trying to get me to dance. I would have been up for it earlier . . . perhaps just after my first sip of margarita, before the lake incident. But now I felt ridiculous. They were all in there in their designer finery, the embodiment of holiday chic, and I was in my ancient cozzie, belly round and soft with pastries and hair in a damp and tangled nest at the back of my head.

I topped up my glass again, aware that I was quite drunk and that it was probably best I didn't talk to anyone else this evening anyway, and walked out of the kitchen towards the back stairs.

The loo door was ajar so I went in and turned on the light, cradling my wine as I let my eyes drink in the photos I'd not had time to look at earlier. My gaze caught on 'Sarah's 40th Bash!' again, before I turned my attention to the rest of the pictures. Rosy-cheeked children blowing out cake candles, the bikini-clad mother . . . Sarah . . . reclining on a sun-yellow lilo. A blonde toddler attempting to hang a snowman bauble on a Christmas tree. I turned around and saw a framed certificate above the door. It read, 'Channel Swimming Association' in swirling serif font, and underneath, 'This is to certify that Isaac Arthur Rivers swam the English Channel, on 2nd September 2014, in 12 hours and 47 minutes.'

It struck me as insane that anyone would do something like that. That they'd even want to, let alone be prepared to put in the necessary training. Looking about the room I found what I was searching for: a photo of a dripping Isaac sporting a wetsuit and an exhausted smile, his hand held aloft in celebration by another man in a hi-vis jacket. Sarah was clinging to his side in denim shorts and a white blouse that stuck to her skin, translucent with moisture from their embrace. Isaac and Sarah. Sarah and Isaac. Mr and Mrs Rivers.

I took another glug of wine and left the toilet, turning off the light. 'Shut up and Dance' rang out through the hallway and I could hear Megs' laugh ricocheting off the walls. I walked up the back staircase to the gallery, but instead of turning towards my room, I approached a different door. Megs had given me a tour of downstairs but I hadn't seen the other bedrooms, and now I felt a burning need to.

I turned the brass handle and walked in. The room was bigger than mine, with plantation shutters and bare wooden floors, draped with artistically haphazard-patterned rugs. A large fern dominated one corner, next to an open, hot-pink suitcase. The clothes inside were in disarray, and several outfits were draped over the crumpled white sheets of the bed. Megs' room, I thought.

Halfway down the corridor I found another door, this one leading to Priya's room – I could tell as the pale-blue linen dress she'd been wearing earlier was on a clothes hanger attached to the shutters, still pristine and crinkle-free. The walls in this room were a dusky pink, and a large Scandinavian-style desk took up one corner, the shelves above occupied by coloured box files, trailing plants, and fat candles. I couldn't see out of the windows, and I didn't want to venture too far into the room, but I guessed it overlooked the front of the house where the cars were parked.

Rachel's door was opposite Priya's and seemed to be a mirror image, but with straw-coloured walls and shabby chic French furniture, with curved legs and embellished swirls. A large wooden sign hung over the bed, vintage letters reading *Boudoir*. The room had no personality at all, and screamed 'guest bedroom', mainly because of the clear French theme. I'd been in rich people's houses before and it seemed an amusing pastime of theirs to decorate a bedroom that wasn't needed to a particular theme that you perhaps wouldn't want to use in the rest of the house. I supposed that was the sort of thing that entertained you when you had more bedrooms than you knew what to do with.

The next door was off the landing at the top of the front stairs. Here the music was louder, and, looking down the floating staircase, I could just about see a swirl of orange fabric and bare feet. I kept back, away from the staircase, in case anyone looked up and saw me.

The door revealed a family bathroom, all beige marble and sparkling glass. There were perfect mini toiletry bottles lined up in the shower cubicle and expensive-looking handwash and lotion in evergreen bottles by the sink.

There was only one door left, and I turned the handle, confident no one could hear me as the music was so loud. But when I pushed, the door didn't budge. I tried again, but still nothing. There was a keyhole next to the handle and I raised my hand, feeling the ridge at the top of the doorframe for a key, but it wasn't here.

I felt an inexplicable surge of frustration. I'd looked in every other room in the house – I had to see this one. I suspected it must be the master bedroom which, I guessed, stretched from the front of the house all the way to the sparkling glass balcony at the back. I wondered if that was the balcony the photograph had been taken from – the one of everyone around the pool at Sarah's seventies-themed fortieth birthday party.

Bending down, I looked through the keyhole. Everything was white, but I was unable to work out if I was looking at carpet or wall or bedspread. I dug my fingernail into the flesh of my thumb, wincing as the pain from the glass cut shot through my hand. I wondered if I'd be able to pick the lock with something . . . a paperclip or hairgrip, maybe. Or perhaps the first thing I should do is try to find the key. Yes, I decided. That would be tomorrow's mission: find the key.

Chapter Four

When I opened my eyes the following morning, the first thing that came into focus was the empty wine glass on the bedside table. I blinked and rubbed my eyes, which were encrusted with sleep. Hitching myself up to sitting, I realised I was still in my swimming costume from yesterday. The door to the fire escape was open and a vague memory of smoking out there before bed flashed across my mind.

My mouth tasted stale and bitter, and my head felt thick and full, a dull pain pressing in around the edges. I got up and went into the en suite, splashed water on my face and brushed my teeth. I looked at my bedraggled reflection, the straggles of hair falling out of the hair tie, the dull brown irises set in bloodshot whites, and the mess of sun-darkened freckles that streaked my cheeks and nose like a grubby constellation. Splashing water on my face was not going to be enough this morning.

Untangling myself from my swimming costume, I stepped from the white tiles into the enormous glass cubicle, and twisted the black control. Cold water blasted from the shower head and I closed my eyes against it, skin tingling as the temperature gradually rose. I pumped soap from a black glass bottle and washed every inch of my skin. Then I used the shampoo and conditioner from the matching bottles, massaging them into my scalp slowly whilst the room filled with steam.

I wrapped myself in the biggest, softest towel I'd ever used, and wiped the mirror to peer again at my reflection, my skin now flushed from the heat and my eyes brighter and less tired. In the bedroom, I dug around in my rucksack and pulled out the only item I'd brought (actually, the only item I even own) that felt suitably Summer Holiday-esque. It was a knee-length black sun dress with hot-pink zig-zags running horizontally across it. I'd bought it in a charity shop about three years ago on a whim, but had never actually worn it. It was slightly too big, but comfortable. I decided to leave my hair down as it looked its best when I'd just got out of the shower and the frizz was dampened down. Propping my sunglasses on top of my head, I reached into the top drawer of the pink dresser and retrieved the Citrus Breeze, giving myself a quick spritz before heading out of the room.

I walked along the corridor towards the main staircase, looking around to check I wasn't being watched, before trying the handle of the main bedroom again. I don't know why I did it; there was no way it could have unlocked itself in the night. But I think I wanted to make sure I'd tried properly, and that it wasn't just drunk Dinny who'd not been able to open it. It *was* still locked, however – unsurprisingly. Last night's determination reignited inside me, and I remembered my promise to myself: I would unlock that door, somehow.

Downstairs, Megs was lounging in a wide, velvet chair in the conservatory, flicking through a magazine.

Rachel was sitting at the long table eating what looked like a croissant, and checking her phone.

'Morning,' I said, trying to sound chipper.

'Morning, Dinny! How are you, lovely? We were worried when you slunk off to bed last night,' Megs said, her hand frozen mid-page-turn.

'I'm fine, sorry about that. I just suddenly had a bit of a headache and didn't want to be a party pooper.'

'I've got painkillers if you need any?' said Rachel, looking up from her phone.

'Thanks, but it's gone now. I'm really OK.'

'Well, help yourself to breakfast. Priya was up at God-Knows-Why O'Clock so she went into the village and bought croissants and now she's swimming.' Megs rolled her eyes in an exaggerated manner and gave me a conspiratorial smirk.

'Thanks,' I said, once again feeling my lack of contribution and wondering what I could do. 'Is there milk? Would anyone like tea?'

'Oh my God, YES, I would kill for a cuppa,' said Megs.

'Lovely, thanks,' Rachel mumbled through a mouthful of croissant.

Buoyed by my new role as Provider of Tea, I went into the kitchen and rummaged through cupboards until I found a large rose gold teapot. I wondered if perhaps it was for coffee, but either way it was big and looked thermal so it would keep the tea hot. I put four tea-bags from a glass jar on the windowsill into the pot and boiled the kettle, then set four blue-blazed mugs on a tray and decanted milk into a white china jug. I even found a packet of sugar lumps in a pull-out cupboard, which I emptied into a small ramekin, then carried the whole thing into the conservatory. Priya had appeared, wrapped in a beach towel and drying her feet before she stepped into the room from the patio outside.

'Oh, wow, we all know we can rely on Dinny for a proper cup of tea,' said Megs, unfolding herself from the chair and throwing the magazine down on the coffee table.

'Well, hot drink preparation is my vocational speciality, after all,' I said, preferring to make jokes about my pathetic job rather than it becoming the elephant in the room. I poured the tea.

'And how's that going?' said Priya, taking a mug by the handle and supporting it underneath with her slender fingers.

I never really knew what to say when people asked me about my job. It was as if they were expecting me to say I was hoping for a promotion, or that I'd actually bought into the franchise and was now the owner of my own branch.

'It's . . .' I shrugged. '. . . going? I mean, there's not much to report really.' All three of them nodded and sipped their drinks. I looked down and filled my own mug, wondering if I should start waxing lyrical about the café more; perhaps I could say, *I get to meet so many new people every day, and it's low pressure, but keeps me active, and suits me down to the ground.* The problem is I don't think anyone would buy that. Because the truth is I hate it. I hate everything about it, from the rude customers, to my pompous boss, to Kate who snitches on me to Hen all the time, to the almost non-existent pay. And the thing I hate the most is that I really should be doing some-thing else. It's not like I don't have a brain. And it's not as if I was thrown out of Oxford two months ago and just need some time to find my feet. My 'disgrace' happened over twenty years ago. I really should have moved on and made an actual career for myself. But what chance did I have now? With a CV that showed nothing but a string of dead-end jobs and short-term temping contracts, what could I possibly go into?

'Have you been doing any tutoring?' Megs asked.

'Not recently, no,' I said, still gazing into my tea.

'I'm surprised at that,' said Rachel, her eyebrows knitted in genuine astonishment. 'I'd have thought all the A level and GCSE lot would have been beating your door down last term.'

'Well, I might get back into it in September,' I said, feeling my insides clench at having to justify myself.

'How do you advertise for pupils? You should put some posters up in local schools and libraries,' said Priya, draping her towel over a wooden chair before sit-ting down on it.

'Or social media, you know, local mums groups etcet-era. I'm sure you'd get loads of English Lit pupils that way,' added Megs.

I nodded, trying to look enthusiastic, or grateful, or whatever the hell they wanted me to look. Trying not to shout *I know how to make bloody posters and use social media; stop speaking to me like I'm one of your sodding kids.* 'There's actually a website I use that specifically advertises tutors to local families, so I'm good for pub-licity, thanks,' I said.

'Oh,' said Rachel, trying to hide her surprise. 'Well, that's perfect then.'

There is no website. There is nowhere I publicise.

In truth, the only reason I'd made even a half-hearted attempt at tutoring was because of a chance conversation one drizzly October day two years ago. One of the more chatty regulars at the café had mentioned her teenage son was struggling with *The Handmaid's Tale* for his A Level coursework. I casually suggested he should start by focusing on Offred's passivity compared to that of the other characters and see where that took him, when suddenly I found myself agreeing to tutor the boy for an hour a week. The mother then gave my name to a couple more parents and there were two blissful terms where I was earning enough extra money to save up for a third-hand Nissan Micra.

But things had become awkward with one family, and with them all being such close acquaintances, the others dropped me within a month of each other. Then I was too nervous to look for more tutoring work. I was worried my name had been sullied and no one would want me. It was a similar feeling to when I'd left Oxford. I wanted to hibernate. To scurry back into an anonymous cave where no one could find me or judge me. The problem was, I'd become so used to living in that cave that now I didn't know how to emerge, and feared what would happen if I did.

I pushed my chair back and made to walk out onto the patio with my mug of tea, desperate not to have to talk about my life any more. Desperate not to feel the weight of judgement and disappointment pressing down on me.

'The email said no crockery or glass out by the pool,' said Priya as I passed. I shot her a look and she glanced down into her own mug. 'Just . . . just so you know.'

I did a U-turn and headed back into the living area, grabbed my shorts from the floor and headed up the floating staircase with them in one hand and my tea in the other.

Looking down at the others, I couldn't resist. 'Am I all right to take a drink upstairs? Was that in the email?'

Three faces turned up towards me; none of them said anything.

I'd had a hazy impression of how the weekend would feel when Megs first invited me. I'd imagined laughing with the girls like we used to at uni, me and Megs trying to get Priya and Rachel to loosen up a bit, drink a bit more, maybe dance. I knew their families would feature heavily in the chat, and I was prepared for that. I imagined sympathising with their stories of parental anxiety and spousal frustration, but then cheering them up with amusing stories about ridiculous customers, and that they'd say I was *so naughty* whilst we laughed and laughed together.

I imagined that part of them would envy my child-free, husband-free, carefree existence. I was the one who was, after all, the most similar to the person I was when we all met, the most recognisable as twenty-year-old Dinny. I was, in so many ways, unchanged. But life had changed these women beyond recognition, and the Dinny who fitted in so perfectly with them when we were all twenty, seemed now to belong to a completely different jigsaw puzzle. Try as I might, I could not reshape myself to match their new curves and angles.

I know my life is pretty pathetic. But I thought that, in its simplicity, I might at least be able to pretend for a couple of days that it was something to be envied, when looked at through the eyes of these friends. But as the weekend wore on, I realised I'd been mistaken. There was no envy in their eyes when they looked at me, only pity. I was a creature to feel sorry for, and also to be kept in line. I was a liability. Someone to be mothered, and spoken down to, and kept an eye on. Once this realisation had fully settled upon me, I decided the best thing to do would be to stop focusing on them, and distract myself with something else: the key to the bedroom.

Once they were all settled by the pool, I began searching in the kitchen. Most of the drawers were immaculately ordered, and the one 'messy drawer' containing odds and ends only held two keys on an Eiffel Tower keyring, and neither were right – I was looking for an old-fashioned mortice key. My search of the games room was also fruitless, and the cupboards in the utility room only contained laundry detergent, cat food, and various household cleaning products and equipment.

I decided to search in plain sight, so headed to the living room. On the stone mantelpiece stood a photo of Sarah and the little girl when she was about eight. They were beaming, their faces pressed together, two brown smudges at each side of the girl's mouth, as if she'd just been drinking hot chocolate. In a terracotta bowl were two marbles, three drawing pins, and a small brass mortice key. My heart lurched but then I realised it was *too* small. My gaze fell on the built-in fireside cabinets. I tried one and, sure enough, the lock turned with a soft click, revealing stacks of old DVDs and CDs as well as fat cream candles. I ran my fingers down the spines of the films, reading Disney titles, *Back to the Future* one and two, a pregnancy Pilates DVD, and *The Remains of the Day* with Anthony Hopkins.

I heard the padding of bare feet and nudged the cabinet closed just as Megs appeared.

'Hi Dinny, what you up to?' she said, dropping her phone onto the sofa and sweeping her hair back into an effortlessly stylish messy bun.

'Just having a nose around,' I said.

'Properly gorgeous, isn't it? Can you imagine living here?'

'I actually can't. It's insane.'

'I know, right? We were saying we should come back again, but next time stay for a week. There's no way a weekend is long enough!'

'Ha, yeah,' I said, half trying to calculate how expensive a week in this place would be, based on what these two nights cost – but it made me feel queasy so I stopped.

Megs went off into the kitchen and I stood up and dropped the key back into the bowl, mentally walking through each room in the house and wondering where they'd most likely keep a bedroom door key. Of course it was perfectly possible the key was at this moment dangling from the ignition of a rented Mercedes as it wended its way through the Italian countryside or somewhere equally beautiful. I imagined the windows open and Sarah's hair being buffeted by the Mediterranean air.

I saw Isaac casting a loving glance in her direction before taking his hand from the steering wheel and resting it on her thigh, squeezing ever so slightly. The little girl in the back pestering for ice cream, and her parents promising they'd stop in the next village and look for a gelateria.

'Why don't you come and join us out by the pool?' Megs voice startled me. I hadn't noticed her walk back in.

'Um . . . yep, I will. I just need to change into my swimming costume.'

'OK.' She beamed at me and swept out of the glass doors with a large glass of iced water.

What happened next, I believe, set everything in motion. It's not that I blame this particular moment for what happened afterwards, or the things I did, it's just that if this thing hadn't happened, then I believe it's perfectly possible I would have simply returned to Hounslow the following day with memories of a slightly awkward weekend in a luxurious holiday house. And that would have been the end of it.

And the thing that happened is that Megs' phone rang. I hadn't realised she'd left it lying on the sofa, so it took me a split second to equate the electro-windchime music with that of a ringtone. I walked over to the phone and looked down at the screen, seeing it illuminated with the words *Sarah Holiday House*.

I twisted dumbly towards the glass doors but already knew I wouldn't have time to get the phone to Megs before the call ended. So I picked it up and pressed the green circle with hands that felt rubbery and unreal.

'Hello?' I said, heart thumping against my ribcage.

'Hi, is that Megan?' Her voice was soft but authoritative.

I swallowed, and made a nonsensical decision. 'Yes, speaking.'

'Hi, it's Sarah Rivers . . . the owner of the house.' Her tone was crisp and clear, even down the phone line.

'Oh, hi Sarah. Is everything OK?' I glanced towards the glass doors again.

'Yes, absolutely. Portugal's fabulous. But I hear you've got marvellous weather in the UK anyway, you lucky things!'

'Yes, it is really lovely.' I heard myself unintentionally mimicking her clipped tone, and wondered if she'd ever spoken to Megs before, and if she could tell the difference.

'Great, well anyway, I was wondering if I could ask you a favour?'

'Yes, of course.' I scurried down the hallway towards the cloakroom, slipped inside and pulled the door closed behind me.

'Well, apparently the cleaners can't get there until Monday now, so I wondered if you could turn the pool heater off tomorrow morning when you leave?'

'Oh . . . yes, no problem. How do I do that?'

'The pump's in the little shed behind the hedge . . . you know on the far side of the pool? Anyway, go in and there's a huge orange lever, can't miss it, just give it a yank down and that turns off the heat.'

'OK, that sounds fine.'

'Lovely. Well, I hope you're having a wonderful time?'

'Oh, yes, it's amazing. I mean . . . the house is just beautiful. You're so lucky.' I felt a swell of embarrassment at the last sentence, but I heard Sarah's grateful sigh and realised I'd made her happy.

'Thank you, yes, we do absolutely love the place. Make sure you leave us a great review online, won't you?'

'Of course, I'll defin—'

'Super, anyway, must dash. Thanks again.'

'No, thank you for—'

'Bye!'

I heard the beep of the call ending but seemed unable to take the phone from my ear. My heart still beat like a butterfly under a glass. I brought the phone down and stared at the screen, wondering if I should try and unlock it and delete the call. But then that would be weird if Sarah spoke to Megs again and mentioned it. It was better there was a record, then if Megs did notice the call I could just pretend I'd forgotten answering her phone.

I wasn't sure why I was over-thinking it, though. Sarah had only phoned to give a very simple instruction. I knew the best thing to do would be to take the phone out to the pool, give it to Megs and say, *By the way, Sarah just called and I answered because I knew I wouldn't get to you in time – she just wants us to turn the pool heater off before we leave tomorrow*. But I didn't do that. And part of the reason I didn't do that, was because I'd just become distracted by a corkboard attached to the cloakroom wall, upon which hung three rows of gleaming silver keys.

Chapter Five

I ran my finger along the rows of keys and watched them swing and tinkle. Most were unmarked, but some were clearly labelled with coloured tags and I read *Garage, Bike shed, Office, Pool shed*, and at the centre of the bottom row, attached to a silver mortice key, *Master bedroom*.

Slipping it off the hook, I pushed it into my pocket and left the cloakroom. I dropped Megs' phone on the sofa as I passed, and walked up the staircase to the landing. Then I stopped. I wondered if one of the girls might have slipped back into the house while I'd been on the phone. I listened to the silence of the house, then crept towards the French room where Rachel was staying. I knocked on the door and, when there was no reply, I went in, crossing to the windows and tilting the shutters so I could see out to the pool.

Megs was lounging in the same spot as yesterday, and Priya was sitting on the edge of the pool, dangling her legs in whilst reading a book. Some of the pool was obscured by the hedge, but as I watched, the water rippled, and Rachel came into view, sunglasses perched on her head as she performed an awkward breaststroke.

I pushed the slats of the shutters back down and marched out of the room, fingers clenched around the key in my pocket. Bringing it out, I pushed it into the lock, hearing the satisfying click as it turned. I slipped it back into my pocket, then turned the chrome doorknob, blood tingling in my veins as I pushed the door open.

The room was much larger than I'd expected, and pristine. The walls and carpet were white, and seemed to glow in the light that poured in through the sliding balcony doors. An enormous bed faced those doors, the oak frame upholstered at the head and foot, with rich blue velvet. There was another modern fireplace opposite the door, and to the right, an open door that led to an en-suite bathroom.

I heard footsteps at the bottom of the stairs and scurried into the bedroom, clicking the door shut behind me as quietly as I could and turning to take in more of the stunning room. I felt the plush carpet under my feet and curled my toes into it. Two huge-leafed plants flanked the glass doors and I headed to the balcony to look out. I watched Priya walking across the patio back to the pool with a glass pitcher in her hand, and three plastic wine glasses clutched by the stem in the other. I placed my palm on the cool glass, remembering how dark the room had looked from outside, and knowing that even if they looked up towards me, they wouldn't be able to see me. I had disappeared. The house had swallowed me up.

The balcony was large and square, with more plants in pots dotted on the sandy flagstones. I wanted to open the sliding doors and step out there, but I knew I couldn't risk the others seeing me. Of all my many misdemeanours this weekend, I knew that unlocking this forbidden room would be the one they most disapproved of, and I'd had enough disapproval for one weekend.

Turning my back on the glass doors, I took in the extravagance of the bed. It was colossal in size, and looked plump and soft with its Egyptian cotton covers, duvet tucked under the mattress all the way round, like in a hotel. I wondered if the cleaners were instructed to make it up like that. Brushed copper reading lights protruded from the bedside walls. The wall behind the bedhead was charcoal grey, and a huge macramé wall hanging stretched the width of the bed, the chunky, woven threads strung from a length of driftwood.

'Dinny!'

I froze. Megs' voice sounded muffled through the door but the following footsteps up the stairs were still unmistakable. *Why didn't I lock the door from the inside?* If I ran now and quietly put the key in the lock and turned it, would she hear from the landing outside? Probably. But that was stupid – why would I do that? Megs would know this room was locked, and it would be the last place she'd look for me. She'd surely try my room first.

I stood in the middle of the room, breathing hard, staring at the door and willing it not to open. I heard the footsteps pad away along the corridor and then a muffled knocking, and 'Dinny? Are you in there?'

I waited for what seemed like endless minutes, until I heard her footsteps get closer again, and then fade down the main staircase. I turned back towards the glass doors and watched Megs emerge into the sunlight, shrugging at Rachel and Priya and shaking her head. I desperately wanted to stay in this perfect, silent room and look around more. But I knew I was on borrowed time, and that if I stayed much longer, they'd get really suspicious. So I made my way back to the door, noticing as I did that my feet had left imprints on the carpet, like footprints in snow. They weren't dirty, just embedded there. I looked around the rest of the room and noticed the faint lines that had been left by a vacuum cleaner, and wondered what kind of strategy and forethought was needed to vacuum a room so the thick carpet looked as fresh as virgin snow.

I stepped out onto the landing and turned back to close the door, eyeing my footprints one last time. At least that had made the decision for me, I thought. I'd have to go back into that room again, if only to make sure I erased those footprints.

'We were looking all over for you!' said Megs when I joined them by the pool. 'You said you were going to put your swimming costume on and then you disappeared into thin air!'

I'd forgotten about that detail as I looked down at the sundress I was still wearing. 'Sorry, I went to get something from my car and got distracted.'

'Well, we were keen you didn't miss out on Pimm's!' she said with a grin, filling up a plastic glass for me. I knew for a fact that Rachel and Priya couldn't have cared less whether I missed out on Pimm's – I remembered watching Priya from the bedroom, clutching only three glasses as she took the jug out to the pool. I knew that Megs had brought an extra one from the kitchen when she'd come in to look for me. It had dawned on me that Megs really was the only one that gave a shit about me. And I decided that was fine, because after this weekend, I didn't much care for Rachel and Priya either.

I basked in the sunshine by the pool, drinking Pimm's and ignoring calls from Hen. Megs tried to tempt me into the pool but for some reason I didn't want to with the others there. I'd enjoyed my swim in the lake (until Rachel had turned up), but for me it was enjoyable because it was a solitary pursuit. I'd no desire to demonstrate a perfect front crawl, nor had I a designer swimsuit to show off.

Rachel and Megs cooked in the evening. They'd bought huge, ready-made pizza bases and topped them with peppers, feta and olives, and piled on torn mozzarella and grated cheddar. As we sat at the long table, tearing steaming slices of pizza with our fingers, I once again felt the pang of uselessness.

'Do we have any more of Dinny's lovely wine left?' Megs asked.

'No . . . I . . . I think it all went,' I said, noticing Rachel and Priya exchange a look. Rachel noticed me looking at her and looked down at her pizza.

'I've got some from the box of six I brought,' said Priya, and I wondered whether her mentioning 'the box of six' was supposed to be an attempt at shaming me for only bringing two bottles. The pizza suddenly felt claggy in my mouth and I had a panicked moment when I wondered if I was going to be able to swallow it. Priya appeared and filled our wine glasses with Merlot, and I took a swig to loosen the doughy mass in my mouth before swallowing it with a painful gulp.

After dinner, Megs dragged us all out to the poolside with plastic wine glasses, having decanted a bottle of wine into a plastic jug so it was in line with the No Glass policy. She set up a playlist on a Bluetooth speaker and danced to Maroon 5 and Toploader, laughing at how embarrassed her son would be if he could see her now. Priya and Rachel danced either side of her like faithful backing dancers, but with a tenth of Megs' energy. None of them attempted to get me to join them, and I think at this point they'd subconsciously let me go, in a way.

I hadn't set out to be the party pooper of the weekend, but by this point I had no energy left to make an effort, and to be rebuked again. So, as the sun sank, I perched at the edge of the pool, sloshing my feet in the water and looking up at the coral sky reflected in the darkening windows of Sarah and Isaac's bedroom.

In the morning, we ate another round of croissants that had appeared in the kitchen, and I made another pot of tea for everyone.

'It's SUCH a shame we have to leave . . . I'm just getting into it!' said Megs through a mouthful of pastry.

'What time is check-out?' Rachel asked.

'Email said 11 a.m.,' said Priya, who was back in her immaculate linen dress and designer glasses.

We gathered our belongings and Rachel stacked the dishwasher and wiped the surfaces.

'Don't kill yourself cleaning,' said Megs, tapping out a message on her phone. 'The cleaners are coming later; they'll sort all that out.'

'I know, I just don't want them to think we're pigs. And we don't want to lose our deposit.'

I suppose this would have been the moment to say, *Oh, by the way, Sarah called yesterday and we need to turn the pool heater off before we leave.* Or else I could have just gone to the shed myself and pulled the lever. But I didn't do either of those things.

It took me about two seconds to throw my rucksack in the car, but I leaned against the bonnet, watching the others fussing in and out of the house, wondering why they'd brought so many belongings for a two-night stay that didn't involve their children. When everything was in the cars, Megs stood by the front door and shouted, 'Bye, house! Thank you!' to appreciative titters from Priya and Rachel.

'OK, everyone got everything? I'm putting the keys back in the safe,' said Megs, pulling the door shut and dangling the keys from her fingers.

'Yep.' We all nodded and watched her cross to the corner of the porch area, shifting a pot plant to the side to access the small box safe that was attached to the brickwork.

I grinned through another of Rachel's pincer-like hugs as we all said our goodbyes. We thanked Megs for organising the whole thing, and I said how much I appreciated being included, resisting the impulse to use the word 'tolerated' instead. We all made the usual noises about how we 'must do it again soon' and how we really 'mustn't leave it so long next time', and when the social nonsense was out of the way, we walked to our cars.

I stood by the driver's side of mine, tapping away at my phone whilst the others blew kisses to each other and slammed car doors.

'You OK, Dinny?' Megs had opened her window and looked up at me through her sunglasses.

'Yeah, it's just I'm going to visit a friend on the way home so I need to work out the best route. Totally forgot until she just texted me.'

'OK, my lovely. See you soon, yeah?'

'Absolutely,' I said, opening my car door and sliding into the seat.

The three cars pulled away, Megs beeping her horn as they disappeared, one by one behind the high trees that flanked the end of the driveway.

I sat in my car, twisted round so I could keep my eyes on the entrance, waiting for one of them to come back because they'd forgotten something. One minute, then two minutes passed. I opened my car door and stepped back out onto the driveway, slamming the door behind me. Looking down at my phone, I scrolled through my inbox until I came to the email from Megs I was searching for. There it was, the subject title *Fw: Riverdean info*. Clicking into the email I scrolled further until I found the right paragraph.

Arriving and leaving
The keys to the front door are located in a small security safe behind a plant pot in the porch. The code for the box is 0310. Please place keys back in the box when you leave on Sunday, and ensure the box is

locked. The cleaners will be arriving late morning, so
please make sure you've checked out by 11 a.m.

I took my rucksack back out of the car, locked the car up, and approached the front door. Glancing towards the driveway opening, I half expected to see a car arriving, either belonging to one of the girls, or to the cleaners. No, I told myself, the girls were gone now. Their minds would no longer be on the holiday house – the sunbaked garden and the dancing ripples of light on the swimming pool, margaritas and late-night wine. They would now be speeding back towards their families or their jobs. Thinking about reading their kids bedtime stories to make up for being away, or what they were going to cook tonight, or what they had to prepare for that important Monday morning meeting. They wouldn't be driving up that drive again. And I had it from Sarah herself that the cleaners couldn't get here until tomorrow, so there was no reason for me to be worried about that.

I moved the plant pot and crouched down, rolling the metal digits under my fingers until the code was lined up, then pressing the release button. The front of the box popped open and I retrieved the keys, heart hammering in my chest as I replaced the plant, rose to standing and inserted the fat Chubb into the lower key hole, turning it until I heard the inner *clunk*. I took the Yale and slid it in, feeling a delicious sort of power as I twisted and pushed, feeling the door give way to me, allowing me, and me alone, access to this blissful sanctuary.

I walked back inside, feeling something relax in me as I turned and pressed the door closed. A sense of peace flooded through me, as if I was finally home. As if the house itself was welcoming me back, wrapping its luxurious arms around me and whispering, *Well done, Dinah. You did it. You got rid of them, and now it's just you and me.*

Chapter Six

Kicking my shoes off by the door, I walked through the corridor and into the open living space. The house was so quiet. There was no Megs throwing her head back and hooting with laughter, no Rachel pacing or whining into her phone, and no Priya bustling about with her superior levels of efficiency. It was just me, and the house. What made it even quieter, though, was the fact that all the doors and windows were now closed. That meant there was no shushing from the trees outside, nor any birdsong or the sound of the wind whipping ripples across the swimming pool.

I crossed to the glass doors and unlocked them, pushing them all the way back and feeling the summer breeze swoop in to thank me. Dumping my bag at the foot of the stairs, I crossed to the kitchen and found a small white china bowl that I took out onto the patio and set on a circular table. I delved into my pocket and brought out my cigarettes, lighting one and inhaling deeply, then blowing the smoke out towards the pool, lifting my feet to rest on the chair opposite, and basking in the sheer audacity of my actions. I couldn't help a short laugh escaping when I imagined what Rachel would say if she could see me now.

When I'd taken my time to smoke two cigarettes and had stubbed them both out in the china bowl, I went back indoors, and headed straight for the cloakroom. The key was exactly where I'd replaced it, in the centre of the bottom row, and I swiped it off the hook and grabbed my rucksack on the way towards the stairs. No back staircase for me this time, thank you, girls.

The door to the master bedroom swung open to reveal my snowy footprints still smudged into the carpet. Closing the door behind me, I threw my rucksack onto the bed and crossed to the sliding doors, unlocking them and pushing them open as I'd longed to do yesterday. I stepped out onto the warm, sandy slabs and crossed to the glass balustrade, leaning on top and taking in the view of the still pool below, the copse of trees that concealed the lake, and the sun-bleached fields beyond.

Along one bedroom wall was a fitted white wardrobe, which I opened. A subtle scent wafted over me, leather and sandalwood. Earth and smoke. I ran my fingers over the clothes and the hangers clicked together. There were light-coloured shirts on one side fading to darker hues, then trousers and jeans. I opened a drawer to rows of rolled-up socks, and another of folded boxers. In slots along the bottom of the wardrobe ran a row of shoes, perfectly polished and all black or tan.

Closing the wardrobe, a question hummed in my mind, but was answered when I noticed a door I'd not seen before next to the main door. It was ajar and I could see streaks of colour through the gap. Crossing towards it, I pushed it open to reveal not a cupboard, but a small *room*, solely for the purpose of storing clothes. I'd never seen a walk-in wardrobe before in real life, and the sheer opulence of it took my breath away. It was about the size of my childhood bedroom. Clothes hung along three walls, and underneath a row of shirts opposite where I stood, there was a chunky white chest of drawers. Above the rails of clothes, there were fitted shelves, housing shoes, boxes, and enough handbags to stock a small shop. A slim stepladder was attached to a rail that curved around the base of the shelves, coasters attached to the feet. It made me think of the bookshop in Disney's *Beauty and the Beast*. I had a sudden, comical vision of myself careening around the room singing, and swiping random handbags from their little nooks.

Smiling, I walked along the racks, running my fingers along the swathes of coloured fabric. Cotton, silk, leather, lace. I pulled out a beige biased-cut dress that looked simplistic enough to be hideously expensive. I checked the label. Dior. I pulled out other items, shirts, skirts, trousers, looking at the labels on each. I recognised names like Gucci and Versace, but there were others I'd never heard of, By Walid and St. Roche. There were even a couple of high street items from Reiss and Hobbs. I opened the top drawer and rifled through an astonishing assortment of knickers and bras in more texture and colour combinations than I thought possible. I owned two bras, one black and one grey. It's possible the grey one used to be white, I can't remember now. But this peacock-like display in garments that were only worn underneath clothes almost made me laugh. Then I remembered Isaac. Perhaps these were for him. Perhaps he liked her in all the colours of the rainbow.

The drawer underneath contained bikinis and swimming costumes. I pulled out a scarlet one-piece with a ruched panel down the front, and built-in underwire. There was a label attached to the shoulder with string, and the plastic panel still in place in the gusset. It had never been worn. I watched my fingers unloop the string and lay the label down on top of the chest of drawers. Then I slowly pealed the plastic panel off and set it next to the label. I pulled my clothes off and let them drop to the floor of the dressing room, then stepped into the red costume, pulling the thick elastane over my body, feeling it embracing the soft parts of me, my stomach and my breasts. Yanking the straps up over my shoulders, I turned, looking for a mirror, and instantly noticed one on the back of the dressing-room door. I pushed the door shut so I could see properly, and stared in amazement at my reflection. The garment was too small for me, and I could feel it digging in around my hips. My breasts were also too large for this cup size. But the overall effect was incredible. It was like looking at someone else entirely. The red brought out the tan in my skin and the copper strands in my hair. The support of the lush fabric flattened my stomach and pushed up my breasts, giving me an hourglass figure I didn't realise was possible. I turned this way and that, caressing the fabric, running my palms over my stomach and hips.

Leaving my own clothes in a heap on the floor, I left the dressing room and the bedroom, and walked down the main staircase and into the kitchen. In a designated fridge was the family's private wine selection, and I opened the door, selecting a perfectly chilled Sauvignon blanc, then a large wine glass from the display cabinet. I poured a generous measure then headed out to the pool, grabbing my cigarettes and the small china bowl on the way.

I sat with my feet dangling in the pool, watching the ripples from my legs dance across the surface. I closed my eyes and listened again to the whisper of the trees, the birdsong, and now, the faint thrum of the pump coming from the shed behind the hedge. The water was cool, but not like the lake. It was refreshing, rather than bracing. It was perfectly, expensively cool.

I sipped my wine and dragged on my cigarette, the tastes of which were as delicious as the imagined shrieks of Rachel and Priya that ricocheted around my mind. *You can't smoke! You can't have glass by the pool! You can't break into the owner's bedroom and wear her swimming costume!*

I grabbed my phone and took a selfie, fag and wine glass in one hand, squinting into the afternoon sun with a corner of the pool and the house behind me. As the alcohol buzzed through me, it took all my willpower not to send the photo to Megs, Rachel and Priya. I even pondered how I'd caption it. *Quiet here without you xxx.* Or simply, *Fuck you all! Xxx*

I felt my lips stretch into a smile as I imagined sitting here, waiting for the manic crunch of gravel as a designated intervener (probably Megs) pulled up at the front, hammering on the door for me to let her in so she could coax me out. Or perhaps she'd slip one of those nooses on a pole around my neck, the way vets bring crazy cats under control. I snorted into my wine, tipped it back to finish the glass, stubbed out my cigarette and slipped into the pool. I decided I'd do ten lengths before lunch.

I found sliced bread in the utility room freezer, toasted it, and slathered on cool wedges of butter from the fridge. I wandered around the rooms as I ate, imagining Rachel berating me for dropping crumbs, and whinging about rules and lost deposits. In the cloakroom, I was surprised to discover an artfully concealed office behind the wall where the corkboard of keys hung. I felt I'd uncovered a treasure trove of information as I rifled through the papers in the in-tray and desk drawers. But I was soon bored by what appeared to be long-winded contracts and letters concerning deeds to buildings and areas of land. I locked up the office and wandered towards the back of the house, stabbing at the control panel on the wall of the steam room until a red light began blinking next to the word 'heating'.

While I waited, I perused the book shelves in the living area, searching for repeated authors that might give me an idea as to what Sarah and Isaac liked to read. Ian McEwan, Jane Austen, John Grisham, Agatha Christie. Obvious, I thought, something deflating inside me. But sprinkled among these bookshelf staples, and overpowered by the likes of *The 7 Habits of Highly Effective People*, I began to see more obscure treasures glinting at me. Marianne Hauser, Alfred Chester. There was a biography of Walt Disney, a message in the front reading, 'Happy birthday, Isaac. Some inspirational reading for you, D'. I scanned the first couple of paragraphs before placing it back and noticing several short story collections by Daphne du Maurier and, as far as I could tell, almost everything written by Ishiguro. I remembered spotting the DVD of *The Remains of the Day* in the cabinet, and pulled down the book. The spine was cracked from repeated reading, and the pages well thumbed. It was an old edition and I flicked through, inhaling the sweetness of the yellowing pages.

When the steam room light turned green, I took a glass of wine in there and sat for maybe fifteen minutes in the stifling humidity, wondering why the hell anyone would want to spend time in a dark, clammy room that felt like it wanted to suffocate you. By the time my wine was warm and my skin wet, I decided I'd had enough and retreated up to the bedroom.

I showered in Sarah and Isaac's en suite, surrounded by sand-coloured marble and expensive products, which I used liberally, from the Shu Uemura shampoo to the La Mer body lotion. His and hers sinks were carved into Carrara marble, and I picked up a clear cubic bottle containing amber liquid, bringing it to my nose and inhaling the scent that had greeted me when I'd opened Isaac's wardrobe. Subtle spice, and wood and smoke. I looked at the label, which read *Terre d'Hermès*. I'm not sure why I did it, but I took out my phone and took a photo of the bottle.

Back in the walk-in wardrobe, I re-threaded the label onto the strap of the swimming costume, and pressed the plastic gusset-protector back on. The costume was still mildly damp, but it would dry in the drawer if I laid it flat. Next I selected the beige biased-cut Dior dress. I only glanced briefly at myself in the mirror this time. The dress did not suit me, the cut giving way to every curve and bump of my body in an unflattering way. It was also several inches too long. But that didn't matter to me in that moment, because I wasn't trying to be Dinah Marshall right now. I was Sarah Rivers. Owner of this luxurious house and everything in it. So I swung open the door of the dressing room, obscuring my view of the mirror, and, in my mind, growing several inches taller and slimmer as I sashayed from the room, and down the stairs to my kitchen to fix myself a drink.

For dinner, I found a pouch of microwave lemon couscous nestled in a cupboard of rice and pasta, stock cubes and bags of dried lentils. I heated it up and ate it with more toast and the rest of the bottle of wine. I remembered then that I'd not properly looked in the cosy living room Megs had shown me when I'd first walked in the door, so I walked down the corridor and into the soft, comforting space. The floors were carpeted in pale champagne, and the walls were a deep blue. The fireplace wasn't modern like the others, but Victorian in style with an ornate black surround and charcoal resting in the grate.

My gaze swept the room and, as it settled, I wondered how I'd only just noticed it. In a corner, to one side of a large window, was a shining black baby grand piano. The lid that covered the strings was closed and on top stood a collection of photos.

There were black-and-white photos of babies, and couples dancing. Some photos looked washed out and I guessed they must be older relatives back in their prime. Sarah and Isaac touched foreheads on a beach at sunset. A young boy picked up a writhing toddler in a pink dress.

Then there was a photo of the girl, but older now. She looked about fourteen, and her face was thin and fragile, her eyes large and golden, like her mother's. Then I realised – if the photo from Turkey had been taken in 2011, then of course she would be much older now. I stared at the photo, and she stared back at me with a look of defiance. She held a dandelion in front of her face, the feathery orb close to her lips. Her lips, although parted, were not rounded into an 'O' as if she was about blow, but set in a line as if she was clenching her jaw. She looked as if she'd been instructed to blow the dandelion, but had refused, and so this was the best photo they'd managed to get. I imagined her dropping the flower onto the floor as soon as the photo was taken and grinding it into the grass with her heel, and I felt a smile blossom on my lips. I liked this photo.

On a low trolley next to the piano sat two crystal glasses and a twinkling decanter of golden liquid. I took out the stopper and sloshed a generous amount into a glass, then carried it back to the piano, placing it on top, next to the photo of the girl. Then I sat on the piano stool and lifted the lid, my fingers sliding into the keys, pressing the perfect weight of them, and closing my eyes as my muscles remembered a song I hadn't played in years. *Someday, when I'm awfully low, and the world is cold, I will feel a glow just thinking of you. And the way you look tonight.*

A beeping sound entered my head like an electric shock, paralysing my fingers on the keys. I drew my hands back, terrified the piano had an alarm fitted that I'd somehow triggered. But as my heart hammered in my chest, I realised the sound was coming from the hallway. *Please, don't be the doorbell. Please don't be a neighbour who's spotted my car and knows the guests should have left today.*

I crept out into the hall, realising with some relief that the sound came from a landline phone unit on the wall. I pressed my body to the wall to one side of the phone, worried it had some sort of camera whereby the caller would be able to see me staring dumbly at it. Eventually the beeping stopped, there was a sharp crackle, and then a woman's voice blurted from the machine.

'Oh, sorry, Sarah, of course you're in Portugal! Totally forgot. Anyway, Duncan's already emailed Isaac about it, but I wanted to call you too, make sure the message was getting through . . . you know what the men are like with anything that's not work related . . . anyway, a week Saturday we're booked into Eden House for Duncan's birthday. I think you're in town that weekend? It's booked under our name. Eight o'clock. Hopefully see you there? Let me know. *Ciao, ciao.*'

I physically flinched at the sign-off, wondering if it was an in-joke, or if this person genuinely used *Ciao, ciao* on a regular basis. But I didn't want to think about that for too long, as I was trying to make sure I didn't forget the gist of the message. I retrieved my drink from the top of the piano, then walked back into the kitchen and picked up my phone, clicking into the notes section and typing, 'Duncan . . .? Birthday week Saturday, 8 p.m. Eden House'.

I'd heard of Eden House, and a quick Google search confirmed my impression that it was a swanky member's club in Soho. I thought back to the voicemail. *You know what the men are like with anything that's not work related.* Then I typed in Isaac Rivers Duncan. The search results sprang onto my screen and I scanned the top three items. The first was Isaac's LinkedIn profile, then a website called Acanthus, then a *Guardian* article entitled 'Top 20 London property investors'. I perched on a bar stool and clicked on each article in turn, reading Isaac's CV, which seemed to consist of three main roles: Property Developer, Marketing Director, and lastly Founder and Director of Acanthus Property. The circular photo at the top of his profile saw him grinning out at me, this time in a navy-blue suit, hair swept back and pale, sea-glass eyes boring into mine.

I clicked back out and went into the Acanthus website.

Isaac Rivers and Duncan Slade set up Acanthus Property in 2012 and have never looked back. From the start, our aim has been to build and develop high-quality residential and mixed-use spaces, whilst sticking to our core beliefs – we are loyal, entrepreneurial, and accountable. Read more about our business approach below.

The gallery section showed a range of impressive photos of gleaming glass structures, tastefully restored Georgian townhouses, and newly built red-brick housing estates. A trophy logo at the bottom of the page informed me they'd been awarded 'Property Developers of the Year' at the 2016 and 2019 Property Investors Awards. The *Guardian* article had a small paragraph about Acanthus, mainly reiterating the information on their website, but headed with a photograph of Isaac and Duncan, holding the golden trophy between them at the 2016 awards. Isaac exuded confidence as he grinned into the lens, but Duncan, much shorter than Isaac and dumpy in stature, gave a tight-lipped smile, as if unsure whether or not to show his teeth. He was clearly the Robin to Isaac's Batman.

I put my phone down then, willing myself not to search more. I wanted to click on every link I could find that contained the words 'Isaac Rivers' and then to do the same for Sarah, and to find out what the daughter's name was, and to see their Facebook and Instagram profiles, but I didn't want to do it all at once. I wanted to savour it, like a bar of chocolate you make yourself eek out, snapping off one small square at a time and letting it dissolve slowly on your tongue before snapping off the next. There would be plenty of time for all that. Right now I needed to make the most of the time I had left in this house. I stood and ran my hands over the fabric of the Dior dress, feeling the silken material yield under my touch. I wondered if I'd ever wear something this expensive again in my life.

I grabbed my drink and walked up the stairs, into the bedroom and out onto the balcony. I leaned on the rail and smoked, and drank the whiskey, relishing the burn of it against my throat, and the warmth of it in my stomach. The pink sky was turning a bruised purple on the horizon, and flecked with distant birds flying home for the night. It was so quiet. I looked out over the pool, which was quietly rippling, the distant hum of the pump in the shed, and I imagined again that all this was mine. I had a husband who was devastatingly handsome, a mountain of money, a beautiful home, and a gorgeous little girl who adored me.

My phone pinged in my hand and I looked down. Hen, asking, *Are you home now?*

I tapped into the message and typed, *Yep. I'm home.*

Then I turned my phone off and stubbed my cigarette out on the pebbles at the base of a pot plant, burying the stub under the stones. I walked into the bedroom and set my glass down on Sarah's side of the bed. I knew it was her side because there was hand cream, lip balm and a shallow blue saucer with two gold rings and a pair of emerald studs set on it. In the bathroom, I picked up the bottle of Isaac's *Terre d'Hermès* and went back into the bedroom. Isaac's bedside table held a pair of silver cufflinks, red Bluetooth earbuds, and a rectangular digital alarm clock. I leaned over his pillow and inhaled but, as I expected, the only scent was that of the same washing detergent I'd smelt on the shirt downstairs. I held the bottle of cologne aloft and spritzed the air, watching the mist arc and fall onto the pillow. Then I replaced the bottle in the bathroom, and went round to Sarah's side, slipping between the sheets and feeling their crisp, coolness give way underneath me. I lay there, where Sarah lay night after night next to Isaac, and I pulled the pillow that smelt of him towards me, digging my fingers into the fabric where he usually lay his head, inhaling his scent again and again as I drifted off to sleep.

Chapter Seven

I woke with a bleary sense of displacement, like you get when you wake up in a strange hotel room, or on a friend's sofa. The light, the smells, the room layout were all alien, but it only took a moment for everything to be pulled sharply into focus, and for the delicious swell of satisfaction to bubble up from my stomach, tingling through my bloodstream. I'd spent a night in their bed, and had slept the deep, untroubled sleep of a child. I stretched out like a starfish, rucking up the duvet and twisting to bury my face once again in Isaac's pillow.

The digital clock showed 10.33, and with a twist of something that felt like grief, I realised I'd soon have to leave. I had no idea when the cleaners would arrive, but they couldn't find me here.

I showered and dressed in the jeans and T-shirt I'd arrived in, spritzing myself with Isaac's cologne before taking one last look around the room. I took my phone out and switched it on, ignoring the voicemails and texts from Kate wondering why I hadn't turned up at work this morning, and took a photo of the room. A memento of the holiday. I made the bed as best I could, but had to give up on trying to smooth over the snowy smudges that were my footprints in the carpet: they now covered every inch of the room and only an expertly wielded vacuum cleaner would obliterate them.

I closed the bedroom door, locked it, and replaced the key on the hook in the cloakroom downstairs. Then I went to the shed and pulled down the orange lever that turned the pump off: I didn't want it getting back to Sarah (or Megs) that instructions had been ignored, especially as Sarah and I had got on so well on the phone.

I took more photos of the pool, then walked through the copse of trees to the lake and took photos of that too, first from the trees, and then from the end of the jetty. Each photo I took seemed to send my mood sinking further, each tap of the screen one photo closer to me having to say goodbye.

I walked back into the house and slid the glass doors shut, then turned to take a photo of the living area. I took more photos of the bookshelves, then of the trio of photos with the one I'd broken. In the cosy living room, I photographed the girl with the dandelion. Then, eyes stinging, and a hard lump in my throat, I walked out into the hallway, took one last look towards the centre of the house, sunlight streaming through those glass doors, as if they were silently pleading with me not to leave. I turned, walked through the front door, shutting it behind me and locking it before depositing the keys back in the box safe and jumbling the numbers. Then I placed my palm on the front door as if feeling for a heartbeat, and whispered, 'I will come back. I will see you again.'

In my car I swiped angrily at my eyes, which were now blurry from uncried tears, and shoved my key in the ignition. The tyres crunched over the gravel and it took all my willpower not to look in the rear-view mirror at the receding house getting smaller and smaller. I felt like a mother leaving her child at nursery for the first time. I'd always listened to that story that came again and again from every parent I knew with so little variance, and I'd always been bored, willing my eyes not to roll with the saccharine emotion of it. *I couldn't bear it . . . she started crying, so then of course I started crying . . . the staff had to take her off me because I just couldn't let her go . . .* Yes, yes, we get that you love your child; do you have to lay it on so bloody thick?

But right then, at that moment, I understood. That's how I felt. I felt as if I were leaving a piece of my heart behind, and it was almost physically impossible for me to keep my foot on the accelerator, knowing I was getting further and further away.

Then a van appeared. It swerved into the driveway and I instinctively steered to one side, scared we'd collide. The van stopped too, and I scanned the words on the side, my blood sluicing cold through my veins. *Diamond Specialist Home Management Services.* The driver's side door opened and a thin woman with a sage-green housecoat, auburn hair and a sour expression emerged. I thought about flooring it and making my escape, but then I had an image of her snapping a photo of my registration number and somehow tracking me down, working out I was one of the weekend guests who must have stayed an extra night. I couldn't have that.

She tilted her chin up and looked down her bony nose at me as she approached, and I plastered on a smile as I wound my window down.

'Can I help you?' she said, in a tone that suggested helping me was the last thing she wanted to do.

I pointed at my phone attached to the dashboard cradle. 'I'm so sorry – GPS brought me to the wrong address. Bloody things.'

'What house are you looking for?'

'Don't worry, I've called my friend – apparently I've driven past it. I know where I'm going now.'

Her gaze slid over the bodywork of my ancient car, and I knew what she was thinking – how could anyone with such a shit car possibly have a friend living in this neighbourhood?

'Have a good day,' I said, winding up the window, desperate to end this exchange.

'You too,' she said, her voice muffled by the glass. She watched me drive away as if she could smell something off, and I felt a pang of satisfaction that I'd forgotten to collect the cigarette butts and shards of glass from under my window, and that she'd have to scrabble around in the gravel to pick them up.

I could barely bring myself to exit my car after I'd parked outside my flat, so great was the impulse to drive straight back to Riverdean. The sun still beat down as I crossed the pavement to the peeling blue door next to the electrical shop, but it seemed incomprehensible to me that this was the same sun that had been shining on me all weekend. This was a sun that shone on chewing-gum smattered pavements, and blistered the pasty skin of pot-bellied shopkeepers. A sun that belched hot, metallic air from Tube stations and brought wafts of rancid rot from roadside litter bins. This could not be the same sun that glittered on topaz swimming pools and softly melted chinking ice in frosted martini glasses. I wanted that sun back. But not just the sun – I wanted all of it back.

I trudged up the threadbare stairs, marvelling (as I did every time) at the smell on the communal staircase. It seemed to be a mixture of fried onions and urine, which was chronically puzzling given there were only two flats, and my neighbour was a clean-shaven man in his twenties who ironed creases into his jeans and didn't seem a prime candidate for staircase urination. But the smell was as strong that day as it had been when I moved in seven years ago. *God, seven years in this dump.*

My moisture-warped door stuck at the bottom as it always did when I tried to push it open so I gave it the usual kick to gain entry. The flat was sweltering, the air stale. I noticed my wilting fern on the windowsill and contemplated throwing it in the bin, but then changed my mind and fetched a cup of water from the kitchen and watered it until its saucer was full. Then I opened the window, petrol fumes wafting into the room.

I slumped onto the grey sofa and dug in my pocket for my phone. I texted Kate: *So sorry, I was throwing up all night then was so exhausted I just slept through my alarm. Think it's a sickness bug so best not risk coming in tomorrow. Be there Wednesday.*

I laid my head back, the thought of having to go and buy groceries, or go to work, or tidy the flat completely overwhelming me. I could barely bring myself to open my eyes and acknowledge the cesspit that was my life, let alone engage in any of the activities required of me in order to keep the hamster wheel of hopelessness spinning. What was the point?

In the end, I was forced to open my eyes by my phone ringing in my lap. Hen. The cherry on top. This time I actually picked up because I realised I couldn't prolong it any longer. Maybe if I spoke to her, she'd leave me the hell alone for a while.

'Hi, Hen,' I said, in a husky whisper, like a child wanting to convince a parent they're too ill for school.

'What's going on?'

'You mean in general or are you referring to something specific?' No matter what the circumstance, I could never shrug off the childish glee I felt at winding up my older sister.

'You know what I'm talking about! Disappearing off the face of the bloody planet, going on a holiday you can't afford, taking time off you don't have, and not showing up for work again this morning!'

'Kate's already called you today then.' The snitch.

'Of course she has, she was worried about you!'

'Well, if you were at all up to date then you'd have heard that I was throwing up all night and that I'm being considerate in missing today and tomorrow's work so I don't infect my colleagues with whatever lurgy I've picked up.'

'I know, she sent me a screenshot of your message.' Bloody hell, that was quick.

'Are you serious? That's like . . . fucking stalking or something.'

'That's rich coming from you.'

Silence. Occasionally Hen slipped up like that and said something too close to the bone, and I always found the best way to deal with it was to let her wallow in the silence of her own embarrassment.

'Oh God, Dinny, I'm sorry. That was insensitive, I didn't mean it.'

Silence. Squirm, Hen. *Squirm*.

'We're just worried about you, you know that. When you disappear like that it makes us worry that you're not feeling well again . . . that you might try . . .'

'To drown myself?'

More silence.

'Is . . . is that what you were . . . doing?' Her tone was now unbearably gentle. 'I mean . . . back then?'

To be honest, I don't even know any more. My memory of it is so blurry around the edges, like the river that day, with the mizzle of rain misting the surface so it was impossible to tell where the air ended and the water began. All I remember is an irresistible urge to be submerged. To feel the frigid oblivion of the water displacing every horrible thought in my head, and smudging out the faces of every person who was so irreversibly, desperately disappointed in me.

When they pulled me out, I've no doubt some of them used the phrase 'cry for help'. And I'm also sure some of them – my friends, my sister – thought I'd chosen this method because of its dramatic literary connotations. I saw myself as an Ophelia. As a Lady of Shalott. But, in actual fact, I'd never thought of it in those terms at all. I just wanted to be under the water.

'Dinny, are you there?'

'Yep, I'm here,' I said, tone falsely bright.

'You don't have to talk about back then . . . I just . . . I was worried you were lying about being on holiday. I know you don't have any money, and you don't see much of the girls any more, so I thought maybe you'd taken yourself off somewhere and were . . . sad.'

She hated saying the word 'depressed', I suppose in case I was sensitive to it, having been diagnosed as such by the NHS psychologist who saw me for three months after the river incident.

I clicked into my photos and selected the selfie Megs had taken of the four of us, and the selfie I'd taken by the pool with the wine and cigarette, and sent them to her.

I heard her phone beep down the line. 'Oh, I . . . OK, I'm sorry. You weren't lying about the weekend. But why did you suddenly take off from work like that? When you haven't got any holiday left?'

'Because I was a last-minute replacement for Neve, if you must know. I only got invited a few days before. And I said I was happy to take some unpaid leave because . . . well, I've got some new pupils I'm tutoring, so I'm actually good for cash at the moment.' The lie should keep her off my back for a while, I thought.

'Great . . . that's really great, Din. But promise me you'll keep in touch and not ignore my calls all the time?'

'OK, if you promise not to freak out every time Kate decides to gossip about me.'

'She's not—' I heard her swallow her own words and take a breath. 'OK . . . I promise I'll be more measured in the tone of my communications in future.'

I snorted into the phone. 'Spot the HR Manager! I'm your sister, Hen, you don't have to talk like that.'

'Well, I'm sorry about that too! Jesus. Are we OK?'

'Yes. Now let me get back to throwing up and I'll speak to you soon.'

'OK, I hope you feel better soon. Drink lots of water.' Poor Hen. All these years and she still didn't know what was a lie and what was the truth.

We ended the call and I peeled myself off the sofa and across the road to Tesco Express. I bought milk, sausage rolls, apples, and bread, then retreated to my flat, and switched on an electric fan in the corner. I set myself up on the sofa with a mug of tea and flipped open my laptop.

The first thing I did was google Riverdean, poring over the online photos from the rental website – photos I'd only given a cursory glance when Megs had sent me the initial details. Back then I'd swiped through the images of opulence with an eye-roll and a bitter snort – of course the girls had chosen this bougie bullshit for their 'mini-break'. But now I felt like a different person, my reaction to the photos incomparable. My heart raced and fingers trembled, caressing the keyboard as I tapped across to the next photo and the next, cross-referencing them against the photos I'd taken myself in each room, playing a strange game of Spot the Difference with myself . . . ah, that candle is on the left of the chimney breast on the website, but in my photo it's on the right . . . the sun loungers are white on the website, but dove grey in my photos – they must have recently replaced them. There was no point to this game, but it made me feel as if I *knew* the house in a way anyone else stumbling across it online couldn't. It made me feel closer to Riverdean.

Next, I googled Isaac and Sarah, separately and together. I didn't use Instagram, my life being the least Insta-friendly one I could think of, so I created an account with the username Jane Smith. I suppose even at this point a plan of sorts must have been forming in a corner of my brain. *Stay anonymous. Don't let them know who you are.*

I found a photo of their wedding day, like a magazine couple in a *Vanity Fair* exclusive, all vintage lace and perfect teeth. There were industry news releases from Isaac's work, detailing new developments to be built or properties restored. Isaac didn't have a personal Instagram account, and I soon grew bored of the impersonal blur of Acanthus's feed: glass, brick, cranes, logos, hard hats, handshakes.

I found Sarah's much more enjoyable, with its healthy lunches, riverside walks, glowing sunsets and scented candles. Most of the photos were of objects, but occasionally her face appeared, sipping a coffee or a glass of wine, laughing with friends. With her marble skin and high cheek bones, she was one of those women who looked much younger without make-up. Although I supposed even in the 'natural' photos she would be wearing something, or have applied some sort of filter . . . wouldn't she? From my googling, I'd worked out she was just over a year older than me. A whole year. It occurred to me that I probably hadn't had skin that smooth and radiant since I was eleven. I chewed my lip, imagining this was my feed, my skin, my expensive candles. Every so often I found myself touching my fingertips to the screen, stroking the photos before me as if I could somehow absorb their essence, their perfection. I was lost in this online world for hours, and didn't notice the time slipping away, the day bleeding into night.

*

On Wednesday, I was back in work, with Kate interrogating me about my holiday and my sickness bug, phone clutched in her pudgy fingers, no doubt a nanosecond away from texting Hen with any information she received. Kate had taken her role as informant with a gleeful earnestness since Hen had asked her to *keep an eye on Dinny* when they'd met at a party three years ago. We were all drunk and, although Kate didn't know the details of the Oxford days, she had gleaned enough to know that Hen believed I was emotionally immature and psychologically fragile. And Kate had latched on to Hen like a duckling setting eyes on its mother for the first time. She'd watched Hen all night with drunken starstruck blinks as Hen waxed lyrical about her career and her kids.

Kate was only in her mid-twenties but had an unnerving energy about her. She was always offering to do more shifts at the café, asking about extra responsibilities, talking about her savings and her 'business plan' for whatever course she was doing at the London School of Economics. I had no idea how she spent so much time at work and still managed to study, but I can only put it down to her being one of those people who seems to have more hours in the day than everyone else. Like Priya.

The café was tucked down a cobbled side street in Covent Garden, in between a shop that sold leather shoes and belts, and a second-hand book shop. It was owned by a man called Giovanni, and was disappointingly called *Giovanni's*. We hardly ever set eyes on the man himself as he owned several other cafés and restaurants in the area, but he'd occasionally waft in, smelling of Old Spice and cigarettes, black hair gelled over an ever-brightening bald patch. He'd kiss us on both cheeks, muttering *bella, grazie*, pat the gelato machine and ask us, *She's OK? Working OK?*, go to the loo, then sweep back out with an *arrivederci*.

Giovanni was someone who played a part very well. He'd found his place in the world and relished it. The quirky, cramped streets of Covent Garden with their well-worn cobbles and their designer shops, their trendy cafés and their plastic-filled gift shops, was the perfect stage for an Italian-born business owner with an eccentric manner and an eye for style.

The green awning outside sheltered two metal tables and chairs and, inside, wooden folding chairs surrounded gingham-draped tables, while two large basket lampshades dangled from a canopy of fake greenery above. The floor, counter and chairs were all artfully distressed, as were the faded peach walls with their deliberately patchy plasterwork that revealed the red-brick beneath. Misha, my boss, preened and purred over Giovanni whenever he came in, and I habitually gritted my teeth through the speech she'd give the moment he left about how in awe she was of *everything he's achieved, given he's not even from this country, and the huge language barriers he's overcome*. I never had the heart to tell her I'd found Giovanni smoking with a delivery driver a couple of years ago and overheard him saying, 'Yeah mate, it's a fucking nightmare,' to the man, with an accent that was distinctly more Millwall than Milan.

My days back at work dragged, and I lived for my lunch break when I'd lose myself down previously unvisited streets, searching for the designer outlets I'd been researching since Riverdean. I recognised some of the names from Sarah's wardrobe ... *Bec & Belle, Piana Vera*. I'd sometimes get my phone out and scan through Sarah's Instagram, wondering if I'd spot any of the outfits she was wearing 'in the wild'. I began to develop a sense of her style from what I'd seen in her wardrobe, combined with the photos I'd taken, and her Instagram. I was confident that if I was about to buy her a gift, I'd know exactly what to go for, and what to avoid. Expensive, obviously. Simple – no flounces or ruffles, definitely no florals. Block colours, no stripes or fussy patterns. Soft fabric that floated or shimmered; no sharp tailoring or hard lines.

After a few days of prowling around outside these shops, I mustered the courage to walk in to one. My hands tingled the first time I crossed the air-conditioned threshold of Piana Vera, the cool quietness like swimming underwater. A couple of shoppers browsed the racks, hangers clicking softly as they sifted through the fabrics. I wondered how long I could hold my breath in here, how long I'd be able to swim with these fish before being forced to surface for air, to rejoin the messy, noisy, dirty world I belonged to.

But soon I found I could breathe. The visions I'd had of a *Pretty Woman* scenario, where I'd be ridiculed by staff and asked to leave, never came to fruition. The two other shoppers didn't acknowledge me, and the shop assistant merely looked up from a clipboard she was marking and smiled, before looking back down again. I walked along the racks, pulling out random items and practising my pondering face, as if I could afford a four-hundred-pound shirt, or a three-hundred-pound pair of jeans. After ten minutes, the price tags started making me feel queasy, so I scuttled back to the café.

But as the days wore on I became more accustomed to those places. I stopped analysing shop assistants' body language to gauge whether or not they approved of my presence. I'm sure Sarah never did that. I'm sure she'd acted as if she belonged in every room she'd ever walked into. And it was with this newfound resolution to walk the walk, that I found myself back in Piana Vera the following Wednesday, at 5 p.m., just a few hours after my June wages had entered my bank account. When I'd checked that afternoon, I was also amused to see a payment of forty pounds from Megs, accompanied by a chirpy WhatsApp.

Hey Din! Amazing weekend, must do it again soon. I've just popped that £40 into your acc. Remember the silly bet about Rachel!? I know, bit of nonsense, but you won fair and square! Xoxo

I felt a swell of gratitude towards Megs that she'd remembered the bet, and a sense of satisfaction that I'd actually gone along with it – and won. Perhaps it was a sign that I was on the right track. That I was doing the right thing. The universe approved of my actions.

Of course, there was no actual money in my bank account: my wages and the money from Megs had simply decreased my overdraft by a few hundred quid, but to me, that was a lifeline. Or rather, a passport to another world.

So, it was on this Wednesday that I entered Piana Vera with the explicit aim of buying something. I wasn't sure what, but it had to be under two hundred pounds if I was going to make my rent and be able to eat for the next month. I ruffled hopelessly through the now familiar racks of feather-soft shirts and tailored pencil skirts, flowing maxi dresses and bizarrely cut tops that left me confused as to which was the front and which the back. It was with a sinking mood I came to the last rack before the shoes, having been unable to find anything for my budget that wasn't a purse or a hairband.

Then I spotted a rack next to the fitting room. I'd thought it was filled with discarded items people had tried on, but now I saw a cream card slotted over the rail that read 'Sale' in sloping black letters. No huge red signs in these posh shops, I thought. A sale was something to whisper, not shout. No need to embarrass anyone who might like to peruse the discounted items. I tried to stroll nonchalantly towards the rack, and not race towards it with hungry eyes. The colours were darker and the materials heavier, but the prices lifted my heart from out of the pit of my stomach. Eventually I found an emerald-green wraparound dress, one size too small, for two hundred and thirty pounds, down from four hundred and fifty. It was a price that would make my eyes sting in normal circumstances, but these were not normal circumstances, and my heart soared in the same way it had last summer when I'd found a faux leather holdall in Primark for two pounds ninety-nine.

I tried it on in the fitting room, marvelling at the way the silky material skimmed my curves, but was also structured enough to show them off. It was a little tight, and the sleeves buttoned at the wrist, which meant it would be far too hot to wear in this weather . . . but it looked amazing. And the thing that clinched it for me, which was more than I could have hoped for, was the two fabric buttons just below the V-neck collar, each embroidered with a simple diamond shape in glossy gold thread – the Piana Vera logo.

With clammy palms, I fumbled for my debit card at the till, a panic flashing through me that I might have forgotten my PIN number, or that my card would be declined because of unusual activity. But the payment went through, and I watched the flawless young woman wrap the dress in snow-white tissue paper, and slide it into a large pale-pink bag with black rope handles.

Adrenalin pumped through my veins as I walked towards Covent Garden Tube station, gripping the bag with a white-knuckled fist, terrified someone would come and grab it from me. I cradled it on my lap all the way home like a baby, stroking the glossy surface with my thumb and feeling a sense of achievement. I had done it. I had set the wheels in motion. As soon as I'd punched in my four digits on the card machine in that shop, I'd set a chain of events in motion over which, I believed, I had complete control.

Chapter Eight

I couldn't sleep the night before the party. I felt a repeated need to grab my phone and check one more detail, or look at one more photo, or search a website one more time. Questions whined like circling mosquitoes around my head, and I'd need an immediate answer. *Is tomorrow definitely 'a week Saturday' from when I heard the message? What do people wear to Eden House? What's their policy on guests?* I researched the answers to these questions (and many more) again and again, until eventually, I fell asleep propped up in bed, phone clutched in my fingers.

My head was fuzzy and my eyes encrusted with sleep when I woke, with a stiff neck and saliva trailing from the corner of my mouth. In the kitchen, I heaped three spoonfuls of instant coffee into a mug and made it lukewarm so I could down it quickly before catching the bus to Richmond.

The hairdressers was one I'd never been to before. In fact, I couldn't remember the last time I'd been to a hairdresser at all, hence the straggles of dirty blonde hair that hung like tassels from my long, grubby roots. I'd decided Richmond was a good place to go, as lots of well-to-do people lived there. Perhaps I'd get a better cut than going to Glam Baby next to the KFC on my road.

Lauren, the hairdresser, smoothed her hands over my mop, pulling the strands and rummaging through the layers. She kept up a professional smile, but I sensed the distaste behind the words, 'OK, there's a lot going on here, isn't there?'

Her suggestions involved colour, cut and taming of frizz. She said I'd have to have an allergy test before she used the dyes, and come back in twenty-four hours to make sure I wasn't going to react to any of the products. *No, no. I need this now, today.* My brain scrambled for something to say, my mouth eventually taking over. 'Oh, actually I already had one . . . last week when I made this appointment,' I lied.

'Oh . . . right. Maybe we just didn't log it on the system.' She walked over to the reception desk and clicked on the computer, scowling at the screen. I felt my plans slipping away from me as I watched her. She returned a minute later. 'I've logged it now. Sorry about that.'

'No problem. It happens,' I said, as if my heart wasn't beating in my ears.

'Shall we get started?'

My hair was pulled and brushed and combed until my roots ached, and that was before the foils were applied. A circular machine on a stand rotated around my head, like some sophisticated medical scanner, before my hair was washed, and combed again, and cut, and cut some more, and blow-dried.

Lauren slathered on some creme, then scrunched and twisted and sprayed. The final effect was mesmerising. The blonde straggles were gone, replaced with chestnut curls that fell to my collar bone, and glinted with auburn and honey highlights. Shorter layers flicked up, framing my face and when I moved my head I could feel the lightness of the waves bouncing around my shoulders. It was perfect.

I thanked Lauren (who looked inappropriately smug) and paid for my haircut, along with bottles and tubes of all the products she'd used on me, in the hope I'd be able to recreate this look at home if I just threw some money at it. That's what Sarah would do, after all. The products almost doubled my bill, but I told myself it was well worth it, even if it meant I could only afford my rent this month, and no food.

Back at the flat I showered – careful to avoid getting my new locks wet – then spent the afternoon watching make-up tutorials on YouTube, and scanning back through key photos of Sarah I'd screenshotted from her Instagram feed. I wasn't trying to look like her – that would be impossible. I just needed to try to work out how she achieved her natural, classy look. I knew not to slather on three inches of foundation then stencil in my eyebrows, but apart from that I was lost.

I'd bought my key products from an online discount retailer, and was proud of my stash: Yves Saint Laurent foundation, Dior lipstick, Bobbi Brown eye make-up. I used the recommended squidgy little sponges to dab on barely-there foundation, then stroked on gold shimmer eye shadow, before applying smoky eyeliner. I swept on a peach blusher I'd had since I was twenty, hoping this one cut corner wouldn't derail my entire plan, and might also save me some money. Besides, *Make-Up by Marie* (5.7 million views) had informed me that the sophisticated colours this season were 'muted nudes and peaches' and that I didn't want to look like 'an eighties pink-streaked Madonna wannabe'. My *Copper Rose* lipstick was dabbed on after a 'whisper of Vaseline', before being 'smudged and blended with my ring finger'.

I stepped into the green dress, pulling it up over my hips so I didn't disturb my new face and hair, then slipped my feet into ancient black strappy shoes that were my only nice pair, admiring the effect next to my Caramel Kiss nail polish (which, of course, matched my fingernails).

Lastly, the *pièce de résistance*: a tiny, black, quilted Chanel handbag with a gold chain strap that I'd spotted slung over a mannequin in the Macmillan charity shop next to the Tube station. I took this to be another sign from the universe, because the bag had cost forty pounds – exactly the amount I'd won from my bet with Megs and Priya. Riverdean had supplied me with the money to buy this handbag. It was as if the house was giving me a sign, telling me I was on the right track, enabling me to do what I needed to do tonight. The house was calling me back. That world was inviting me in.

I arrived on Wardour Street at eight forty-five. I hoped everyone else would have arrived before me, although I realised I couldn't be certain. Everything about this evening was a gamble, so I needed to keep my nerve and just do the best I could.

My heart throbbed inside my dress as I wove through the Saturday evening hordes of Soho. The air was thick with car fumes and cigarette smoke, and stale beer wafted from pubs along with the laddish shouts of sweaty men.

The ribbon of sky above was pinkish blue, the air still muggy from the heat of the day. A trickle of sweat ran down between my shoulder blades and I resisted the urge to unbutton the cuffs of my sleeves and push them up, to feel the air on my skin. A gaggle of bubblegum-pink girls shrieked past me wearing fluffy tiaras and silky bridal sashes. A lad with a too-tight polo shirt crossed from the Queen's Head and slung an arm around the bride, to honks of approval from his mates and gleeful giggles from the girls. I stepped into the road to avoid them, the smell of sweat and Sambuca washing over me as they lurched past.

At last the black railings I recognised from Google came into view. There was no sign outside the glossy black door saying 'Eden House', because it didn't need to advertise. Its members knew where it was and if you didn't, then you didn't belong here. Next to the door was a large brass doorbell, and my mouth dried up as I wondered if I'd have to press it to gain entry. Then I noticed a modern-looking unit on the other side of the door, and became even more concerned I'd need to press a buzzer and plead for entry from the street. But as I stood, paralysed by my first hurdle, the door opened and a couple came out, hand in hand. I darted forwards, extending my hand to hold the door open, prepared to have it closed on me, and to have them gesture towards the buzzer as the official method for gaining entry. But as the man let go of the door and I lurched towards the gap, he took a step back towards it and took its weight.

He smiled at me. 'I'm sorry! Didn't see you there.'

I smiled back. 'Thank you so much,' I said, taking the weight of the door from him and noticing how my voice had become clipped and bright. It was the voice I'd used on the phone to Sarah at Riverdean. The couple walked off and I turned towards the dark marble foyer, stepping over the golden threshold and letting go of the door so it softly clicked shut behind me.

I found myself facing a low-lit reception desk. There were two men talking to the woman behind the desk, all three of them nodding and smiling, sharing an in-joke as if they were regulars. My heart had expanded and was now pounding in every part of me from my stomach to my head. It numbed my fingertips and tightened my jaw, and sounds became muffled as I watched the two men walk up the sweeping marble staircase, as if St Peter had approved their souls for ascension. The receptionist's eyes turn towards me, a warm smile blossoming on her lips.

'Hello,' she said.

I approached the desk and beamed at her with what I hoped was relaxed confidence. 'Hi. I'm not a member,' I said – then forgot everything else I was supposed to say. I'd been rehearsing in the mirror for the past week, but at this precise moment all my thoughts and intentions and plans seemed to implode inside my brain.

Her smile dimmed then brightened, like a lightbulb on the blink. When I didn't continue, she nodded her encouragement. When I still didn't say anything, she looked down at the desk and shuffled some papers around. 'And, are you hoping to become a member? I can run you through the process if that's what you'd like?'

'Umm . . . I, actually no.' *Think, Dinny, you absolute idiot! Think*. 'I'm so sorry, I'm not explaining myself properly. I think it's the heat!' I fanned myself with an elaborate waft of my hand and watched her face relax.

'Oh goodness, isn't it unbearable?' She matched my joking tone with perfect professionalism.

'Completely, although I supposed we shouldn't complain.' And there it was, the British social staple coming to the rescue. The ever-reliable conversation saver: The Weather.

'Anyway, what I meant to say was – I'm here for Duncan Slade's party. As a guest. Because I'm not a member.' *Shut up, stop talking.*

Her face immediately lightened. 'Ah, I see, let me get that reservation up for you.' She clicked at the keyboard and I felt a sudden terror she was about to ask me for a form of ID. 'You're not the first to arrive.'

'Thank goodness, I hate that!' I said, in my new voice, with my new confident humour.

'Doesn't everyone?' she said, turning to the desk and hefting a large book onto the ledge in front of me. 'If you could just enter your name and contact number in the book.' She gestured at the page, which was scrawled with rows of strangers' details. I picked up a heavy black pen and wrote Jane Marshall, and my phone number with two digits changed.

'And can I just log you on the system?'

'Um . . . of course.'

'What's your name please?'

'Jane Marshall.' I'd wanted a different name from my new Instagram handle, so decided my own surname was common enough to be convincing but not stand out. It's not that I was planning on doing anything wrong, or even being dishonest . . . this was just a necessary step in order to gain access to them. To see them, and hear them talk in real life. To feel their presence, and to imagine I was part of their world, even if just for one evening.

The woman tapped again on the keyboard, her face illuminated by the white light of the screen. Then she turned her warm-but-professional smile towards me. 'They're on level one in the Garden Lounge. Have a wonderful evening.'

And that was it. I said thank you and followed in the footsteps of the young men I'd watched earlier, ascending the marble staircase, heels clicking on the stone, palm gripping the cool brass curve of the bannister.

I reached a half landing, and an archway over which was a sign reading 'Garden Lounge and Bar'. I walked through, trying to affect the swagger of someone who had been here a hundred times and knew where they were going. But if my body language was convincing then I imagine my eyes would have given me away, as my gaze darted about like a restless fly, alighting on objects and people with erratic energy.

I drank it all in. Dark-blue wood-panelled walls, hanging plants, velvet chairs in tangerine, circular tables with small gold lamps. Clumps of people huddled around these tables, and the air buzzed with conversation, punctuated with laughter. There was background music that reminded me of a mixed tape I'd made at uni called 'Chill-out music' – a piano tinkling over relaxed electronic beats. The bar glistened with coloured bottles and amber light along the wall to the right, and a barman prepared a drink, the ice crunching in the cocktail shaker.

On the many occasions I'd imagined this moment, I'd envisioned myself walking in and immediately spotting Sarah and Isaac within a huddle of people, including Duncan, who would be accepting birthday drinks from people with drunken joviality. I'd sidle up and perhaps take the vacant table next to them, where I could listen to their conversation whilst slowly sipping the cheapest drink on the menu, and pretending to check my phone. But in reality, the room was much busier than I'd anticipated. Every table seemed to be taken, and a sick feeling churned inside me as I imagined the group settled in a dark corner, cocooned by occupied tables, and me on the outside, no way of infiltrating.

There's no rush, just take your time. I tried to slow my breathing, reaching into my bag for my phone so I had something to look at while I considered what to do next. As I stared at my home screen, it occurred to me that the first thing I should do was buy that cheap drink. I set my gaze firmly on the bar and once again attempted to click into 'I belong here' mode.

The bar was lined with tanned leather stools, and I gratefully perched on one, glad to take the pressure off my feet that were struggling in shoes they'd not worn for at least fifteen years. I swivelled on the seat and reached for a drinks menu, returning a nod and a smile from the barman. *He thinks I belong here. He thinks I'm like all these other people.* I turned my attention to the menu, immediately discounting the cocktails, which were fifteen pounds each, and turning instead to the wine. It was extraordinary to me that I wouldn't be able to buy a small glass of wine for less than nine pounds. That was more than I'd spend on a bottle.

The barman looked at me but I wasn't ready. I gestured towards a man in a white shirt who'd just arrived at the bar. 'I'm still thinking, you can serve him.'

White Shirt gave his order and I was relieved it comprised three cocktails, which would give me time to collect myself before ordering a glass of tap water.

'Would you like a recommendation?' I looked up into the eyes of the barman who, to my annoyance, had decided to multi-task and prepare White Shirt's drinks while also interrogating me. I stared back at him. He must have been about thirty, with jet-black hair and a small scar from a nose piercing on his left nostril.

'OK.' I shrugged, feeling it would have been rude to say no.

He turned over a page in my menu and tapped a cardboard insert upon which purple italics read *Forbidden Fruit* above a printed sketch of a martini glass. 'Our speciality cocktail this week, which is made with Belvedere vodka, apple syrup, lychee, and cinnamon.'

For some reason my hairdresser's words from that morning came back to me. 'Wow, there's a lot going on there.'

He smiled and nodded. 'And it's delicious.'

I felt pressured, and awkward, and my dress was tight and clammy around my waist. I just wanted a drink, and suddenly wished I'd downed a few glasses before I got here, or smuggled in a miniature of cheap vodka. My annoyance turned to petulance, and I couldn't resist it.

Jane receded and Dinny resurfaced. 'Does "speciality" just mean two pounds more expensive than the other cocktails?'

His smile dwindled, but he managed to pick it up again and give a polite laugh. 'Or our signature margarita is also very tasty.'

'Can I give *you* a recommendation?' I said, willing myself to keep my tone light and jokey.

He gave an uncertain nod.

I leaned across the bar, raising my hand to my face to feign a stage-whisper. 'Happy hour with half-price cocktails would go down a storm.'

A deep, chesty laugh startled me, but it wasn't the barman, it was White Shirt next to me. The laugh pulled everything into focus and I looked up, mortified that I'd just said something so cheap and inappropriate in a high-class venue like this, but also dizzy with gratitude towards this stranger for laughing at my joke.

We made eye contact.

It was him.

His eyes were pale green, the tanned skin around them creased into a smile. His hair was longer than I'd seen it, the black waves swept back and greying at the temples. I tried to still my gaze, which darted over his features, drinking in every detail of him like a starving woman faced with a mountain of food.

'That was funny,' he said, his voice rich and holding the trace of an accent. I hadn't expected an accent that wasn't generic, posh.

I looked down, searching every corner and crevice of my paralysed brain for something to say. *It doesn't have*

to be funny or brilliant, Dinny. It just has to be words.
'Thanks,' I said, then looked towards the barman. 'Sorry, I didn't mean to be rude. Long day.'

The barman smiled. 'No problem, all suggestions are welcome!'

I was hyper aware of Isaac next to me, his white-sleeved arm on the bar next to my hand. I hadn't planned it like this. I hadn't planned on engaging straight away, or perhaps even at all. This was an observational activity. I hadn't intended on being thrust into conversation with one of them before I'd even had a sip of alcohol. I needed Jane back. Dinny did not have the confidence and suavity to pull this off. *Come on, Jane. Come back to me.*

'What cocktails are you ordering?' I said, nonchalant, blunt. I looked back at my menu and then up into Isaac's face.

'Well, my personal favourite is the Poisoned Bramble, but my wife is drinking an Eden Mess.'

I nodded thoughtfully at my menu clutched in my numb fingers, pretending I still had the ability to decipher letters and words and make sense of what they meant. I wondered if he'd deliberately mentioned his wife in case I thought he was chatting me up. *As if the idea of chatting me up would even enter someone like Isaac's mind.*

There was no way I could order tap water now, not in his presence. 'I think I'll take your recommendation and go with the Poisoned Bramble,' I said, my voice calm and clipped again.

'Are you ordering a round, or just for you?'

Scottish, that was it. A very faint Scottish lilt.

'Just for me. My friend stood me up so—'

'James, add another Poisoned Bramble. I'll get this,' he said, leaning very slightly towards me as he dug in the back pocket of his jeans for his wallet.

I felt a surge of heat through my body, and my mouth moved uselessly before finding words. 'Errr . . . no, you can't . . . no, honestly, it's fine.' This was too much, this was not the plan.

'Don't be silly. You've been stood up; the least I can do is buy you a hideously overpriced cocktail.' He grinned and winked at me and it was almost too painful to look at him. He was buying me a drink. Isaac Rivers was buying me a drink within five minutes of me getting to the bar. He was talking to me as if I belonged in this place, and making jokes with me, and recommending cocktails, and my heart felt like it was going to burst out of my chest. Tears prickled my eyes for some reason I didn't understand, and I looked down, the words on the menu blurring and merging. *Do not cry, you silly bitch. Do not spoil this. Do. Not. Spoil. This.*

'This is so kind of you, thank you so much,' I managed, the words seeming inadequate.

'It's really nothing,' he said, as the barman placed the four drinks in front of us. 'Come and join us. It's my friend's birthday.'

'I can't gatecrash your friend's birthday!' I said, panic sluicing through me. *I'm not ready for this. I'm not prepared for it.*

'Nonsense, it's not gatecrashing. We're just in a bar.' He shrugged and picked up the two martini glasses. 'Plus, I can't carry these drinks on my own so you're going to have to help me.'

He started walking away, so I had no choice but to slip off the barstool, grab our Poisoned Brambles and follow him.

He stopped and turned back towards me, whispering. 'I haven't asked you your name – and I can't introduce you as the random woman I picked up at the bar.'

I laughed, my guard slipping in the delirium of the moment. 'Dinah,' I said, heart instantly lurching at my mistake.

He nodded. 'Isaac. Or Zac – whichever you prefer.'

We wended our way between tables. I looked down at our identical, purple drinks. Mine and Isaac's. They were full to the brim with a stirrer in each, topped with a tiny golden apple, and two blackberries on cocktail sticks resting across the rims. As we walked, I dipped my head and took a small sip from each glass. I didn't want to spill any.

In a corner of the room, four round tables had been pushed together. Champagne bottles in silver ice buckets sat on each table along with bowls of olives and nuts. An extra table on the end held gifts and cards, and someone had brought a glossy rainbow helium balloon that read *Birthday Boy!* and gently swayed on its taut gold ribbon.

As Isaac got to the tables, a woman in a pale-pink shirt twisted in her seat to look up at him. He bent down and handed her a martini glass, and her profile sent shivers across my skin. It was Sarah, her perfect golden hair cascading in waves to a tapered curve between her shoulder blades. I stopped walking and just watched them. She said something, the smooth line of her chin tilted up towards her husband, who whispered something to her before dabbing a feather-light kiss on her lips. Sarah took the other glass from him and handed it to a woman sitting next to her all in black. I didn't recognise her.

Isaac looked up and beckoned me forward, Sarah twisting further round to see who he was summoning. I strode towards them, holding Isaac's drink out. He took it from me, his cool fingers, wet from the cocktail glasses, brushing against mine.

Most of the people around the table were absorbed in their own conversations, some standing in clusters, others sitting in the velvet chairs.

'This is Diana,' he said to Sarah. *Diana?* He must have misheard me. My mouth moved, wanting to correct him before the moment was gone. But as I stalled, Sarah pushed her chair back and stood, smiling widely, her familiar amber eyes gleaming in the glow of the lamps.

'Nice to meet you, Diana. I'm Sarah.'

And then it was too late. I couldn't go back. I wasn't Dinny, or Dinah, or Jane any more. I was Diana.

Chapter Nine

'I found her at the bar making trouble for the staff so I thought I'd bring her over here and keep her out of the way,' Isaac said, casting me a sly smile that flipped my insides.

'Very thoughtful of you, darling.' Sarah furrowed her brow at her husband in mock earnestness, then turned to me, her expression brightening.

I'd never understood what people meant when they said they'd had an 'out-of-body experience' but I suppose that's what happened to me in the moments that followed. I felt like a spectator in my own life, watching someone who wasn't me accepting smiles and handshakes from strangers. Sarah introduced me to Duncan who was sitting opposite, older and stockier than in his photos. His wife, Evangeline, was the woman in black next to Sarah. She was thin and pale, and wore a slash of scarlet lipstick that was striking against her chalky complexion. Her hair was cropped and black, and a couple of locks had been twisted into contrived curls at her forehead and cheek, reminding me of Jodie Foster in *Bugsy Malone*. There were some peripheral people whose names and faces began to merge and blur . . . Felicity from Isaac's work, or perhaps it was Fiona. David and Harriet from 'next door'.

I tried to ask questions as soon as they occurred to me, desperate to keep the spotlight off my own pitiful life. *So, how long have you lived next door to Isaac and Sarah? And where is that? Sussex? Beautiful . . . I've always been very fond of Sussex. Do you have to commute in to London for work?*

I sipped at my cocktail as everyone answered my questions, seeming happy and confident to wax lyrical about their own lives in minute detail. I couldn't imagine talking about myself for any length of time with even a quarter of the gleeful confidence of Duncan's guests, but as I'd observed many times before, money makes people confident, even when there's little else of interest about them. I don't mean to say the Rivers' friends were boring, but their appeal was dulled by the presence of Isaac and Sarah. It was like trying to focus on tying your shoes when you were in the Sistine Chapel . . . fine for a few moments, but eventually impossible not to look up and around, eyes seeking out the beauty. And as a couple they were both so beautiful. There seemed to be a golden glow about them . . . the way they smiled, and talked and moved. When one of them was actually speaking to you, and looking you in the eye, it was almost too much to bear. It was like trying to look at the sun.

Isaac noticed I'd finished my cocktail before I did, and reached out to take my empty glass, replacing it with a fizzing champagne flute.

'I . . . I should really be buying you a cocktail back . . .' I stuttered.

'Well, I think Duncan's ordered enough of this stuff to get Soho drunk so unless you really want another cocktail, I'm happy with this.'

I took a sip, the dry tang of the bubbles tingling on my tongue. 'It's delicious,' I said, a wave of relief washing over me that I didn't have to engage with that barman again, or spend an insane amount of money on two cocktails.

My insides felt warm and my head fuzzy as I listened to the hubbub of voices around me, the chilled beats of the music woven through the voices, and the pockets of laughter that broke out across the room. I'd had time to gather my thoughts, my story, while people were talking at me, so when the inevitable question came, I was ready for it.

'So, what do you do, Diana?' It was Evangeline who asked the question, tilting her delicate head to one side, her feathered black hair shining like ravens' wings in the light.

'Oh, I'm an English tutor. I generally work with teenagers who have their sights on Oxbridge.' I'd toyed with the idea of completely fabricating an exciting and high-flying career, but was worried about getting caught out, so decided to stick as close to the truth as possible, hoping the mention of Oxbridge would lend a whiff of class. I didn't mention the café.

'Interesting,' she said, eyes narrowing slightly. Her response unnerved me, but Isaac came to my rescue with the next question.

'So – were you Oxbridge yourself?'

'Yes. Oxford actually. Many moons ago!' I smiled and sipped my champagne.

'Wow, that's so impressive.' He smiled and my insides turned to liquid. He was impressed by me. And so far I hadn't told a single lie.

107

'Do you have an office where you're based or do you move around?' asked Sarah.

'I generally like to go to pupils' houses; I find that teaching them in their own environments keeps them more relaxed and receptive.' This time I was impressed with myself. I was speaking with authority and nodding at my own words, emphasising their truth and importance, as everyone else here seemed to do. And I had to admit, it really did make me sound as if I knew what I was talking about. And from the nods that bounced back to me from Isaac, Sarah and Evangeline, I knew they were buying it.

'And how far are you willing to travel?' said Evangeline.

'Oh my God!' said Sarah, and I flinched at the sudden exclamation. She gripped Evangeline's arm. 'I'm so slow at putting two and two together. Of course – Freddie!' Sarah turned her full-beam smile towards Isaac and then me, as if we would know what they were talking about.

'Of course!' Isaac had clearly experienced his own light-bulb moment and now I was the only one in the dark. 'Duncan, come over here.' He beckoned Duncan, who stood and shuffled his stubby legs between two round tables, coming to stand next to Isaac and sucking a drip of spilt champagne from his hand. I had a disconcerting feeling that I was falling, with nothing to grasp on to to save myself. Whatever was about to happen was being taken out of my hands.

Isaac placed a chummy arm around Duncan's shoulder and gestured towards me with his own glass. 'So – bit of a revelation. Diana here runs a tutoring company that specialises in English, and specifically teenagers wanting to get into Oxbridge. How about that?'

My mouth opened and shut like a goldfish. How quickly and effortlessly I had gone from being an English tutor, to *running a tutoring company that specialises in English*. I had been gilded by Isaac, and looking at his wide-eyed smile I knew he didn't even realise he was doing it. The confidence that flowed freely amongst this shiny group was *so* rich and unstemmable, it even extended its gloopy reach towards outsiders, encasing them in its golden liquid and making them shiny too. I felt like a fly cast in amber, and unable to move so much as a wing or a leg to free myself. And if I had been able to, would I have wanted to? I knew in that moment that I was a willing and submissive prisoner. This was a gilded cage of my own making, and I was delirious to be trapped.

'Really?' said Duncan, an unsynchronised blink giving away the effects of the champagne. 'Where are you based?'

'London, but . . . I sometimes travel.' My heart had broken out of its fuzzy drunken cocoon and was beating its ferocious rhythm again.

'Sussex?' he said.

'Could do.' I nodded, unable to think of longer answers. Unwilling to risk saying something that would spoil this.

'Bet you'd charge an arm and a leg for that, though, wouldn't you?'

'I . . . ummm . . . I hadn't really—'

Evangeline interrupted. 'She'd still probably be better value than that bloody awful man we hired last year.' She raised a thin eyebrow as she sipped her drink.

'Guys,' Isaac interrupted, 'I don't think we should be assuming things about Diana's rates and services before we've even asked her.' He rolled his eyes at me, mocking his friends. Bringing me into his joke. He was on my side, not theirs.

'Quite right, don't be so vulgar, Vangie,' said Duncan, before turning to me. 'So what are your rates?'

'Well . . .' I swallowed. *Come on, don't wilt now. Stand strong. You're one of them. You are one of them.* I narrowed my eyes and cast what I hoped was a wicked smile at 'Vangie'. 'I'd rather like to hear more about this awful man you hired last year.'

'Ha! Don't!' she chortled, casting a conspiratorial grimace at me. 'He was abysmal. Freddie hated him, he smelt like over-cooked carrots, and he charged eighty pounds an hour.'

I swallowed. Eighty an hour.

'I mean, don't get me wrong,' she continued. 'I'd happily pay that for someone good. It's just he didn't strike us as really . . . worth it . . . if you see what I mean?' Her voice petered out as if she was embarrassed. She was embarrassed that I might think her cheap for moaning about spending eighty pounds an hour on a job I'd always done for thirty.

'Well, perhaps we could negotiate—' I suggested.

'But hang on,' Isaac said, 'not to interfere or anything, but Carrot Man lived around the corner, didn't he? Diana would be travelling.'

'Oh, of course, travelling costs on top,' Duncan said, with a nonchalant wave of his hand. 'I mean – could we do a few weeks as a trial? See if Freddie's not a complete lost cause?'

'Duncan!'

'Well,' said Duncan, ruffling his mousey hair, 'he does drift a bit, doesn't he? With his studies?'

Vangie sighed, her red lips tightening in reluctant agreement. 'Whoever tutors him probably will need to work on his focus a bit.'

I nodded slowly, a concerned professional who'd seen it all before. 'Well, he wouldn't be the first reluctant teenage boy I'd tutored, that's for certain.' Still no word of a lie had left my lips. I sipped my drink and absorbed Vangie's grateful smile. She appreciated the reassurance. Freddie would be fine. In the right hands.

'I mean . . . do you have availability?' she asked.

'I have some. I'd have to check my work diary.' *Play it cool, Dinny.*

'Where would you be travelling from?'

'I'm . . . I'm based outside Richmond.'

Duncan nodded. 'Right, so probably take you best part of an hour to get to us.'

'And we'd want two hours, like we had with Bill, or whatever his name was. That's quite a chunk of time for you.' Vangie looked at me with a worried frown, and I realised they'd talked themselves into this. They *really* wanted me now. Even more so now there was a possibility I wasn't available.

'Four hours in total.' I pursed my lips and looked sky-ward, as if working something out. I felt four pairs of eyes trained on my face and for a fleeting moment imagined this morning's version of me seeing a photograph of this moment, with Isaac, Sarah, Duncan and Vangie encircling me, watching me, waiting for me to say something. This morning's me would have hyperventilated herself to death in her sweltering flat. Amazing how far a haircut, three drinks and a new name can take you. 'Right . . . it might just about be doable, but I'll have to double-check and get back to you.'

Vangie snatched up a black clutch bag she'd left on her seat and retrieved her phone. I sipped my drink, willing my hands not to shake as I watched her tap at her screen, the blue light emphasising her Bugsy Malone curls.

She looked up. 'What's your surname?'

'Malone,' I said.

'Great.' She handed me her phone to type in my number, which I did with the painstaking precision of someone diffusing a bomb. I checked and double-checked before handing the phone back to her. She gave me a missed call and I made a show of saving her number.

'Vangie Slade,' she said as I did so, and I nodded, casting wary glances at Isaac and Sarah in case either of them had noticed I'd entered her surname before she'd said it. But Sarah was beaming at Vangie, and Isaac was talking to Duncan, so my minor misstep had gone unnoticed. But I knew I'd have to be careful now. So, so careful. Because *Malone* had been my first real lie.

'Do you have a website?' Duncan asked.

I felt a panicked lurch in my stomach, but Diana gave a soft, knowing laugh. 'Actually, no. We got rather flooded with enquiries when we first set up, and inevitably had to let a lot of people down. So now I like to keep things word of mouth.' They all nodded. 'I've also found that's the way to get the best quality clients too. That . . . and gatecrashing strangers' birthday parties,' I added with a wink at Duncan.

They all burst into laughter at that, and I felt a shot of pure euphoria surge up, coursing through my bloodstream and setting off fireworks in my brain. For the second time that night I felt I was about to cry, and realised it was because these feelings were too big, too huge, too unfamiliar to be contained inside me. I was being accepted by these people. They were laughing at my jokes and asking me about my life and not looking at me like I was an embarrassing liability who needed to be kept in check. Where Dinny Marshall would have sunk, Diana Malone was only just beginning to rise.

I lay on my bed that night, staring at the orange slits of light on my ceiling from the streetlamps that shone through my blinds. I still wore my emerald dress, because I couldn't bear to take it off, to step out of my new persona and return to being dowdy Dinny.

Words and images from the evening buzzed around my room, echoing in my mind and dancing in the shadows. *What cocktails are you ordering? I can't carry these drinks so you'll have to help me. I haven't asked you your name. Isaac, or Zac . . . whichever you prefer. Nice to meet you, Diana. Are you staying in town tonight? Do you need to share a taxi? Are you sure?*

I heard Sarah's bright laughter echoing down the spiral staircase as we made our way out of Eden House. I smelt the waft of Isaac's familiar scent as he kissed me goodbye on both cheeks. I watched Vangie's sheer black sleeve billow in the cool night breeze as she waved before disappearing into a black cab.

And then I was back at the beginning again, standing outside Eden House with no idea how to gain entry, or what awaited me if I did. A couple emerged, the man holding the door open from me. *I'm here for Duncan Slade's party.*

This delicious cycle of events went round and round until I didn't know if I was thinking or dreaming, awake or asleep. Perhaps I was all those things all at once, because at some point the next day I noticed the orange light had gone, and the rosy summer morning was painting my bedroom walls a frosted pink.

I imagined this must be how Cinderella felt the morning after the ball. Delirious, but bereft. Grateful it had happened, but grieving it was over. But no, it wasn't over. And it was this thought that propelled me into the living room, and saw me flipping open my laptop, searching *Microsoft* and clicking *create new account*. There I gave myself a new email address using the name *Diana Malone* and the password *Riverdean0310*. The box safe combination had stuck in my head, and it gave me a thrill to use it along with the name of the house . . . things none of them would ever guess I knew in a million years. Buoyed by my shiny new email address, I clicked into PayPal and added it to my account. I didn't want to tempt fate, but if it ever came to taking payment from Vangie, I couldn't give my bank details and reveal I'd been lying about my name. This way she could pay me just using my new email address. It was perfect.

My new account gave me an excuse to text Vangie, but I didn't want to be hasty. So I went back into the bedroom and reluctantly peeled my green dress off and hung it in the wardrobe, stroking the fabric one more time before closing the door. In the shower I stood under the hot water, eyes pressed shut against the flow, calculating what my text should say. It needed to be friendly but professional. A courtesy text that had no agenda other than to impart information. It was not a plea for work, or an excuse for contact. I was not begging for this tutoring job. I was simply being polite.

In my bedroom, I threw on a black T-shirt and my denim shorts. I'd washed the shorts after the weekend at Riverdean, but there was still a dull brown smear of blood on the left thigh. I knew there was no chance of getting them clean now, but I liked the shorts, so I didn't want to get rid of them.

I sat on the sofa, staring at my phone and the blinking blue cursor under Vangie's name. *Hello!* I typed, instantly cringing and deleting it. Too chirpy. Too 'Pick me!'

Hi Vangie. That was better. More classy.

It was great to meet you all last night, I hope Duncan had a great birthday. No, 'great' twice was not good. Especially from an elite English tutor.

I hope Duncan had a fabulous birthday. Yes, 'fabulous' was a Diana word. She'd definitely use 'fabulous'.

If you'd like to give me a few more details about Freddie, and confirm what sort of tutoring sessions you're looking for, I'd love to . . . No, not 'love'. Too desperate.

115

I'll see if I can squeeze you in anywhere. Yes.

If you'd prefer email, that's fine too. Good – informative, brief.

Dxx. No, not yet.

Diana. Perfect.

After adding my new email address in brackets, I pressed send.

I threw my phone onto the coffee table, chewing my lip, wondering if the Hotmail email address was too unprofessional. But I didn't have my own website, so I supposed any email address was going to look amateurish. *Stop over-thinking.*

I made my way, zombie-like, to the kitchen. The flat was tiny, and the kitchen a cramped arrangement of plastic-coated units in one corner. The worktops were chipboard covered in a grainy, faux-marble pattern. I thought back to the cool, silky kitchen surfaces in Riverdean, the dense luxuriousness of the delicately veined stone. I picked at a corner of the plastic that was peeling off to reveal the flaky wood crumbs underneath. It reminded me of the stuff Hen and I used to line our pet mice cages with when we were children. There was a two-ring gas hob, a small oven with a broken door that only stayed shut once wedged with a ball of tin foil, and a fridge that smelt of burnt plastic.

Thoughts swirled in my head, and not positive ones. I dreaded reading a message back from Vangie saying something like, *It was lovely to meet you, but I don't think we'll be taking the tutoring any further*, or *Gosh, I don't even remember talking about that*, or *Perhaps we'd all just had a bit too much to drink and got a bit over-enthusiastic!* I told myself that of course she would dismiss my text, either with one of those comments (or similar), or by simply not replying at all. People like the Slades and the Rivers don't find tutors for their precious offspring by chatting to random strangers in Soho bars. The threads of these doubts and worries wove themselves into a tight knot in my stomach.

I made myself an instant coffee, ignoring the anxiety that curdled the liquid the moment I swallowed. I flicked on the electric fan, wondering whether to open a window, or let the glass and the thin orange curtains do their best to keep out the burgeoning heat of the day. It was as I touched my hand to the curtain fabric that my phone pinged, sending a slosh of coffee over the rim of my mug as my whole body jolted. I crossed to the sofa, plonked my mug down and swiped up my phone. Vangie Slade's name illuminated my screen within a green notification banner. With tingling fingers, I tapped on it.

Fab to hear from you, Diana. We'd love you to come and do some sessions with Freddie. Email with details to follow. Vxx

The relief that washed over me made me feel almost sick. I read and reread the text with a pounding heart, analysing every character in minute detail. I was thrilled she'd used 'fab' which echoed my own use of 'fabulous', and reassured me I'd set the right tone with my own message. The abruptness of the text was also reassuring: they wanted me, that was definite. And the two kisses were just perfection. This wasn't how you'd end a text

117

to a new tutor you'd found online. This was a text to someone for whom you felt a certain degree of affection. Perhaps a new friend. And the fact that Vangie felt this way made me realise Isaac and Sarah probably did too. *I was their new friend.*

I felt as if my heart were floating inside my body, like an astronaut in a space shuttle. I couldn't remember the last time I'd felt this sense of pure happiness. Of weightless joy. Even contemplating going to work in the café tomorrow didn't bring me down. Work would be easy, maybe even fun. Because now I had something new to focus on. I could make coffee and serve customers and make inane chit-chat with Kate, all with a smile on my face, because now I had new, better things to think about. I had access to a new world, and in the new world lived all my new friends.

The joy inside me was too big for the four walls of my stifling flat, so I swept into my bedroom and grabbed my rucksack, then knelt on the floor to retrieve my writing box from under the bed. It was ancient and battered. At some point in my teens I'd covered it with floral wallpaper my parents were using to redecorate the hallway, but now the corners were ripped and tattered, the sticky tape browning and brittle. I slid the box out and lifted the lid, taking out my latest correspondence set. I'd found it in a WHSmith a couple of months ago, and loved the raspberry-red edging of the cream paper. Gold vines wound their way up the sides, with miniature leaves and gold berries ornamenting them.

I'd always loved writing letters – whether it was to my French pen pal, or to our cousins who lived on the

Isle of Wight, or as thank you notes for Christmas and birthday presents. Back when I was growing up, we were always encouraged to write proper letters. I'd found it heartbreaking when email took over. I still used to write letters at university; back then it was still just about acceptable. But now, if anyone saw me doing it, they'd comment or make a joke. As Kate had done when she'd caught me writing a letter on my lunch break. But I didn't care. Dad had always maintained that letters were the most rewarding form of communication. Which is why he was my only enduring pen pal.

I slipped the writing set into my rucksack and headed out of the flat, tugging the warped door hard shut behind me.

Chapter Ten

Heron Park is a sprawling, messy patchwork of woodland, grass, marshy ditches and babbling streams. By midday on that particular Sunday, it was already teeming with picnicking families, boisterous dogs, and displaced teenagers. I walked across an open common, towards a shady cluster of trees. Some kids had slung a rope over a low branch and an older boy pushed two blonde girls who shrieked as they swung from the creaking bough.

I slunk past them and squeezed through a gap in the bushes, stepping over a trampled barbed-wire fence and making my way down into the gully, the sound of the burbling water and the chill of the damp air rising to greet me. The slope was a tangled mess of twigs and brambles, and the earthy tang of damp soil and crushed leaves met my nostrils. The river was more of a brook that day, having been dried out by the hot weather. It's not always like this, though. After heavy rainfall, the river swells into an unrecognisable beast that tears along the slope, grabbing trees as it goes and oozing over the opposite bank, turning the flat grasslands into marsh. But when the water runs low, a large flat stone is revealed in the shade at the water's edge, and now I headed towards it, sinking onto its hard surface and relishing the cool tingle of the rock against the bare skin of my legs.

I could hear children's laughter in the distance, and if I craned my neck, I could see families settled on picnic blankets along the opposite bank. But no one came to this part of the river. The barbed-wire fence at the top was too unwelcoming for families, and the bank too steep and knotted to attempt with small children. So here I was safe.

I took out my writing set and rummaged in the bottom of the rucksack for a pen, eventually finding a chewed blue Biro. I had a gold fountain pen back at the flat. My parents had given it to me as a 'well done' gift when I'd been accepted to Oxford, along with some thick, cream writing paper. The pen in particular had been uncharacteristic of them in its extravagance; they'd never really bought into things that were ostentatious or unnecessary. But I suppose that was the point. The luxuriousness of the pen symbolised how proud they were of me. I guessed the whole gift had been Dad's idea – acknowledgement and approval of my love of letter-writing – and I also took it as an invitation to write to him when I left home, a tradition I'd continued through to the present day.

But I hadn't used the pen in more than twenty years. It was too painful. After I'd been forced to leave Oxford, I felt I didn't deserve to use it. The glossy weight of it was only a reminder of how much of a disappointment I was. So I kept it under a stack of letters from Dad, in the battered box under the bed, in its navy-blue case with the claret velvet lining.

I shifted on the stone slab, resting the pad on my knee and writing the date in the top right-hand corner. Then I watched my pen form the slopes and curves of those two familiar words that always seemed to calm me. *Dear Dad*.

I never really planned what I'd say, other than vaguely in my head. Sometimes something would happen and I'd think *that needs to go in my next letter to Dad*, but other than that I just let my news pour out onto the page. On this occasion I had so much to say, and was excited to share news that was more than just a string of trivial stories about the café. I started by elaborating on the text I'd sent him at Riverdean, explaining how I came to be on a mini-break with the girls, then painting a detailed picture of the house in all its magnificence. (I didn't mention staying on an extra night). I then went on to explain how I'd secured a brilliant tutoring job that would earn me more than twice as much as my previous tutoring work, and that I hoped this would be the start of getting back into it . . . perhaps more pupils would follow, and then maybe, if I saved enough money, I could see a way towards finishing my degree. I felt my lips curve into a smile as I wrote those words, imagining a day when I might feel able to take the fountain pen out again, and write Dad a letter with it. A day when I felt I deserved it.

I signed off as I always did, *Dinah xxx*, and folded the paper before sliding it into an envelope and sealing it shut.

*

The two weeks following my night at Eden House felt blurry and fragmented. Emails and texts pinged back and forth between Vangie and me, but every time I saw her name on my screen, everything else around me faded to black, so all I could see were her words, and all I could think of was my response. Misha gave me a warning at least three times for ignoring a customer and staring at my phone.

'What's got into you?' she asked, her mousey fringe quivering with annoyance above her magenta cat-eye glasses. When Misha wasn't around, Kate would tease me about having a new boyfriend, something I strenuously denied, not because I didn't want her thinking that, but because I couldn't bear the humiliation of being teased on such a subject by someone twenty years my junior. I finally snapped as we were shutting up one day, after she'd asked me who I was texting in a flirtatious, sing-song tone that made me want to suffocate her with a gingham tablecloth.

'Can you just fucking drop it?' I said.

There was no one in the café but still she cast her gaze wildly around the room, as if for witnesses. I stared at her until she looked down and continued wiping coffee rings off the counter. That evening I waited for the inevitable *ping!* of a text from Hen, who Kate would no doubt have contacted in order to report on my unhinged behaviour. Sure enough the text came at about eight o'clock.

How are you doing Dinny? x

Oh, you know, fine. Just a normal day with a colleague who looks over my shoulder to read all my texts then reports on me to my big sister when I tell her to fuck off. You?

She's just worried about you, Din. Are you OK?

I'm totally fine! I'm trying to sort out a new tutoring job, if you must know. And every time I look at my phone, your number one secret agent is in my face asking me what I'm doing and trying to look at who I'm texting and it's driving me insane! Call off the dogs, or I'm going to chuck her mobile under a train. Preferably whilst she's holding it.

That's great you're getting back into the tutoring. Why didn't you just tell Kate that?

Because it's none of her fucking business! I don't owe her, or you, an explanation every time I text someone.

OK. I'm sorry you feel she's over-stepping.

But you're not sorry she *is* over-stepping?

Don't be pedantic.

Fuck off, Hen.

There followed an incoming call from Hen that I cancelled. I wanted to turn my phone off but I couldn't in case Vangie texted.

Back at work the next day, Kate was subdued with me, but I didn't apologise. If anyone was owed an apology, it was me. But none was forthcoming, so I met Kate's sulking with my own silence, relishing the lack of inane conversation.

A few days later I noticed her tapping at her phone in a lull between customers, before laying it face down and disappearing into the stock room. I grabbed it quickly, before it had had time to lock itself. Clicking into her texts, I saw Hen's name at the top, and opened the conversation. There was a stream of observations and updates, almost as if Kate was my counsellor and was being paid to psychoanalyse me.

Dinah was quite grumpy today. Might need a cheer up call from big sis? Xx . . . She was late for work third time in a row – Misha's furious. Perhaps check in this eve xx . . . Dinah's been very distracted at work. I'm worried something's on her mind. Xx

Rage boiled inside me. Who the fuck did she think she was? She was nothing to me. She wasn't family and certainly wasn't a friend. How dare she treat my life as if I was in some sort of controlled experiment, and she a psychoanalyst on the other side of a two-way mirror, observing and making notes and reporting back to her boss about how the patient was doing? Hen was one thing – she was a control freak of an older sibling – but Kate . . . how fucking dare she?

Her observations were met with short responses from Hen: *thanks Kate xx* and *that's great, I'll give her a call this evening xx* . . . and what was with these constant bloody kisses? As if they were best friends or something. I heard the slash of scissors through packing tape, and the cough of a cardboard box being opened in the stock room. I turned away with the phone, shielding it from view in case

Kate came out. The latest message had been typed only two minutes ago. It read, *Dinah's still very sullen at work. Perhaps depressed? Still being very secretive on her phone. Xx*

Three blinking dots appeared at the top of the screen and I knew Hen was replying. Sure enough, the swooping sound of a new message came, and a response appeared: *Thanks Kate. I'll call her tonight. Xx*

I chewed my lip, an idea flickering. I clicked into Kate's contacts, found my own phone number and swapped the last five digits for new ones. Then I found Hen's number and blocked it. Lastly, I swiped back out, locked the phone and replaced it face down on the counter, just as Kate rounded the corner carrying two stacks of paper cups. I didn't offer to help her with the teetering stacks, but squeezed past her and into the stock room myself. There, I unlocked my own phone and texted Kate.

> *Me again. Just so you know I've got a new phone so you can delete my old number and just use this one. Thanks. Hen Xx*

I knew this was a gamble, and in all likelihood I'd get found out eventually. But somehow I couldn't muster the energy to give even the tiniest shit. My phone pinged in my hand. Kate.

> *No worries, will do! Xx*

Perfect. Now I'd be able to read and respond to every little observation Kate made about me, and Hen would be getting nothing. The added bonus was that Kate no longer had my phone number either, so I wouldn't have to endure any more *where are you?* texts when I was running five minutes late. Perhaps those texts would now go into the ether, never to be read by anyone. Or perhaps they'd bounce back as an unrecognised number. Or perhaps a random guy in Glasgow would type some angry expletives back to her, asking who the fuck she was and why she was texting him. I decided I was happy with any of those eventualities.

But despite my ongoing fury at Hen and Kate, they were not the main subjects of my thoughts and dreams in those two weeks. The more emails and texts I swapped with Vangie, the more solid a plan became. Evenings would be difficult, as I'd have to travel from the centre of London to Hounslow, pick up my car, then drive to Sussex. Then there were the added complications of Freddie's after-school activities – mainly sports clubs, it seemed; he was clearly an active young man, and pinning him down for tutoring was not an easy thing. We eventually landed on the idea of Saturday mornings. Vangie was concerned that this would eat into my weekend, and I'd end up cancelling often when family or social commitments came up. I assured her I often worked at the weekend, and that it was a necessary part of maintaining a successful tutoring company.

So the date for Freddie's first session was set for the second Saturday in July. I was aware that it was almost the end of term, and that school would be breaking up soon after. When I mentioned this to Vangie in an email, wondering how she wanted to play it with summer holidays, she said it was important he maintained his studies throughout the summer break so he could hit the ground running in September. I wondered if Freddie agreed with this theory, but doubted he had much say in the matter, for which I was grateful. It meant I would spend my summer Saturdays earning more money in four hours than I would in two days in the café, and be able to keep contact with the Slades, and Isaac and Sarah too. I thought of the girl with the dandelion. Perhaps she also needed a tutor? But I didn't want to get ahead of myself. Baby steps.

*

The morning of my first session with Freddie, I was flustered and panicky. My heart pounded in my ears as I spooned coffee into a mug, splashing boiling water over my hand and spilling the contents of the mug as I lurched for the cold tap and held my raw skin under the flow of the water. It seemed a bad omen. I stepped away from the kitchen and had a long shower instead, trying to get my thoughts straight, trying to remember what I'd need to take.

I had no money to buy anything new to wear, so had dug around in my wardrobe for my most presentable ensemble. This was a pair of basic black trousers and a sky-blue shirt I'd bought from H&M ten years ago. I hoped the Slades wouldn't get close enough to notice the cheap, synthetic sheen of the trousers, or the shabby stitching in the shirt-sleeves. I used my expensive 'curl defining' shampoo, and slicked the hairdresser's cremes and oils over my clean hair, scrunching and twisting as the stylist had done, then spritzing with a finishing spray. I applied a lighter-handed version of the make-up I'd worn to Eden House, and stood back to see as much of myself as I could in my tilted dressing table mirror. I didn't look as polished as I had for Eden House, but it was still ten times better than my everyday look. I'd washed an old canvas tote bag that sported the words 'London Books' with a sketch of a bookshop in blue ink printed on the front, then filled it with a large pad of lined paper, a slim, transparent pencil case of blue Biros, an A5 spiral-bound notebook, and a printout of the current A Level English Literature syllabus. I hooked the bag over my shoulder, then slung the miniature Chanel handbag across my body. I didn't really need it, but it was my talisman, and lent me, I hoped, an air of sophistication. I looked smart, professional, and in control.

'Diana Malone,' I said to my reflection, using that organic, clipped tone that had surfaced naturally on the phone to Sarah, and again in Eden House. 'Diana Malone, owner of a tutoring company that specialises in English, for students applying to Oxbridge.'

The car journey was sweltering, with the air conditioning broken and only circulating warm air around the car. The polyester fabric of my clothes made me sweat, and I felt the small of my back sticking to the car seat through my shirt. I had allowed two hours for the drive, desperate not to be late.

I arrived forty minutes early in the village of Broadsham, and parked by a parade of shops – I had no intention of clunking up the Slades' driveway in my clapped out, peeling Micra. I slipped into an air-conditioned café and drank a bottle of chilled water, before going to the tiny toilet at the back of the café (careful not to catch my pale sleeves on the grimy walls) and washing my hands, holding my wrists under the cold water, and feeling the blissful drop in my body temperature. I wiped melted mascara from under my eyes and blotted the sheen from my face with dry tissue paper. I was ready. Or at least, as ready as I'd ever be.

I'd studied Google Maps so many times I knew how to get to Blackworth House from the parade, but I still didn't want to take any chances. I followed the blue line on my phone as I crossed the main road, passed a row of sandstone houses, and turned left onto a road shaded by high, thick-trunked trees. Unlike the narrow road that brought me into Broadsham, there were no chocolate box cottages here, or cute wooden gates hung with plaques embossed with names like *Honeycomb House*, and *Wisteria Lodge*. The houses along this road were hidden from view, set back from the road, behind red-brick walls or wrought-iron gates.

Eventually I found myself standing in front of a modern-looking, solid timber gate, flanked by a high wall, and topped with a security camera that winked its red eye at me from above. A familiar twist in my stomach reminded me of the feeling I'd had outside Eden House two weeks ago. The feeling of being an outsider. An intruder. But no, I told myself, I was neither of those things. I had been asked to come here. I was being paid to come here. Diana Malone had a job to do, and she was going to do it.

I strode over to a silver unit attached to the wall, and pressed the buzzer.

The unit crackled and a woman's voice came through. 'Hello?'

'Hi, it's Diana.' There was a pause, and I suddenly wondered if it was Vangie I was speaking to, or someone else who might not know who I was. I faltered. 'I . . . I'm Freddie's tutor. I think they're expecting—'

The unit gave a harsh beep, and I flinched away from it as a grinding noise sounded from behind the wall, and the heavy gate began to slide back, revealing tramlines in the gravel.

Blackworth House eased into view, and it was extraordinary. It looked like a giant glass Rubik's cube held together with black aluminium. Wide slate steps led up to the black front door, which opened as I approached.

'Diana! Wonderful to see you.' Vangie spread her arms and I felt my shoulders sink with relief. I'd made it, I was here, she was expecting me.

'Fabulous to see you too!' I chimed, trying to match her confident tone. If we were going to be friends, I needed to be an equal, not a meek employee.

She clasped my shoulders and planted an air kiss either side of my face before stepping back to let me in. The space was cavernous, the pale marble floor stretching forever across the immense open-plan room. It was like an airport lounge or a huge hotel lobby. Where Riverdean was soft and luxurious, this was stark and striking. A white island stood near freestanding kitchen units in black. Sofas in gunmetal grey were dotted about, and ferns in chrome pots stretched up towards a glass walkway that could be reached by a spiral staircase in the centre of the space. It was impossible not to say something.

'Gosh. This is just absolutely stunning,' I said, and it was true – I was stunned. I also knew my face was set in an incredulous expression.

Vangie gave an appreciative sigh. 'Thank you so much. It's taken a bit of work . . . it's been a labour of love, shall we say . . . but we're thrilled with how it turned out.'

'You had it built then?'

'Yes – Duncan's an architect by trade, although now of course he's mainly into property development. He's made so many contacts over the years it seemed inevitable he'd design and build us a house one day.'

'Well quite,' I said, wondering how anyone got to a place in their life when a house like this was 'inevitable'.

I tried to make sure I smiled as my eyes swept over the sharp angles and monochrome palette. I was terrified that something in my face would give away the question that hummed inside my brain: if you had millions of pounds to build your dream home, why on God's earth would you want to live in a vast, soulless, greenhouse? There was no doubt it was a striking display of wealth: every detail seemed stamped with invisible pound signs. At least, that's how I looked at it, with my cash-strapped eyes. Perhaps if you were also wealthy, you'd just see good taste. But then I thought back to Riverdean, and my impressions of that house. Yes, it was obviously the home of a very rich family, but it exuded a warmth, colour and softness that Blackworth House was completely lacking.

'I'll make us coffee,' said Vangie, as we walked the length of a tennis court to get to the angular kitchen.

My shoes reverberated on the marble as we walked, and I wondered if I should have offered to remove them. When we arrived at the kitchen I felt like I was standing in the middle of an art installation at the Tate Modern. Vangie placed small porcelain cups in a chrome recess in a wall unit and pressed a button, and I watched the silky brown liquid flow in two perfect streams. She opened a black cabinet to reveal a fridge, and I caught a bright flash of milk, eggs, Babybel, Fanta. The items seemed incongruous, comical even, in this environment. I wondered what it said about a home when groceries looked laughably out of place.

She walked me to an endless chrome trestle table set at the back of the space, and I sat, looking out at black decking that led to a rectangular swimming pool surrounded by more white marble, and six black sun loungers. A low box hedge bordered the pool on three sides, and I watched a man with a chainsaw trimming the perfect edges.

'He normally comes on a Friday but could only do Saturday this week.' Vangie scowled through the glass. 'If he's too noisy we can ask him to stop?'

'No – I think he's fine. It's actually very quiet through the glass.'

'Yes, well, thank goodness for air conditioning or we'd be sweltering keeping these things shut.' She gestured towards the towering glass wall, and I assumed she meant 'these things' to be some sort of doors, but looking at the vast glass squares I couldn't tell where wall became door or door became wall. 'I'll just go and get Freddie.'

She jogged up the spiral staircase and disappeared through a door that led off the gallery. I arranged my notepad, pens, and syllabus in front of me and then sipped my coffee, waiting for two sets of echoing footsteps to emerge from the cool silence. When they did, I looked up and watched Vangie walk back down the staircase, followed by a slim, loping figure in green cargo shorts and a black T-shirt. His dark hair fell forwards over his eyes and he swept it back with his fingers before pushing his hands back into his pockets. He was smaller than I'd expected.

'This is Freddie,' said Vangie, with that tight-jawed expression parents use to introduce children who may or may not embarrass them. I'd noted it was usually reserved for teenagers.

'Hi Freddie,' I said, stepping forward and extending a hand. He peeped through his fringe at me and offered a limp hand back. I shook it firmly. 'I'm Diana, and I'm really excited to meet you.'

'Hi,' he murmured, shuffling his feet.

'Freddie's excited too, aren't you, Freddie?' Vangie said.

I'd never seen anyone look less excited about anything.

During the short exchange that followed, I learned that Freddie was smaller than I expected because he wasn't seventeen and about to embark on his A Levels, but fifteen, and about to begin his GCSE year. The downside was that the syllabus I'd printed out and diligently pored over was useless, but the upside was that this job was going to be a walk in the park. Vangie and Duncan had decided that as GCSE English took up two whole GCSEs (literature and language), they were keen to tick them both off with one tutor. And that was absolutely fine by me.

Freddie was, as I'd been forewarned, a bit of a day-dreamer. The body language I'd first taken to be surliness was in fact just shyness, so I spent some time chatting to him about school and his subjects. It seemed he had a natural ability at maths, which I told him I was in complete awe of, being a mathematical dunce myself. He liked sports too, but didn't do well with English, Art or History. He became more vocal the more we talked, and I noticed him pushing his hair from his eyes more frequently in order to make eye contact, which I took to be a good sign.

The texts he was studying (*Silas Marner* and *Twelfth Night*) were ones I knew inside out, so we chatted in general about the stories and the characters, and did some short comprehension exercises I made up on the spot, pretending this was an 'informal assessment session' rather than admitting I'd printed the wrong syllabus and was completely unprepared. We had a short break after an hour when Vangie brought me more coffee and a squash for Freddie, but apart from that we were uninterrupted. I made sure I over-ran by ten minutes or so, so I could make a point of saying, 'Gosh, I've been so engrossed in our session I didn't notice the time!' to Vangie when I spotted her in the kitchen.

She approached, scarlet lips set in a thin crescent smile. 'How was that, Freddie?'

I willed him to offer some form of muted enthusiasm, something that would set me apart from his previous tutor, or Carrot Man as I'd now come to think of him.

'Yeah. Good.' He nodded, once again looking at his shoes, hair flopping over his eyes.

I felt my hopefulness dissolve. But Vangie's smile broadened and she nodded at me. 'Good? Gosh, I don't think I've ever heard you give such high commendation, Freddie.'

'Am I to understand I've been damned with faint praise?' I said in my best affable voice.

'Oh no, I'm serious,' Vangie said, thin eyebrows raised. 'Carrot Man used to get a grunt at best, isn't that right, Freddie?'

Poor Freddie scuffed his shoes on the marble floor, and I remembered what it was like at that age – understanding a joke but unsure where exactly it was aimed, or how to join in.

'Well, I think I eased you in gently today, so I'm fully expecting my review rating to plummet in the coming weeks when we really get down to work!' Pushy parents loved terms like *really get down to work*. And clearly Vangie was no exception.

Her deep brown eyes glittered and she gave a vigorous nod. 'Fabulous,' she said. 'Well, we'll see you the same time next week then?'

'Absolutely, looking forward to it.'

We agreed I'd invoice once a month because that's how I said I usually worked. That sounded more Diana, when the truth was Dinny would really have liked cash in hand every week. But still, it was money (and a lot of it by my standards) so however it came was fine by me.

It was only as Vangie was showing me out that the question that had been churning inside me finally escaped my lips. 'How are Isaac and Sarah?'

She looked up at me. 'Oh, good, I think?' Her eyebrows dipped as if she'd been caught off guard. But I needed to make sure I was tethered to them – tethered to that night in Eden House when we'd all been so friendly. I couldn't risk coming here week after week and becoming like the man with the chainsaw outside: a member of household staff who could be rescheduled or told to be quiet or dismissed at the drop of a hat. No, I needed to make sure from the outset that they saw me as one of them, as a friend who was doing them a favour by finding time in her busy schedule to tutor their son.

'To be honest,' Vangie continued, 'I don't think I've been in touch with them since Duncan's birthday.'

'That was a really fun night,' I blurted, catching myself at the phrasing. *Really fun night* wasn't quite the way Diana spoke. *Really fun nights* were what Dinny had.

Vangie looked at me, and in the beat of silence I swear I saw her eyes narrow. But we were outside the front door at this point, so I told myself it was probably a reaction to the sun as she looked up into my face.

'Yes, it was rather fun.'

'We should go again,' I said, clinging to this moment, desperate to delay my exit and my departure once again from this new world. Desperate to make a connection with Isaac and Sarah again. 'I love Eden House,' I added, hoping to convey my familiarity with the venue.

'Yes . . . yes, it is good,' she said, but her words seemed faded, and her eyes held something I couldn't quite decode. She was looking directly at me, but it was as if her mind was elsewhere. 'Anyway, thanks for today. See you next week.'

Her smile was tight as she closed the door, and I felt something shift in the pit of my stomach. Something uncomfortable. She hadn't addressed my suggestion of going back to Eden House. I'd expected something like, *Oh, gosh, that would be fabulous!* or *I'm sure Isaac and Sarah would love to see you again!* But she hadn't said anything like that. I felt a sinking sensation as I wondered if the two couples weren't as close as I'd thought. Perhaps this tutoring job wasn't the gateway to a friendship with Isaac and Sarah. Perhaps Isaac and Duncan were purely work colleagues who politely invited each other to birthday parties, and that was it.

I walked back to my car, my elation at how well the tutoring had gone dissipating as a gnawing anxiety took over. I'd pushed it too hard with Vangie. I needed to back off and not mention the Rivers for a while. I decided to concentrate on being the best tutor I could be, winning over Freddie, securing my position in the household. Then I could work my way back to Riverdean.

Chapter Eleven

The next four Saturday mornings established a routine for Freddie and me. I'd park on the parade, walk to the house, and be met by Vangie. She'd make us both a coffee, go and get Freddie from upstairs, bring me another coffee and a squash for Freddie after one hour, and then leave us for the remaining time. Freddie was intelligent but uninterested. There were moments I'd assume he was considering a question I'd posed, only to find myself tapping his shoulder three minutes later and discovering he hadn't even heard me, or had been thinking about something else entirely. This was rather frustrating, and I found myself trying to keep my tone in check, scared he might decide he disliked me, or that Carrot Man might be preferable, after all.

My anxiety was compounded by the fact that Vangie had been polite but distant with me since the first session. She didn't air-kiss me now when she opened the door, and there was no warm conversation on the way to the coffee machine. She might ask something vague along the lines of *how was your week?* but nothing more. A couple of times I ventured a carefully planned question or two, intended to sustain the feeling I'd had at Eden House . . . the pretence we were equals. *These plant pots are spectacular. Where are they from? I'd love to get something similar for the house.* That sort of thing. It implied not only that I shared her taste, but also that I would be able to afford them, and that I had a house big and grand enough for such bulbous monstrosities. But she always seemed to shut me down, with a *gosh, I can't remember now*, or some such answer.

One Saturday I asked if I'd be seeing Duncan any time soon, and she said he was working very hard at the moment on a huge deal in the city. Something about luxury apartments and foreign investors. And then I realised that was probably the reason she seemed distant and distracted: she was at home, her husband was working so hard she hardly ever saw him, and there was a big deal on the table that might fall through – and the stress was getting to her. I thought about Duncan and Isaac working together, and wondered if Sarah was experiencing a similar thing over at Riverdean. I realised then that I didn't know what Sarah and Vangie's jobs were, so overshadowed were their professional lives by those of their husbands. Obviously Duncan and Isaac's business brought in the bulk of the money, but I wasn't sure if Vangie and Sarah had professions or projects of their own. I made a mental note to frame some questions on the subject for my next visit.

We were now well into August, and the sweltering weather continued. I'd been paid by the Slades for the two sessions in July, and subsequently spent several happy lunch hours back in the posh shops of Covent Garden, fastidiously curating a capsule wardrobe based on my continued trawling of Sarah's Instagram feed.

But my time in these shops was bittersweet. It reminded me of those heady days before Eden House, when I'd searched with adrenalin coursing through my bloodstream, unsure of what I was seeking and of what use it would be when I found it. Part of me longed to be back there, before I first set eyes on Isaac, so I could experience it all again. And my longing for those days (and that night) only increased my desire to see Isaac and Sarah once more – and to return to Riverdean.

As the weeks went by, and I visited Blackworth again and again, it was like I was drifting further and further away from them. Each week Vangie seemed more distant, and I felt more and more like a member of staff. She didn't laugh when I made a joke as she'd done at Eden House. Her eyes didn't glitter with appreciation when I praised Freddie's progress. She didn't make physical contact with me, or say *fabulous* when I said *see you next week*, and I felt my confidence receding like a tide on the sand, slowly pulling me away from that day (and night), that life, and those friends. I had been doing so, so well. But now I had no life raft or rope to cling on to to pull me back.

That was until the third Saturday in August.

My session with Freddie was nearly over, and I was pointing at an extract from *Twelfth Night*: *She pined in thought, And with a green and yellow melancholy she sat like patience on a monument, smiling at grief.* We'd been over Viola's speech the previous week and I was frustrated but unsurprised to learn that Freddie had retained little of what we'd discussed. I'd just asked him to get his notepad out and look at what he'd written, when a harsh buzzing sound ricocheted through the space.

I looked up to see Vangie walking towards the front door, peering at the screen attached to the wall, and pressing a button that gave a loud beep. Freddie was rummaging through a pile of books and paper with the laborious apathy of someone playing for time, and in this instance I didn't care. It gave me the opportunity to watch his mother. She opened the door and stood silhouetted by the sun, before stepping back and saying something to whoever she'd just opened the gate for.

And then he was there, his figure framed by the rectangle of daylight. He stepped over the threshold and bent to air-kiss her on both cheeks. But they were still so far away I couldn't hear what they were saying. Or perhaps I was deafened by the muffled pounding of my heart.

Isaac and Vangie stood by the door, talking and nodding. *Look up. Look at me. See me.*

'Are you OK?' came a voice next to me, and I startled to see Freddie staring at me, notebook open and eyes wide. He'd never asked if I was OK before, and for one terrible moment I wondered if I'd said the words out loud.

'I'm fine! Do I not look fine?'

'Not really.'

'Thanks.' My thoughts were melting into a puddle like an ice cream in the sun. I had to do something to make Isaac see me. He couldn't just turn around and leave after all these weeks. Who knew when I'd next see him? I wanted to shout *I'm here!* but realised that wouldn't be appropriate. I didn't want to look desperate.

I needed it to come from him, for him to notice me, not the other way round.

'I just need a glass of water,' I said, rising from my seat. 'You . . . you read that speech again and look over your notes.'

My legs felt unsteady as I walked towards the kitchen, aware that every step was taking me closer to them. They still didn't look up, deep in conversation as they were. I turned to a black cabinet and opened it. Plates. I shut it with more force than it needed, and cast a sideways glance towards the door, but they still didn't glance over. I opened another cupboard. After taking out a smoky glass tumbler, I turned towards the sink.

'Are you OK? Do you need something?' It was Vangie. At last she'd seen me.

I looked up with what I hoped was a casual smile. 'Oh, I just needed some water.'

She was walking towards me and, over her shoulder, I watched Isaac pull out his phone. I tried to keep my gaze on Vangie but it was impossible not to watch Isaac, frowning at the screen, head bowed and a lock of hair falling forward. But then he straightened and slid the phone into his back pocket, looking up and towards the kitchen. Our eyes met, and I was rewarded with an instant brightening of his expression.

'Diana! Amazing to see you again.' He strode towards the kitchen and I thought my body would spontaneously combust when he held my shoulders and kissed me on each cheek.

'Isaac, so nice to see you,' I said, amazed to find my voice steady and confident.

'This is so great that the tutoring thing worked out. Who'd have thought a drunken night in Soho would have been the answer to Freddie's GCSE success?'

A trill-like laugh escaped my lips and I threw my head back as I'd seen Sarah do on several occasions. Whilst Isaac beamed, Vangie cast me a sour look. 'Well, let's not get ahead of ourselves,' she said, folding her arms across her chest and glancing at Freddie who was trying to fish something small out of his glass of squash. 'He's not done the exams yet.'

Isaac took a step towards me and placed an arm around my shoulder. Adrenalin surged through me, making my legs quiver. 'I have every faith in Diana's tutoring abilities, and you should too,' he declared.

I decided I was being too passive, so placed a hand on my hip and gave an exaggerated frown. 'Absolutely, and you should also have more faith in Freddie. He's doing brilliantly!'

We all looked over at Freddie who seemed to be smearing something onto the table with his index finger.

'Well, anyway, I didn't mean to interrupt the tutoring session,' said Isaac, stepping away from me. 'I just came to get the gazebo for this afternoon. You said it doesn't fit in your car?'

'Yes, that's right, boot's too small. It's in the driveway shed.'

'OK, I'll grab it on the way out.'

Vangie looked at her watch, then at me. 'I think you've got about ten minutes left, Diana?'

'Oh . . . yes. Sorry. Yes, I have,' I said, looking at my own watch and trying not to feel the sting of her dismissal.

'And then what?' said Isaac. I looked up and noted a mischievous twinkle in his sea-green eyes.

'I . . . what do you mean?' I stuttered, feeling a flush creep up my chest.

'I mean, what happens after you've finished with Freddie?'

'I . . . I go home,' I said, a wave of grief washing over me at those desperate words. *I go home.*

'Or . . .?' He raised one eyebrow as if in a question, and I felt my lips curling into a smile, despite not having the smallest clue what he was talking about. I cast a quick glance at Vangie whose arms were still folded, lips clenched in a thin line. 'Or,' Isaac continued, 'you come to a barbecue at our house and join in the fun?'

If emotions could express themselves then mine would have begun back-flipping down the street at that moment, setting off fireworks and streamers. It took every ounce of willpower I possessed not to throw myself on Isaac and sob into his beautiful smelling neck. Not for the first time in his presence I felt my eyes prickle with tears. Desperate not to reveal my true feelings I grabbed my phone from my pocket and tapped into the calendar . . . the calendar I'd never used, didn't know how to use. The calendar that contained nothing but pre-entered UK bank holidays. 'Let me just—'

'I'm sure Diana has places to be. She's probably got back-to-back tutoring appointments. We're already taking up four hours of her day, you know.' It sounded as if Vangie was giving me an excuse to say no, but her tone was not the same as she'd used previously when concerned I was being inconvenienced, and she didn't search my face for signs I was being polite as she had at Eden House when we'd first talked about Freddie's tutoring. It was almost as if she didn't want me to come to Riverdean.

Isaac watched me making random stabs at my phone screen with my thumb, and when I looked up, he raised his eyebrows again. 'So, any other pressing engagements this afternoon?' He leaned towards me and spoke in a stage-whisper. 'And by that I mean, any pupils you can't cancel?'

Vangie tutted. 'I'm sure Diana is more professional than that. Aren't you, Diana?'

I locked my phone and slipped it back into my pocket before addressing my lie to Isaac. 'I usually have a pupil in Richmond this afternoon but they're on holiday at the moment, so no, I do not have any pressing engagements. I'd love to come to Riverdean.'

'Great!'

'How did you know their house was called Riverdean?' Vangie looked at me with narrowed eyes and I felt a single thud of my heart against my ribs.

'Um . . . I think Sarah mentioned it, when we were at Eden House.' My palms prickled with sweat.

'I don't remember her mentioning the house at all.'

'I think you were talking to Duncan at the time.'

'Vangie . . . you're not a barrister any more. The prosecution rests.' Isaac turned and gave me a wink over Vangie's head so she couldn't see, and my heart gave a responsive squeeze.

'Right, you finish with Freddie,' he instructed. 'Vangie, call Duncan and tell him to get off the phone to that bloody company again and get over to Riverdean, and I'll get the gazebo in the car.'

I watched him stride to the front door, only aware that Vangie was still watching me when I glanced at her.

'I'll just give Freddie his last ten minutes,' I said, turning to go back to the table.

'Aren't you forgetting something?' she said.

I turned back towards her, shaking my head as if it might be a trick question.

She nodded towards the empty glass still clenched in my hand.

'Oh, yeah,' I said, stepping towards the tap. 'I got completely distracted.'

She took it from me and filled it up. 'I can see that,' she said, handing it back, our eyes meeting for a moment. 'Easily done.'

Fifteen minutes later, I was walking back towards my car on the parade. Isaac had offered me a lift to Riverdean but I'd said it was better if I fetched my own car. Both Isaac and Vangie had looked puzzled when I said I liked to park on the parade instead of in the driveway, but I had an excuse ready – I always liked to park and then walk, as a way of increasing my step count. It wasn't a perfect excuse but it seemed to satisfy them.

I quickly popped into a pretentious organic shop next to the café and perused the pine shelves, laden with over-priced crisps made from chickpeas, and locally sourced honey. I chose the most expensive bottle of wine I could find, then, armed with a full heart, a bottle of Picpoul, and a postcode, rushed back to my car. I didn't need the post-code, of course. I knew it by heart. I also knew the route from Blackworth House to Riverdean from the many times I'd looked it up on Google Maps. I didn't drive all the way to the house, of course; I didn't want to park my battered Micra there any more than I did at the Slades'. Luckily for me, I knew of a quiet cul-de-sac about five minutes' walk away, where I could leave my car.

When I arrived at Riverdean, the gates were open, and Isaac was taking the folded gazebo from the boot of his black Range Rover. Vangie's slate-grey sports car was parked next to it, but there was no sign of her. I took a minute to stand near the gate and survey the scene. The house was just as I remembered it. The dazzling white façade, the sandstone fountain, the curve of the driveway, the gravel underfoot.

I was back. I'd made it back.

I watched Isaac carry the gazebo towards the open front door and felt my heart quivering like a butterfly about to take flight. I savoured that moment of anticipation. I'd been invited by Isaac. He and Sarah would be there, welcoming me. I wanted to mark this moment somehow, so I delved into my pocket for my phone and found my dad's number.

Hi Dad. The tutoring is going really well. It's even made me some new friends! I'm about to head to a barbecue at their house. Will write to you again soon. Lots of love, Dxx.

I looked back towards the house, once again feeling overwhelmed and tearful. So I cleared my throat, forcing my legs to stride in that confident, purposeful way of Diana's.

The front door was still open so I walked straight through, feeling the house envelop me in a cool white hug. I knew I had a silly grin on my face but I didn't care. I felt like I was home.

'Knock, knock!' I called, as the space opened up into that beautiful open-plan living area.

Sarah bustled out of the kitchen. 'Diana!' She grinned at me, clenching my shoulders and planting kisses on my cheeks, her soft golden hair brushing my skin. 'It's so lovely to see you again. Isaac said he'd managed to persuade you to come. How wonderful.'

'Thank you so much for having me. It's an absolute joy to see your beautiful home!' I enthused in my plummy voice, gesturing at my surroundings with my bottle-holding hand.

'Thank you; yes, we do love it,' she said, and I remembered her saying the same words that time I'd spoken to her on Megs' phone. She obviously received a lot of compliments about the house, and this was her standard reply.

'I'm so sorry,' I said, handing her the wine. 'This was all I could find last minute on the parade.'

'Oh my goodness, don't apologise, thank you so much. I adore a Picpoul. How perfect. I'll just pop it in the fridge, you go out.' She nodded towards the glass doors.

I dropped my tote bag next to the sofa, and quickly crossed to the mirror hanging on the wall. I was delighted I happened to be wearing a sleeveless dusky-pink Piana Vera top that was a new addition to my collection, as it had been on sale last week. My face was glossy with sweat so I blotted it with a tissue from my handbag before sweeping tinted lip balm onto my lips. Perfect.

I headed out of the glass doors onto the patio and found Isaac extending the legs of the gazebo on the grass.

'Let me help,' I said, rushing over to him and grabbing an aluminium pole.

'Ah, thank you, darling. Nice that someone wants to help.' He said the last sentence louder as if hoping Sarah and Vangie might hear from inside, but I didn't give the appreciative laugh I perhaps should have, because I was still light-headed from the *darling*.

We erected the tent, then pushed the pegs through the feet to keep it steady.

'So . . . if you don't mind me asking,' I said, 'what's the gazebo for?'

'As well you might ask,' he said. 'Sarah's concerned there's a lack of shade out here, so she thought it would be nice for the people with paler complexions . . .' He glanced sideways at the house then whispered, 'Vangie and Duncan . . . to have a little place they can sit if they feel they're burning up.'

'Very considerate.' I nodded, feeling that familiar warmth that bloomed inside me every time Isaac brought me into a joke about other people. Feeling like a confidante.

'What would you like to drink, Diana?' Sarah called from the patio. 'I've just opened a rosé, but there's anything you like, really.'

'That's so kind, um . . . I'm driving, but I guess one rosé wouldn't hurt. Thank you.'

Sarah gave me an affectionate, wrinkle-nosed smile and headed back towards the kitchen. Isaac was now retrieving a wooden bench from the side of the house, so I decided to leave him to it, not wanting to look like I was too keen to buzz around him.

I walked to the pool area, wondering what the girls would think if I sent them a photo of me now. *Guess who's been invited back to Riverdean?* But however tempting it was, I knew I wouldn't tell them about this. This was my secret. It was my happy place, not theirs. Yes, they'd enjoyed their weekend here, but I knew they hadn't connected with the place in the same way I had. It didn't stir the same feelings in them as it did in me. They wouldn't understand the hard work it had taken to get back here as a guest – no, *friend* – of the owners.

Sarah came to deliver my wine, but left me to go straight back inside, citing barbecue prep as the reason. I asked if I could help but she insisted I relax. I glanced over at the kitchen window and could just about make out the dark blur of Vangie behind the reflection of the pool in the glass. I wondered what they were talking about in the kitchen, and if Vangie had mentioned me, in relation to either Freddie's tutoring, or why Isaac had invited me. I wasn't too worried about either possibility: the tutoring mattered far less now I was back in Sarah and Isaac's circle – and if Vangie did question my presence, I was confident Sarah would come to my defence with something along the lines of *I'm sure Isaac invited her because she's our new friend and he wanted her here!*

Now I was here, though, I had one job to do. I had to make sure that today, right now, I cemented myself as a part of the Rivers' lives. I was their new, their best, their most fun and exciting friend, and they couldn't possibly go back to life without me. If I managed to make them realise this, then it didn't matter what Freddie or Vangie thought of me. Tutoring Freddie could go to hell. I wasn't interested in the Slades. Today was about my relationship with Isaac and Sarah. Today was about Diana belonging at Riverdean.

Chapter Twelve

A trickle of guests began arriving, squawking and air-kissing. Isaac and Sarah had both changed, her into a floaty pale-green dress and cream ballet pumps, and him into a crisp white shirt, pale-blue chinos and tanned loafers. They flitted between their guests, topping up drinks and laughing. Touching backs and complimenting outfits. Dinah wanted to creep towards the copse of trees, to cast her shoes into the undergrowth and dangle her legs in the cool water, listening to the babble of the guests in the distance, knowing she was unseen and unmissed. But Diana couldn't do that. Diana needed to make her mark. So every time I felt the need to hide, I dug my fingernail into the cut on my thumb – the cut from the glass in the picture frame. After I'd left Riverdean that first time, I found myself with a constant impulse to play with it, pressing it until it burst open afresh, or picking at it until it bled. It was a souvenir of my weekend here, and I somehow felt that if I let it heal up, then something of the weekend would be lost. Something special. Now it had become a sort of comfort blanket when I was anxious, or needing to concentrate. The pain when I dug my nail into it focused my mind. And at that moment, staring at the newly formed clusters of guests that had gathered on the lawn and around the pool, it reminded me of the reason I was here.

So I launched myself. I strode over to these cliques, each in turn, and introduced myself with a broad smile and a loud voice. I'd noticed that volume was a key component amongst people of Isaac and Sarah's social standing. The louder the better. I kissed cheeks and shook hands and told the story of how we all met in Eden House at Duncan's birthday, and how *amazing* it was that the Slades happened to be looking for a tutor at that particular time. I found that the louder I spoke, and the more I moved my arms around, the bigger the smiles I received from my listeners. I squeezed arms and fetched drinks. I chinked glasses and took photos.

At one point, I recognised a woman from Duncan's party. It was Felicity or Fiona, who worked with Isaac. She was in her twenties, wore floral Palazzo trousers and a white shirt tied in a knot at the front. Her long black hair cascaded down her back and I watched her looking up into Isaac's face as he amiably nodded at whatever it was she was saying. I wondered what a twenty-something intern, or whatever she was, could be saying that was of interest to him. But as I watched them, I realised he *wasn't* interested. He was casting his gaze around the sunbaked garden, as if looking for someone. Felicity or Fiona was on a roll now, gesturing with her hands and nodding to emphasise the importance of whatever she was saying, as if she thought she was the most interesting person at the party. I wondered if she was smitten. I wondered if Isaac wanted saving.

I strode over and planted myself between them, relishing the way Isaac's eyes rounded as they settled on me, a smile blooming on his lips. 'Diana,' he said.

I turned to the woman and decided to gamble. 'Felicity, isn't it?' I beamed.

'Oh my goodness, yes! I'm so sorry . . .'

'We met at Duncan's party at Eden House. I'm Diana.'

'Oh goodness, of course. Diana! How wonderful to see you again,' she drawled in that public school voice that told me she probably had a double-barrelled surname, and a horse. I knew she didn't remember me.

'That is so impressive,' said Isaac. 'I don't know how you can meet someone once and remember their name like that.' He smiled at me with an affection I could feel on my skin.

'You remembered mine,' I said, blaming the four glasses of rosé for my raised eyebrow and flirtatious tone.

His smile broadened, eyes crinkling as he swept his fingers through his greying curls. 'Well . . . some people are more memorable than others.'

He stared at me then, for a moment too long.

'So, are you going to Duncan's *Investing in Architecture* event next week?' Felicity said to Isaac, bringing us out of the moment. We both turned to look at her, and I imagined tipping my glass of wine over her glossy hair.

'Felicity's one of our bright sparks in the design team,' Isaac said, and I felt a twist of surprise and annoyance. She wasn't just an intern. And Isaac thought she was a 'bright spark'.

'Come on now, Zac, don't try and fob me off by distracting me with compliments.' Her elongated vowels sounded like a rusty door and I felt my fists clench. And how did someone so young, so early in their career, have the bald-faced cheek to call her boss *Zac* and to speak to

155

him like he was an equal? The bloody gall of people in their twenties.

'I'm not fobbing you off at all,' he said. 'I'll quite happily tell you I've no intention of attending anything called *Investing in Architecture* because it would all go completely over my head. I'm not on the architecture side of things. I'll leave that up to you and Duncan – design genii that you are.'

'There you go again, trying to disarm with complim—'

'Flick!' A gangly man who looked about the same age as her began tugging at Felicity's arm. 'Martin's here, come and say hi.'

'Oh God, sorry. Must dash!' She trotted – was semi-dragged – away, raising her glass to us as she went.

Isaac breathed out a sigh through pursed lips. 'Thanks for saving me,' he said.

'I didn't realise you needed saving,' I said with what I hoped was an innocent expression. 'She seems lovely.'

He raised an eyebrow at me. 'Where do young people today get their confidence? When I was her age, I'd have had a panic attack at the idea of hanging out with my employers in their home.'

'That's exactly what I was thinking!' I said, elongating my own vowels, just to try it out.

'But she's waltzing around like she bloody owns the place. I mean . . . good on her and everything, but jeez.'

We both shook our heads then, in silent acknowledgement of our like-mindedness.

The afternoon staggered on and the yellow sun turned orange. At some point I noticed the gazebo had been decked in garlands, the bench slung with furs and scatter cushions, and mirrored side tables set up on either side. A long table appeared on the patio laden with sausages and burgers, Cajun chicken legs and corn on the cob. Side dishes materialised, salads, couscous, coleslaw. I don't remember when I looked down and noticed I wasn't holding a wine glass any more, but a cut-glass tumbler containing a ruby liquid and a sprig of rosemary. I recognised the tumbler as one of the ones I'd drunk whiskey from, the night I'd stayed here alone. I stroked the starburst grooves in the glass with my thumb, and was about to take a sip when Sarah was at my elbow.

'There you are, darling,' she said, her floral perfume wafting over me. It was that or honeysuckle on the evening breeze. 'Have you eaten? Help yourself, won't you?'

'Of course . . . thank you. It looks amazing,' I said, concerned at the way my words blurred at the edges. My crisp tone was slipping. I must make sure I tried harder.

'Well, Duncan loves it when he's in charge of a barbecue. Look at him. In his element.' She nodded towards the patio and I noticed Duncan for the first time. Had he been here all along? When did he arrive? I looked up and realised the sky was bruised at the edges, and a dusting of early stars streaked the treeline.

Sarah dragged me to meet David and Harriet from next door, and I recognised them from Duncan's party too.

'Ah, the tutor!' said David, his flushed face beaming with pride for remembering who I was. His wide face had a balloon-like quality, and his piggy little eyes peeked from pale folds of skin.

I nodded and laughed sporadically as they spoke to Sarah, their words washing over me as the effects of the cocktail took hold. I plastered on what I hoped was an interested smile, and tried not to sway as I inspected Harriet. She had wavy red hair that was held back with a gold clasp, and she wore an outrageous amount of make-up, including thick eyeliner and claret lipstick. Her dress was also outrageous. It floated around her in several layers of what looked like chiffon or tulle in jungle vibrant colours, with a bow at the waist and a frill at the low-cut neck. It was no doubt eye-wateringly expensive, but it was fussy and sultry, and not at all Sarah-like. She was also eccentric in her gestures and facial movements, gasping and frowning like an over-animated Disney character. I found my gaze flicking to Sarah, taking in her serenity and grace, which was all the more pronounced next to Harriet.

Eventually, another couple pulled David and Harriet away and Sarah turned to me.

'They've been our neighbours for donkey's years. They're sweet.' She swallowed and I sensed she wanted to say something else but was weighing it up.

'You get on with them?' I said, hearing the slur of my words but not really caring any more.

Sarah cocked her head to one side. 'They're fine; I mean, they're good neighbours.'

We both took large sips of our drinks, and I felt the ground tilt and took a step to correct my balance.

'Harriet is quite eccentric, you know. She has her own sort of style.'

'Yes, she certainly does!' I said, trying unsuccessfully to stifle a giggle.

'What? What are you laughing at?' Sarah's eyes glittered at me, as if she wanted me to say more.

'Nothing, it's just she's very sort of . . . flouncy, isn't she?'

'Yes.' It was Sarah's turn to stifle a giggle now. 'She does like her flouncy sort of dresses.'

I took another sip before continuing. 'I think she looks like a sort of . . . sexy jellyfish.'

Sarah gave a sharp shriek, before clamping her hand over her mouth, her round eyes bulging as her skin turned pink. This set me off and I let out a squawk of my own, sloshing my cocktail over the rim of my glass, which made us both erupt again. I noticed a couple of people turn to look at us, grins on their faces as they watched us giggling helplessly.

'What on earth has got into you girls?' Isaac appeared, draping one arm around each of us. 'I have to know what's so funny.' He was mock stern as he glared at each of us in turn.

Sarah stepped away from him, trying to control herself, before glancing around to check we weren't being overheard. 'Diana just . . . Diana just described Harriet as . . .' she held her fingers to her lips and squeezed her eyes shut for a moment before taking a deep breath. 'Diana just described Harriet as a "sexy jellyfish".'

Isaac snorted and pressed his lips together before glancing over at David and Harriet who were now deep in conversation with Vangie and Duncan. 'I don't think I've ever heard such an accurate description of anyone.'

Sarah and I started giggling again, and I watched her wipe her fingers underneath each watering eye, happiness simmering inside me, sending bubbles through my veins so I felt I might burst.

'Right! More cocktails,' said Isaac, taking my glass, which I hadn't noticed was empty. I watched him walk towards the house, my gaze catching on Vangie who was standing with Duncan, David and Harriet. But she wasn't listening to their conversation, or looking at Isaac. She was staring straight at me. Our eyes locked and I smiled, then waved, but she just stared, her red lips in that hard line, before turning away.

I was in the kitchen, talking to a tall, deliberately grey woman I'd not met before about the problem with second homes. I was surprised at my own conviction on the subject, and gratified by her enthusiasm when I said, 'And don't get me started on gardeners!' which prompted an avalanche of criticisms of staff, specific and general.

'Oh God, don't.' I heard Isaac's voice and noticed him standing next to me for the first time. How long had he been there? 'Sarah's on the war path with our cleaners after she found cigarette butts in the plant pot on our balcony.'

'Oh my God!' I scowled and clutched my chest.

'But don't you rent the place out sometimes?' said Grey Hair.

'We do, but we always lock up our room, so it could only have been the cleaners. Seriously, Sarah really laid into them about paying them to clean, not have fag breaks on the balcony.'

'So disgusting,' I said, shaking my head. Then I couldn't resist. 'I didn't know you rented the place out.'

'Well, we've been giving it a go,' said Isaac, his nose crinkling as if smelling something off. 'Sarah thought it might be a good idea – friends of ours talked her into it. But now Vangie's been telling Sarah we should get CCTV and motion sensors and all that paraphernalia if we're going to have strangers staying here, and to be honest, it all just sounds like such a faff. I think we've decided it's not worth the pocket money.' He gave a nonchalant shrug.

My brain scrambled to work out how much they'd have made from the four of us staying at Riverdean that weekend. Somehow I couldn't reconcile that amount with the term 'pocket money'. But I smiled up at Isaac. 'Well quite,' I said. 'If it's stressful it's just not worth it.' Everyone nodded at me and I sipped my drink, which I was surprised to note was now Prosecco.

Felicity's tanned midriff elongated as she stretched her arms over her head and executed a perfect dive into the glowing aquamarine pool. There were cheers from the sun loungers, and the gangly man I'd seen her with earlier followed her dive with a comedy cannonball.

I was wondering where Isaac was and if he'd noticed Felicity's midriff, when his voice was in my ear.

'So they actually brought swimming things with them too . . . bloody cheek of it.'

'Very cheeky,' I slurred, looking up into Isaac's face and stumbling into him.

'Whoa, are you OK?' He half laughed.

'I'm just great,' I said, waving a thumbs up in his face and trying my best reassuring smile.

The music was something Spanish or South American, guitars and drum beats, thick, guttural singing. I twirled and twirled and people clapped. A meaty hand grabbed mine and I was pulled into an embrace as we swayed, our hips in time. It was Duncan, red-faced and shiny with sweat. Felicity was there too, winding her sinewy arms above her head and sashaying to the music, flicking her damp hair around her shoulders. I didn't mind though, because I knew I was dancing better than anyone. I was whirling and laughing, my hips moving in sultry swirls, my feet in perfect rhythm. The patio and the faces of the people watching blurred as I spun round and round, and, when I stopped, it was Isaac's face I found in the crowd. It was Isaac who was watching me, a faint smile on his face, his green eyes glittering in the darkness.

I was in the downstairs toilet, standing on the lid so I could see the photos high up near the ceiling that I hadn't inspected properly last time I was here. Isaac and Sarah's beautiful faces beamed out at me and I touched each photo in turn, leaving invisible fingerprints on each rectangle of glass. I reached up high and felt the toilet lid shift under my feet, slipping sideways with a loud clunk. My arms flew out and my fingers made a frantic grab for the only thing they found, the hand towel, which wrenched the rail from the wall with the weight of my falling body. My lower back slammed into the floor at the same time as my head cracked against the cupboard, my legs left draped over the toilet seat above me.

Loud knocking.

'You OK in there?' said a posh voice.

'Oh yes. Fine, darling, fine.' I had no idea who I was talking to, but had become very comfortable with the word 'darling' over the last few hours.

I slowly hitched myself up to sitting. I was fine.

The kitchen looked empty. The grey-haired lady sauntered in and began stretching clingfilm over a plate of sausages. I'd never seen anything so depressing. Ignoring her, I walked over to the fridge and pulled out a bottle of wine before slamming the door and walking off towards the conservatory, grabbing someone's empty wine glass from the table as I went.

The room swayed as I walked and I ignored the dull throb at the back of my head. Isaac, Sarah, Vangie and Duncan were on the patio, talking in a huddle.

'Hey! This is where the party's at!' I said, holding the bottle aloft as I strutted towards them.

'Diana,' said Vangie, looking me up and down. 'You're still here.'

'Yes!' There was no music any more but I bobbed up and down as if there was, hoping to keep the party spirit alive. The others were talking again, but quietly and their words were blurry around me so I couldn't work out what they were saying. I cradled the bottle of wine in the crook of my arm to open it and sloshed a large measure into the glass.

'Don't you think you've had enough?' said Vangie.

I looked up to see four pairs of eyes on me. 'But . . . it's a party?'

There was a moment's silence before Isaac spoke. 'She does have a point,' he said, casting an earnest look around the group. 'It *is* a party.'

'Oh, for God's sake,' muttered Vangie. 'Duncan and I are leaving, so . . . enjoy the rest of your night.'

I stood back and watched the four of them saying their goodbyes, deciding I'd take a swig every time there was an air kiss. I'd had to refill my glass by the time Vangie and Duncan made their way inside. Once they'd disappeared, I felt a wave of relief. 'Right,' I said to Isaac. 'We need more music. We need more dancing. We need more drinks!'

He smiled down at me, reaching his phone from his back pocket and tapping at the screen. For one desperate moment I thought he was calling me a taxi.

'Your wish . . .' he said, giving the screen one more tap, 'is my command.' The Bluetooth speaker erupted with the unmistakable trumpet intro to 'Livin' La Vida Loca'.

Chapter Thirteen

The knocking sound was relentless. It was only when I squeezed my eyes open that I realised it was my pulse, throbbing inside my head. But that knowledge became of lesser interest as I attempted to make sense of my surroundings. A white fireplace, cream candles, a bookshelf. I was still here. I was still at Riverdean. I pushed myself up, swallowing a wave of nausea as my body adjusted to the new position. My neck was stiff and painful as I looked around the room, which was bathed in the warm sunlight of a well-established summer's day. The glass doors were open, and I could hear a faint chinking sound from the kitchen.

I swung my legs off the sofa, making an involuntary moaning sound as a pain flared in my lower back. I rubbed the area, wondering what the hell I'd done to it. My mouth tasted sour and metallic and, pressing my hand to my chest to burp, I felt a stickiness on my skin. There was a dark purple streak down the front of my pale-pink top, and I had a sudden image of a dark cocktail, a sprig of rosemary. My stomach lurched and I clamped a palm over my lips, willing myself not to throw up.

I needed to get to the bathroom. But I had to get past the kitchen to get there, and there was someone in the kitchen. I pulled my phone from my pocket and clicked into the camera, reversing it to use as a mirror. The sight that met me made the nausea so much worse. My freckled face was pasty, and the dark shadows under my eyes were speckled with dried mascara. I licked my finger and rubbed at them, but this simply added to the redness of the rims, and the bloodshot appearance of the whites of my eyes. My hair had reverted to a frizzy mess and my lips were cracked and pale. It would seem that try as she might, Diana couldn't keep Dinny at bay for long.

'You're awake.' The voice startled me and I twisted towards the kitchen. Sarah had emerged, her hair tumbling around her shoulders as if freshly washed and dried, and a knee-length silk dressing gown with a print of exotic birds wrapped around her. Her face was bare of make-up, and she looked younger and more fresh-faced than I'd ever seen her. She handed me a steaming mug of tea in a turquoise, crackle-glazed mug.

I wrapped my trembling hands around the mug, offering an apologetic smile. 'Thank you . . . you really shouldn't be bringing me tea. I don't deserve it.'

'Everyone deserves tea,' she said, perching on the arm of the sofa and giving me a gentle smile, which perhaps contained a hint of pity.

'I . . . I can't even remember . . . when did I go to bed? I mean . . . when did I pass out on your sofa?'

She laughed in the carefree way of someone whose brain wasn't pulsating against the inside of their skull. 'I have to admit I'd already gone to bed at that point, so you'd have to ask Isaac.'

I winced and looked down into my mug. 'Oh my God, I'm so sorry.'

'Don't be sorry. I'm glad you had fun.'

'But, did everyone have fun? I mean, was I . . . was everyone else really drunk too, or was I the only one—'

'Oh my goodness, there were plenty of drinks consumed by everyone. You were by no means the only drunk person at the party.'

'But was I the most drunk?'

She smiled again and I sensed her weighing her words. 'You were the person I would say was enjoying themselves the most.'

'Oh, fuck.' The Diana part of my brain startled at the swear word. 'I'm sorry, I mean—'

'Don't apologise. You were the life and soul—'

'Oh God, I don't want to be the life and soul . . .' I groaned and doubled over, inhaling the steam from my mug and wishing for the first time that I could teleport away from Riverdean. I straightened up and looked into Sarah's smooth, rose-tinted face. 'You look like you've been on a spa weekend and had ten hours' sleep. How have you done this?'

She giggled then and I had a flashback to us laughing in the garden. Something about a dress . . . or a jellyfish . . .

'Who's up for bacon?' It was Isaac.

'Oh God.' I plonked my mug down on the coffee table and launched myself towards the kitchen, pushing past him and on to the downstairs toilet, slamming the door shut and throwing up the fizzing, purple contents of my stomach into the toilet bowl. I held onto the seat as I continued to wretch, unable to control the volume,

and wincing with every heave, knowing they could probably hear me from the living room. When I'd finished,
I slumped back, bringing the toilet seat with me. *Shit!*
It had come away in my hands. I desperately slotted
the screws back in and attempted to tighten the bolts
with my hands underneath the toilet bowl at the back.
Having done my best to tighten it, I went to the loo, then
washed my hands, noting the handrail had also come
away from the wall and was lying on top of the towel on
the floor. Images and sensations shifted in my brain but
they were blurry, and wouldn't come into focus.

I splashed cold water on my face and ran my wet
fingers through my hair, attempting to tame it. But my
reflection was grotesque in the mirror, like a pale corpse
dragged from a lake, skin leached of blood and eyes
sunken to shadows.

In the kitchen, Isaac stood over the hob, wet hair
slicked back and wearing a white T-shirt over blue
pyjama shorts. The crackling of the frying bacon along
with the extractor fan made me think I might get away
with rushing through the room without making conversation, but I barely made it to the breakfast bar.

'Ah, Diana,' he said, turning to me with an unbearable, sympathetic grimace. 'How are you feeling?'

'Absolutely bloody awful,' I said, unable to bluff this
one. 'I . . . I'm so sorry. I was such an embarrassment
last night.'

'Were you?' He looked at me with that twinkle in his
eyes and I couldn't work out if he was teasing me, or wanting me to elaborate. Regardless, the hangover combined

with my self-loathing was sapping me of my ability to deal with either scenario.

Unable to form an answer, I sidled over to a bar stool and pulled myself up onto it. I placed my palms on the white veined marble, resisting the urge to flop over onto it and feel the cool stone against my cheeks and forehead. I felt tears sting my eyes and made a feeble attempt to blink them back, but the balloon of shame inside me was expanding, pushing them up and up, causing them to spill silently down my cheeks. Isaac was turned back to the bacon so didn't notice. I swiped at my cheeks and sniffed.

He reached to turn off the extractor fan and tipped two slices of bacon onto an oval of buttered toast, then placed the plate in front of me. 'It'll do you the world of good.'

I nodded, relieved the sight and smell of it no longer made me want to vomit.

'You know,' he said, plating up two more portions, 'you don't have anything to be embarrassed about.'

'Oh please, I think I know when I've made a complete fool of myself,' I said, making a renewed effort to keep my voice clipped and Diana-like.

'How exactly? By having a few drinks and dancing?'

I shifted in my seat. 'I think I had a few more drinks than anyone else.'

'There were people swimming, Diana. People who had not been invited to swim.' He cast me an earnest look and I remembered Felicity's midriff. 'And Duncan twirled around when he was dancing, lost his balance and smashed a glass.'

'Did he?' I said, uncontrolled hope in my voice.

'Yes. Everyone had a bit too much drink. You didn't do or say anything embarrassing.'

'Didn't I?'

'Absolutely not. And I was the host. I'd know if you'd offended anyone.'

I had another flashback, this time to Vangie's face, her lips in a thin red line. *Haven't you had enough to drink?* 'I think I offended Vangie,' I said, tearing off a piece of bacon and placing it tentatively on my tongue, feeling the salt flood my tastebuds.

Isaac laughed. 'Vangie loves being offended. I wouldn't use that as a benchmark for your shame.'

Buoyed by these words, I wanted to ask more questions, seek more reassurance, but at that moment someone walked into the kitchen. It wasn't Sarah, but at first glance it could have been. The figure was lean, with blonde hair tied up in a messy bun. She wore a black vest top and jeans that hung in shreds from skinny hips. She flashed me a look with round amber eyes and I knew it was the girl with the dandelion from the photo.

'Camellia,' said Isaac. 'To what do we owe the honour?' His voice held a stiffness I'd not heard before.

She crossed to a cupboard and took out a tumbler, filling it from the tap and gulping it down. I watched her, noting the line of a spidery black tattoo on the inside of her wrist. I couldn't work out if it was letters or numbers before she put the glass in the sink and went to the fridge. She looked about eighteen.

Camellia still didn't answer Isaac, and I felt the atmosphere in the room solidify.

Isaac cleared his throat. 'Camellia, this is Diana. Diana . . . Camellia. My daughter.'

The girl turned and stood with a plate of cold sausages, peeling back the clingfilm and taking a large bite of one as she looked me up and down with exaggerated disdain before glancing at Isaac and raising her eyebrows. I didn't know what was going on, but felt an overwhelming urge to speak, to relieve some of the tension somehow.

'It's nice to meet you, Camellia.'

'Actually, it's Cam,' she said through a mouthful of sausage.

'Oh . . . sorry—'

She swallowed. 'No need to apologise. Not your fault. It's Isaac who been consistently ignoring the fact I've been asking to be called Cam since I was ten.' I glanced at Isaac's fingers gripping the edge of the worktop. Cam continued, her tone measured and calm. 'Note he also introduces me as his daughter – that's another method by which he attempts to rile me.'

'Come on now, Cam. Diana's a guest and doesn't need to hear this nonsense. Especially from someone who treats this house like a hotel.'

'That's rich, coming from someone who's been freeloading for the past twelve years.'

'I'm warning you, Camellia—'

'Fuck off, Isaac,' she said, pushing the fridge shut with her elbow and striding from the room with the plate of sausages.

In the silence that surrounded us after she'd left, I thought of the bedroom I'd slept in, with the fairy lights, pink dressing table and Citrus Breeze Body Shop spray. The shell-encrusted jewellery box and the rainbow hair tie.

'What did she mean about you introducing her as—'

'She's my stepdaughter,' Isaac said, releasing his grip on the worktop and offering me a stiff smile. 'Camellia is Sarah's, not mine.' Sadness flickered in his eyes and he looked down. 'As Cam regularly likes to remind me.'

I nodded, a hundred questions crowding into my brain and making my tender skull throb harder. 'I've heard stepkids can be tricky . . .' I offered, unsure what I meant by this bland wisdom, but knowing I wanted to make Isaac feel better, to comfort him.

'Yes, I think any kids can be tricky. But the role of stepdad is fraught with danger – and many pitfalls, as you've just witnessed. Using a full name or trying to show affection with the term "daughter" . . . all ways a bumbling stepfather can enrage a spirited teenager!' His voice had become more lively and I sensed he wanted to make light of the situation.

'I can only imagine,' I said.

'Well, stick with us and you won't have to, I'm afraid.'

Despite the awkwardness of the exchange with Camellia, my churning stomach, pounding head and burning shame, those words soothed me like a balm. *Stick with us.* OK, Isaac, I'll stick with you.

I went over the interaction between Cam and Isaac as I dangled my legs in the pool. The protectiveness I'd felt towards Isaac in the kitchen was tinged with a strange sort of gratitude towards Cam for coming in at that moment and making things so resolutely about something other than my embarrassment and my hangover.

Isaac had disappeared whilst I was eating my breakfast, and I hadn't seen Sarah since she'd given me the mug of tea. No one had asked me to leave, so I decided I'd stick around a bit longer. The coolness of the water tingled against my skin and I longed to slip under the surface and feel it envelop me. My headache was receding now and the bacon had settled my stomach. I just needed to feel clean again.

I gazed around the pool, noting dirty glasses dotted around the sun lounger legs, an abandoned pink pashmina crumpled on a chair. I wondered if I could get away with slipping into the cold water, then lying out to dry in the sun.

'Oh, sorry. I'll come back in a bit.'

I turned towards the voice and was met with a figure in a sage-green housecoat. Our eyes met and something connected in the back of my brain. The auburn hair, the bony nose. I'd seen this woman before. It was the cleaner I'd met on the drive as I made my escape that first weekend.

I jumped up. 'No, don't worry. Carry on,' I said, gesturing awkwardly towards the pool area.

She stood with a black bin bag hanging from one hand, and a jay-cloth and spray bottle in the other. I looked down, pretending to dust something off my legs, hoping she'd just get on with whatever she was about to do. But I could feel her eyes on me, inspecting me. I straightened up, flashed her a brief smile and walked past her and through the gap in the hedge, onto the grass.

She just stood there, gazing after me.

What if she recognised me? What would I say if she told Sarah she'd seen me here before, when they were away? I'd just deny it, I thought. I'd say she must be mistaken. Yes, that's what I'd do.

I didn't want to go back into the house. I needed air, and the movement of the breeze. Besides, a small part of me wondered if I'd be asked to leave if Isaac or Sarah noticed me. There were clearly issues with Cam, and if they were having a big family argument inside then I didn't want to make them feel awkward by witnessing it. But I also wasn't ready to leave. Not quite yet.

So I headed towards the copse of trees that surrounded the lake. Remembering the cool serenity of the place, it was just what I needed at that moment.

When I emerged from the trees where the jetty began, though, I was surprised to find I wasn't alone. Cam sat at the end of the jetty, her back to me, legs dangling in the water. My assumption that she was inside involved in a family confrontation of some sort had been wrong. As I watched her still figure, a curl of white smoke rose above her shoulder, dissipating on the breeze.

'You know, if you want a fag, Diana, you just need to ask,' she said, without looking round.

'I . . . I wasn't . . .' I couldn't find words, despite what I really wanted to say – God, *yes please, can I have a fag?*

I walked down the jetty towards her and lowered myself onto the decking, slipping my feet into the icy water. Bliss.

'Occam's razor,' she said.

'What? I . . . I'm sorry, I don't know what you mean.'

She looked at me with her round amber eyes that were almost gold in the sunlight. 'It's a philosophical principle that states one should search for an explanation constructed of the fewest elements.' She took a drag of her cigarette and tilted her head to blow the smoke out, over the water.

'What do you—'

'I heard someone trampling through the undergrowth. Now, I know the only people on the premises are my parents, the cleaners, and you, Diana. The cleaners have no business coming to the lake, and my mother and Isaac haven't set foot here for two years as it upsets them too much. Therefore the explanation with the least number of assumptions attached to it, is that it would be you approaching, rather than anyone else.'

I stared at her, vaguely aware that my mouth was hanging open in what I suddenly worried was a gormless fashion. I closed it and turned to the water. 'Occam's razor.'

'Precisely.'

'I like it.'

She nodded. 'I mean, we usually apply it automatically, but sometimes it's good to use it consciously.' She pulled a packet of Marlboro from her pocket and offered it to me. 'There you go. Save you sucking in my second-hand smoke every time I exhale.'

I took a cigarette. 'Oh God, was I that obvious?'

She lit my cigarette and we sat in silence, swishing our legs in the water.

'So, what's your story then, Diana?'

I felt a strange splitting inside myself then. She called me 'Diana', but here I was, my legs in the water, a cigarette clenched between my fingers. I didn't feel like Diana in that moment, and I knew I wasn't speaking like her. I needed to claw this back. I needed to retain this persona I'd so carefully crafted.

I straightened up, and tried to gently steer my voice back towards the crisp efficiency I'd been cultivating over the past few weeks. I told her about meeting Vangie and Duncan and tutoring Freddie, about how I was at Oxford, and how I lived in an apartment just outside Richmond. I tried to impart as much as I could without gaps so she couldn't ask questions, then I turned the subject back on her.

'What about you? You don't live here?'

'Not really. I mean, I keep my stuff here, but I try to avoid the place if I can. I move around, stay with friends, you know.'

Ah, that made sense of the room that seemed to belong to a much younger child. 'Is your mother OK with that?'

'Not really, but I'm nineteen so she can't really say anything, can she? And before you ask, no, I didn't want to go to university.'

That *had* been what I was going to ask. She was clearly intelligent and perceptive and I wondered why she didn't see university as an option. But before I delved into that, there was a question burning inside me.

'Why does coming to the lake make your mum and Isaac upset?'

She flicked the glowing butt of her cigarette into the water and exhaled loudly. 'Because a boy died here two years ago. Drowned.'

I felt ice through my veins. 'What? I . . . who?'

'Jamie Kerr. He was nineteen.'

'But . . . what happened?'

Cam stares out over the water, her voice steady and expressionless. 'There was a big house party for Mum and Isaac's wedding anniversary. They said I could invite some friends so I got some mates from college to come along. Jamie was one of them.'

'God, Cam, I'm so sorry. That's horrific.'

'We'd all been drinking. But no one knows why he was here – none of us were with him. We weren't swimming or anything. He was still in his clothes . . . even his shoes. They think maybe he fell in and got tangled in the reeds or something.' She nodded towards the red 'Danger' sign at the base of the jetty, the one Rachel had pointed out to me when she'd found me swimming here. 'That's when the sign got put up. And now I'm the only one who comes here.'

'I don't know what to say.'

'You don't have to say anything.'

'Were you close?'

'We weren't together, if that's what you mean. I fancied him. I think he thought of me more like a little sister, though. But you know when you're seventeen, and a girl, it's quite rare to find a boy that actually listens to you. I mean, one that isn't just pretending to listen so you'll have sex with them. But Jamie used to listen. He'd *actually* listen to what I was saying, you know, take me seriously.'

She looked out over the twinkling water as if she was reminiscing about things that happened decades ago, not two years. I reminded myself she was only nineteen. She seemed much older.

'He'd listen to me banging on about Isaac, and all that shit, and he'd never look bored, or tell me I was being stupid. He'd take it all in.'

'What type of stuff would you say? I mean . . . why don't you get on with Isaac?'

Her face broke into a twisted grin and she gave a dark laugh. 'Oh, where to begin,' she said, shaking her head.

Something was niggling in the back of my brain, something I hadn't been able to grasp. But now, several elements merged and took shape – the shape of a photograph in the downstairs toilet, to be precise.

'So . . . you said Isaac had been "freeloading" for twelve years. What does that mean?'

'It means that's how long he's been skulking around.'

'Skulking around, as in . . . he got together with your mum twelve years ago?'

'Yes.' She shifted her position on the jetty so she was facing me, and I noticed a glint of interest in her eyes, as if she were a teacher watching a student trying to work out a mathematical riddle.

'Are your mum and dad divorced?'

'No, my dad died when I was six.'

'I'm sorry.'

She shrugged and gave a quick shake of her head, as if this was a distraction from the meat of the conversation. 'Mum and Isaac got together shortly after he died.'

This was the sticking point. 'But . . . the photo in the downstairs toilet . . .'

The corners of Cam's mouth twitched with the hint of a smile. 'Yes?'

'There's a photo of you all on a beach, and . . . you're a toddler.'

She took another cigarette from the packet and lit it, inhaling deeply and nodding as she blew out the milky cloud. 'You are very perceptive, Diana.'

I frowned. 'But I don't understand . . . your father was still alive when that photo was taken?'

'Oh yes. He was still alive, and he and my mum were still very much together. We were all on holiday together in Cornwall, you see – me, my parents, the Slades, and Duncan's best friend . . . Isaac.'

I blinked, trying to piece together this new dynamic. My vision of this idyllic family unit had just been blown apart. What was left was something much more complicated.

'So, the photo was taken when your father wasn't there?'

'Of course, I mean how would a photo like that have come about if my father had been there? He was probably further along the beach, or back at the holiday house, or in the pub with Duncan or something. Unaware that another man was having a family portrait taken with his wife and child. And now that family portrait is hanging in our house. Fucked up, right?'

I frowned at Cam, images and scenarios still shifting and slotting into place in my head. But no matter how I looked at it, or how many allowances I made, I had to admit . . . yes . . . that was a bit fucked up.

Chapter Fourteen

Cam left, citing 'places to be', and I ambled back towards the pool, relieved to see the cleaners had also disappeared. I went over our conversation about the photograph as I stood alone on the stone steps at the shallow end, my feet in the water. And the more I thought about it, the more I realised my reaction to Cam's revelation about the photo had been hugely influenced by Cam herself. As I'd attempted to piece together the timeline of Isaac and Sarah's relationship, Cam was already awaiting my outrage with barely concealed glee. Which made me wonder if perhaps I'd only been so shocked because she'd wanted me to be. After all, there could be a perfectly reasonable explanation for the photo. For example, if Cam's father hadn't been present at that particular moment, it was quite possible a well-intentioned passerby had offered to take the photo assuming they were a family. We've all been on the receiving end of a stranger's misunderstanding before. And sometimes it's too awkward to correct, and much easier to nod and smile, so as not to make them feel silly.

I wondered vaguely if there was a friendly local woman in Cornwall, who still walked along that beach to this day, remembering the beautiful family whose photo she'd insisted on taking one cloudy summer's day.

Then I wondered how she'd feel if she knew the golden-haired toddler in the beautiful woman's arms would one day describe the photo she'd taken as 'fucked up'.

I decided I needed to see the photo again, so walked in through the glass doors and towards the kitchen. I heard running water from the bathroom at the top of the stairs, but didn't encounter anyone on my way. In the loo, I locked the door, then turned to stare at the large photo on the wall. It was the first photo that had caught my eye when I was here for my weekend with the girls, and it had certainly been positioned in pride of place, opposite the door and right at eye level. I tried to glean anything I could from the body language and expressions of the three subjects. Sarah and Isaac stood comfortably next to each other, his arm around her shoulder in a stance that looked completely natural. Sarah's face held an easy smile, as did Isaac's. Neither of them looked as if they'd been cajoled into posing for an awkward photo based on a stranger's assumption. Cam was a toddler, and therefore oblivious to everything other than her own pudgy hand, which she waved in front of her face.

Did Isaac's smile hold something else? Was there something mischievous behind his barely raised eyebrow? It was an expression of his I was now familiar with in real life, and I knew the accompanying glint so well from the times he'd turned it on me, making my stomach somersault. But he was a charismatic man, and it was obviously an expression he used regularly when he was having fun. But was that what was happening in this photo? Was he enjoying the fact he'd been mistaken for Sarah's husband, and the father of her child?

Turning the frame over, I prised up the metal clips with my fingernail. My mother used to make notes on every photograph she took, and I wondered if there were any clues on the back of this one. It transpired there were no names or dates, but there *was* an inscription. It was scrawled in black ballpoint and had quote marks around it, although there was no indication whose words they were: *All our dreams can come true, if we have the courage to pursue them*. What did that mean? Something stirred at the back of my brain, as if I'd read this before somewhere, but I couldn't work out where. It was sort of romantic . . . as if Isaac had given the photo to Sarah as a gift, implying that she was a dream come true. *The courage to pursue them* . . . had Isaac pursued Sarah? Did this imply he'd had his sights set on Sarah before her husband died? No, that was unthinkable. And yet, it was what Cam had insinuated. This – this inscription – had to be what had formed the root of her mistrust, didn't it?

It was then that I heard the front doorbell chime. I wondered about staying hidden, but curiosity got the better of me, so I quickly reassembled the frame and repositioned it on the wall, before opening the door, and walking through to the kitchen. There were voices in the hallway, and I recognised Vangie's hard vowels punctuating Isaac's low, soft lilt. I crept towards the kitchen door, then out and under the treads of the floating staircase, shielded from the hallway by the wall.

'. . . absolutely, and great to catch up with David and Harriet,' she said.

'Indeed, they're always asking after you. Look, why don't I just bring the gazebo round another time if you're not in a rush for it? It's still up in the garden.'

'Well . . . OK, if you don't mind?'

'Of course not. Might save dismantling it until I'm not quite so worse for wear.' I couldn't see Isaac, but I could imagine him running his fingers through his tousled hair as he said this.

'God, yes, I bet you're not the only sore head this morning. I'm sure poor Diana is absolutely broken!' Despite the word 'poor', Vangie's tone conveyed rather more glee than sympathy.

'She was a bit fragile, but nothing a bit of bacon couldn't sort out.'

I felt a surge of gratitude towards Isaac in that moment, for downplaying the sorry state I was in.

'What? You don't mean . . . she didn't *stay the night*?'

'Well, she couldn't very well have driven home, could she?' Isaac said this on an easy laugh, which contrasted with Vangie's shrill indignance.

'For God's sake, that's so . . .'

'So what?'

'So . . . inappropriate!'

Isaac outright laughed at this. 'It was a party, she was drunk and crashed on the sofa. That's what happens at parties, Vange.'

'But we hardly know her!' Vangie's voice fizzed with disapproval.

'What are you talking about? You probably know her better than anyone. She's been tutoring your son for weeks.'

183

'Yes, and a fat lot of good that's doing. Anyway, that's beside the point. She appeared out of nowhere, she's got absolutely no online presence, no website, no reviews, no nothing. All we've got is her word that she is who she says she is. And suddenly she's getting invited to birthdays and barbecues . . . for God's sake, you'll be inviting her to France next!'

France?

'Actually . . . maybe that's not a bad idea.'

'Oh, you cannot be serious, Isaac. Don't . . . don't you look at me like that, this is not a joke.'

'Why are you being such a bloody spoil-sport?'

'Why are you such a fan of this new . . . *limpet*, who's attached herself to us from out of nowhere?'

'Because she's *fun*!'

The word rang out, bouncing off the hallway walls and ricocheting towards me, forcing me to clamp my hand over my mouth in a sort of delighted horror. *I'm fun.*

There was a silence then, during which I sensed Vangie collecting herself. 'There's more to life than just fun, you know, Isaac.'

'Oh God, you sound just like Duncan now. Birds of a feather, I guess.' His voice was laced with something sharp, but I didn't know why.

'Don't you . . .' She sounded almost as if she was going to cry. 'If you invite her to France then I won't be coming. And Duncan and Freddie won't either.'

The bitch. Anger writhed in the pit of my stomach. How dare she threaten Isaac. How dare she trample on the opportunity for me to join them on an actual holiday. The fact that Isaac wanted me there filled me with such euphoria. Images flashed through my mind of me sitting in the shade of an olive tree on a cobbled patio, a glass of crisp dry wine on the table. Isaac sweeping out of the doorway with a tray of cheese and placing it on the table before pulling up his own chair to join me. Chinking glasses as we watched the breeze ripple the leaves of the vineyards that dotted the hills around us. And Vangie wanted to take this away from me. Why? Because I was 'new'? Because I didn't have an 'online presence'? *What utter bullshit.*

'Diana, what are you doing?'

'Oh, shit!' I jumped, clutching my hand to my chest as I twisted to see Sarah who must have just walked down the stairs just above my head. I'd been so absorbed in Isaac and Vangie's conversation I hadn't heard her coming.

'Are you OK?' Her eyes flickered with concern.

'Yes . . . I'm sorry, I was . . . I heard Vangie at the door and was just about to go and say hi, but . . . she and Isaac sounded like they were having a bit of a disagreement, so I stopped.' I thought that perhaps it would help my case if Sarah asked Isaac about the disagreement, then Sarah could side with Isaac and decide that, of course they wanted to invite me to France with them . . . the holiday wouldn't be the same without me. After all, I was *fun*.

I left Riverdean about an hour later, after showering in the barely used family bathroom at the top of the stairs, and having been lent a clean top by Sarah.

'Are you sure I can't wash your top for you?' she'd offered.

'No, really, please don't go to any more trouble for me – I really don't deserve it.'

Then, to my delight: 'Is that . . . Piana Vera?' she'd said, fingering the tiny gold diamond embroidered on my collar.

'Yes, it is; how did you know that?'

'It's one of my favourite brands, actually. Not many people seem to have heard of it.'

'Oh my goodness,' I'd chimed. 'That's one of the reasons I love it so much. I always pop into the shop whenever I'm in Covent Garden. I just adore it.'

She'd winked and disappeared into her bedroom then, reappearing with a pale-blue wraparound top that had a matching diamond on the collar. 'Borrow this. You can't go home in a cocktail-encrusted top. What would the neighbours say!'

It was these glimpses of camaraderie that occupied my thoughts on my journey back to Hounslow. I tried to cling to these moments, stacking them up in my mind like a tally of reasons why the Rivers would want me to continue to be their friend, and why they would ultimately decide to invite me to France. I replayed Sarah's expression when she'd spotted that my top was Piana Vera, I remembered Isaac's relief when I'd saved him from talking to Felicity, I half-recalled Sarah laughing wholeheartedly at a joke I'd made . . . possibly about shellfish or something. Admittedly, the memories of the previous night were patchy, but my shame had dissipated when I'd overheard Isaac insisting I should be invited to France, and his annoyance when Vangie had objected.

So, with a receding headache, a borrowed top that smelt of Sarah's perfume, and a new sense of belonging, I drove my clunky Micra back to Hounslow in a bubble of hope.

I wore Sarah's top to work for the next three days, until the perfume smell was replaced by the scent of milk that had spilled and gone sour. There were also a couple of small espresso splashes on the front, and I decided I'd get it professionally cleaned so I could hand it back to her in pristine condition, preferably in one of those plastic covers they used in dry cleaner's shops.

It was Thursday lunchtime when I dropped it off, requesting a twenty-four hour express wash so I could pick it up on Friday and take it to Riverdean on Saturday, after Freddie's tutoring session. I walked past Piana Vera on the way back to the café, noting the autumn styles in the window. I hadn't yet been asked to France, but checked my phone regularly in excited anticipation of Isaac's text, or perhaps Sarah's phone call, which I knew would come soon. I wondered when the holiday would be. Perhaps October half term. But whenever it was, I was sure there'd be some discounted summer items at the back of the shop that would be perfect for lounging around a villa pool, giggling with Sarah and accepting cocktails from Isaac. I felt my insides melt with a contented warmth, and couldn't keep the smile from my face that afternoon.

When the last customer had gone and I'd locked the café door, I took out my phone, desperate for an outlet for my jubilant mood.

Hi Dad! I hope you got my last letter. Things are going so well this end. Tutoring's going brilliantly, and I might even be off on holiday soon with the new friends I was telling you about. Promise I'll call by soon and see you. Lots of love, Dxxx.

It was as I clicked out of WhatsApp that I noticed the email notification. It was from Vangie, and the subject title was *Apologies, late notice*. Having expected the France invitation to come from Isaac or Sarah, it surprised me that it would now be coming from Vangie. But then I thought back to Isaac's insistence that I was fun and should be included in the holiday arrangements, and wondered if, once Vangie had cooled down, he'd been able to persuade her that it really would be wonderful to have me there. After all, I could even do a couple of tutoring sessions with Freddie, to keep up the impetus over the holiday. Yes, I wondered if that had been part of Isaac's argument in my defence.

I opened the email, ready to drink in the words.

Dear Diana, I'm so sorry to give you such late notice, but we've decided the tutoring isn't really working out for Freddie. We really appreciate your efforts with him, but I think as of next term we're going to ask about availability for extra sessions at his school instead. This is in no way a reflection on your work with him, which has been excellent. It's just that weekends tend to get rather busy, and a time slot at school with one of his existing tutors would certainly be more time efficient for us.

I felt the blood leave my face in an icy trickle through my veins. But there was more.

I would say let's do one more session this Saturday, but we're off to France early next week with Isaac and Sarah, and there's so much packing to do! We'll be away for ten days so that counts out the following weekend too. I should have told you about this before the summer, so I apologise for being so disorganised, and of course I will pay you for the next two sessions anyway. I'll add the amount on to the transfer I'm about to make so you get it in one lump sum.

Anyway, it's been lovely meeting you, and I wish you all the best with your tutoring business, and for the future in general.

Kind regards

Vangie

I was dismissed. Just like that. And not only from the tutoring sessions, but from her life, it would seem. *I wish you all the best with your tutoring business, and for the future in general.* Could there be a sentence more certain to mean *I never want to see you again*? I only noticed I'd slipped down onto the floor when my bottom landed with a jolt, my back pressed up against the stainless steel counter. Not only was she trying to eject me from their friendship circle, and put a stop to the easy money I'd been getting used to, but she'd made sure I knew for certain I was not, and never would be, invited to France.

I stared at my phone, limbs paralysed, until the screen went dark. Then, from somewhere small and hard inside me there surged a white hot fury that electrified every nerve in my body. I stared down at my right hand, suddenly aware it felt slick, and realised a trail of dark blood was oozing from the freshly opened gash in my thumb where I'd dug in my fingernail. I pressed harder and felt the delicious pain of it flare under my skin. But that wasn't enough. The door to the dishwasher was open next to me and I felt myself lunge forwards, swiping a cup from the rack and smashing it into the tiles next to me, pounding and pounding until there was nothing left of it. Then I grabbed more. I grabbed plates and glasses and mugs with both hands, smashing them into the floor. I smashed and pushed and ground them into the surface with my hands and somewhere distant I heard a screaming sound, like someone in pain on the other side of a door. It was only when there was no crockery left in the dishwasher that I stopped, and realised the sound was coming from me. But now there was another sound. It was my name, over and over again.

'Dinah, Dinah, Dinah, Dinah.'

I twisted on the floor – limbs slipping on the powdered fragments of glass and china strewn across the kitchen – and looked up into Misha's horrified face as she stared down at me. Her open mouth quivered and she held up her hands as if reassuring a stray dog that she was friend not foe.

'Dinah . . . just . . . just stop, OK? You're OK. You're OK.'

I wanted to laugh at her; she looked so ridiculous, standing there in her silly pink glasses with her arms outstretched, repeating the same thing over and over again. I looked down at my own hands, which were streaked with a sort of chalky red substance which I guessed was my blood mixed with powdered china. The same substance was smeared all over my jeans and shirt. Thank God I'm not wearing Sarah's top, I thought.

My thoughts seemed to shut down at that point and I observed myself being helped to my feet by Misha. My hands were placed under cool running water, and a first aid kit appeared. Wipes, cream, bandages, plasters.

'I should really get the brush and clean up this mess,' I said as Misha tucked in the end of a dressing she'd wound around my right hand.

'Kate will do that. You just need to get home. I'll drive you.' She spoke slowly as if I were a child who might have trouble understanding. It was only as her words sunk in that I turned to the door of the store cupboard and noticed Kate standing there, peeping from the darkness like a frightened mouse.

I didn't speak much in the car. Misha did, though. She told me I needed to take some time off, and of course I would be granted statutory sick pay. I needed to call someone, preferably a psychologist or counsellor. Had I used one before? Yes, I assured her. Was there a relative I could go and stay with? Didn't I have a sister? Yes, but I wouldn't be going there. Could I stay with my father then? I always spoke very fondly of him? Yes, I said. That might be the best thing. I'll speak to him.

It was as we were pulling up outside my flat that my phone pinged with a message from Kate. It took me a moment to remember she thought she was texting Hen because I'd swapped the numbers around.

> *Hi Hen, Dinah absolutely LOST IT at work just now. You need to call her ASAP because she does not look like she's in a good way. I think she just had a complete breakdown. Don't worry, Misha and I took good care of her. She's at home now. Let me know how she is when you've spoken to her. Lots of love, Kxx*

I congratulated myself on having had the presence of mind to swap our numbers, and felt tremendous relief that this was one update Hen would not be getting, and one episode she would never find out about. I tapped on the reply box.

> *Thanks for the update, Kate. But from now on I think it would be best if you would just mind your own fucking business. Lots of love xxx*

Chapter Fifteen

The smell of cooked onions and urine seemed particularly strong in the hallway as Misha escorted me up to my flat. It was weird seeing her there. I watched her pottering around, making tea, opening the curtains, making one-sided conversation about a cousin of hers who swore by cognitive behavioural therapy. She said she'd get me a phone number. She wanted to wait whilst I called my sister or my dad, but I said I would call both of them later, after I'd had a shower and a rest. She seemed doubtful about this, but also too scared to push the subject. Eventually she left.

The yellow light that filtered through my grimy windows eventually dimmed to a dull orange, before turning cool grey, then black. My hands throbbed under the dressings and my clothes stuck to me in patches where the bloody paste had congealed. Eventually I fell asleep there on the sofa, in the amber glow from the streetlamps outside.

The next morning, I woke at ten, joints creaky and head pounding to a pulse. I could also feel stinging in the lacerations in my palms. I crossed to the bathroom and peeled off my crusty clothes, showering carefully so as not to get my bandages wet. In my bedroom, I took three paracetamol washed down with an old glass of dusty water, before dressing in the black and pink zigzag dress I'd worn my first weekend at Riverdean. It was the easiest thing to throw on over my head.

All the while I was berating myself for my stupidity. Once I'd engaged with Isaac and Sarah again, I'd thought of my relationship with Vangie as almost inconsequential. She'd served her purpose as my gateway to Riverdean. But how stupid of me not to understand that she was both gateway and gatekeeper. And once I'd fallen out of favour, she had no qualms about pulling up the drawbridge, leaving me alone outside the castle. All this time I'd been focusing on Isaac and Sarah, when I should have been winning over Vangie.

Exhausted by these thoughts, and the small tasks I'd managed to complete, I collapsed back onto the sofa and picked up my phone. There were three messages. One was from Kate and was a mortified response to my message yesterday, in which she apologised for 'over-stepping', and pleaded with Hen to let her know of 'absolutely anything at all' she could do to help. I ignored it. The second was from Misha asking if I was OK, and whether I'd called my therapist or my dad. I replied saying I planned to visit my dad later today. The third was an automated text from *Lily White's Laundry* in Covent Garden, informing me my item would be ready for collection from midday today.

Sarah's blue top.

A thought bobbed up from somewhere. *I had to return Sarah's top.* Suddenly I felt my thoughts clear, like clouds scudding away to reveal a clean blue sky. Why should I skulk away with my tail between my legs on

Vangie's say-so, when Isaac had been so clear that he wanted me to go to France? What was it he'd said while he was cooking breakfast on Sunday morning? *Vangie loves being offended.* This was just her. This was how she was. She was judgmental and suspicious and she didn't like other people muscling in on her friendship with Isaac and Sarah. She was controlling and jealous and took easy offence when anyone threatened the boring balance of their four-way friendship. It made me wonder why amazing people like Isaac and Sarah would be friends with someone like her in the first place, but then I reasoned it was probably just because Isaac and Duncan worked together. Yes, the more I thought about it, the more I realised theirs must be a friendship born of necessity. There's no way Isaac and Sarah would be friends with such a stuck-up kill-joy if they didn't have to be. And it was this realisation that reawakened the fire in me. Tomorrow was Saturday, which meant they were more likely to be at home. I would go to Riverdean to return Sarah's top, and once there I'd ask them both about the France holiday, wax lyrical about how much fun it sounded, mention I spoke decent French, then wait for my invitation.

Feeling re-inflated by my plan, I grabbed my handbag and headed towards the Tube station. Fellow passengers stared at my bandaged hands, which were now patchy with dried blood that had seeped through, but at this point I didn't really care what a bunch of gawping strangers thought.

Once I'd collected the shirt in its see-through plastic cover from the dry cleaners, I called at a pharmacy and bought new bandages and antiseptic cream, before heading home. Then I decided to keep my promise to Misha. I got out my phone, and texted *Hi Dad. I'm on my way to see you! Hope that's OK. Be there in about half an hour. Dxx.*

The traffic on the M4 to Slough wasn't too bad at two o'clock on a Friday afternoon. As was my routine when I went to see Dad, I parked at the bottom of the hill so I could pop into the newsagents and buy a bottle of Pinot Grigio, a bunch of carnations, and a family-sized bar of Cadbury's Dairy Milk.

I walked up the hill, feeling the sun on my shoulders and the familiar tingle of anticipation as I ordered my thoughts, working out what news I would share and in what order. I turned into the tarmacked driveway, marvelling as I always did at the immaculate grass, the edges trimmed with impressive precision. At the yew tree I took a shortcut across the lawn, arriving only fractionally later than I said I would.

I knelt down on the velvety grass and set my carrier bag next to me. Leaning forward, I touched my fingers to the black stone, an action that had become habitual over the course of my visits.

'Hi Dad,' I said, running my fingers over the gilded lettering. *Frank Joseph Marshall. 1951–2017.* 'Sorry I've not been for a while. I've actually been really busy.'

I reached into the carrier bag and brought out the carnations, slotting their stems into the holes in the small silver pot.

My visits to Dad always churned up the same thoughts and memories. I'd always leave the cemetery remembering how he'd been my biggest cheerleader, telling me I could do anything, be anything. But this had always been said against the backdrop of Hen's successes, which made me wonder if he actually believed it, or just felt bad for me because I wasn't as good as her. She was the top of the class. The winner of the bake-off. The highest jumper or fastest runner. I didn't concentrate, or was unpredictable – and 'not a team player', as one of my school reports once said.

I'd always drive home from the cemetery thinking about how Mum, Dad and Hen had all been completely floored when I got into Oxford. They hadn't realised that A Levels had allowed me to focus on the subjects I *wanted* to take, and that's why I succeeded. Because when I focused on something I *actually wanted*, everything else faded away, and I'd do exactly what I needed to do to get it.

After musing on these points, I'd usually arrive back at my flat and spend the rest of the evening ruminating on how unfortunate it had been that my first semester Modern Classics professor had decided to lie to his wife and the faculty about my mental state so I'd get thrown out – or *encouraged to leave* as one of the letters they'd sent me had phrased it. And it was because of these predictable, spiralling thoughts that, after visiting Dad, I always treated myself to a dinner of white wine and chocolate.

After that particular visit, I watched whatever it was that popped up on my TV screen . . . a quiz show with B-list celebrities, a house makeover programme, the news . . . then, deciding there wasn't much point trying to change into my pyjamas, I crawled into bed wearing my zigzag dress, gulping down three more paracetamol before drifting into a sickly sleep.

The next day, I dressed in a discounted Piana Vera top in cream, with black ribbon detail, and long black trousers. It was perhaps overly smart for a social visit, but I'd been in such a state the last time they'd seen me I wanted to claw back some of the dignity Eden House Diana had managed to conjure. I had new clean dressings on my hands, and tried to ignore the stretching and stinging of the flesh underneath as I gripped the steering wheel.

I parked in the same cul-de-sac as I had before the barbecue last weekend, then retrieved Sarah's top from the hook in the back of the car, and walked to Riverdean. The gates were open, welcoming me. I thought of Vangie and Duncan's house, and the unfriendly entry system. The way they made every visitor stare into a monitor and justify their presence. How the open gates of Riverdean contrasted with the unfriendliness of Blackworth House. Well, to hell with Blackworth House. And to hell with Vangie. I knew when I wasn't wanted. And I knew when I was wanted. Here I *was* wanted. At Riverdean I would always be welcome.

Isaac's Range Rover was parked on the driveway, an emerald-green Mini next to it. They were home. I had thought about phoning ahead, but then I worried Sarah would say something like, *Oh goodness, keep the top for as long as you like, don't worry about returning it today*, and then it would have been difficult for me to turn up.

I pressed the doorbell and heard the muffled chime behind the thick front door. I tried to arrange my heavily made-up face into a relaxed and happy expression. The expression of someone completely at ease with calling in on her close friends unannounced. At last I heard footsteps in the hallway, and the door swung open to reveal Sarah.

Her eyebrows lifted in surprise when she saw me. 'Diana, what . . . we weren't expecting you?' It was phrased like a question, as if she was worried she might have forgotten an arrangement we'd made.

'No, no, you weren't, don't worry. I just called by to return your top.' I held up the garment in its rustling cover. 'And to say thank you so much for lending it to me.'

'Oh goodness, don't mention it. You didn't have to return it so soon. And you certainly didn't need to get it cleaned, bless you.'

'Well, it was the least I could do.' I cursed myself at that moment for not thinking to bring wine or flowers as a gesture of thanks.

I'd expected Sarah to ask me why I was in the area, but as she didn't, I thought I would break the silence by offering up my lie anyway. 'I'm visiting some old Oxford friends on the other side of Broadsham, so thought I might as well call in on my way.'

'Right . . . lovely.' She nodded again.

'Because I'm not tutoring Freddie any more . . . I'm not sure if Vangie told you?'

Her eyebrows dipped into a sympathetic frown. 'Yes . . . yes, she did mention that. I mean, I think Freddie's got so much on at the moment; it sounds as if it was a case of bad timing really. I know she thinks you've done absolute wonders with him.'

Now I *knew* Sarah was just being kind. I happened to know Vangie thought nothing of the sort, from overhearing her telling Isaac my tutoring was doing *a fat lot of good*.

'Well, that's very kind. Like you say, I suppose just a case of bad timing.'

Sarah reached for the top and took the hanger from my grip. 'Oh goodness, what are these bandages? Have you hurt yourself?'

'Oh, it's nothing,' I said, noting the real concern etched into her face. 'I stupidly tripped in a café the other day when I was holding a tray. Put out both hands to save myself, naturally, and ended up with some cuts from the broken china.'

'Gosh, that sounds painful!'

'It was. But they're on the mend now.'

'Good,' she said, nodding again. 'Glad to hear it.'

For one awful moment I thought she was going to say *well, thanks for dropping the top off. See you sometime!* but just as I was trying to think of a way I could prompt an invitation into the house, Isaac appeared from the cloakroom door at the side of the corridor.

'I thought I recognised that voice,' he said, a grin spreading across his face as he came and stood next to Sarah. 'I was trying to get some work done in the office and this exchange was all very distracting.' He frowned in mock consternation and I felt my insides soften as they often did when Isaac was joking around.

'Well, I'm terribly sorry to interrupt your work. I just came by to return Sarah's top,' I said, trying to match his jovial tone.

'I hope you'll come in for a coffee now you're here?' He looked hopeful, and just like at Vangie's house when he'd invited me to the barbecue, I wanted to leap onto him and cry *thank you, thank you, thank you!*

'I'm sure Diana has a million things she has to be getting on with, Zac,' said Sarah, and I was rather stingingly reminded of Vangie saying almost exactly the same thing when Isaac invited me to the barbecue. It was as if Sarah didn't want me to come in. But that couldn't be right. I realised I must be getting paranoid because of the unfortunate way things had ended with Vangie.

'No, I'm free as a bird actually.' I directed my smile at Isaac, who clapped his hands together.

'Wonderful! Well, come on through then.'

Sarah closed the door behind me and we followed Isaac down the hallway and into the kitchen. She fiddled with dishes and cups at the sink whilst Isaac breezed around, boiling the kettle, fetching down mugs, grinding coffee beans in a sleek version of the industrial-looking grinder we used at the café.

Sarah and I perched on bar stools with our coffee, and Isaac stood sipping his. Glancing around the kitchen, I noticed three passports at the far end of the island, fanned out as if on display. This was my moment.

'Oh, off on holiday?' I said, eyeing the passports.

'Yes, France,' said Sarah. 'I think Vangie mentioned it to you?'

201

Right, I thought. Vangie had told Sarah everything she'd written in that email. What else had she said, I wondered. Had she mentioned that Isaac was planning on inviting me?

'Ah, that's right. Yes, she did mention it,' I said, with a concentrating frown, as if I was trying to remember something so wholly inconsequential it had barely made an imprint on my brain. 'When are you off?'

'Tuesday morning, for ten days,' Sarah said. 'We have a villa over there that we share with Vangie and Duncan, so it's become a sort of yearly tradition.'

'How lovely,' I said, feeling a compulsion to say more. 'My parents used to own a villa in the South of France when I was a child. We spent many a happy summer down there.'

'Oh my gosh! Whereabouts?' This was the first time Sarah had sounded genuinely enthusiastic since I'd arrived, so I knew the lie had been the right decision.

'My goodness, I can't remember now. They sold it when I was nine, and you know when you're that age you don't really concentrate on the geography of your holidays.'

'No, well quite.' Sarah nodded. 'Well, we're flying into Bergerac and it's a little village just outside called Beaumont-sur-Lede.'

'Right . . . that's Dordogne, isn't it?' I said, desperately trying to remember my French geography. 'Yes, I'm sure that was the region where our villa was. I think I remember them talking a lot about Bordeaux, so it wouldn't have been far—'

'Yes, Bordeaux is the nearest city.' Sarah beamed.

I nodded and tried not to show my utter shock and delight at having dredged that knowledge from somewhere. 'Absolutely gorgeous area. Those vineyards . . . the quaint little villages.'

'It is very picturesque, yes,' Sarah agreed.

Isaac wasn't contributing to the conversation, but had lowered his gaze to the dregs of coffee in his mug, which he swirled round and round. I would have given anything to know what he was thinking. Perhaps he was wondering whether this would be a good moment to invite me, but worrying about how Sarah would react. Which was ridiculous, because I knew she'd love to have me there as much as he would. Perhaps the thought just hadn't occurred to her yet. I had to make sure the thought made its way to the forefront of her mind.

Suddenly I had an idea. '*Il y a longtemps que je n'ai pas parle français. Pêut-etre je dois visiter la France pour practiquer.*'

'Wow, that's impressive!' Isaac's eyes had lit up. He turned to his wife. 'Isn't it, Sarah?'

'Very,' she said, with a muted smile. 'I'm afraid we're all hopeless. Every year we say we'll take a course or use an app or something and be able to speak French by the following year, but of course we never do. Are you fluent?'

'I did take A Level French, so I suppose I'm not bad,' I said, making sure to give a self-deprecating shrug. 'But "useful on holiday" is probably a more accurate description than "fluent".' I looked at both of them in turn, wondering if I'd said enough for Sarah to have the epiphany that I'd be an amazing addition to the party.

'Have you finished with that?' she said, holding her hand out to take my empty mug.

'Um . . . yes. Yes, I have.' I passed her the mug and watched her turn and put it in the dishwasher.

I looked at Isaac who tapped his fingers on the worktop a few times before announcing. 'Right, I'd better get back to work. Duncan wants these papers signed and emailed back to him this afternoon. Slave driver that he is.' He rolled his eyes in mock annoyance.

I felt the blood draining from my face as it had in the café when I'd read Vangie's email. My veins tingled with the iciness of it, and my breaths quickened. This was not panning out how I'd envisaged. This was ridiculous. How could they not see what was right in front of them? How could they not appreciate the importance of this new friendship we all shared? Was this all Vangie's doing?

The spark of white hot fury flickered inside me, stuttering like a faulty cigarette lighter. But before the flame could take hold, someone walked into the kitchen. It was Cam. Her hair was hanging in wet mousey straggles around her shoulders and she wore a baggy black smock and black Doc Martens. Her eyes were smudged with eyeliner that looked a day old.

'Diana,' she said, seeming almost amused to find me there. 'Nice to see you again.' Her tone also held a trace of the amusement, and I wondered what was so funny.

'I didn't know you'd met?' said Sarah, looking between both of us as if wondering whether or not she should be concerned.

'Yes, Diana and I met the other day. When she was horrifically hungover.'

'Oh God, please don't remind me.' I cringed inwardly.

'We had a good chat, didn't we?' Cam said as she reached into the fridge, bringing out a carton of apple juice. For an awful moment I thought she was going to bring up the photo we'd discussed, and that I would have to bear witness to the ensuing awkwardness.

'It was a good chat,' I said, deciding to keep the subject light. 'I learnt a new philosophical principal ... which wasn't bad for a hangover day.'

'Really?' Sarah looked at me then and her eyes twinkled as she smiled. Her face looked open and surprised as her gaze flicked towards Cam and back to me.

'Yep,' agreed Cam, filling a large tumbler with juice. 'I mean, Diana was clearly only listening so she could bum a fag, but still, she seemed to understand the concept.'

I was mortified that Isaac and Sarah now knew I smoked. It was so completely unfitting with the Diana I'd created.

'I didn't know you smoked?' Sarah said, disbelief flashing across her face.

'Ah, well ...' I felt my palms prickle. 'I'm trying to give up actually. It was a moment of weakness ...' I said, trying to sound offhand.

'Perhaps you should both be giving up?' Sarah looked at Cam, a tentative expression flashing across her face, as if she was scared to suggest how Cam should behave any more strongly than that. Something inside me clenched on Cam's behalf, having been on the receiving end of exactly that expression and that tone of voice whenever Hen scooped me up after an 'episode'. It was the voice that said *you know I love you, but please allow me to*

explain exactly why you're incapable of making deci-
sions for yourself.

Cam ignored Sarah's comment and put the juice back in the fridge. Isaac, I'd noticed, had taken a sudden interest in cleaning out the coffee grinder with a small brush. He put the lid back on and turned around as if none of us had been speaking. 'Well, I'm back off into the office. Lovely to see you, Diana.' And with a subdued smile he left.

There was a beat of silence. 'I need a fag,' said Cam, flashing Sarah a pointedly defiant look before stalking out of the room.

Sarah sighed and ran her fingers through her hair. Then she turned to me. 'Actually, I should probably get back to my packing.' She gave an apologetic grimace. 'I'm sorry, Diana. Thank you so much for the shirt. It was really kind of you to take the time to return it.'

'Well, it was really kind of you to lend it to me.' I smiled back at her before realising she'd moved towards the kitchen door and was holding her arm out ever so slightly, as if ushering me towards the front door. This was it. Just like Vangie, she was dismissing me.

Numbly I slid off the bar stool and followed her into the hall. We said goodbye at the door. 'Perhaps we could catch up again soon?' I heard my voice say with a pathetic hopefulness.

'That would be lovely,' she said, but she was already closing the door. 'Bye bye.' Click. It was shut.

I stood, looking at it, as if I could will it to open again. But it stood resolutely still and silent.

'They bored of you now?' The voice made me physically flinch and my head snapped round to see Cam leaning against the side of the porch, cigarette burning between her slender fingers. 'I know how that feels.' She took a drag and tilted her head to blow the smoke up in a diagonal cloud.

I didn't know what to say so gave an awkward laugh. 'I think . . . I think they're probably just a bit busy for visitors at the moment.'

She turned towards me and leaned her shoulder against the wall, fixing me with a steady gaze. 'I think they're really fond of you, Diana. They like you.'

'Do you think so?' I realised I sounded pathetically desperate for further confirmation, but I didn't care.

Cam's lips twitched into that mischievous smile I'd seen by the lake. It made me wonder if I was being mocked, or whether that was just the way she smiled.

'I definitely think so,' she said, giving an earnest nod. 'I've heard them saying how much fun you are, and how pleased they are they met you.'

'That's . . . that's just great. I mean, I think they're fun too.' I smiled and shrugged, feeling a bit like a child making friends in a playground.

'I'm surprised they didn't invite you to France, actually.'

This statement injected a shot of adrenalin through me. 'What do you mean?'

'But I heard Isaac and Vangie talking last weekend and I realised it's probably just because of her. She's jealous someone else has come into their exclusive friendship group, so she's being a bitch.'

I knew it!

'I'm sure they'd have invited you otherwise.'

'That's kind of you to say.'

'They gave me a plus-one, you know. For France. I think they wanted someone to occupy me over there so I'm not constantly in their space making Isaac feel awkward by calling out his bullshit.'

I nodded slowly, unsure where this was going.

She dropped the glowing cigarette butt on the floor and ground it under her boot. 'I think I'd like you to be my plus-one.'

'What?' Disbelief had sharpened my voice and quickened my pulse.

'I say screw Vangie. I've been given a plus-one, Mum and Isaac would love you to be there – what's the problem?'

The way she gave a nonchalant shrug as she said this made me think, *actually, what* is *the problem?* Then I remembered. 'Vangie said she wouldn't go if I was invited.'

'So let's not tell her. Why don't you just show up as a surprise? It'll be perfect.' Cam stood up straight, eyes glittering. 'Vangie won't have to follow through with her pathetic threat not to come, I get my plus-one, Mum and Isaac get the pleasure of your company. It's a winning scenario all round.'

'Do you . . . do you really think your mum and Isaac would be pleased if I just turned up out of the blue?'

'Oh my God, they'd love it.' She emphasised the word love by scrunching up her eyes. 'You know what Isaac's like . . . Mr Life and Soul.' She rolled her eyes as she said this. 'A fun friend turning up as a surprise when he thought he was going to be stuck for ten days with Dull

Duncan and Vangie Bitchface? He'll love you forever.'
Her eyes bore into mine as she said this.

I could see it. I could imagine rounding that corner to
the pool and seeing Isaac turn towards me, his eyes widening, his face brightening in thrilled disbelief that I was
there. Sarah exclaiming *Diana!* and enfolding me in her
arms. Vangie . . . Vangie fuming under a sun umbrella.

'Vangie would not be impressed.'

'I've got to admit, Diana . . . that's kind of the best
part of the plan.' Her lips curved into a proper naughty
smile then, and I tried to stifle my own.

She was right. That would be the best part of the plan.

Chapter Sixteen

The taxi rolled through the undulating countryside, a patchwork of striped green vineyards and sunbaked fields. High poplars flanked the roadsides as we wound our way through sleepy stone villages. I'd written the address on a piece of paper and handed it to the driver so there'd be no error in translation. *Manoir Segantin, 55 Route des Arbres, 47993 Beaumont-sur-Lede.* The driver, a rotund man in his fifties with thinning black hair and a pockmarked face, had only given the sheet a cursory glance before nodding his head and swerving the car around and away towards the exit. This had reassured me he knew where he was going. Perhaps, I thought, he'd even driven the Rivers and the Slades to the property earlier in the week.

I'd decided to give them a couple of days to settle in before making my surprise entrance. Cam and I had swapped phone numbers so I could keep her informed of my progress, and she could make sure they weren't all out when I arrived. I had to admit a small part of me was nervous about my arrival, but a larger part was fizzing with excitement as I anticipated Isaac and Sarah's reactions. I got out my phone and texted Cam: *Driver's GPS says we're 15 mins away. x*

Her reply came almost instantly: *Great. See you by the pool.*

I felt the prickle of sweat and pulled the fabric away from my armpits to try and get some air to them. I'd dressed in a Breton-striped T-shirt from the Jigsaw sale, and cropped white trousers from Gap, which I'd managed to keep spotless on the journey by refusing all snacks on the plane and only drinking water. I wanted to turn up looking fresh and clean.

A wide opening in a pale stone wall indicated the gravel driveway, which was short and led to a large two-storey building with ivy growing around the doorway. Duck-egg blue shutters flanked the windows, which were set in old limestone walls – walls my internet research told me were at least four hundred years old. It was a charming, quintessentially French building, and I couldn't wait to explore inside. But first, I needed to make my grand entrance.

The driver pulled my black suitcase from the boot and I paid the fare plus a generous tip.

'*Merci.*' It was the first word he'd spoken to me the entire journey.

'*De rien,*' I replied, excited to get my first opportunity in twenty-four years to use my French. I felt a quiver of excitement as I anticipated impressing everyone over the next week, perhaps if we went on day trips, or ate out in the local village.

I picked up my suitcase as it was impossible to pull along on the gravel. The oak front door opened onto a large, square flagstone hallway with wooden stairs sweeping up to a gallery where I could just about make out a rust-coloured tapestry and a door that stood ajar. Cam had said everyone was around the pool so I left my

211

bag at the foot of the staircase. Wide French windows in front of me let in the natural light, and led to a sloping lawn that ended in a thicket of trees. A door to my right revealed a large room with a pool table and shelves stacked with board games. I walked back through the hallway, and found myself in a comfortable living room. On the dark varnished floorboards sat two large cream sofas either side of a white stone fireplace. A low glass coffee table crouched in the middle where an aquamarine vase displayed a bunch of white pompom flowers. Beside the vase was a small china cup with coffee dregs at the bottom.

At the far end of the room was an elegant baby grand piano made from a polished golden wood. I ran my fingers over the smooth surface, admiring the intricate side panels, separated by carved laurel wreaths. A gilded inlay just above the keys read *Gaveau, Paris*. It was a stunning instrument and I longed to sit on the claret velvet stool and let my fingers wander over the keys . . . but that would have to wait until I'd greeted everyone. *Or would it?* Perhaps this was the perfect way to announce my arrival.

I peeked out of the window. I could just about see where the sand-coloured flagstones gave way to the turquoise ripples of the pool. Peeping into the next room – a kitchen, I realised, with tall units that stretched across one wall, a large stove centre stage, and a massive dining table that dominated the space – I spotted two huge blue-framed doors that opened up to reveal the pool area. Voices drifted in from outside and, as I watched, Duncan waddled across the doorway, his round belly protruding over baggy lime-green trunks. My heart fluttered as I heard Isaac's voice say, *yes, perhaps tomorrow?* I couldn't work out who he was talking to, but Sarah's laugh tinkled from further away, maybe from the opposite side of the pool.

Retreating into the living room, I sat down at the piano, running my fingers silently over the keys before sliding them into position. I filled my lungs with a calming breath, trying to still the quiver of excitement inside me. Then I played. It was the same song I'd played on the piano at Riverdean, the extra night I'd stayed there alone.

The arpeggios sang out, round and rich from deep within the instrument, and I could hear them fill the room before carrying through to the kitchen. I envisaged them winging their way out to the poolside, conversations stopping as Isaac and Sarah turned their heads quizzically towards the music. I saw Duncan's confused expression, and Vangie's vexed frown. I imagined Cam reclining on a sun lounger, her lips curving into her signature smile of amusement.

With each word your tenderness grows, tearing my fear apart . . .

There was the padding of bare feet on stone, and muffled voices. I brought my gaze up from the keys and kept my eyes on the door. Sarah appeared first, a gentle frown creasing her porcelain features. Her eyes locked onto mine and I smiled as I continued to play. *And that laugh that wrinkles your nose, it touches my foolish heart . . .*

Sarah's expression flashed with something hard – something I hadn't expected. Was it fear? It was certainly

213

shock. She stood stock-still in the doorway, her sunglasses perched on her head, and her white cover-up stirring in the breeze. Hands appeared on her shoulders and Isaac followed, guiding her into the room so he could push through himself. *You're lovely, with your smile so warm, and your cheeks so soft. There is nothing for me but to love you . . .* He was laughing and saying something to someone behind him as he entered, but when he turned and saw me, his smile faltered too and he froze where he stood.

Cam sauntered in next, barely giving me a glance as she made her way around Isaac and Sarah whilst tying her hair up in a messy bun. She kept her eyes on the door, perhaps waiting for Vangie and Duncan to appear. They both strode in then, Duncan looking sweaty and puzzled, Vangie already looking furious. But her anger warped into something else when she saw me.

'*Diana?*' she said, her voice a horrified rasp. Her already frowning face contorted into something grotesque. *Just the way you look tonight . . .*

I let the chord die away at the end of the cadence and rested my hands in my lap. My gaze flitted from face to face, waiting for at least Isaac and Sarah's expressions to break into the delighted smiles I'd been envisaging since I'd decided I would take the plunge and book my ticket. But none of them smiled. Sarah cast frantic glances at Vangie, who looked like she was about to explode. Isaac opened and closed his mouth as if he had a question but didn't quite know how to frame it. Duncan looked more bewildered than anything as he stared at each of his friends in turn, eyebrows raised questioningly.

'What the fuck are you doing here?' It was Vangie again, a sheen of sweat on her pale face and a burgeoning patch of red invading her upper chest and neck.

'Vangie . . .' Isaac said with a hint of warning in his voice. But he didn't continue.

'I don't understand what's going on,' said Sarah, shaking her head and searching her friends' faces. Her gaze came to rest on me. 'I . . . has there been some sort of misunderstanding?'

Vangie snorted. 'I think that's a bloody understatement.'

A misunderstanding? I felt a sudden surge of anger, and was surprised to find it was directed at Sarah. How could this possibly be a misunderstanding? Did she think I was stupid and didn't know if I'd been invited on holiday or not? The first thought to occur to her was not that my presence could be a 'surprise', but that it must be a 'misunderstanding'? I felt as if I'd been punched in the stomach.

'Actually, there's been no misunderstanding.' It was Cam who spoke now, and I felt awash with relief that she'd taken the role of explainer. 'I invited Diana.'

All eyes were on Cam.

'What do you mean, darling?' said Sarah, her face still seemingly unwilling to relinquish its frown.

'You gave me a plus-one, and I chose Diana.'

'You're not serious?' Vangie spat the words and I noticed the redness had spread all the way up her face.

'I am serious, Vangie. If you've got a problem with that arrangement, perhaps you should take it up with Isaac. It was his idea Freddie and I should be allowed to bring someone.'

'I . . . I suppose it's just that we would have expected it to be one of your friends . . .' Isaac said meekly, flashing me a glance that looked almost apologetic.

'Diana *is* my friend. We get on like a house on fire.' Cam's voice was a deadpan drawl, her expression dark and serious. 'House on fire' was definitely not the vibe.

'What absolute bullshit,' said Vangie, giving a slightly unhinged cackle. Despite my unease I was pleased to hear her sounding so deranged. 'You invited her to stir things up and watch the fallout because you just love messing with everyone!'

'Vangie!' It was Sarah's turn to look livid. 'That's incredibly unfair. Cam would never do something like that.'

'And yet here sits Diana!' Vangie gestured to me with a triumphant sneer.

'I'm sorry . . .' It was the first time I'd spoken, but I felt I couldn't stay silent any longer. 'But what does that mean? That my presence specifically is somehow controversial?' I cast a confused look around the group. 'I'm a friend of the family, and a friend of Cam's. She approached me privately and asked me to come, saying she thought it would be fun if I turned up to surprise everyone.' I kept my voice soft and calm. All eyes were on me. 'If I'd realised my visit would be seen as "messing" or "bullshit" or that there would be "fallout", I wouldn't have made the effort.'

There was a silence then, and it was saturated with embarrassment. I'd thrown Vangie's words back into the room and made everyone see how hurtful and aggressive they were, when I'd actually gone to a lot of trouble to be here at Cam's request. I looked at Cam who nodded her head solemnly. 'So rude,' she said.

I decided to take a gamble then. This whole scenario had not panned out in any way as I'd hoped or expected, but I could perhaps claw it back if I doubled down on how insulted I was, and made them realise how poisonous Vangie was being.

I sniffed and put my fingers to my mouth as if willing myself not to cry. Then I stood, the scraping sound of the stool against the wooden floor sending a collective flinch through the group. 'I . . . I can see this was a mistake. I'm sorry, Cam. Perhaps you should have chosen a different plus-one.'

I looked down, and Cam extended a hand towards me, which I instinctively reached for. We squeezed and then let go in perfect synchronisation. The gesture was so out of character for both of us, I knew in that moment that Cam and I were playing the same game here.

'I'm so sorry, Diana,' she said. 'I really thought they'd—'

'I know . . . I know. So did I.' I cast a tearful glance around the group, taking in Vangie's furious stance with her arms folded across her chest, Duncan's enduring confusion, Sarah's terrified gaze that flicked between Cam and me, and Isaac's embarrassed hair tousling.

'I'll walk you out,' said Cam, and we both turned away from the group and headed towards the far end of the room and into the hallway. We didn't speak as I lifted my bag and carried it out of the front door. We stopped at the top of the driveway and made brief eye contact before Cam checked her watch and dug in the pocket of her denim shorts.

'Well, Vangie's reaction was beyond my wildest hopes and dreams,' she said, pulling out a packet of cigarettes. She lit one then offered me the pack. I shook my head.

Mortification writhed inside me. Cam still thought this was all a joke, but Isaac and Sarah's reaction had left me feeling physically bruised.

As if she'd read my mind, Cam said, 'You know Mum and Isaac only reacted like that because of Vangie, right? If she hadn't been there they'd have been all over you.'

'Do you really believe that?'

'I know that,' she said, blowing smoke over my shoulder. I wondered if the game was over for her, if Vangie's reaction was all she wanted out of this, and whether she couldn't care less now whether I stayed or left.

The front door clicked open and I grabbed my phone from my pocket and pressed it to my ear. '*Oui, oui*,' I said as Sarah crunched over the gravel towards us. I took several paces away from Cam and pressed my finger to my other ear as if trying to hear the person on the other end of the phone. '. . . *taxi pour l'aéroport s'il vous plaît*?' I watched Cam and Sarah, observing Cam's sullen detachment as Sarah spoke to her in hushed tones, occasionally gesturing towards me. I pretended not to notice and turned my back on them. '*Oui, maintenant. Bergerac, oui.*'

A gentle hand was placed on my arm and I spun around to be greeted with Sarah's beautiful face, her eyes sad and pleading. '*Un moment, s'il vous plaît*,' I said, pressing the phone to my chest so the imaginary taxi company couldn't hear.

'Diana, please . . . I'm so sorry about what happened in there . . .'

'No need to apologise,' I said. 'I'm the one who should be apologising for intruding like this. I knew Vangie didn't want me tutoring Freddie any more, but I had no idea she disliked me so much. It just came as a bit of a shock, I think.' I needed to make sure I kept Vangie's hysterical outburst at the centre of this. Make sure it was her behaviour under the microscope, not mine.

'I . . . I don't know what to say.' Sarah gave a hopeless shrug and pressed her hand over her eyes. 'Oh, gosh, this is all such a mess.'

I rubbed her arm then. 'It's not your fault.'

She lowered her hand from her face and set her amber eyes on mine, and I was once again struck by how similar they were to Cam's. 'Vangie does wear her heart on her sleeve sometimes, and I suppose she can get rather over-protective of us as a friendship group. I mean . . . Duncan and Isaac's business has made a lot of money over the years, and sometimes that means people come into the frame who aren't really offering proper friendship, but are more . . .' She sighed.

'More what?' I asked, horrified that Sarah would think my interest in them was anything other than genuine. That I would want anything from them other than proper friendship.

She looked down at her shoes as if embarrassed. 'My parents are what you'd call "old money", I suppose, so we've had a fair few cling-ons. Then there are people like Felicity—'

'From the barbecue?'

'Yes, that's right. She's very young but she's always on at Isaac about promotions and opportunities. She always shows up if she gets a whiff of a social gathering, but we know she's only there to bend Isaac's ear about how she can climb the ladder at Acanthus. Then there are my candles—'

'What?' I'd been thinking about Felicity and how grateful Isaac had been for me saving him from talking to her at the party, so the mention of candles completely disorientated me. 'What candles?'

'Oh . . . the company I set up, Moss & Dean—'

'Moss & Dean is *your* company?' I stared in disbelief. Moss & Dean candles were everywhere. They were the nationwide go-to gift for female friends for any occasion. I'd given one to Hen last Christmas. This was Sarah's company. I felt myself gawping at her.

Sarah gave a soft laugh and shook her head in a self-deprecating way. 'It was a project I started years ago, which took off suddenly when I got into some good shops. Anyway, when it started doing well on social media, I used to get all sorts of people wanting to "team up". And the ones who approached me directly with business propositions were fine. But then you'd get sneaky ones who tried to befriend me, or started chatting to me at parties. I suppose it was just a bit of an invasion. That's why I tried to distance myself by going back to my maiden name, Dean. That made it a bit easier to sever the link online.'

All the time Sarah was talking I'd been trying to work out why I'd never found this out in all my extensive online research, but now it was clear. She was Sarah Rivers on her personal social media, but Sarah Dean when it came to the candles.

A new thought popped into my head. 'Riverdean . . . you merged your surnames.'

Sarah smiled, and I saw a relaxed expression ease onto her face for the first time since I'd arrived. 'Yes, you've got it.'

'Who's "Moss" then?'

'That's my mother's maiden name. My parents helped me set up the business, you know, financially. I thought it would be a nice nod.'

'OK,' I said, 'I understand all the reasons you and the Slades would be wary of newcomers into your friendship group. But honestly, why on earth would I be interested in any of those things? I'm an English tutor, for heaven's sake! I don't want a promotion in Isaac's company, and as wonderful as your candles are, I don't have a related product to promote. In fact, I never even knew you owned a candle company.'

'I know . . . I know all that. I just wanted to explain to you why Vangie sometimes gets wound up. Not that that excuses her awful behaviour in there.' Sarah squeezed my arm. 'Or the horrible welcome we all just gave you.'

I felt something mellow inside me then. 'There's no need to apologise.'

'I also had no idea you and Cam got on so well.'

I turned towards where Cam had been standing but she was gone.

'Cam's quite . . . troubled,' Sarah continued. 'She probably told you she doesn't get on very well with

Isaac, which can be very stressful for all of us. I'm so glad she's opened up to you, though. It's so important she has someone to talk to. Perhaps it's because of your experience with tutoring teenagers . . . maybe that's why you have such a way with her?'

It was my turn to give a modest smile and look at my feet.

Sarah continued, 'And as far as I'm concerned, it's brilliant that you're someone Isaac and I get along with too. When we offered her a plus-one, we were worried we'd end up in France with one of her dark and moody friends. Which of course we'd have gone along with . . . but it's so much nicer that it's you. It just . . . it took us by surprise, that's all . . . when we didn't think she'd invited anyone.'

'I totally understand.'

'So please say you'll forgive us all for being such an unfriendly bunch, and stay?'

It only now occurred to me that I was still clutching my mobile to my chest. I looked down at the screen. 'Oh . . . the taxi company's hung up.'

'Please don't call them back.' She squeezed my arm again. 'Please come inside, and we can tell Cam you're staying? If she's chosen you and you leave because of us . . . she'll never forgive me.'

Her eyes were pleading. She was begging me to stay. How quickly things can change, I thought. Especially when you work really hard to make them.

Chapter Seventeen

My room was perfection. The floor was dark wood, and the double bed-frame gleaming brass with a feather-soft mattress. The walls were papered with blue pastoral scenes – a young couple on a hay bale, a picnic by a river, sheep grazing. The room smelled sweet, like wood polish and clean cotton. My casement window framed a view across the plush green valley from just above the sloping lawn.

I took my time settling in, aware that conversations needed to be had downstairs. I knew Sarah was smoothing over the cracks, for which I felt a swell of gratitude. I'd been harsh on her in my mind earlier, blaming her for using the word 'misunderstanding' when of course she was only responding to Vangie's unfounded fury, and her own ignorance of the fact that I'd been invited, and by none other than her own daughter. But of course I accepted her apology, and now all was forgiven. That's what friends did, after all – they forgave and moved on. And Vangie would just have to deal with that.

I peeled my clothes from my clammy skin and showered in the en suite, keeping my hair dry so I wouldn't have to spend time reapplying all the products I'd slicked and scrunched and teased through it this morning. I dressed in my new turquoise St. Roche swimming costume, and a sheer black cover-up that reminded me of something Megs or Priya would wear – classy and expensive. As much as I hated Vangie right now, I couldn't have managed without the advance payment for the last two tutoring sessions she'd cancelled. That money had paid for my holiday wardrobe as well as my flight. I felt my lips twist into a smile, wondering how Vangie would feel to know it was only because of her money that I was here at all.

I crept down the creaking stairs, feeling like a child after bedtime, worried about a scolding from angry parents. I wanted to sashay out to the pool and stretch my newly salon-tanned legs along a sun lounger. And I knew if I'd had more of a positive welcome, that's exactly what I would be doing now. But despite Sarah's pleading and her reassurances, I still felt embarrassed. I wanted to bump into Cam so I could ask her to walk out there with me, but then I realised that was ridiculous and childish, and was not the way Diana would behave. So instead I sidled into the large stone kitchen, taking in details I'd not had the chance to earlier, like the oversized sofas pushed back against the walls, and the bare wood breakfast bar.

Taking a seaglass tumbler from a cabinet, I noticed the enormous black fridge was one of those fancy ones with the ice dispenser in the door, so I took some time to investigate that, pressing the buttons to change from 'cubed' to 'shaved' to 'crushed'. I was about to press the button for 'chilled water' when an arm slid around my shoulder, making me start. It was Isaac.

I looked up into his eyes, the same translucent green of the cool glass I held in my hand. He stared at me, the corners of his eyes creasing into an expression that was more of a wince than a smile.

He sighed and squeezed my shoulder. 'I'm so sorry about what just happened. We were all just . . . surprised to see you, and I think Vangie . . . Vangie over-reacted.'

I nodded, pleased that Vangie's behaviour was still being apologised for, although doubting she'd be providing any of the apologies herself. 'You don't have to say sorry. It's fine.' And everything *was* fine, because Isaac had his arm around my shoulder, the weight of it sinking through me, and I was having trouble feeling anything but the molten pleasure that swirled inside me.

He looked down at the glass of melting ice I was holding. 'What are you about to put in there then?'

'Water,' I said.

He gave me his twinkle of a smile then. 'I think we can probably do better than that. Especially as you've just had a long journey and a horrible welcome. Plus, it's the first day of your holiday.' He released me and ducked down to fetch two bottles from a low cabinet, then proceeded to make us both cocktails, topping each with a sprig of mint from a pot on a shelf over the sink.

'To a wonderful holiday,' he said with a wink, and we chinked glasses.

I took a sip and had a flashback to the barbecue at Riverdean and the dark cocktail with the sprig of rosemary. I watched him taking another sip and nod with approval at his own creation, and marvelled at how effortlessly he made everything OK. Just as he had at Eden House that first night we met. I'd been alone, nervous and out of place, and instantly he'd put me at ease.

It was the same when he'd invited me to the barbecue at Riverdean, and he'd done it again today. When he looked at me it was as if I were the only person in the world. Like I was important. And after the welcome I'd just received from everyone, I couldn't work out what magic he'd woven that had turned my anxious mortification into this warmth that now glowed inside me as we stood sipping cocktails in the kitchen.

'Come on, let's get you out into the sunshine for God's sake.'

And so, with slightly less trepidation than I'd descended the stairs, I walked out to the pool with Isaac. Duncan lay under a sun umbrella, a silky sheen on his pink belly. His soft snores fluttered the pages of *The Times* that rested on his chest. Vangie reclined on a sun lounger next to him, scrolling on her phone. The dark lenses of her sunglasses were impenetrable, and she made no movement to suggest she'd noticed our arrival, even though she must have. There was no sign of Sarah or Cam, so Isaac and I settled on sun loungers next to each other.

The pool was enclosed on two sides by the stone walls of the house, and on another by a hedge that bordered the sloping lawn. On the opposite side of the pool were black iron railings that gave way to the spectacular view of the plush green valley in which we were nestled.

Despite the silence, the atmosphere was tense. I could sense Vangie seething, like a pan of water coming to the boil. I tried to concentrate on the view but in my periphery I saw her clench her red manicured toes, swat a midge away from her face, scratch her knee. Every movement was quick and agitated and I wondered how long she'd be able to sit there before the pressure became too much. It wasn't long.

She stood and slipped her feet into white flip-flops before marching to the kitchen doors. 'I'm going to make a start on dinner, as it's my turn tonight. I'm told you're staying, Diana?'

'Yes,' I said, unsure what else to add.

'Right, so one extra then.'

'I . . . do you need any help?' I said, desperately hoping she'd say no so my abysmal kitchen skills weren't discovered.

'No thank you.' She gave us both an icy smile, then marched off into the kitchen with as much authority as her flip-flops allowed. The large doors had been left open but she slammed one of them shut as she passed, in a bizarrely childish outburst. Isaac and I exchanged grimaces, and Duncan stirred on his sun lounger before waking and sitting up, rubbing his eyes as the newspaper slid to the floor. He noticed us, heaved himself up and walked over.

'Hello, Diana. Staying, are you?' His face was blotchy and there was a white patch across the bridge of his nose from sunglasses. His upper chest bore ink markings from the newspaper that had been resting there.

'Um . . . yes, I am.'

He nodded then glanced at Isaac as if for clues as to what his reaction to this news should be. Isaac's face remained impassive. 'Right. Well, very good.'

'Vangie's making dinner for everyone,' Isaac said, lying back and closing his eyes.

'Right. Well, I . . . perhaps I should help her.' He ruffled his sweaty hair, making it stick up like a baby bird's feathers, then shuffled off into the kitchen.

I stared down into my cocktail, stroking the mint leaves between my fingers, wondering if Vangie's frostiness would ever thaw. If she remained this hostile for my entire stay, how could any of us enjoy ourselves? Was the rest of the holiday going to be permeated by her foul mood and punctuated by snide remarks and dirty looks? That wasn't quite what I'd envisaged when I'd imagined drinks by the pool and day trips to quaint little villages.

'Don't worry,' Isaac said, as if I'd voiced my concerns to him. I'd thought his eyes were shut but when I looked he was shielding his face with his arm, and squinting at me against the sun. 'It'll be OK.'

I nodded. I believed him.

Freddie appeared just before dinner with a gaunt, pasty-looking friend who was apparently called Alastair and was Freddie's plus-one for the holiday. Vangie swept Freddie away to 'bring him up to speed' while the boy cast terrified glances at me, as I suppose any teenager would upon the unexpected appearance of his English tutor.

At dinner, Cam sat with a serenely smug expression, contributing nothing to the conversation. Isaac poured drinks and flashed reassuring smiles around. Duncan supplied random unprompted facts about local historical sites, but I couldn't work out if he was trying to dissipate the awkward atmosphere, or whether he was oblivious to it. Sarah picked at her food, casting worried glances at Vangie, who only spoke when an opportunity to make a dig presented itself. *Of course now we're a seat short in the hire car, so someone will have to stay behind*, or *we'll have to change that dinner reservation . . . and they're so busy, I'm not sure they'll be able to fit any extras in*. It was all extraordinarily immature, but I still couldn't help the swell of satisfaction I felt every time her comments rewarded me with a wink from Isaac, or a conciliatory smile from Sarah.

After dinner, I dutifully helped with the washing-up, relieved to be free of Vangie – she and Duncan had excused themselves, having cooked the dinner. When everything was put away, I noticed Sarah pour two glasses of wine and sidle out to the poolside. The turquoise water glowed with the underwater lights, and lanterns shone from the brickwork. It was an inviting scene, but as I watched Sarah cross to the other side of the pool and hand Vangie a glass, I knew I needed to stay away. If Sarah was on a mission to placate Vangie, then I should probably leave them to it.

Freddie and Alastair were side by side on a sun lounger, hunched over a phone screen, and Isaac and Duncan were playing chess in the living room. I slipped through to the entrance way, following the smell of cigarette smoke out of the French doors and onto the sloping lawn.

The light was nearly gone, and the black shadows of trees swallowed the end of the garden. I looked along the wall and saw a floating pinprick of orange light. Cam was standing on a stone patio that wrapped around the games room. There were no lights on inside or out, the only speck of light the end of her cigarette. She didn't acknowledge me as I came to stand next to her, but leaned on the wrought-iron railing and flicked ash onto the grass.

'Goodness me, Diana,' she seemed to address her cigarette as she spoke. I wasn't sure whether her persistent over-use of my name was supposed to unnerve me, or whether she did it to everyone. 'I'd have thought you'd be inside, soaking up the adulation of your newfound friends.'

'No, you didn't,' I said, unsure why Cam's spikiness didn't bother me. Perhaps because I knew it was a reflection of her own deep-rooted family issues, and not a personal attack on me. 'Can I have one?'

She pulled a cigarette from the packet and as she handed it to me an automatic light clicked on above our heads, casting our shadows onto the grass below. She lit my cigarette and I breathed in, closing my eyes as the nicotine tingled through me.

'If you're trying to avoid Vangie then it's a bit late for that.'

'I'm not really. Just giving them a bit of space, I suppose. She's not going to calm down with me in her face the whole time.'

Cam didn't answer, but continued to stare out towards the invisible forest beyond.

I took a breath. 'I wanted to ask you . . . have you told anyone else about your suspicions about Isaac?'

She turned towards me, casting her pale eyes on mine for the first time, her mouth curving into that amused smile. 'And what "suspicions" would those be?'

'Well . . . the photo we talked about. I thought that must be the basis of some sort of suspicion?'

'That's interesting . . . I suppose I think of the photo as more of a pictorial representation of my suspicions, rather than as evidence in itself.'

I sighed, worried that Cam was about to go off on a philosophical rant I wouldn't be able to keep up with, and that I'd miss something important. 'But . . . I mean, what actually are your suspicions? Because it seems to me that—'

'Oh gosh, let me guess!' She pressed her cigarette-holding hand to her chest in theatrical glee. 'It seems to you that Isaac is such a loving, wonderful, kind, charismatic man, that he could never be suspected of doing anything untoward . . . is that close?'

I turned away from her gaze, annoyed at how close she'd been to what I had indeed been about to say.

'See, the thing is, Diana, you've latched on to an interesting part of the last conversation we had . . . the photo. When really, there was something much more important we talked about.'

'That philosophical principle you told me about . . . Occam's razor?'

'That's certainly relevant, but no, wrong again.'

'What then?' I was getting frustrated and just wanted her to speak plainly.

'Jamie Kerr.'

'What?'

'Jamie Kerr. Do you remember *anything* I told you about him?'

I felt a surge of shame. I'd thought so much about our conversation by the lake, but those thoughts had been almost exclusively about the photo, and the implications

231

it had for Isaac and Sarah's relationship. I'd hardly spared a moment to go over the other thing she'd shared with me: the horrific death of one of her best friends, at a party at her family home.

'Of course . . . of course I remember.' I felt the heat in my face. 'But what's that got to do with Isaac?' A trickle of ice chased the nicotine through my veins as I asked the question.

'Well now, that's a tricky question. All I can give you are the facts.'

'And what are the facts?'

She placed the cigarette between her lips, her cheeks hollowing as the tip glowed.

'Like I told you by the lake, Jamie knew how much I disliked Isaac. I didn't have anything solid on him, but I'd never trusted his motives with Mum. Anyway, I used to drip-feed Jamie daily snippets . . . trivial gripes that really only amounted to a heap of annoyances any stepdaughter might voice about her stepdad. There was never anything more . . . other than this deeper instinct I've always had that something's not quite right.'

'But . . . Cam—'

'Yes, yes I know. I'm sure there are hundreds of step-children around the country who have "funny feelings" about their stepparents. I'm not naive enough to argue against that point. But the night he died, Jamie sent me a text.'

She didn't continue so I prompted. 'What did it say?'

'"Fucking hell, Cam, I've just seen something. If you want to bust Isaac then you've got to hear this. Meet me by the jetty asap. JK."'

A queasy feeling churned in my stomach and I dropped my cigarette and stamped on it. I wasn't sure if I wanted to hear more. But at the same time, I couldn't bear not to. 'So did you go to the jetty? Is that when you found him?'

'No, I didn't go. Because I didn't get the message until the next day, after he was dead. Every day since, I've imagined what could have happened if I'd got that message at the time and raced to the jetty to meet him. Perhaps he'd still be alive. Perhaps he'd have told me the one thing that would have shown us the truth about Isaac. But you see, I was never going to get that message that night.'

'Why not?'

'Because Isaac had confiscated my phone the day before.'

I heard a breeze rush down the valley, shushing the darkened mass of trees all around us. It tingled against my skin, bringing goosebumps to my arms.

Cam dropped her own cigarette and scraped her shoe over it before nudging it off the patio onto the grass. 'I can't remember why now,' she continued. 'Some misdemeanour I'd committed . . . not sticking to a curfew, or swearing at him or something trivial like that. It was just a power thing. I mean, who locks away a seventeen-year-old's phone? As if I was a child? Anyway, I didn't give him the satisfaction of putting up a fight, just made a comment about how I hoped it made him feel like a big man . . . you know, Lord of the Manor . . .' Her voice had risen and agitation fizzed in every word. '. . . but that's not really important. What's important is that my phone wasn't with me that night. It was with Isaac.'

'So when that message from Jamie came up on your phone . . .'

She turned and looked into my eyes; hate and pain swirled through those golden irises. She nodded. 'When that message came through, it was Isaac who saw it, not me.'

Chapter Eighteen

I thought about what Cam had said as I lay on my soft mattress and watched the moonlight creep across my blue patterned wallpaper.

The following morning, her words played through my mind as I ate the fresh croissants Sarah had bought at the bakery, and when Isaac leaned over me to top up my coffee cup. Cam's recollection of the details of the night Jamie died haunted my thoughts, in the same way the photograph had.

And yet I couldn't quite pin down why it should bother me so much, when everything she'd said could easily be attributed to chance. A teenager at a party had had too much to drink and drowned. It was tragic, but it wouldn't be the first time an accident like that had happened. And it certainly wouldn't be the first time a stepdaughter's mobile phone had been confiscated. But the fact that Isaac had possession of the phone when the text from Jamie came through . . . and that Jamie died less than an hour later . . .

It was ridiculous. This was *not* how this was meant to pan out. Isaac and Sarah were new friends, and I'd worked bloody hard to bring us together. To think about how they'd embraced me, and included me . . . it made my heart ache with happiness. I wasn't going to throw all that back in their faces because a teenager was trying to stir things up. No, I would not risk my newfound happiness by doubting Isaac for a second longer.

In the afternoon, there was talk of visiting a local vineyard. Vangie seemed particularly taken with this idea as it was another opportunity for her to emphasise that the hire car was only a seven-seater, and therefore we were *one person too many*. Oblivious, Duncan interjected that he wasn't going to come anyway because he had work to do.

'You're on holiday, Dunc,' said Isaac, patting him on the back as he hunched over his mobile at the kitchen table.

'Yes, Isaac,' he replied, in a sharp tone I'd not heard him use before. '. . . but Moorgate Solutions and the German engineers aren't, so someone has to keep the deal afloat.'

Vangie's jaw tightened, clearly unhappy at the extra space in the car that had suddenly been supplied by her husband.

I relished her moment of discomfort before speaking. 'Actually, I think I'll leave you all to it and stay here too.'

Isaac looked over at me, and I felt a flush of pleasure at the disappointment on his face. 'Really? But there's room . . .'

'I know, I'm just quite happy to stay here and sunbathe. Maybe read my book.' I shrugged and smiled, knowing my calm nonchalance was contrasting beautifully with the poisonous waves of hatred emanating from Vangie. 'You've all been so generous, welcoming me on your gorgeous holiday – I don't mind giving you a bit of time to enjoy it with the original crew. Well, the original crew, bar Duncan, of course.' I kept my tone light and jokey.

'To be honest, Duncan was probably never going to come along anyway, were you, Duncan?' said Sarah with an affectionate smile.

Duncan was checking his phone whilst scribbling on a notepad, and hadn't heard her.

'That's true.' Isaac nodded. 'All work and no play, this one.' He rolled his eyes at me and I smiled back, noting the look of disgust that flashed across Vangie's face.

Once they'd all bundled into the car and I'd waved them off down the driveway, I got myself a glass of iced water, took it out to the pool, and sank onto a sun lounger with my head in the shade of a large umbrella.

The sun tingled on my legs and the only sounds were the ripple of the filter system in the pool, the shush of the surrounding trees, and, from the kitchen, the tap-tapping of Duncan's fingers on his laptop. I felt myself drifting in and out of sleep, half aware of an insect landing on my thigh then flying off, the flapping of the umbrella in a gust of warm wind, a door banging somewhere inside, the pssht of a can being opened, someone speaking.

I opened my eyes and watched Duncan pacing along the opposite side of the pool, mobile pressed to his sweaty face. 'Yes, it should be with you tomorrow morning at the latest . . . Nicola needs to sign it but she'll email it straight off to you . . . yes . . . it's all confirmed with Isaac . . .' The professional tone was at comedic odds with Duncan's yellow trunks, which I only now noticed bore the black silhouette of Mickey Mouse on the left leg. I wondered what the movers and shakers on the other end of the call would make of Duncan if they could see him at this moment.

He hung up and scratched his head before noticing me. 'Oh, hello, Diana. Didn't see you there. Hope I didn't wake you up?'

'No, not at all, I was just resting my eyes.'

'Can I get you a drink or anything?'

'No, I'm fine, thank you.'

He wandered off into the kitchen and I could hear him rummaging in cupboards. He emerged five minutes later with a thick white sandwich over-stuffed with glistening ham, and a pint of orange squash. I felt a twist of disappointment when he came and lowered himself onto the sun lounger next to mine, aware that small talk would probably now be on the cards. Then I felt a pang of guilt. I liked Duncan, in spite of his wife, and I was quite content with his company when it was diluted by a larger group. But one-to-one I wasn't sure exactly what I would say to him.

He swallowed a large mouthful, leaving a smudge of mustard at the corner of his fleshy mouth. 'Didn't fancy the vineyard then?'

'No, not really. Thought I'd just relax here.' It came to mind that perhaps I'd test the water. 'Anyway, I'm sure Vangie could do with a break from me.'

He gave a humourless laugh. 'Don't mind Vangie. Her bark's worse than her bite.'

I gave an inward shudder, imagining a bite from Vangie to be painful at best, rabid at worst.

'So how did you both meet?' I asked, unable to imagine either of them falling in love, or lust with the other.

'Oh, we were at uni together. She was studying Law and I was doing Architectural Engineering. Isaac and I were out in the student union and bumped into her and her law buddies.' He gave a wistful smile before taking another bite of his sandwich.

'Was Isaac on the same course as you then?'

He shook his head and swallowed. 'No. Isaac did a Marketing degree. But we always planned to go into business together at some point.' He gave a wry smile. 'When I realised he had something special.'

'What do you mean?'

Duncan chuckled. 'I remember telling Isaac I was running a department fundraiser in our first year, and watching him double the sponsorship in about an hour just by chatting to people. Then there was the time he DJ'd for campus radio and listener numbers went through the roof.' He shrugged and shot me an affectionate smile. 'He's just one of those charismatic people. And fortunately for Acanthus, his charm is as effective in the boardroom as it is with the ladies.' He frowned. 'I mean – before Sarah, of course.'

I felt a pathetic twinge of jealousy, which made me realise that, despite knowing Isaac was a happily married man, I had, for some reason, been giving weight to his flirtatious behaviour. Behaviour I now realised was probably not even conscious. A raised eyebrow, a conspiratorial smile, a gaze that lingered a second too long. For someone who'd presumably spent their entire life behaving this way in exchange for the things they wanted, perhaps it all just became as automatic as breathing in and out. So even when you encountered someone who was of no use to you at all, like a dowdy English tutor, you just couldn't be bothered to switch it off.

'Are you OK?' Duncan's words came thickly through a mouthful of ham and bread.

'Yes, I'm fine. I was just thinking about what you were saying about Isaac's charisma. I suppose Sarah fell under that spell whilst you were all at uni too?' I knew they'd met later, but I wanted to hear it from Duncan.

He shook his head before swallowing then thumping his chest with a fist and coughing. 'Oh, sorry. Went down the wrong way. No . . . no, actually . . . Isaac met Sarah years later. She was already married, in fact. We were just trying to get Acanthus off the ground and there was a networking event in London.' He frowned and looked off towards the horizon as if trying to remember something. 'Yes, that's right . . . her husband was trying to drum up clients for a business idea he had . . . something to do with artisanal whiskey or some such trendy endeavour. Always trying to think of the next big business venture, was Archie. Anyway, we all got on like a house on fire, went on a couple of holidays together, that sort of thing. After Archie died, Isaac was a rock for Sarah . . . they grew close. Truth be told—' he hitched forward on the sun lounger and glanced towards the kitchen doors before continuing '—I think Isaac probably had feelings for Sarah from when they first met. Would never do anything about it obviously, happily married woman and all that. But I think he sort of felt they were . . . meant to be, perhaps? If you believe in that sort of thing!' He chuckled as if embarrassed by the concept, then took several large gulps of his squash.

The jealousy was back and gave an unpleasant twist in my stomach. I decided to change tack. 'Was he ill for a long time? Archie?'

Duncan's face darkened. 'Ill? No, he wasn't ill at all. He died in an accident. God, I'd have thought Cam or Sarah would have told you about that?'

'No . . . I . . . I just assumed he had a long-term illness.'

'No, no. Fit as a fiddle, was Archie. Well, maybe not quite as fit as he thought he was. No . . . it was a terrible business. He drowned.'

'What?' I felt all the air leave my body as the blurry image of Jamie Kerr flashed through my mind. 'How?'

Duncan shifted on the sun lounger as if working out how to start. He cleared his throat then swallowed. 'Well . . . we were all on holiday in Cornwall and the three of us – me, Isaac and Archie – had all had rather too much to drink and . . . oh God, it was so stupid. If we'd known Archie was going to take the chat that seriously we'd never have started talking about it.' He rubbed his hand over his face.

'Talking about what?'

'About swimming and triathlons and all that bloody stuff.' He sighed. 'Isaac and I used to do quite a lot of open-water swimming. I mean, I was nowhere near as good as Isaac, of course—'

'The certificate.' I spoke the thought out loud. Duncan looked puzzled. 'I mean . . . at Riverdean, there's a Channel swimming certificate in the downstairs bathroom.'

'Ah, yes, that's right. I never attempted the Channel, but yes, that's the sort of thing we were banging on about that night. Sarah and Vangie got bored and went to bed. Then I nodded off outside by the fire pit . . . woke up and the fire had nearly gone out. Must have been hours later. No sign of Isaac or Archie. Anyway, I trundled off to bed, woke up with a horrible hangover, as did Isaac. But Archie never appeared.'

'Oh my God,' I said, folding my arms across my stomach where an uncomfortable knot was forming.

'Sarah said he hadn't been to bed so she'd assumed he'd passed out on the sofa or something, but turns out he'd taken our stupid macho chat about open-water swimming rather more seriously than we'd intended and gone down to the beach on his own. We think he must have tried to swim out to Mor's Rock . . .' his voice trailed off and his eyes seemed to mist over. He cleared his throat.

'I'm so sorry. That must have been horrific.'

'God, that was the worst day. Sarah was obviously inconsolable. The police were everywhere. The body . . . Archie . . . he washed up pretty quickly, so almost as soon as we realised he was missing he'd been found. And then Sarah had to tell little Cam . . .' He made a guttural sound and looked down.

I didn't know what to say. How could I not have known about this? I was surprised Cam hadn't said anything. She'd told me about Jamie, but perhaps talking about her father and that day was one step too far. Perhaps it was too painful.

'But Sarah and Isaac have built a wonderful life together,' Duncan said, a muted smile on his lips. 'I suppose everyone just has to . . . move on, really. Make the best of things. Follow their dreams. . .' His voice trailed off, as if his attempt to end the conversation on a lighter note hadn't quite worked. I nodded, but his words had brought a vision to mind – the quote scrawled in black ballpoint on the back of that photograph at Riverdean: *All our dreams can come true, if we have the courage to pursue them.*

'We're back!' The shout startled me and I looked up to see Isaac in the kitchen doorway, hugging a large brown paper bag to his chest. 'Mexican for dinner, if that's OK? Obviously with margaritas.'

He smiled and his eyes twinkled at me like the rippling surface of the pool. I felt my insides tingle, and made a conscious effort to push aside any unwanted thoughts that my conversation with Duncan had provoked. 'Great, I love Mexican,' I called back, '. . . and margaritas.'

'I knew I could count on you, Diana.' Isaac grinned, then turned and disappeared into the kitchen.

I felt the same quiver of excitement I'd felt when he'd invited me to the barbecue at Riverdean. He was in a playful mood, he was making cocktails, he was looking for someone up for a good time – and relying on me to be that person. I remembered overhearing him talking to Vangie that time, remembered him telling her he wanted to invite me to France because I was *fun.* But I took a breath, willing my excitement down. There could not be a repeat of my hideous behaviour that night.

I was already persona non grata as far as Vangie was concerned, and I knew she'd take a vicious delight in watching me embarrass myself again. This time I was not going to give her the satisfaction.

My conversation with Duncan swam around my head as I made my way to my bedroom, but I also reminded myself why I was here – to spend quality time with Isaac and Sarah, and get to know them better. They'd embraced me like one of the family, and for that, I owed them loyalty. The fact both Archie and Jamie had drowned was a coincidence, sure, but coincidences happen – and when I thought carefully about it, it didn't seem that suspicious. After all, both died in different circumstances, different places, and many years apart. Yes – the more I considered it, the more I realised Cam's conspiracies were making me see connections where there were none. I wouldn't waste any more time thinking about it.

Instead, I concentrated on thinking about the evening ahead, taking a long shower and giving myself further instructions: drink slowly, don't get drunk, don't dance, don't be loud, don't give too much away. I sat at the walnut dressing table and took particular time over my hair, teasing and twisting it into waves. I applied Sunkissed Holiday Make-Up as per another *Make-Up by Marie* tutorial I'd pored over before my departure from Heathrow. Then I slipped into a cream V-neck dress by Wolf & Rose (a new designer Sarah had recently tagged on Instagram), with covered buttons all down the front and an A-line skirt. My skin had already caught the sun, and I was pleased with the contrast of my tan against the pale, soft fabric. I pushed small gold hoops through my ears and three gold bangles onto my wrist. As a finishing touch, I fastened a thin gold chain around my neck, so the minuscule pearl nestled just below the hollow at the base of my throat. We weren't going out anywhere, so I decided to stay barefoot, hoping that would give me an air of effortlessness.

I went downstairs at six thirty to find Isaac in the kitchen pouring margaritas from a large frosted jug into the seaglass tumblers, their rims ready salted, before placing a sliver of lime on top of each. He bent over the worktop as he did this, like a chef at a five-star restaurant.

'They look delicious,' I said, walking over to the breakfast bar and sliding up onto a stool.

He looked up at me with a grin, his smile faltering as his gaze swept over me. 'God . . . you, you look nice.'

My stomach lurched. I'd not heard Isaac stutter before.

'Sorry,' he said, straightening up. 'I didn't mean to sound surprised, I mean, you always look nice. I just meant, you look particularly nice.' He gave a more confident smile then, having regained his suavity. He dipped down to place a lime on the final drink before changing his mind and straightening up again. 'Also, please substitute "nice" for a less pathetic word . . . maybe, "lovely" or "beautiful".'

'Consider "nice" duly substituted,' I said, still feeling my insides flutter and reminding myself of what I'd learned from my conversation with Duncan – this was just Isaac. This is what he did. He charmed. Whether you were male, female, friend or potential investor, it was all either a subconscious habit, or an idle game. It was meaningless. I just wished my brain would tell that to my hammering heart.

He passed me a drink and we chinked glasses and sipped. The salt and lime stung my tongue and I remembered the margaritas Priya had made at Riverdean. I wanted to reminisce with Isaac, but of course he hadn't been there. That was before I'd ever met him. That seemed so strange.

'Margaritas are served!' he shouted, and, to my disappointment, Vangie slunk in from the pool, casting me a dirty look before Sarah, Freddie and Alastair followed, shattering my intimate moment with Isaac. Cam sidled in from the living room, looking at her mobile, and Duncan followed, holding his laptop and still wearing his Mickey Mouse shorts.

'Grab a drink,' said Isaac, making sure everyone had one, including Freddie and Alastair (who had been served a weak version, Isaac assured Vangie). 'While we're all gathered, I just wanted to raise a toast to Duncan, actually.' Duncan folded his laptop under his arm and placed it on the table, keeping his drink steady in the other hand. He looked at Isaac, his cheeks flushing. 'Seriously, Duncan has been working like an absolute demon on this deal we're about to make, from its inception . . . God, at least two years ago . . . right through to the finish line, which is almost in sight—'

'God, don't jinx it, Zac!' Duncan said, and Sarah gave an appreciative giggle.

'No, but honestly. You work so bloody hard – missing out on stuff like the vineyard today, or having to turn up late to barbecues, or working through social occasions . . . you're an absolute machine, and we're all so grateful. I mean, I know I talk a good talk, but I've got nowhere near the expertise you have. There'd be no Acanthus without you.' Isaac's eyebrows dipped in a sincere frown.

'That's really kind of you, Zac,' said Duncan. 'But don't underestimate your value to the company. Everyone knows I'm completely rubbish at all that schmoozing. I think it's fair to say this deal wouldn't have even come close to being a reality if you hadn't seduced them all in that initial consultation.'

'Oh, for fuck's sake.' It was Cam's voice that cut through the appreciative laughs like a knife through butter. All eyes went to her, and I observed the redness in her cheeks and the glittering hatred in her eyes. 'Can we please stop with this alpha male back-slapping bullshit and thank the *only* person in the room who should be taking any credit for the existence of Acanthus? My bloody mother!'

Cam jabbed her arm out, extending her long fingers with their chipped black polish towards Sarah, who stood next to Isaac. 'Never mind this "working all hours" and "seducing people in the boardroom" bullshit. If my mother and her parents hadn't become the main investors in the company, both of you clowns would still be trying to renovate three-bed terraces in Devon. So, where's Mum's thanks?'

'Cam, please.' Sarah's eyes were pleading.

'Oh God.' Isaac held up a hand as if in surrender. 'I'm such an idiot, Cam, I'm so sorry. You're absolutely bloody right.' He turned to Sarah and took her hand, pressing it to his lips for a moment before releasing it. He looked at his wife with the same sincerity he'd directed at Duncan a moment before. 'You and your amazing parents took a huge leap of faith investing in Acanthus, and the trust and encouragement you've given us from the very beginning are the entire reason we're still here. Cam's completely right. Without you, we'd never have got past that rented office in Tiverton, and we'd certainly not be about to sign one of the biggest deals on the London property scene this year.'

Sarah smiled back at him, her expression now serene. Isaac had worked his magic. Cam shook her head, disgust etched into her features.

'So let's raise our glasses, to . . . what shall we say?' Isaac looked around the room, his face open and bright, as if Cam had never spoken. 'To dreams coming true!'

We all held our drinks aloft and echoed, 'To dreams coming true!'

Chapter Nineteen

Isaac set the meal out on the breakfast bar and told everyone to grab a plate, serve themselves, and mingle. I loaded my plate with chilli, rice and guacamole, before refilling my tumbler with iced water, and heading out to perch on a sun lounger. Isaac got the Bluetooth speaker going, and some clichéd French café music drifted from the kitchen, an upbeat guitar rhythm, a jazzy violin solo.

'I know the music doesn't match the food, but I love it!' he announced, appearing at the doorway with a newly filled margarita jug. I sat alone, eating, and watching him topping up everyone's glasses, an arm around a shoulder, a hand on a back. I watched faces turning to him, the reciprocal twinkle he received from everyone as he bestowed his attention on them. Freddie's usually dour face peered up at him with wide, gleaming eyes. Sarah fixed him with an adoring gaze. Even Vangie drew herself up and curled her red lips into a smile when he approached. I'd never noticed the effect he had on people until my conversation with Duncan earlier. I'd been too busy thinking about the effect he had on me.

'Diana, don't hide away over here,' Isaac said now, coming over to sit next to me. His hair was tousled to perfection, his usual unruly lock falling forward. He was wearing a white shirt and navy chino shorts, and he sat so close, his leg pressed against the length of mine. I could smell the tequila on his breath.

'I'm not hiding, I'm just watching all you beautiful people . . .' he turned towards me when I said that '. . . and feeling very lucky to be here.'

'Well, we're very lucky to have you,' he said, looking at me for one second too long. My sober brain tried to push down the quiver of excitement inside me.

The warm breeze washed a wave of his aftershave over me, and I found myself speaking. 'That's . . . *Terre d'Hermès*, isn't it? The scent you're wearing?' I held his gaze, remembering the photo I'd taken of the bottle that sat in their en-suite bathroom in Riverdean. The scent I'd spritzed over the pillow I'd slept on, and over my clothes the following morning.

'What? How the hell did you know that?' His eyes frowned but his mouth curved into a delicious smile.

I attempted an embarrassed laugh. 'My ex-boyfriend wore it. Scents are quite evocative, aren't they? Difficult to forget.' I don't know why I mentioned the scent, or why I lied about an ex-boyfriend. Perhaps I wanted to test his response . . . find out what was charisma and what was flirtation.

'I think I need to hear more about this ex-boyfriend.' His expression had turned mock stern. 'The man with great taste in cologne and women, but who was stupid enough to let you go.'

It was really the cheesiest line, and not even terribly well delivered. But I'm embarrassed to say I still loved every word of it. 'Actually, it was me who let him go,' I said.

'I'm glad to hear it. Can't have you all broken-hearted, can we?' He gave me a gentle nudge with his shoulder and we swayed together. Then he cleared his throat and held the margarita jug aloft. 'Top up?'

I downed the rest of my water. 'Sure,' I said, holding my glass out for him to fill.

I sipped the cocktail, trying to keep the promise I'd made to myself. *Don't get drunk. Don't embarrass yourself.* Isaac sauntered back to the others, and I carried my plate to the kitchen. Laughter bubbled in from outside in between music tracks. Margaritas were replaced with crisp glasses of rosé, and I joined the group, making small talk with a tight-lipped Freddie about whether or not he was looking forward to going back to school. Alastair stood next to him, like a lanky ghost with his pale skin and white-blonde hair. I was about to direct the same bland line of questioning in his direction when Isaac's voice cut through my train of thought.

'. . . well, I am . . .' he said, his voice rising above the hubbub. I looked over to see him pulling his shirt off over his head.

Duncan laughed and Sarah put a hand on Isaac's arm. 'But . . . you've not got your trunks on!' She was protesting, but looked as amused as everyone else.

Isaac stepped backwards towards the edge of the pool, shrugging as he reached the ledge, before twisting and executing a perfect dive into the glowing water. He surfaced, flicking his hair out of his eyes and grinning up at his adoring audience. 'Come on you lot, it's gorgeous!'

Duncan, whose only attempt at changing for dinner had been to add a salmon-pink shirt to his yellow trunks, began to undo the buttons. Vangie watched him and rolled her eyes. I was pleased to learn I wasn't the only person who met with her disapproval. Duncan cannon-balled into the pool, to hoots of laughter from Freddie, while Alastair cast terrified glances around the group as if he were about to be made to walk the plank. Vangie lowered herself onto a sun lounger, clutching her glass of wine to her chest like a shield.

'Come on, Diana, I'm sure you can swim in that dress!' Isaac called, and I felt a shiver of pleasure at being singled out. I couldn't imagine Sarah's perfection lending itself to night swimming, and I could no sooner see Vangie jumping in fully clothed than I could envision her stripping naked and dancing the Macarena. No, I was the fun one. And perhaps if I'd had more to drink . . . as much as Isaac clearly had . . . then I would have dived straight in fully clothed, just to impress him. Even relatively sober, the lure of his approval was that tempting.

But I made myself flash him a coy smile. 'I will come in, but I'm going to get changed first.'

I ignored Vangie's tutting as I walked past her, and headed up to my room. I poked my head out of the hallway doors as I passed and saw the glow of Cam's cigarette in the darkness by the games room, but tonight I had no inclination to join her. Upstairs, I changed into my turquoise costume, tied my hair in a topknot, and hurried back down, keen not to miss the fun. Isaac and Duncan were in the water, throwing one of Freddie's footballs to each other. Freddie had clearly declined the water play in favour of sitting next to Alastair on a sun lounger, hunched over a glowing phone screen.

Sarah passed me on my way to the poolside. 'I'm just going to check on Cam,' she said, her forehead creased with a worried frown.

'I think she's outside on the games room patio.'

'Lovely,' she said, face brightening. 'Thank you, darling.' She squeezed my arm as she walked away and I felt a surge of warmth. It was quickly dampened, however, as I looked over at Vangie who glowered at me from her shadowy sun lounger. She was dressed in her habitual black, which blended into the shadows, and bar her single slash of lipstick, leached her face of colour.

Isaac cheered as I slipped into the water. I batted the ball a few times in a feeble attempt at joining in, but then left them to it and swam lengths. The cool water was delicious against my clammy skin, and I forgot my plan to keep my hair and make-up perfect, and gave in to my urge to duck under the surface, letting the water caress my entire body, tingling my scalp and rushing in my ears. I pushed off from the side and swam down as deep as I could, untouchable by the muffled shouts and splashes of the ball game above. I did this twice, three times, four times. Each time I surfaced for air my lungs burnt hotter, until I could barely catch my breath.

I swam to the shallow end to surface, pushed my hair back from my face, and opened my eyes to see the game had stopped. Vangie had disappeared, and the boys still sat like zombies, rapt faces illuminated by the phone screen.

Duncan was hauling himself out at the deep-end ladder, water cascading down his belly and rippling his Disney shorts. 'Gosh, bloody cold when you get out,' he muttered. 'I need a shower.' He grabbed a towel from a chair and waddled off into the kitchen.

Then Isaac caught my eye. He was treading water at the deep end, and staring straight at me. A smile flickered on his lips and he pushed away from the side, his muscular arms slicing through the water as he made his way towards me.

'You're quite the mermaid, aren't you? Ever swim on the surface?'

I laughed. 'I just prefer it under there. It's quiet.'

'Come on, then . . . let me see you do a length. Front crawl.'

I thought once again of Isaac's Channel swimming certificate at Riverdean and felt a flutter of nerves. He was an expert, and I was about to make a fool of myself. But I also knew that Isaac saw me as game. A willing participant in his fun. So I launched myself as gracefully as I could towards the deep end, trying to emulate the precise strokes I'd just seen him perform. At the deep end I clung to the edge, and he was at my side a second later.

'Not bad, actually,' said Isaac. 'But look . . .' He took my arm in his hand and extended it in front of me. Under the water our legs nudged together as I rebalanced myself so I could hold on to the edge with my other hand.

I looked over my shoulder. Freddie and Alastair remained on their sun lounger, transfixed by the phone.

'Your arm should extend like this . . .' He dragged his fingers the entire length of my arm, sending an electric current through me. I couldn't help the short gasp that escaped my lips. Our faces were so close I knew he'd heard, but he pretended not to. '. . . And your fingers should be like this . . .' He cupped my hand, tilting it so my thumb entered the water first. '. . . Then it's a circular motion, around and past your thigh . . .' As our joined hands brushed my thigh, I felt the fingers of my other hand lose their grip on the ledge, and my whole body slipped down. His hand let go of mine and he clamped his arm around my waist, pulling me towards him. We were still, just looking at each other, and I wondered if he could feel my hammering heart against his chest. He didn't speak, and he didn't release his grip. He stared at me like I were as transparent as a pane of glass. In that moment I felt he knew everything about me. His gaze drifted from my eyes and fell to my lips, then to my neck. His chest rose and fell quickly like mine, and his lips parted as if he was about to say something, but no sound came out. I felt the smallest stroke of his thumb at my waist, and my insides turned to liquid.

'Fucking idiot!' We both startled, snapping our heads towards Freddie and Alastair who were guffawing at something on the phone. Freddie looked up and saw us then. 'Oh God, sorry. I . . . I didn't know you were there. It's just our mate back home being a . . . being really stupid.'

I laughed, trying not to hate Freddie in that moment. He stood, raised his eyebrows at Alastair, and they both scurried indoors.

I looked at Isaac. We weren't touching any more. 'We should probably get out now,' I said, wanting to lock everyone else in the house and stay in the pool with him all night.

He nodded and gave a heavy sigh. 'I suppose you're right.'

I watched him pull himself out of the pool and rub a pine-green beach towel over his hair, his muscles flexing under the tanned skin of his arms. I climbed the ladder and stepped onto the flagstones, looking around for another towel, realising there wasn't one. Isaac stopped drying himself and came towards me, and I stood still as he draped his own towel over my shoulders, clasping it in his fist under my chin.

'Gosh, fancy you two still being here.' It was Vangie's voice that had us turning towards the French doors. She walked over to her sun lounger, and I thought I could detect the tiniest sway to her gait. She picked up her half-finished wine and took a large swig. 'Surprised you've not got a drink in your hand, Diana.' Her words were smudged, and I wondered if she'd been drinking inside while we'd been in the pool.

'Is Duncan all right?' asked Isaac, his voice bright, as if he was trying to change both the subject and the mood.

'Oh, he's fine,' she slurred. 'He's passed out on our bed, snoring his head off, so the absolute life and soul as usual.' She gave a bitter snort and tipped the remaining contents of the glass down her throat before swaying back into the kitchen.

'I've not seen Vangie like that before,' I said. The bitterness was familiar, but I'd never seen it mixed with drunkenness. This was a much more pitiful spectacle.

'She gets like this sometimes. I don't know if it's something to do with Duncan, if they're OK as a couple . . .'

He shrugged. 'But anyway, this is definitely nothing to do with you, so you don't have to worry. She can just be a bit . . . troubled, sometimes.'

I nodded.

'I should probably go and check she's OK.'

'Of course.'

Then he was gone, leaving wet footprints on the sandy flagstones.

Something deflated inside me, but this feeling was mixed with a hundred others I couldn't process all at once. I was disappointed, both at how unfinished my moment with Isaac felt, and also in myself and how easily he made me want him. I was confused about how he was feeling . . . Was this really just a game for him, or was he attracted to me? And even if he was . . . so what? He was happily married to the most beautiful woman I'd ever seen . . . A woman with whom I was enjoying a blossoming friendship.

I padded through the empty kitchen and living room. There was a burst of laughter from the games room and through the open door I could see Freddie and Alastair playing pool. Beyond them on the patio outside, Cam sprawled over a wicker chair with a cigarette while Sarah leaned towards her, talking earnestly, a glass of wine cradled between her palms. The pool balls clacked, and the boys laughed. I made my way upstairs to my room, feeling displaced now everyone had split up and regrouped into pairs I didn't belong to.

It was nearly ten o'clock, and felt too early to go to bed, but I wondered if the evening had run out of impetus. I wasn't sure if anyone would reappear downstairs to pour another drink, or put on more music. Perhaps everyone would give up and call it a night. I showered and put on the new short pyjamas I'd bought in case lounging around all morning in nightwear had been on the cards. (I'd left my greying Stereophonics pyjamas with the holes in the armpits back in my flat.)

I was twisting my damp hair back up into a topknot in front of the mirror when I heard it. A short, sharp cry. I'd have thought it was a cat if I'd seen one around, but as I lowered my hands from my head it came again. I tiptoed to the door of my room and poked my head out into the hallway.

My room was about halfway along the corridor. At the staircase end was Isaac and Sarah's room, opposite it was Cam's. The door to Vangie and Duncan's room was opposite mine, and as I listened I could hear Duncan's faint snores from inside. Further along the corridor was a twin room that had been allocated to Freddie and Alastair, across from a door that concealed the steps to the roof terrace. And then right at the end of the corridor, hidden in shadow, was the door to what everyone referred to as 'the old nursery'. It was unused, and in need of decorating, but when I'd explored, I'd noticed an artfully distressed wardrobe, vintage suitcases, and an old rocking horse that Sarah had said she fancied restoring.

I was about to retreat into my room when I heard another noise, this time a muffled sniff, followed by mumbled words. The voice was deep, and I assumed belonged to Isaac. Careful to keep to the edges of the corridor so the floorboards didn't creak, I crept along to the old nursery.

I halted where the door was ajar. Through the crack I could tell there was no light on in the room, just silvery shadows cast by the moon.

Another sniff, a muffled sob. 'I can't do it.' It was Vangie, and she sounded distraught.

'What are you talking about? No one's asking you to do anything.' It sounded as if Isaac was trying to stay calm, but his patient tone was forced through gritted teeth.

'I mean . . . I can't live like this . . .'

'Oh, for fuck's sake.' This was a hiss that made me flinch away from the door. I'd never heard him sound like that before. Harsh and furious. 'Why do you do this? Why do you get so bloody upset like this?'

'Well, I'm sorry that I have feelings, Isaac. I'm sorry that I'm not just devoid of all emotion like you!'

'Will you keep your bloody voice down. Jesus.'

Back away, just go back to your room. This has nothing to do with you.

Vangie gave another muffled sob.

'Look . . . you need to stop doing this to yourself, OK?' His tone was softer now, and his voice quieter, as if he'd moved further away from the door. I lowered myself to a crouching position so I could keep myself hidden in the shadow of a bulky chest of drawers that sat just inside the room. Peering around the door I could see them both, outlined in silver from the moonlight that filtered through the windows behind them. Vangie leaned against the wall, her arms hugged around her body and her pale face smudged with mascara. She looked down as if trying to avoid eye contact. Isaac stood opposite her, arms hanging limply at his sides, head tilted as if questioning an unreasonable child. He was still bare chested and wearing the damp shorts he'd been swimming in.

'I just don't think you appreciate how it affects me when . . .' She broke off into pitiful sobs.

'I do, I do.' He took a step closer to her and she looked up into his face. 'I'm sorry, OK?' His tone was almost tender now.

There was something about the weak smile she gave him then that twisted my stomach. I couldn't put my finger on what it was, until Isaac moved. He brought his hand up from his side and touched his fingers to her face. She closed her eyes and leaned her head back against the wall. His fingers trailed down her cheek, stopping at her chin, which he tilted up towards his face.

The blood froze in my veins. He leaned forwards and kissed her thin red lips, softly at first, then harder. She responded, her hands sliding around the back of his head, fingers weaving into his hair. My breath turned to stone in my lungs. His hands pushed under her shirt and she moaned against his neck.

'Sshhh,' he said. 'They can't find us.'

'Oh God, Isaac,' she whispered.

Bile rose up in my throat and I clamped my hand over my mouth. I wanted to be anywhere but here, seeing anything but this. But my limbs were paralysed, and I couldn't look – or walk – away.

He pulled up her skirt and clamped his hand over her mouth as he pushed against her.

I'd hardly had anything to drink but my vision seemed to tilt, and I felt my body sway to one side. I grabbed for the door to steady myself but it moved as I gripped hold of it, creaking on its ancient hinges. Isaac's head snapped around, locking me in his gaze before I stumbled into the hallway.

'What? What is it?' I heard Vangie's frantic whisper from inside the room, the creak of footsteps across the floorboards.

I looked along the corridor towards my bedroom but it seemed impossibly far away. I lunged for the closest door – the one that led up to the roof terrace. I ran up the stone steps and out onto the terrace, flinching at the automatic light that clicked on as I headed for the opposite wall. The space was large and square, with nowhere to hide. High walls enclosed the terrace on three sides, but the front wall was built like the battlements of a castle, the raised sections at waist height, with gaps in between.

I stared across the terrace at the door I'd just come through, silently praying Isaac wouldn't come up here and find me. *Had* he definitely seen me? I knew Vangie hadn't by the way she'd asked him what he was looking at. Perhaps he hadn't been able to make out who it was? Perhaps it had been too dark in the shadows. But I knew I was fooling myself. His eyes had caught mine, widening just a fraction as recognition hit.

I waited. The automatic light clicked off and I felt the instant relief of the darkness enshrouding me. If I stayed statue still, perhaps the light would stay off, and I could remain invisible up here in the shadows.

The image of Isaac and Vangie played in my mind on a sick loop. Isaac's fingers on her face, Vangie's smeared lipstick, the sounds they made. I would never, in any ridiculous, fantastical moment, have imagined Isaac and Vangie to be having an affair. But now I thought about it, her behaviour made so much more sense. Sarah had said she was being 'protective' of the group, but it was more than that – she was being possessive of Isaac. She could see he liked me. She'd reacted like a stroppy teenager when he'd suggested I was invited to France. In fact, I remembered her frostiness towards me beginning the first time I asked after Isaac and Sarah whilst I was teaching Freddie. Perhaps even at that stage she worried about us getting too close. And after Isaac had been so enthusiastic about inviting me to the barbecue at Riverdean, she'd turned positively hostile. Yes, I could see it all now. How could I have been so blind as to completely miss the fact that Vangie's behaviour was obviously down to good old-fashioned jealousy?

A door creaked. The sound came from inside the building but I couldn't work out whether it was the door to the staircase, or a bedroom door. I strained to hear footsteps, but all had fallen silent.

Why was I hiding here? Why were my palms still tingling with sweat? I realised it was for the same reason I hadn't stayed in the old nursery and confronted them. The same reason I hadn't stood there and said *what the fuck are you two doing?* and threatened to run and tell Sarah. It was because I was terrified.

And the reason I was terrified was because as soon as I'd backed out of that room, my brain had made a connection that I knew I couldn't sever by drinking too much wine or flirting with Isaac or putting on a new designer dress. It was a connection between what I'd seen tonight, and what Jamie Kerr had seen at that party two years ago. *I've just seen something. If you want to bust Isaac then you've got to hear this.* I could say those exact words to Cam right now and they'd be true. But would Isaac try to stop me first?

I heard footsteps scuffing up the stone staircase, and felt a surge of nausea mixed with adrenalin. I was about to find out.

Chapter Twenty

The door to the terrace creaked and I pushed my back up against the opposite wall. The automatic light clicked on, and there he was. He stood still, staring at me. I was reminded of how he'd watched me from the deep end of the swimming pool, less than an hour ago. But now the playful smile had been replaced by something dark. He was still wearing his damp shorts but had thrown on a pale-blue shirt, his wet hair darkening the fabric around the collar. He gave the door behind him a gentle push until it clicked shut, then he approached, his gait disconcerting in its slow steadiness.

He stopped in front of me and ran his fingers through his hair, his expression troubled. 'I wish you hadn't seen that, Diana.' He searched my face as if he was judging my reaction.

'I'm sorry. I shouldn't have been creeping around in the dark . . . I . . . I could just hear that Vangie was upset . . .' My voice trailed off.

Isaac nodded, as if considering my words. 'We were stupid. I was stupid.' He walked towards the battlements, resting his hands on the stone. A faint blue light reflected on his face, and I realised the terrace must look down onto the swimming pool.

I glanced across the terrace towards the door. If I ran, perhaps I could get to it and run to my room before he caught up with me. I tried to remember if my door had a lock on it. Yes, I was pretty sure there was a brass bolt near the top. I looked at Isaac's profile, his shoulders rounded as he peered down to the pool, his expression almost dejected. Despite shadowy thoughts of Jamie Kerr, my overriding impulse at that moment was to comfort Isaac. How bizarre that was. I feared him, but didn't want him to be sad.

I made my way across the terrace with the tentative steps of a tightrope walker, and stopped beside him. Beyond the swimming pool was the darkened valley of whispering trees, and I had a sudden vision of Macbeth, surveying Birnam Wood from the battlements of his castle. But who was I in this vision? Perhaps the *poor player, that struts and frets his hour upon the stage, and then is heard no more*. I shook my head, trying to quell these dramatic thoughts. Ridiculous thoughts.

I had a question, and it felt naive and silly, but I had to ask it. 'Are you and Vangie . . . I mean . . . do you love her?'

The monosyllabic laugh that came from deep down in Isaac's chest was enough of an answer, but I wanted to hear what he had to say anyway. 'No. No, nothing like that. It's all been very trivial, really. Well . . . it was trivial, until Vangie made it into something bigger. I thought we'd just . . . you know, mess around. Then she started getting like this. Getting almost possessive. God knows why, I mean, I'm married, and so is she. Possession was never on the cards here.' He turned to me and ruffled his hair, genuine confusion knitted on his brow, as if he expected me to provide some insight.

But I had none. At least, none I could share with him. Because, if I was honest, Vangie's possessiveness wasn't as mysterious to me as it was to Isaac. I remembered my first feeling upon seeing Isaac and Vangie together in the nursery. It had taken some admitting, even to myself, but my first reaction was not indignation at their adultery. It was jealousy. White hot, searing, excruciating jealousy. This meant that, in a strange way, I understood Vangie more now than I ever had. But understanding Vangie's feelings wasn't top of my list at that moment.

'I just don't understand. I mean, Sarah's . . .' I took a breath, wondering how to phrase it. 'Sarah's perfect. Why—'

The laugh came again, that low, humourless sound. 'She certainly is, Diana. Can't fault her. She is perfection in everything she does.'

'You're mocking. You mean, she's not perfect?' I'm embarrassed to admit my own question caused a swell of hopefulness to bubble through me. I stared at him, willing him to explain Sarah's failings, but he wouldn't meet my eye. He remained staring into the dark distant hills.

'Do you know?' he said. 'I don't think I've ever met anyone as faultless as Sarah.' My hopefulness simmered down. 'She's unquestionably beautiful, clever, talented, kind, a brilliant mother and a caring wife.' He turned to me then and shrugged. 'And I'm sleeping with one of her closest friends. So what does that make me?'

He looked at me as he had in the pool, as if he was looking straight into my soul. I tried to hold his gaze but it was unbearable to feel that exposed, given how much I'd always tried to hide from him. I also wasn't sure what he wanted from me. Did he want me to call him a bastard? Threaten to tell Sarah?

I decided to change tack. 'From what Cam said downstairs, it sounds like Sarah and her parents are rather tied up in Acanthus.' I felt my heart accelerate as Isaac's expression hardened.

He nodded. 'Yes. Tied up is the right term. They've invested millions in the company over the years, and if they pulled out now, Acanthus wouldn't survive. Everything we've worked for would go up in smoke.'

'So this thing with Vangie . . . you're really playing with fire there, aren't you?' Just like I'm doing now, I thought.

'Yes, that's a fair assessment.'

'Is that part of the thrill?' This question sounded more petulant than I'd intended, and contained traces of my own hurt that I wished I'd disguised better.

'Probably.' He nodded. I'd expected more defensiveness. He looked down again, leaning slightly over the battlements to view the flagstones below. Between us was a gap, about a foot in width, and he scuffed his foot on the floor, sending a cluster of tiny stones over the edge. They skittered onto the patio below, and I instinctively took a step back.

He didn't move quickly, but his reaction was decisive. He put his hand out and took hold of mine, bringing it up to the stone wall and resting there, his own hand on top, the fingers curved around mine, cold and hard. My whole body had gone rigid. But it wasn't like in the pool, when his touch had sent a spasm of pleasure through me. This time the adrenalin that shot through my veins was almost painful. I felt like a hunted animal. Fight or flight.

He looked at me, his head slightly tilted as if wondering if I had any more questions. A breeze ruffled his hair, and brought the sting of goosebumps to the skin on my arms.

'So what's the plan then?'

The question caught me off guard. 'What do you mean?' My voice quivered.

'Are you going to go and wake Sarah up to tell her, or wait until tomorrow?' His eyebrows lifted as if this was an innocent question.

His words were muffled by my beating heart. He was challenging me. He was testing me. I moved to take my hand from the stone, and felt his fingers tighten around my own. He looked down to the patio below, then back up to me. Perhaps he was checking to see if anyone was down there, anyone who might look up at any moment and spot us. Or perhaps he was wondering, as I was, whether it was possible to fall from this height and survive. I supposed it depended on how you fell. I had a vision then of blue flashing lights on the gravel at the front of the house. Of a sour-faced French officer interviewing a tear-streaked Vangie. *Yes, yes officer, she did like a drink. She'd had a few margaritas.* I imagined Isaac, his face sallow and shocked. *She was rather tipsy.*

I'd had to get her out of the pool earlier as I didn't think it was safe for her to be swimming. Vangie interjecting. *Yes, that's right, I saw Isaac wrapping a towel around her.*

I met Isaac's gaze, searching the familiar rockpool green of his eyes for what he was thinking, but could decipher nothing. His expression was alien to me; he wasn't being jocular, suggesting drinks or music. He wasn't on edge because Cam was needling him. He wasn't flirting with me. His eyes were grave and penetrating, and I couldn't work out what was behind them. He shifted his feet, but didn't release my hand.

'Come on, Diana. What's stopping you? What's stopping you going down those stairs right now and telling Sarah?'

To my shame I felt tears prickling my eyes, and I tried in vain to blink them back.

'Hey, why are you crying?' His eyebrows dipped with concern and he released my hand to wipe a falling tear from my cheek with his thumb. Confusion writhed inside me. Should I run? Should I allow him to comfort me? Was my fear ridiculous? I didn't even know why I was crying . . . I could only think it must have been a mixture of fear, adrenalin, and an overriding sense that something was utterly and irretrievably ruined. But one thing I knew for certain, and if my fear of Isaac in that moment held even the smallest justification, I needed him to know.

'I'm not going to tell Sarah.'

He blinked. 'Why not?'

'Because it's none of my business.'

He regarded me for a while, his eyes wide and child-like. Then he looked down at his feet and blew out a lungful of air, nodding his head slowly. He didn't speak. Didn't thank me. I withdrew my hand from his grasp, relief washing through me when he didn't flinch. I took a tentative step towards the terrace door, still expecting him to reach out and catch my hand again. But he didn't move. I kept my eyes on him as I walked, twisting around to walk backwards the final few steps, keeping him squarely in my vision. He stayed turned away from me, shoulders slumped like a puppet whose strings had been cut. I stepped through the doorway into the coolness of the stone stairwell, and slowly pulled the door, staring at Isaac in the narrowing wedge of light, until with a click, he was gone, and I was left in darkness.

It was only when I'd slipped into bed and pulled the cool, cotton bedspread up to my chin in the silvery darkness, that I realised I couldn't do it. Silent tears spilled down my cheeks, and my heart ached in my chest. I could not stay here knowing what I knew. I couldn't take any more snide comments and poisonous looks from Vangie, whilst simultaneously keeping a secret for her. I couldn't smile and laugh with Sarah, knowing what I knew about her husband and her friend. How could I casually chat to a bumbling Duncan when I'd seen his wife like that with his best friend and business partner? And what was I supposed to say to Cam? She already had plenty of suspicions about Isaac, but how was I supposed to keep this new knowledge from her, knowing it would validate all her instincts about Isaac? Knowing I had the key to everything she needed? The small half-truths I'd cultivated over the past weeks in order to maintain my friendship with the Rivers were one thing, but to enter into this level of subterfuge in order to protect Isaac and Vangie, the extended family, plus a multi-million pound business, was too much to bear.

So I found myself getting dressed and packing my things. It proved impossible to order a taxi in the middle of the night from our remote location, so I wandered towards the local village, pulling my wheelie suitcase behind me. I was quite sure no one had seen me leave, as all the lights were out when I left. As I cut across the grass so as not to make a noise on the gravel, part of me hoped to hear the front door bang open, and to see Isaac or Sarah running across the lawn towards me, begging me to stay, asking me what was wrong, pleading with me not to desert them. But the house stayed dark and quiet as I turned out onto the road.

I sat on my case in the cobbled village square, under cover of an ancient wooden structure that housed the weekly market. Now it was empty, the coloured bulbs hanging dark and forlorn from the rafters above. Dawn emerged, the pinkish rays whitening the lichen-dusted rooftops. Eventually I got through to the same taxi company that had brought me here, and a younger version of the surly driver I'd had two days before collected me.

I briefly imagined the early risers back at the house, making themselves coffee and wandering around the pool. Sarah walking to the village to get croissants. Isaac eventually mentioning that Diana must be having a rather luxurious lie-in this morning. Perhaps it would be midday before anyone thought to check on me. Would they be alarmed by my departure? I could only imagine that Isaac would be relieved. Vangie certainly would. Would Sarah be worried, and try to contact me? Yes, I was sure she'd be in touch soon to check I was OK.

*

As I trudged up the foul-smelling staircase to my flat, I tried to imagine the sentiment I'd heard so many people profess over the years – *Yes, it's wonderful being on holiday, but isn't it lovely to get back home?* No, it was not. There was nothing lovely about the slate-grey sky that met me at the airport, or the stale, mouldy smell that billowed out to greet me when I kicked open my warped front door.

I dumped my bags in my bedroom and went through to slump on the sofa, noticing a hardened dollop of ketchup on the coffee table that I must have forgotten to wipe away before I set off for France. For some reason, the sight of it prompted a surge of emotion so strong, I burst into tears. I could hardly bear it. I hadn't wanted to stay in France, but now I couldn't face my flat either. Once my pathetic sobs had subsided, I pulled my writing set from under my bed and stuffed it into my old rucksack, which lay near my overflowing laundry basket, and headed for the door.

Heron Park was almost deserted, although it was Saturday. Ominous rainclouds bore down on the common, and only a small group of teenagers had risked the impending weather to play a game of football on the grass. A smattering of dog walkers dotted the pathways, casting occasional wary glances at the sky.

I took my usual route towards the trees, trampling the undergrowth until I came to the broken barbed-wire fence that I stepped over. The ground underfoot, and the roaring of the river below as I approached, told me why the usual park-goers were either absent or wary-looking today – there had clearly been a substantial amount of rainfall while I'd been away. The ground was spongy and waterlogged, the brambles and ferns cowering close to the ground as if they'd been pummelled by a ferocious downpour.

Wet thorns tore at my linen trousers, and scratched at my sandalled feet. I hadn't bothered to change since I'd left Manoir Segantin in the middle of the night. But I didn't really care. Of what use were these clothes now? Hen would probably laugh if she saw me in any of the finery I'd collected since meeting Isaac and Sarah. She wouldn't extend an appreciative fingertip like Sarah sometimes did, complimenting a garment I was wearing and beaming with approval when I mentioned a designer we both loved. No, Hen would more likely snort and say something like, *Oooo, look at you trying to be all posh!* And then try to retract the comment when I looked offended and say something bland and placatory like, *No, it actually looks lovely, it's just . . . just not your usual style, that's all*, and expect that to make me feel better.

No, I couldn't wear these clothes any more. And I doubted I'd be invited back to Riverdean again, knowing what I knew. Isaac had always been the instigator of my involvement with the group. He was the person who'd dragged me over to meet them all on that first night at Eden House. He'd invited me to the barbecue. It had been his willingness to invite me to France that had given me the courage to book my ticket. Without his insistence on my inclusion, no one else would think to invite me. Not even – and it hurt to admit this to myself – Sarah. Yes, Cam had supposedly invited me as her 'plus-one', but looking back with some perspective, I now saw that Vangie's assessment of her actions was probably correct – Cam just liked winding Vangie up, and knew that my unexpected appearance would do that. I think I'd known that as soon as I'd arrived in France, but hadn't wanted to think about it.

I stopped further down the bank and looked, awe-struck, at the rushing river below. I'd seen it swollen before, but never surging and bubbling with such feroc-ity. The flat stone I usually sat on was submerged, and the water tore at the brambles and ferns just a few feet below where I stood. I sank to the ground, feeling the thorns underneath me and the damp seeping through my clothes. I felt, rather than heard, the bass roll of thun-der far away. Fat raindrops began to peck at the leafy canopy above, but I slung my bag down and pulled out my writing set.

Dear Dad, I had a lovely time in France with my friends. I couldn't tell him the truth. I couldn't say what I'd seen, and that it had ended my friendships as quickly as they'd begun. *The villa we stayed in was beautiful.* I set about a good, long description of the French house, with its uneven limestone walls, and its pale shuttered windows. I knew he'd appreciate that. Circles of water spattered on the page as I wrote, smudging some words, obliterating others. The river roared and writhed beneath me.

My phone pinged, the sound piercing through the white noise that filled my head. I delved into my pocket and swiped at the screen that was already flecked with rain. It was an automated text from my bank: *Account ending 2566 is £10 from its overdraft limit. If you go over your limit you will be asked to pay back your entire overdraft immediately.*

Fuck. Leaving France early had meant buying another plane ticket, and at the time I hadn't thought anything of it, because I'd been so desperate to escape. But now I wanted to kick myself. I should have stayed. Just laid low for a while. Maybe spoken to Isaac again and reassured him I wasn't going to say anything. But no. As usual, I had made the wrong decision.

I stared at the rushing river, tears and raindrops blurring my vision. My phone pinged again. Hen.

Hi Dinny. How are you doing? Not heard from you for a while? Xx

The knot of hopelessness in my stomach grew heavier, and sank further.

I stared at the river. Putting the phone down beside me, I folded up the letter and pushed it into an envelope, sealed it, and wrote *Dad*, on the front. I usually posted the letters. I know, stupid. It just felt good to take them to a letterbox and push them inside, like a child sending a letter to Father Christmas, with the unshakeable belief that he would actually receive it. I'd always imagined my letters to Dad winging their way off into the ether. I'd felt the act of posting them meant that, somehow, their essence would reach Dad, wherever he was. I hadn't really believed it, of course. Just felt it. But now, for the first time, I imagined a bunch of bored Royal Mail workers whose job it was to dispose of all the crackpot letters that bore no attempt at a discernible address. I saw a pack of burly men huddled round a Formica table in their red T-shirts, sipping milky tea. One of them shouting, *There's another one!,* and reading out my letters to hoots and guffaws. *It's not even written by a child! How the fuck does she think her dad's going to get this without an address? Seriously, some people just have no fucking brain cells.*

I held the envelope, running my finger over the word, smearing the ink with rain. Then I threw it, like I was skimming a stone, into the raging water. I watched it dashed away by the river, valiantly remaining buoyant for a good few metres, before it was dragged down by the broiling froth.

I shuffled further down the bank, brambles clawing at my skin, thorns scratching my palms. I stretched out one sandal-clad foot, observing the Caramel Kiss polish that still coated my nails. Just like France, and my clothes, and my letter to Dad, the nail polish made me feel like an idiot. How ridiculous I was. What a pathetic, stupid, sad individual. I shuffled down further so my feet were right at the river's edge, then stretched them both out, watching them disappear beneath the muddy surface, feeling the ice-cold water pulling at them and seeping into the hem of my trousers. I tried to keep my feet still, but it was impossible as the water tugged and jostled them. Gradually I slipped further down, until my legs were submerged to my knees, and I was unable to sit straight, as the current dragged my legs sideways. I felt the heel strap of one sandal slip under my foot, then the whole shoe come away. It felt strange to only be wearing one sandal then, so I kicked off the other one too. They didn't surface as they were borne away. I wondered how long I could stay above the surface if I went in. As long as the letter? Or would I stay under like the sandals?

I couldn't take my eyes from the river. It was mesmerising. My legs were numb, and I realised I was now submerged up to my thighs, and the rain really was coming down. The field on the other side of the river was a blur of green and grey. My hair and clothes stuck to my skin.

Ping. I almost didn't hear it through the roaring in my ears. I turned my head and saw the rectangle of light in the undergrowth further up the bank. Stretching out I grabbed the phone with wet fingers, expecting to read a follow-up message from Hen with a demand to call her as soon as possible. But it was from an unknown number.

Diana, where are you? You didn't have to leave. Everyone's worried about you. Are you OK? Isaac.

I stared at the dirt-streaked screen. *Everyone's worried about you. Are you OK?* A painful wave of tears surged up from deep inside me, erupting in a moan I couldn't even hear above the sound of the river. But the feeling of it doubled me over, and I wrapped my arms across my stomach.

Everyone *wasn't* worried about me. But maybe Isaac was. Or was he just worried I wasn't there where he could keep an eye on me? Was he just worried about what I might say? Who I might tell?

I hauled my legs out of the water and huddled against the trunk of a tree, sheltering my phone screen from the rain. I typed with quivering fingers: *Thought it was time to leave. Vangie can enjoy her holiday now, and you can relax too*. Yes, that was it. A simple explanation, no emotions.

I watched the three undulating dots telling me he was typing, then, *Do you hate me?*

Fresh tears sprang to my eyes.

Of course I don't hate you.

Vangie doesn't know what you saw, by the way. So you don't have to worry about that.

She loathes me anyway, Isaac, so that doesn't really make any difference.

And it's over. I've told her there's nothing between me and her any more, and it's not going to happen again.

That's none of my business.

Will you stop being so fucking reasonable!!

I let out a sound that was half sob, half laugh. If he'd been watching me for the last half an hour, 'reasonable' would not be the word, I thought, casting a glance at my bare muddy feet.

He was typing again.

So if it's none of your business, and Vangie hates you anyway, then we're all good? We're still friends?

Oh God. Even after all this, after France, after discovering him and Vangie, after my desperation at no longer being welcome at Riverdean, the only happy place in my life, Isaac still managed to set off fireworks inside me. *We're still friends*, I typed.

So you'll come to our anniversary party at Riverdean in a couple of weeks?

What the fuck? *Why would you want me to do that, Isaac?*

Because I like you! Because you're FUN! Because the whole party will be stuffed full of boring Acanthus people and Sarah's ancient family members!

And there it was. A tiny flicker in the darkness inside me. A spark from a flint that caught the kindling. I felt my blood glowing with a warmth that hadn't been there moments before. It was OK. All was not lost. I could get back to Riverdean.

My hands shook as I struggled to type. *OK. I'll come.*

Great! It's at the house on Saturday 3rd October. You're free?

I'm free, I replied, not even waiting to pretend I was checking my diary.

He texted back a smiley face emoji and I closed my eyes, leaning my head back against the tree and feeling the rain speckle my face.

Something clicked into place then. The date. Saturday 3rd October. 0310. It made sense – the combination of the box safe that held the keys to Riverdean was Isaac and Sarah's anniversary. In truth, that date really was the key to everything.

Chapter Twenty-One

I went back to work. I couldn't face two weeks of stagnating in my dingy flat, going over and over the events of the past few weeks. The delirious highs and the crushing lows. I needed to occupy my mind with the mundanity of operating a milk frother, stacking a dishwasher, asking *regular or large?* repeatedly.

Misha and Kate had stared at me like I was an apparition that had just walked through the wall of the café when I first showed up.

'I . . . I thought you'd . . . I mean, how lovely you're back! I just . . .' Misha stammered. What she was trying to say is that she thought I'd be taking more time off. *Hoped* I'd be taking more time off. Her eyes flickered towards the dishwasher as she spoke, and I knew she was silently wondering if Giovanni's crockery was safe.

I smiled my calmest smile and blinked in what I hoped was a serene manner. 'I understand you're concerned for my mental health, and I have to say I've felt so supported by you, Misha. Both as a boss, and as a friend.' I watched her eyes crease into a twinkly smile behind her magenta glasses as I said this. 'And I'll definitely be telling Giovanni how amazing you've been.'

I watched her chest swell then as if she were being inflated by an invisible bicycle pump. 'Well . . . you know, you do what you can.'

I knew she'd relish any possibility of Giovanni hearing about how wonderful she was, and hoped that would be enough for her not to send me home. I just needed to seed another idea. 'I'm going to tell him it was you who made me realise I needed to see a counsellor too.'

'Oh good, you've found someone?'

'Yes, someone who comes highly recommended. She's expensive, but I've already had two sessions and honestly, it's like a fog has lifted. She's worth every penny.'

Misha nodded with wide-eyed enthusiasm. I knew she was about to launch into her speech about her cousin's cognitive behavioural therapy, at which point I'd say that's what I was having, then she'd say she was thrilled she'd set me on the right path, whereupon I'd ask for an advance on this month's wages, or sadly I wouldn't be able to afford to continue with my therapy.

It worked like a charm.

I spent my lunch hours wandering the cobbled back streets of Covent Garden, exploring the designer shops I now knew so well. Sometimes I'd notice a glimmer of recognition in a shop assistant's eyes as they greeted me. Occasionally I'd receive a *how are you today?* I remembered how terrified I'd been to cross these thresholds that first time I'd needed an outfit to wear to Eden House. How certain I'd been that I'd be rejected by the perfect people who either worked or shopped there. But that hadn't happened. I'd been allowed access again and again. I'd been accepted. And now, all these weeks later, these places felt inextricably linked to Riverdean, and Isaac and Sarah. Therefore, like Riverdean, they too were my happy place. I felt my breathing calm and my pulse slow as I walked through the expensive stream of air conditioning at each doorway. The cushioned quietness felt like a library, or a church. The muted clacking of hangers on rails and the soothing whispers of the shop assistants were zen-like music to me. Sometimes there was actual music playing, but wafting from somewhere invisible, and always unobtrusive. I suppose telling Misha I needed the money for therapy wasn't a complete lie . . . this was my therapy.

It was on my second week of searching that I lighted upon the perfect dress for Isaac and Sarah's party. It was from a small boutique called Bec & Belle, and was a sleeveless, navy-blue midi dress, with white embroidery down the front, and around the waist and hemline. It was classy, but understated. I was not going to make a statement in this dress. I was going to look sophisticated, but un-noteworthy. This was not a party I would be getting drunk at. I would not dance. I would not draw attention to myself. I wanted to be at Riverdean, and spend time with Isaac and Sarah, and see if I could get our friendship back on track. There was no reason to think about Isaac and Vangie, especially since Isaac had assured me it was now over. Who was I to mess things up by spilling secrets that weren't even mine? And as for the Jamie Kerr conspiracy . . . having had time to think, I realised Cam's suspicions were nothing short of preposterous. Isaac was no murderer. Yes, he was a charismatic flirt who'd cheated on his wife, but a killer he was not.

The two weeks leading up to the party were peppered with text messages from Hen. She'd obviously not heard from Kate since I swapped the numbers around, which meant the messages were less frantic than they had been when I'd had an informant working against me. *Have you had a good day? How's work?* I responded levelly to each message, and even called her a couple of times, reporting that work was boring but that I had a couple of new pupils I was tutoring . . . stuff I thought she'd like to hear.

Messages from Kate had dried up since 'Hen' had told her to fuck off, and it pleased me to imagine Kate observing me at work, itching to reach for her phone but terrified of another reprimand from Hen. I didn't tell Hen about France, or mention Riverdean or Isaac and Sarah. Sometimes I felt like Alice in Wonderland. There was an entirely separate world I was part of, that no one in this one would understand. I was a different person there, and I meant something different to those people. I wasn't a sad, pathetic, crazy person who needed constant surveillance. To Sarah I was a new friend. To Isaac I was fun. To Cam I was a confidante. To Vangie I was a threat. Yes, she hated me . . . but she didn't pity me. I could live with that. I could live with anything but the constant pity.

*

Make-Up by Marie (5.4 million views) informed me that 'smoky eyes' were *the* look this autumn. But not the charcoal panda effect we'd seen in seasons past, no, no. This season it was all about subtle smudges of gold. Think changing leaves. Think the last glow of an autumn sunset. Based on the price tag, the minuscule pot clenched between my fingers contained what must surely be twenty-four-carat powdered gold. I dabbed at it with quivering, newly Caramel-Kissed fingertips, and 'swept' it across my eyelids, which had already been 'prepped' according to a previous tutorial.

Eyeliner smudged, cheeks rouged, lips dabbed nude, I stood back to admire my reflection. It was understated and classy, the gold of my eyes contrasting with the navy fabric of my dress. My black Chanel bag didn't match the blue, but I'd decided if I wanted to splash out and buy milk to go on the cornflakes I was living on this month, it would have to do.

My heels clicked on the damp pavement as I approached my car. The sky was silver grey and the streetlamps flickered on along the parade, a bite of distant winter in the air. I felt as if I'd been in a dream state since Isaac had invited me to the party, but now as I drove towards Riverdean, a tingle of adrenalin began to simmer inside me. How would everyone react to seeing me after I'd made a midnight flit from the villa? How would I explain my unexpected disappearance to Sarah?

I parked in the cul-de-sac near Riverdean, checking the rear seat for the sleeping bag I'd slung in there earlier. If I had a few drinks and didn't want to drive back, I'd decided I would sleep in the car. Anything but stick around and make a fool of myself like last time. I shrugged on a dove-grey summer jacket I'd found in the St Roche sale, which was paper-thin but better than nothing, and headed towards the house.

I needn't have worried about being unfashionably early – the driveway was already crammed with cars, and a mini cab blinked its hazards in the lane as a couple emerged, thanking the driver. I wove my way towards the front door, careful not to scratch the gleaming body-works of a BMW and Mercedes that were parked close together.

It was only as I rang the bell that I noticed the couple who had emerged from the taxi were making their way around the side of the house, where a hand-painted sign read *Come this way!* with an arrow towards the back garden. But before I could follow them, the door opened. Sarah stood there, her face creasing into what looked like a relieved smile as she enveloped me in a hug. I felt my insides melt with my own relief. It was the welcome I'd hoped I'd get in France, but had been deprived of thanks to Vangie's hostility. I wrapped my arms around Sarah's back, fingers gliding on the soft folds of her maroon dress. The loose waves of her hair smelt familiar and floral.

'I'm so glad you came, darling,' she whispered into my ear. 'So sorry you had to leave France early.' She drew black, holding me by the shoulders, face a concerned grimace. 'Isaac told me about your sister. Is she OK?'

'I . . . um . . .'

'Oh God, was he not supposed to say anything? I'm so sorry, it's just we were all rather worried about you—'

'Diana!' Isaac's voice boomed down the corridor and he strode towards us. He wore a pale-blue open-necked shirt and caramel chinos. His hair had been trimmed since I last saw him, but his signature lock still fell forwards as he bent to kiss me on both cheeks. I filled my lungs with his scent – wood and spice. My fingers held his taut upper arms as I felt his hands on my waist. I pulled myself away as he drew back to stand next to Sarah.

'I hope you don't mind,' he said, with an earnest expression. 'I told Sarah about your family emergency with your sister . . . that she was having a bit of a crisis and you had to get back to the UK to see her.'

'No, of course I don't mind. It's . . . it's fine, it's just she sometimes has these . . . episodes, I suppose you'd call them . . .' Sarah nodded as I spoke, and I found myself trying to imagine how Hen might talk to a stranger about me. 'So anyway, she was going through something, and needed a shoulder to cry on . . .'

'Well, she's very lucky to have you watching out for her, ready to drop everything and run to her side.'

'Thank you,' I said, hoping that would be the end of the conversation.

Isaac was on the same wavelength. 'Anyway, let's not keep you on the doorstep!' he said. 'We need to get you in and get you a drink.'

The house was breathtaking in a way I'd never seen before. Tonight, Riverdean was resplendent. Candles glimmered on every surface, set in saucers, encased in glass, nestled in nooks. The table in the conservatory was heaving with food, and had been pushed back against one wall to open up the space. Above it hung a large structure of autumnal leaves, ferns and white flowers. Glass orbs hung from it, containing flickering tea lights that twinkled on invisible threads.

The glass doors were thrown wide, and the patio had been enclosed in a white marquee. Kilim rugs were strewn over the flagstones, on which sat plush sofas and fluffy footstools. Plants in large pots were dotted about, and glowing lightbulbs were strung in lines across the ceiling.

'Cocktail?' said Isaac.

'Always.'

It was only when I stepped into this new space that I noticed a makeshift bar had been set up along one side. A man in a white shirt was placing two coffee beans on top of an espresso martini. A large chalkboard behind him listed six cocktails in swirly writing, and at the end of the bar, the frosted emerald necks of beer bottles protruded from an oversized bucket of ice.

'I can recommend the classic mojito, or if you're feeling brave, a cocktail of my own design called the Ruby Rose . . . Belvedere vodka, a hint of ginger . . . and perhaps I'll let you try and work out the other ingredients.'

I watched his eyes twinkle as he spoke, like a little boy explaining what he wanted for Christmas. 'You really love a cocktail, don't you?'

'What's not to love? I think if I'd not started Acanthus I'd probably be a mixologist or something . . . own a high-end bar in Soho that does specialist cocktails for ridiculous prices.'

'I can see it. You'd be good at that.' Isaac would be in his element running a bar, talking all night, flirting with customers. I could tell from the way he was speaking that although he was joking, there was an element of truth to what he was saying. I watched him watching the barman making our cocktails. He was chipping in with nuggets of advice on how much ginger to add, and how much to stir the syrup. I could tell he was dying to make them himself.

'Diana!' The voice sent a bolt of adrenalin through me, and I turned to see Vangie's pale face, her thin lips curving into a smile. She was wearing her signature black, and her cropped black hair was teased into contrived messiness.

'Vangie,' I said, trying to unstick my voice from my throat.

She moved towards me then and I found myself flinching as her cheek found mine and she kissed me, once on each side, her thick perfume enveloping me and confusing my senses even further. 'I . . . it's nice to see you,' I said, trying to compensate for the fact my body had gone completely rigid.

Her scarlet smile broadened, her gaze darting towards Isaac then back to me as he handed me my cocktail. 'It's lovely to see you too, Diana. I'm absolutely thrilled you could make it.'

I cast a glance at Isaac, whose gaze flicked towards me, before he looked back at Vangie with narrowing eyes. He was as confused as I was.

'I was so sorry to hear you'd had some family troubles. But anyway, tonight's not about that, is it? Tonight's about friends all being together, and catching up with each other.' Her smile was almost clownlike in its breadth, and I wondered if she'd taken something.

'Are you all right, Vange?' Isaac clearly felt the same way I did.

'Oh, I'm just great!' she said, without the hint of a drunken slur. 'I'm just really looking forward to catching up with Diana, and having a good old chinwag. At the right moment, of course! Not now. Perhaps later. Perhaps we can all have a little catch-up, you know . . . me, Duncan, you, Sarah . . . and Diana.'

She held my gaze, her dark eyes glittering. Something inside me fell. A tingle of ice that slithered down my back. The way she'd said my name. Diana. As if it wasn't my name. It *wasn't* my name. Did she know that? No, she couldn't possibly. And anyway, what did it matter? It was *almost* my name. People used nicknames all the time. Dinah and Diana sounded more similar than Vangie and Evangeline. So what if I used a nickname? Admittedly I'd invented a surname, but what did that matter? Who cared about a surname? I hadn't told any other lies. I was a tutor. I had been at Oxford. I did live near Richmond. All these thoughts flicked through my mind like pictures in a projector.

'Where's Duncan?' I asked, trying to change the subject.

'Oh, you know Duncan.' Her face turned into a sneer as she said his name. 'All work and no play. Think he's in your office finishing off some paperwork.'

Isaac sighed. 'Well, for God's sake, get him out here! It's our anniversary party, not a chance to catch up on contracts.' He rolled his eyes in mock frustration, and I wondered if he wanted to dispel Vangie's strange mood as much as I did.

'Oh, I'm sure he'll come out at some point, don't worry. I know he'll want to spend time with Diana as much as I do.' She smiled with an unnerving serenity, and we watched her slink away.

Isaac turned to me with a frown. 'What's going on with her?'

'I was going to ask you the same thing. Are you sure you haven't said anything to her about . . . about France?'

Isaac cast wary glances at the people around us and bent towards me as he whispered. 'Of course not. I promise she doesn't know you saw anything. And anyway, if she did, why would she be preening like that? If anything, surely she'd be on the back foot?'

I nodded, hating to admit he was right. The idea that Vangie was acting strangely because of France would have been a relief, though, when the alternative was that she suspected I'd been lying. *But I haven't been lying. Not really. Not about anything important.*

I sipped my cocktail and watched Isaac circling the room, chatting to people, batting away compliments, laughing. I remembered my desperation to fit in when I was here at the barbecue, and how I launched myself on the cliques of people, introducing myself and trying to be extrovert, entertaining, worthy of their company. But tonight I couldn't bring myself to do that. Vangie had unsettled me. I wanted to find a quiet corner where I could hide and collect myself without falling within her sights.

That's when I knew where I should go.

I shuffled between the chattering groups of people towards the back exit of the marquee, and out onto the grass. Fairy lights twinkled in the hedge that bordered the swimming pool, and a couple of people huddled on a sun lounger, smoking cigarettes.

291

It was dark now, and the copse of trees a shadowy mass. Once I knew I was out of sight of the marquee, I lit the torch on my phone, shining it on the soggy undergrowth so I could find my way.

The trees opened up and the lake shimmered in front of me, a full moon dusting the circle of trees with silver, and casting an eerie light on the figure hunched at the end of the jetty. Wispy curls of smoke rose above her head as if she were a dampened fire, smouldering in a forest.

'You should start buying your own cigarettes, Diana,' she said, looking up at me as I arrived at her side.

'But then I wouldn't have an excuse to come and talk to you.'

I lowered myself onto the damp planks of wood and folded my legs underneath me, grateful I'd chosen a dark-coloured dress. Cam handed me a cigarette and flicked her lighter, the flame steady and straight in the still night air.

I blew out a cloud of smoke and watched it disappear like a phantom above the glassy water. 'Do you not have any friends here tonight?'

She gave a dull laugh. 'Strangely enough, I don't invite mates to this particular event any more. Don't think any of them would fancy it, somehow.'

'Oh God . . . was it . . . was it Isaac and Sarah's anniversary party when it happened? When Jamie died?'

She nodded, her skin like porcelain in the moonlight. Her expression was hard, but there was a subtle hurt behind her eyes. It reminded me of the photo of her with the dandelion.

I turned and stared out over the mirrored surface of the lake, at the reflection of watery trees and sunken silver moon. I felt that if I slipped off this jetty into the water, I would fall down, down, down into the sky below. Like Alice into another world. Like Jamie.

I felt a bubbling unease inside me as I swallowed down the knowledge I had. The knowledge Jamie had been so eager to share with Cam. I could tell her now. I could tell her at this moment, in the very place Jamie had intended to, on the two-year anniversary of his death. Wouldn't that be somehow so beautifully *right*?

We sat in silence, the weight of my secret silently expanding inside me, growing so big I knew it couldn't come out. My throat tightened and I coughed.

'Time you gave up?' Cam said, gesturing to the cigarette and raising an eyebrow.

'Probably.' The moment was gone. I stood up, flicked my cigarette stub into the water, and smoothed down my skirt, picking off tiny splinters of damp wood that had stuck to the back. 'Are you OK here by yourself?'

'By myself is what I do best, Diana.' The tip of her cigarette glowed orange as she looked out over the lake.

I made my way back to the house.

The party was bubbling along merrily, the voices louder now more cocktails had been consumed. I noticed Harriet from next door wearing a ruched jungle-print dress with golden orbs on her ears. She was talking overbearingly to an audience of three women who nodded silently, casting tight-lipped smiles at each other. Caterers weaved between the guests, circulating mouth-sized canapés on silver trays. A cork popped and I looked over to see Felicity pouring champagne into the outstretched glasses of two gormless young men who were both trying to catch her eye. Soft jazz floated from discreet tower speakers concealed behind plants in the corners.

My eyes darted around the room as I passed through it, wondering where Vangie could be. I felt like a rabbit emerging from a burrow, desperate to avoid the midnight prowling of a hungry fox. I slipped into the conservatory, admiring the table laden with every finger food you could imagine, from cheese to grapes, cold meats to melon. There was even an artful display of sushi with accompanying chopsticks, and a mound of ice upon which perched curled pink prawns. I made a promise to myself to eat something later, when I was feeling less on edge.

I wandered towards the trio of photographs that hung from the length of driftwood on the wall, noticing with some amusement that the glass over *Turkey 2011* still hadn't been replaced. No one had noticed it was gone. It struck me as funny in that moment, how oblivious we can be to things that are right in front of us. I brought one hand up to my face and inspected my thumb, where a silver starburst of a scar streaked across my skin.

'Lovely photo,' said a woman at my shoulder.

I flinched and turned to stare at her. I didn't know her. 'Yes . . . yes, it is.'

I don't know if she'd expected me to say something else, to start a conversation perhaps, but I couldn't think of anything else to say. She nodded, her smile faltering slightly before she moved off.

I darted into the kitchen to see it had been completely taken over by the caterers. A tall woman in a white apron beamed down at me. 'Can I help you with something?'

'Oh . . . errr . . . I was just looking for some wine, actually.'

'Is there none out at the bar?' She looked panicked for a moment. 'Nathan should be sending someone in to restock if—'

'No, I'm so sorry, I'm sure there is wine out there, I just didn't think. Came straight in here, you know – force of habit.'

Her expression softened. 'Ah, you must be a good friend if you know where to help yourself to wine!'

I gave a polite laugh, but before I could reply, I was cut off.

'*Such* a good friend.' The voice came from behind me, and I whirled around to see Cam standing in the doorway to the kitchen. She stared at me with a hardness that sliced straight through me.

'Cam . . . are you OK?' It was a stupid thing to ask. She was clearly not OK. Her chest rose and fell rapidly as if she could barely contain her fury.

As I watched, she brought up her right hand to reveal something I, at first, took to be a packet of cigarettes. But it wasn't cigarettes – it was a mobile phone. It was *my* mobile phone. Then I remembered . . . I'd used the torch to find my way to the lake, then I'd turned off the torch and set the phone down between us when I'd sat next to her.

'You really should use a passcode, Diana.'

Chapter Twenty-Two

Cam stalked past me towards the doorway that led to the back staircase. A taut kind of energy emanated from her as she passed, like static electricity. I felt that if I reached out and touched her, a spark would ignite us both. Heart hammering, I followed her, aware of the tall caterer gawping at us as we went.

Cam strode along the corridor and up the curving staircase to the gallery above, me scuttling silently behind. My mind raced to work out what the hell she'd found on my phone. The many photos I'd taken of the house when I stayed here with the girls? Photos of her mother's wardrobe, Isaac's aftershave, her own bedroom? Or perhaps it was my Instagram account with the username *Jane Smith*. Had she discovered Diana wasn't my real name? She flung open the door to her bedroom and marched inside, leaving me to follow and close the door behind us. I turned to her and she rounded on me, holding my phone aloft like a weapon.

She recited from memory. '*Do you hate me? Of course I don't hate you.*' She voiced Isaac with a booming exaggeration of his faint Scottish accent, and me with a plummy, childlike whine.

'*Vangie doesn't know what you saw, by the way. And it's over. I've told her there's nothing between me and her any more, and it's not going to happen again.*

'*That's none of my business.*'

I'd never seen Cam like this before. It was as if she'd lost control. She'd always been so calm in her contempt for Isaac. But now, her despisal of us both poured out of her like gushing river water.

'*None of your business*, Diana?' Her face was contorted with hatred.

'It . . . it *is* none of my business.' My voice was feeble. It stood frail next to hers, no match for her ferocity.

'*None of your business* when you knew that Isaac was shagging my mother's best friend? *None of your business* when you sat next to me on that jetty and sympathised with me about Jamie? When you knew how desperate I was to know what he could possibly have meant when he said he had something on Isaac? None of your *business*?'

'I didn't know . . . I . . . I only just found out. In France.' My voice was shaking almost as much as my hands.

'That's why you left?' She stared at me open-mouthed for a moment. 'Instead of coming to me?'

'I couldn't come to you and . . . it would have meant the end of—'

'The end of *what*?' She flung her arms out to the sides, gesturing wildly about the room. 'The end of this sham of a marriage my mother has lumbered herself with? The end of Isaac's fucking property development dreams? So fucking *what*?' Her normally pale face was a blotchy, livid red, her eyes glittering with fury. Then her expression changed. She drew back into herself and her eyes widened. 'Or . . .' Her lips curved up into a hateful smile, and a mocking twinkle appeared in her eyes. 'Or is it that it would mean the end of you and Isaac?' She tilted her head, as if this was an innocent question.

'What do you mean, me and Isaac?' A new heat flared in my chest, spreading out towards my limbs.

Her smile grew. 'You know exactly what I mean. You're a little bit in love with him, aren't you?' Her voice dripped with derision, a vicious sneer curling her lips.

'Of course not. I don't know what—'

'Oh, come on, Diana. Why else would you be hanging around like a bad smell? Poor little Diana has found herself basking in the infinite charisma of Isaac Rivers, without the faintest inkling that he doesn't give a fucking shit about anyone but himself!' She laughed and the sound was like punches to my chest. 'You know he's the same with everyone, don't you? You know you're not special?'

'I . . . I don't think for one minute that I am—'

'All his flirting and charming . . . it's just something he does. And it's either to get his way with useful people, or just because he likes feeling like a king among adoring peasants. You do realise he sees you as a peasant, don't you?'

A hard lump was pulsating in my throat and I tried to swallow it down but it wouldn't budge. The strain of it brought tears to my eyes. 'Look, Cam.' My voice was thin, strained. 'I know you're angry, and you're right, I should have told you—'

'It's too late for apologies now. From you, from Vangie, or from him.' She marched past me towards the door.

'Cam, please, don't do this in front—'

'Don't tell me what to do!' she shrieked, spinning around to glare at me. It was the most livid I'd ever seen her, and despite the rage that radiated from her, she had never looked more desperate or more lost. 'You think I'm going to go down there and do that to my mother in front of all these people?' She spat the words, jabbing her finger towards the door. 'In front of her friends and family? After sacrificing everything I have so I could stay close and make sure she was OK, you think I'd go down-stairs now and throw a tantrum in front of all these people just to get back at Isaac and Vangie?' She winced at me with incredulity.

Then I realised where it all came from. All the hard-ness and hurt inside Cam, the contempt that fizzed on the surface of her skin; it was all because she wanted to protect her mother. She'd lost her father when she was six, and the person who'd replaced him was a loud, laughing, flirt of a man who had secrets she hadn't been able to unearth. And when she'd lost her best friend, she'd flailed around in the dark, desperate for it to be linked somehow to Isaac, to mean an end to his rela-tionship with her mother. Her protective instincts had gone into overdrive. That's why she hadn't moved away, hadn't gone to university, was always around the house. She was waiting for something to happen. Waiting for the fallout of what she saw as a catastrophic relation-ship. And now the fallout was here.

'Let me deal with this,' she said through gritted teeth. She threw my phone at me and it glanced off my shoul-der with a thwack before she slammed the bedroom door on her way out.

I rubbed my shoulder as I bent to pick up my phone, then sank onto the bed. I looked around the room, the first room I'd stayed in when I'd been at Riverdean with the girls. The pink dressing table was the same, as were the fairy lights in the fireplace. If I'd had any cigarettes on me, I think I'd have walked out onto the fire escape and smoked for a while, listening, invisible, to the party in the distance. But I had none, and no reason to stay in Cam's room. I tried to imagine how I would have felt on that first night in Riverdean, if someone had told me I'd be back here a few months later, being screamed at by the grown-up little girl whose room this was, about an affair her stepfather was having with her mother's best friend. *Oh, what a tangled web we weave, when first we practice to deceive.* Sir Walter Scott was right, I thought. But I was about to realise that sometimes the tangle you see in front of you is only one small corner of the knot.

Even though Cam had said she wasn't going to make a scene, she'd been in such a state I didn't know whether to believe her. That's why I felt my palms tingle with trepidation as I crept down the back staircase, across the Moroccan-tiled floor, and into the kitchen. The caterers were bustling about, bringing fresh platters from the oven, and carrying in empty plates from the conservatory. The tall woman in the apron cast me a wary smile before looking down to fiddle with a plate of crudités.

In the living area, I felt a swell of relief – the atmosphere was unchanged, with clusters of people holding drinks and chattering. Chilled electro pop music wafted through the space, reminding me of something you'd get in a hotel lobby or in the reception area of a gym. I scanned the room and spotted Sarah sitting on the coffee table, talking to an elderly couple who were folded amongst the sofa cushions. She caught my eye and beckoned me over.

'Diana, come and meet my parents.' She beamed as she spoke, which told me she hadn't seen Cam yet.

I attempted an engaged expression as Sarah introduced us. Mrs Dean's eyes were embedded in folds of skin, but the amber colour was definitely that of her daughter and granddaughter. Mr Dean stared at me with more of a shrewd look in his dark eyes, and I found myself over-smiling as if to prove myself in some sort of superficial way.

I was aware of Sarah's voice explaining to them that I was an English tutor, but I couldn't stop my gaze roaming the room, searching for Cam, Isaac or Vangie. Trying to find some clue or indication that something had been said.

That's when I spotted Isaac by the buffet table in the conservatory.

He was smiling down at Felicity, who I now saw was wearing a skin-tight black dress that stopped just above her knees. She had her back to me, but I watched her waving her arms around – a cucumber stick clenched between the thumb and forefinger of her right hand – and knew she was trying her best to keep Isaac engaged. I thought back to earlier when I'd seen her popping champagne, oblivious to the hungry gazes of the young men she'd poured the drinks for. But now it was she who was hungry – hungry for Isaac's attention. And as I watched him, his eyes creasing into his twinkle of a smile, I remembered what Cam had said upstairs . . . *A king amongst adoring peasants*. He was loving it.

A beautiful young woman was showing him attention and he was basking in her admiration. Of course he was. My heart sank further in my chest. How stupid of me. I mean, why else would she be invited? She wasn't a relative or a proper friend. And she certainly wasn't useful for the business as an investor. She was here because she adored Isaac, and he liked being around people who adored him.

People like me.

He invited me to things because he liked to watch me pandering to his ego. I wasn't young or beautiful like Felicity, but I was pathetic enough to hang on his every word, jumping and pawing at him like an infatuated puppy. I remembered he and I mocking Felicity together . . . mocking her young, vibrant enthusiasm for her job, and her audacity for jumping in the swimming pool, and calling him *Zac*. But now a new thought reared up, and it stung more than all the others – he and Felicity probably mocked me. This was probably part of his fun, playing each concubine off against the other, in an endless game of 'who's the favourite?' Was it this game that had driven Vangie mad? Was it this game that had laced her voice with the desperation I'd heard in the nursery in France? *I can't do this any more.* Yes, I could see, if you were infatuated with him, perhaps even in love, then watching his constant flirting with other new 'favourites' would slowly drive you insane.

Ting, Ting, Ting. Somewhere a glass was being struck to get everyone's attention. I looked towards the kitchen door and saw Vangie standing with a champagne flute and a knife, a manic grin across her pale face.

The hubbub died down and someone killed the music. I watched Isaac's face darken, saw the bob of his Adam's apple as he swallowed. His expression did nothing to alleviate the sound of blood rushing in my ears. He knew the strange mood Vangie was in as well as I did, and this did not bode well.

'Oh goodness,' said Sarah next to me, a carefree smile on her face. She leaned over to her parents and whispered, 'Darling Vangie's going to make a speech, I think.'

'Thank you, everyone! This won't take up much of your precious drinking time, don't worry!' There were titters around the room, and more people pushed in through the glass doors from the marquee to see what was happening. I felt something curdling in my stomach.

'I just wanted to take a moment to honour the happy couple! I hope no one minds me taking it upon myself, but you see, I've been friends with Isaac and Sarah from almost the beginning. Nearly as long as Duncan!' There were more laughs as she nodded towards the hallway where I turned to see Duncan's round, sweat-sheened face, glowing in the light from a candle. 'I was there for their budding romance, the inception of Acanthus, the birth of children, the holidays and high days . . .' she cast her eyes down '. . . and the more difficult days . . .' She looked towards Sarah whose turn it was to lower her gaze and give a sad nod into her glass. 'But, we've always been in it together, the four of us – Isaac, Sarah, Duncan and me. And it's fair to say that none of us in this room would be here today if it wasn't for this truly inspirational couple!' There were cheers and shouts of *True!* from the crowd.

'Isaac and Sarah . . . what can I say? You truly are the most beautiful, kind, caring, *fun-loving* . . .' she gazed pointedly at Isaac as she said this and everyone laughed, Isaac raising his glass towards her with a smirk '. . . couple I think any of us have ever met. And I'm so proud to call you both my best friends.' Vangie's voice caught on the last two words, and there was a muted chorus of *awwww*s from the audience. Sarah sniffed next to me and shot Vangie a watery smile. The duplicity of the woman was astounding. Everything about her words and her manner spoke of her being the most devoted best friend. I couldn't keep the image of Isaac pushing her up against that wall out of my mind. The desperate ecstasy on her face.

'I know this yearly get-together is a bit of a tradition . . . an excuse for a "knees-up", as Isaac would say . . .' Isaac nodded approvingly and Felicity flashed him an ice-white smile '. . . or "a lovely way of ushering in the autumn", as my beautiful, self-deprecating friend Sarah would say . . .' Sarah gave a soft laugh and there were murmurs around the room '. . . but this year I thought it would be nice to put something together for Isaac and Sarah. Something to celebrate their relationship, not only with each other, but with all the wonderful friends and family who are here tonight. After all, each one of you is here for a reason.'

She held something black up in her hand and pointed it towards the wall just behind where Sarah and I sat. I twisted around on the coffee table, looking up at the ceiling from where a mechanical whirring sound came. Then, from a recess above the huge painting that hung above the fireplace, a strip of white cloth appeared. It was a projector screen, and it was enormous, eclipsing the oil painting completely, and concealing half of the bookcases either side as it slid into place.

There were whoops and cheers from the tipsy guests, and I drew in a mouthful of Prosecco, unsure if it was even my glass. The liquid burned my oesophagus as it bubbled down, past my hammering heart and into my churning stomach. I willed myself to calm down. This was ridiculous. Vangie was about to present a slideshow, a perfectly ordinary thing to happen at such an event, and something which had nothing to do with me. *How could it? Just sit back, and calm down.*

The screen flickered to life, and italic black words came into focus: *Happy Anniversary, Isaac and Sarah.* The words faded and a wedding photo appeared, the bride and groom smiling into the camera. The next one was the same, this time with a blurry Cam running across the screen, Sarah reaching out a hand to catch her. There were appreciative murmurs from the crowd, and I turned to see Sarah beaming up at the screen. My pulse slowed. This was going to be OK.

Then the tinkling of piano keys came from the speakers either side of the room. It was an introduction to a song I knew well. A song I could play on the piano myself. In fact, it was the song I'd played to everyone when I arrived in France. *Someday, when I'm awfully low, and the world is cold, I will feel a glow just thinking of you . . .*

I turned to look at Vangie. Her eyes locked on to mine, her lips curving into a malicious smile. Heart thumping, I turned back towards the screen, trying to focus on the stream of images that faded and warped into each other. Isaac and Sarah kissing on a beach . . . Isaac, Sarah, Vangie and Duncan standing in front of a gleaming 'Acanthus' sign . . . Cam and Isaac in a canoe . . . Isaac and Duncan playing chess . . . the whole Acanthus team holding champagne flutes aloft . . .

There were photos of people I didn't know, of course. Dinners and birthdays that elicited laughter or murmurs from various pockets of the room . . . a man with cream on his nose and cheeks . . . Sarah with two women I'd not met, all brandishing golf clubs . . . a photo of Oxford University. It faded without comment, replaced by a gurning ten-year-old Cam. Something shifted inside me. Who went to Oxford? It was as I mused on this that the next photo came into focus, like a slap to my face. It was an image of a bed strewn with rose petals. My breath caught in my throat.

'I don't remember that . . .' laughed Sarah next to me.

I remembered it. It wasn't that particular bed, which looked like a stock image, but I remembered a bed, and handfuls of petals, cool and pink. I felt sick.

More photos . . . Mr and Mrs Dean in front of a sprawling, white mansion . . . David and Harriet holding martinis . . . that photo faded, then it was there.

My face, blotchy from the sun, semi-bleached hair a straggly mane, holding a red wine glass aloft, surrounded by Megs, Priya and Rachel, in the conservatory, not five metres from where I sat now.

My skin turned to ice.

'When was that?' Sarah was asking next to me. 'Who are those people?'

I didn't answer. The next photo came into focus . . . me, wearing my black swimming costume with the rotten elastic, stomach spilling over denim shorts, standing with a plastic martini glass, squinting in the sun. Priya sitting on the edge of the pool just to the right of the shot.

'I don't understand when this was,' Sarah whispered, leaning to catch my eye. I kept my head firmly twisted away from her, my eyes trained on the screen. My mouth was dry, but I couldn't drink. I knew I wouldn't be able to swallow.

The next shot was mercifully a huge group shot, but my relief was short-lived as on closer inspection the banner strung between two Christmas trees read *Oxford English Department Christmas 2000*. I remembered that night. The photo stayed up long enough for me to locate myself, leaning on Christopher's shoulder as we sat on the bottom step. The photo faded, replaced by a photo of him. It was a professional headshot, possibly from the university website. Christopher looked older than I'd ever known him, his hair greying at the temples and deep creases furrowing his brow. But I knew that office, knew that desk, knew that chair he was sitting on as well as I knew that smile. The smile I'd fallen for as a fresher over twenty years ago, but hadn't seen since.

'Who's that? Is that one of Isaac's friends?' Sarah muttered, more to herself than me as she turned to look for Isaac. I did the same, but he wasn't there. Looking towards the back of the room, I saw him next to Vangie, leaning to whisper something to her with a frown. He gestured towards the screen with a shake of his head, a confused shrug. But Vangie's focus remained on the slideshow, her smile unwavering.

A photo of me at eighteen, empty shot glass in hand, face glowing blue with the club lights, skin glossy with sweat. A couple of people cheered at this photo, perhaps thinking it was a university friend of Isaac or Sarah's. More photos of Isaac and Sarah, more *awwww*s.

A broken window. Some awkward laughs. Like the rose petal photo, it looked like a stock image, but it didn't matter, the message was clear – Vangie knew the whole story.

The broken window faded and the black-and-white exterior of Cowley Police Station came into focus, to guffaws from a couple of men at the back of the room. Nausea surged up inside me.

'What's the story there then, Zac?' a deep voice boomed.

I turned towards Isaac to see he was watching me, his expression stern but puzzled. 'Tell you later, mate,' he called out, with an attempt at joviality. More sniggers.

I turned back. The slideshow ended with a string of photos of the happy couple . . . at the villa in France . . . on a double lilo in the pool . . . chinking glasses on a tartan rug . . .

Fade to black, then . . . *Happy Anniversary xxxx*

There was applause and a smattering of whoops and cheers. Someone shouted *To Isaac and Sarah!* and everyone echoed it back, raising their glasses. I watched Sarah next to me take a hesitant sip of her champagne before glancing at me, her eyebrows dipping into a frown.

'I . . . I don't think I understand . . .' She stared at me a moment longer, before casting her gaze up and down, as if appraising me in some way. Then she set her glass on the coffee table and stood. 'I need to speak to Vangie.'

I wanted to run. I wanted to run to the front door, and out into the night. To get into my car and drive as far away as I could get. But something told me I couldn't do that. So I set my own glass down next to Sarah's, nodded to her parents, and followed her towards the back of the room. Towards Vangie and Isaac.

Chapter Twenty-Three

Sarah smiled and nodded at guests as she weaved her way to the back of the room, fielding compliments and well wishes. *Wonderful photos . . . Such happy memories . . . What a lovely thing for Vangie to do . . .* But I could tell from her tight smile she was distracted, not capable of absorbing the comments and their meanings.

When we reached Vangie, Isaac was whispering to her, a confused frown on his face. Vangie's arms were folded across her chest and she looked up at him defiantly.

'Vangie,' said Sarah, 'I don't understand those photos, and I don't know what's going on with you and Diana, but I really want someone to explain.' Her voice was almost pleading.

'Of course you do,' Vangie said, looking directly at me. 'Diana? Care to enlighten Sarah?'

The four of us stood in our little circle, a pocket of stillness amongst the jostling guests.

'Jesus!' I'd not heard Sarah sound so angry before. 'One of you better tell me what the hell is going on right now! This is our party . . . mine and Isaac's . . . and if there's something going on between you two that you need to get off your chests then bloody well spit it out.'

Vangie drew herself up and looked at me, her expression hard and full of hatred. 'I think we need to have a little chat with Diana, but I don't think here is the right place. Let's go outside.'

She spun towards the glass doors and marched off, Sarah casting me a wary glance as the three of us followed, Isaac loping along with his hands in his pockets like a child off to detention.

Vangie exited the marquee and turned towards the swimming pool, crossing the patch of grass and passing through the opening in the hedge. The pool glowed aquamarine, but the sun loungers were deserted. The temperature had dropped in the last couple of hours, and any guests who'd braved the cold earlier were now huddled in the marquee or the house. Damp night air bit at the bare skin on my arms. I wanted to go back inside and find my jacket, but knew I couldn't. This was happening now.

Vangie stopped and spun round to face Sarah. 'I'm so sorry, Sarah. I didn't want this to spoil your evening, but there are some things that need to be addressed . . . need to be said . . .'

'Does it need to be now, though? Right in the middle of our anniversary party?' Isaac stared at Vangie with an almost fearful expression. I knew what he was thinking. Whatever she was about to say, whatever revelations she had about me, I had some pretty explosive revelations of my own. But of course Vangie didn't know that.

'Yes, Isaac, it does need to happen now. This has gone on for long enough! I'm only doing this because I love you and Sarah. You're my best friends and I'd do anything for you. I'm doing this to protect you . . . to protect us all!' She looked wild, her eyes wide as she glared at each of us in turn.

'Protect us all from *what*?' said Sarah.

'From the liar in our midst!' she announced with a dramatic glare. 'Do you know,' she said, turning to me, 'I had a feeling about you from the very first time we met, at Eden House. Something just didn't add up. Call it a gut instinct, or intuition or something . . .'

'But you hired me to tutor Freddie—'

'Well, more fool me!' she shouted.

'Vangie, I think you should just calm—' said Isaac.

'Don't you dare!'

'OK, OK . . .' Isaac lifted his hands in surrender.

'So, I did a bit of digging,' Vangie continued. 'I didn't have a plan as such – it was more instinctual than that. Perhaps something from my days as a barrister . . . something kicked in and told me the questions I needed to ask. So I got in touch with an old colleague of mine. He's a part-time Law lecturer at Oxford University.' She waited a beat, watching me for a reaction.

I felt a faint tingling in my fingertips, but couldn't tell if it was from the cold, or from the anticipation of what I knew was coming.

'I asked him if, in the twenty-five years he'd been working there, he'd ever come across a student named Diana Malone. Of course he said no . . . He'd have come into contact with hundreds of students, and names come and go. I mentioned she would have studied English, rather than Law, and asked if he could check the alumni records for the name. It was very easy for him to do.' She smiled, pleased with herself. 'And do you know what he found? No one named Diana Malone has ever attended Oxford University.' Her eyes widened with satisfaction and she looked from Isaac to Sarah with a gleeful smile.

'I . . . I don't understand . . .' said Sarah, looking at me with a wounded expression.

'I did go to Oxford University,' I said, my voice weak.

'Oh, I know you did,' said Vangie. 'Don't worry, there's more. He wanted to know why I was searching for a past student, so I told him I was suspicious about a newcomer to our friendship circle. I said this newcomer's stories didn't ring true with me. She'd appeared out of nowhere, and despite no one else being able to see it, had latched on to my friends in a way that seemed almost parasitical. She gatecrashed social events and family holidays, she lurked around long after she should have left—'

'Hang on, that's not really fair—' Isaac interjected.

'And do you know what he said?' Vangie continued as if Isaac hadn't spoken.

I shook my head, cheeks burning hot with shame and fury.

'He said, "Are you sure you haven't misheard her name? Are you sure it's Diana, and not *Dinah*?"'

My stomach plummeted like I was on a rollercoaster. 'But . . . I . . . how . . .'

'Because he recognised the pattern of behaviour I'd described as being very similar to that of a Dinah Marshall. You see, *she* attended one year of an English degree from 2000 to 2001, but left before completing it. Diana Malone. Dinah Marshall. I just knew they had to be the same person. Especially after he told me all about Dinah.' She stopped talking and made eye contact with each of us in turn, her jaw clenched defiantly. She was enjoying this.

Isaac and Sarah both looked at me then, and I couldn't bear it. I had to look down at my feet, even though I knew that was as good as an admission.

'What did he tell you?' said Sarah, her voice hard and emotionless.

Vangie took a deep breath, relishing the exhale before continuing. 'He told me that Professor Christopher Thorpe was one of his closest friends all those years ago. And Edward, my colleague, had front row seats to the whole drama.'

'What drama?' Despite Isaac's previous attempts to silence Vangie, he'd clearly become more invested in this story the more Vangie told.

'Christopher Thorpe, it seems, was plagued by a first-year student who became completely obsessed with him during her first semester.'

Indignation flared inside me. 'That's not how it—'

'Of course, it wasn't unusual for students to develop crushes on their lecturers – everyone knows that's a tale as old as time. But in this instance the crush became somewhat out of control. Didn't it, *Dinah*?'

I felt my lips quivering as I tried to speak, the tingling in my fingers spreading up my arms. 'That's not what happened. It wasn't like that. Christopher and I were in a relationship—'

'A *relationship*?' Vangie's face twisted into a disbelieving sneer and she threw her head back and laughed, her whole body seeming to shake with it. 'What kind of a *relationship* involves a student breaking into a lecturer's house and scattering rose petals everywhere whilst his wife is out? Climbing naked into their marital bed? Do those sound like the actions of someone who's in a relationship? Or someone who's a mentally unstable stalker?'

'I was not stalking him!' My voice was not my own, it was vicious and shrill.

Vangie took a step back, gaping at Sarah and Isaac as if I was dangerous. As if my outburst was proof of how unhinged I was. She was in full barrister mode at this point, examining a witness, pinpointing weaknesses, exploiting emotions.

'We . . . we *were* in a relationship.' I took two deep breaths. *Calm, stay calm. She wants you to lose it. Don't let her play you like this.* 'We were in a mutually consensual relationship. Yes, it was an affair, and no, his wife didn't know about us. But I didn't break into his house . . . I borrowed a spare key . . . it was supposed to be a surprise because I knew his wife was away . . .'

'But she wasn't away, was she? Her plans had been cancelled, so she came home early and found you sprawled on their bed, surrounded by rose petals. God, that must have been the most excruciatingly embarrassing moment . . .' She screwed up her face as she peered at me through the slits of her eyes.

I felt my own eyes stinging, a hard lump forming in my throat.

'Or was it?' she said. 'Perhaps a more embarrassing moment was being thrown half-naked from their house by Mrs Thorpe? Or perhaps it was some weeks later when you returned to the house to vandalise it—'

'I didn't! I just threw—' *Calm, calm.* 'I was just trying to get Christopher's attention . . . I didn't mean to break the window. It was an accident!'

'Why were you trying to get his attention? Why didn't you just call him on the phone?'

'Because . . . because he wasn't returning my calls . . .' My voice trailed off. Once again she'd handed me the rope to hang myself. What kind of freak threw stones at someone's window when they didn't answer their phone?

'So then, understandably, Mrs Thorpe called the police, didn't she? You were taken in handcuffs to the station because when the officers arrived you went berserk and resisted arrest. And that's when Mr and Mrs Thorpe filed for a restraining order against you, thus terminating your *relationship* with Christopher Thorpe, and your time at Oxford University.'

She straightened up, like a peacock displaying her beautiful plumage. Isaac and Sarah stared at me as if they'd never seen me before. Isaac frowned, and Sarah's face bore a wide-eyed almost fearful expression. I swallowed, willing myself not to be sick.

'But of course, my investigations didn't end there,' Vangie continued with relish. 'I did a simple Google search for *Dinah Marshall* and hey presto, there you were. Of course, you don't really do social media yourself, do you? But Megan does. Megan Finch had a wonderful weekend away with her university friends recently, did you know that, Sarah? And she very thoughtfully tagged each of them in a recent Facebook post.'

Sarah tore her eyes from me and gazed at Vangie as if stunned. 'Why do I know that name? Megan Finch?'

'Because she's the woman who booked Riverdean in June for a weekend whilst you were in Portugal.'

'Yes . . . yes, that's right,' said Sarah. 'She booked for four guests, two nights.'

'And guess who the fourth guest was?' Vangie beamed as she asked this question.

All eyes turned towards me.

I swallowed. 'It was just a last-minute . . . I wasn't supposed to . . .' But of course all my protestations were in vain. What did it matter why I'd come to Riverdean, or who had cancelled? The only thing that mattered was that I'd lied.

'You'd been to the house before?' I could only glance at Isaac as he said this, because his face was incredulous. Appalled.

I looked down, squeezing my eyelids together and shaking my head. I opened them to see a fat teardrop spatter onto the ground and seep into the flagstones. I wanted to double over, then sink to the floor, then disappear through the cracks. I wanted to slip into the glowing water of the swimming pool, and never surface. Of all the excruciating moments in my life, this was the worst.

'But . . .' Sarah sounded like she was trying to catch her breath. 'But we met you for the first time at Eden House?'

'Yes.' I nodded, looking up, pleading, a chink of light, a new lie that could save the old. 'That's right . . . I bumped into you at Eden House and it was only after that night I realised where you lived and—'

'What absolute bullshit,' Vangie said, her savage grin widening. 'You found us. I don't know how you tracked us down, but you knew we'd be at Eden House that night. You stalked us, just like you stalked Christopher Thorpe.'

'No! It wasn't like that!' But what else could I say? How could I make them understand that I'd never wanted anything from them other than friendship. Approval. Love. I didn't want to hurt anyone . . . I just wanted to be in their lives. Just like I'd wanted to be in Christopher's. My eyes darted frantically between Isaac and Sarah, desperate for them to see me – see the real me. Their friend. But all I saw on Sarah's face was horror. All I saw on Isaac's was pity.

The sickness squirmed in my stomach, writhing around and twisting my insides into knots. Cam's words from earlier still reverberated inside me, the shame of my betrayal of her still raw. My heart still ached from what she'd said about Isaac . . . the realisation that of course she was right . . . of course I wasn't special. Of course I was only here because I was needy and adoring, and Isaac liked that. And now I'd had every embarrassment of my life laid out in front of me by the woman who hated me most of all, in front of the people I'd come to love. My only friends. Every part of me felt bruised, from my skin to my heart.

'I . . . I just can't believe it.' Sarah's voice was small and breathy. An appalled whisper. 'Why? I mean . . . this is just such awful, crazy behaviour . . . and after I told you in France how difficult we found it to trust people . . . How could you be so deceitful?'

I stared at Sarah as these words of disgust poured from her lips, and something inside me shifted. I turned to Vangie, the triumphant smirk curving her blood-red lips, and I had a flash of a memory. Those same lips twisted in ecstasy. That same lipstick smeared across her jaw. The nausea subsided as a hot ball of anger grew bigger and bigger, taking over my insides as if my blood were boiling in my veins.

Vangie is calling me a liar. Vangie is calling me disloyal. How fucking dare she?

I glanced at Isaac, and he looked terrified. The pity had gone, perhaps wiped away by something he was seeing in my own face. I looked from him to Vangie, and felt my mouth opening, my own lips curling upwards. A monosyllabic laugh erupted from me, loud and manic. Sarah took a step back like someone scared of a wild animal. Vangie's smile faltered.

'You—' Another laugh jolted through me, making it hard to speak. I felt light-headed. I was beside myself, out of control, unable to feel anything but sheer fury at Vangie's hypocrisy. 'You want to talk about deceit, Sarah? You want to talk about people who *betray your trust*?'

Sarah's face flickered with confusion.

'Diana . . .' Isaac's voice was a warning. I looked at him and he shook his head.

'It's too late, Isaac. Cam knows. I didn't tell her, but she knows.'

Isaac didn't speak, but squeezed his eyes shut. He knew what was coming just as I'd known what was coming when Vangie marched us out here. Because there was no reason not to say it now. It was all going to come out anyway. At least if I said it here, now, I could have the satisfaction of wiping that smug grin off Vangie's face.

I turned to Vangie, relishing the confusion now set on her features as her gaze flickered between me and Isaac. 'What are you talking about?' she snapped.

'I'm talking about the biggest betrayal of all, Vangie. I'm talking about you droning on and on about protecting loved ones, and the value of friendship, and the importance of Sarah in your life . . . while all the time you've been fucking her husband.'

Vangie's face twitched, the skin shining pale blue in the light from the pool. Isaac crumpled onto a sun lounger, leaning forwards and running his hands through his hair and whispering *shit, shit, shit,* over and over.

Sarah's eyes were huge and round, her mouth opening and closing as she gaped at Isaac, then at Vangie.

'Sarah . . .' Vangie's voice was a whisper, as if she didn't mean to be heard.

'I . . . I don't understand . . .' Sarah looked like a lost little girl as she stepped backwards, her head shaking as if of its own volition. 'You and Isaac?'

Vangie turned to me, her face contorted with hatred. 'You fucking *bitch*!'

My manic laugh was back. 'I'm sorry, Vangie – are you calling *me* a bitch?' I wanted to say more, but staring back at her livid face, at Sarah's stunned expression, at Isaac's crumpled form, I knew I didn't have to.

I backed away, towards the hedge that bordered the pool.

'I just can't . . .' Sarah whispered.

Isaac stood up, took a step towards her. 'Sarah, please—'

'Don't you come any closer to me!' She raised her hands in defence.

'Sarah,' Vangie whined, 'you need to know that—'

'Don't you fucking dare tell me what I need to know!' Sarah hissed.

I turned away, and walked back towards the marquee. When you've thrown a grenade, the best thing to do is get as far away as possible. I pushed through the tent, past the raucous voices of the tipsy guests, past the rattling cocktail shaker in the barman's hands. I kept my head down, not wanting to engage with anyone. My thoughts were blurry and unfocused as they sped through my brain. What just happened? What did this mean for us all?

Inside the downstairs toilet, I locked the door and leaned against it with my eyes shut.

They knew. They knew everything. All about my past, about my lies, my real name, my visit to the house, and now Sarah knew about Isaac and Vangie. My heart was like a bass drum in my chest, pulsating against the fabric of my dress, making my whole body quiver. My fingers were numb from the adrenalin, my legs shaking. I ran my hands under warm water, hoping to get some feeling back. Then I lowered myself onto the toilet seat, waiting for the rushing sound in my ears to stop.

Cam would be furious with me. She'd told me to let her deal with this. She didn't want to make a scene here tonight, for her mother's sake. And I'd gone and done just that. I wondered where she was, where she'd gone after she'd screamed at me in the bedroom.

I tried to slow my breathing, to compose myself. I looked around the room, trying to focus on different photographs to distract my mind from its racing thoughts. It worked because I immediately noticed a photo I'd not seen before. It was next to the beach photo and must have been newly placed there, because it was of everyone in the villa in France. It was of the four of them, Isaac in his chino shorts, his face golden from the sun, Sarah in a floaty blue dress, her hair falling in soft waves. Duncan was wearing his Mickey Mouse trunks, and had his laptop still clamped under one arm, and Vangie sported a black one-piece and a scarlet smile. They held cocktails aloft towards the camera.

My gaze returned to the beach photo, the photo of Sarah, Isaac and Cam, which portrayed Isaac as a father figure, despite Cam's real father still being alive at that point. I remembered the inscription on the back: *All our dreams can come true, if we have the courage to pursue them.*

Something flickered at the back of my brain then – the same thing had happened when I'd first read that quote on the back of the photo. I'd recognised it from somewhere, but hadn't been able to place it. Something stirred again, just at the edge of my consciousness. It tickled like a hair caught in a shirt . . . I couldn't quite reach it, but it was there. Now I looked at the new photo next to it, the tickle grew into an itch. There was something about these photos, something that linked them, but I couldn't work it out.

Thinking about the beach photo turned my mind towards Cam again. Perhaps I should try to find her – warn her of what I'd done, and that Sarah knew. I imagined her sitting alone on the end of the jetty, dangling her feet in the freezing water, silent tears sliding down her cheeks as she thought about Jamie and the anniversary of his death. But that didn't sound like Cam. She'd been furious. She'd seemed as if she was about to leap into action. *I'll deal with this.* Those weren't the words of someone about to skulk off alone to cry.

I looked back at the photos, my eyes darting from one to the other. The beach, the villa, the beach, the villa.

The threads of several seemingly unrelated thoughts then came together, the ends finding each other and twisting themselves around and around into a thick spiral . . . a mobile phone, a locked door, a photograph, a gift. Then it was there. I felt my breath freeze in my lungs as every hair on my body stood on end.

No. No, this was ridiculous, this was stupid, I was being crazy.

Before I could decide what to do, a bolt of pure adrenalin had me on my feet. I saw my hands reach out and grab the beach photo from the wall. I had no time, there was no time. I raised my arm and smashed the frame down on the sink, sending shards of glass in all directions.

'Are you OK in there?' A voice from the corridor.

I shook the frame so the loose glass fell out, splintered fragments stinging my fingers as I pushed them aside. Freeing the photo I tossed the frame into the sink, unlocked the door, and ran.

Chapter Twenty-Four

The house was thick with people, music and chatter. I pushed through, ignoring the withering glances and disgruntled tutting of the guests. Outside I sped up again, desperately hoping they were still by the pool. I rounded the hedge and collided with Isaac.

'Shit!' He drew back.

Sarah was sitting on a sun lounger, sobbing, Vangie pacing in front of her. They both looked up as I steered myself around Isaac and stumbled onto the patio.

'What the fuck are you doing here?' Vangie said. 'No one wants to hear anything you've got to say!'

'This photo!' I said, waving it in the air. 'It's . . . it's from the downstairs toilet . . .' I knew I looked like a lunatic, my movements too wild, my voice too loud.

'Diana . . . or whatever your name is . . .' Sarah's face was blotchy and tear-streaked. 'You need to leave right now.'

'Not until I've said this. This is important.'

'Diana . . .' Isaac said it like a warning. 'We need space now. You have to—'

I pushed the photo in front of his face. 'Who wrote the inscription on the back of this photo?'

'What the fuck does that matter?' he snapped, looking at me like I was mad.

I had to make sense. I had to make them see what I saw. I turned towards Sarah, collapsing on the floor in front of her and holding the photo up. 'When I first saw this inscription, I thought it was because Isaac had given this photo to you as a gift . . . *All our dreams can come true, if we have the courage to pursue them.* That's romantic, right?'

Sarah frowned at me, her face wrinkled with disgust. 'I haven't seen that message, and I don't know who wrote it! Now can you just leave us alone!'

'That's what I thought.' I felt myself nodding mania-cally, willing myself to calm down, to seem credible. I spun around to face Isaac. 'But you know who wrote it, because the photo was a present for *you*. The quote was for *you*. And I think it was written by the same person who took the photo.'

Isaac squinted at me as if I were a page covered in very small writing. 'I think we need to call someone . . . I don't think you're OK.'

'Just tell me who took the photo!' My voice came out shrill and hysterical and there was nothing I could do about it.

'Duncan!' he shouted back at me. 'Duncan, OK? He took the photo of us on the beach, and wrote the inscrip-tion on the back and gave it to me as a gift. Is that what you wanted to hear? Is that what's so important right now?'

I took a step back, my heart hammering in every cell of my body, echoing around my brain, throbbing against my skull.

'Duncan gave you that book in the living room – the Walt Disney biography. That's where I first read the quote. The shorts Duncan was wearing . . . the Mickey Mouse trunks . . . that's how I made the connection.'

'The swimming trunks were just a joke present,' Isaac said. 'Diana, you need to stop, OK?'

'But it's not a joke, Isaac.' I stared into his eyes, my gaze as steady and serious as I could make it. 'This is not a joke.'

The three of them fell silent, and stared at me in mute terror. They were scared of me. I had silenced them with my madness. But I knew I wasn't mad. I knew I had to follow this through.

I addressed Isaac again, trying to keep my voice even. 'The night Jamie Kerr died . . . you'd confiscated Cam's phone?'

'Yes.' He gave an exasperated shrug.

'And where did you put it? Cam said you "locked it away" somewhere.'

'Oh, for fuck's sake. In my office! Why?'

'The office that Duncan was using tonight? Was he working in there that night too?'

'For fuck's sake, *Dinah*!' Vangie stood and took a step towards me. 'I've had enough of this. I'm calling someone to get you removed. You're fucking insane.' She strode past me, then disappeared around the corner.

I ignored her and continued. 'Cam has always thought that you saw that message from Jamie on her phone. The one that said he'd seen something incriminating.'

'I never even looked at her bloody phone!' Isaac shouted. 'I just threw it in the office and locked the door!'

I nodded, willing them both to believe me, to understand. 'Then you gave the key to Duncan so he could work in there. It was Duncan who saw the message on Cam's phone. And I think he either already knew about the affair, or he went to meet Jamie by the lake, and Jamie told him.'

Sarah's face contorted as if she was in pain. 'Duncan knew about the affair? All this time?' She began sobbing again.

'Sarah, that's not the point . . . the point is that Duncan didn't want *you* to find out.' My voice was harsh, sympathy being the last thing I could offer at that moment. In desperation I turned to Isaac. 'The most important thing in the world to Duncan is Acanthus. Like you said to me in France, without Sarah, Acanthus crumbles. He couldn't let Sarah find out.'

Isaac's face was grey, like all the blood had seeped out of it. That's when I knew he was listening to me.

He began shaking his head, biting his bottom lip. He raised his hand and tugged at his hair. 'No . . . no . . . I mean, he's driven. He's very driven. But no . . . that can't . . .' It was as if he was talking to himself, trying to convince himself of his own words.

'He made you and Sarah pose on that beach with Cam, didn't he? He knew Sarah and her family were wealthy, and could probably sense a connection between the two of you even before Archie died.'

'That's not fair,' Sarah wailed. 'Nothing ever happened between Isaac and me whilst Archie was alive!'

'I know, I know . . . and it never could. You would never have left Archie. Duncan knew that.' I looked at both of them, hoping they'd see what I saw. '*All our dreams can come true, if we have the courage to pursue them. Not your*

327

dreams as a couple . . . but Duncan and Isaac's dreams. And Duncan was the one who pursued them.'

Now it was Sarah's turn to shake her head, her eyes wide and watery. 'But no one could have known that Archie was going to . . . that he'd have that awful accident . . .'

'Just like no one could have known Jamie would have that awful accident?' I hadn't meant to shout but I needed them to listen.

I left the words hanging between us, looking from one face to the other, hoping that now they saw everything I saw, even if they didn't believe it yet. Neither of them spoke, they just stared at me, and I couldn't work out if they were processing what I'd said, or whether, like Vangie, they thought I was crazy.

'Where's Cam?' I asked.

Sarah flinched at her daughter's name. 'Why? Why are you asking that?' Her delirious expression was replaced by a frantic, wild look.

'I saw her,' Isaac said quietly. 'She was in the hallway for the slideshow . . . talking to Duncan.'

Panic sluiced through me. 'What happened then?'

Isaac's eyes darted between me and Sarah. 'She . . . she whispered something to him and they walked towards the front door. They must have gone outside.'

Cam had told him. She'd decided she didn't want to make a scene, so she'd gone to the only other person who needed to know, whom she could rely upon to be as furious and sickened by the revelation as she was. Duncan knew that Cam knew.

I didn't wait to ask if they were coming with me. I ran back towards the marquee, aware of Isaac and Sarah following behind. We pushed through the crowded tent and the conservatory, on towards the hallway and out of the front door. The driveway was still crammed with cars, and the gate was shut.

'Their car's still here,' said Isaac, a hint of relief in his voice.

'But, I don't understand,' Sarah said, her face a picture of panic as her eyes roamed the driveway as if for clues. 'Are you saying Cam and Duncan have gone somewhere?' It was as if Sarah was functioning in a dream state. She knew she needed to be worried but she couldn't work out why.

Isaac took his phone from his pocket and called Cam's number, then shook his head. 'Straight to voicemail.'

Could they have walked somewhere? Out into the lanes, or into the forest?

No. In a flash, I knew where Cam would have taken Duncan to talk. But she'd have taken one look at the crush of guests, all watching the slideshow, and decided there was a quicker, less noticeable way to get there.

'Follow me.' I ran onto the gravel driveway, weaving between parked cars, and around the side of the house. We came out in the back garden next to the marquee, and ran across the grass to the darkened copse that led to the lake. For the second time that night I trampled through the undergrowth. I felt for my phone but realised I must have left it back at the house.

I could hear Sarah and Isaac striding after me, hear Sarah's soft panting and confused whispers. 'Where's Cam? Why are we going to the lake?' But it was as if she was talking to herself, not expecting answers.

'Diana, you can't be serious about this,' Isaac hissed behind me. '. . . This is just absolutely bloody insane.'

But I'd seen his expression by the pool. I'd seen my theory hit home, and leech the blood from his face. Isaac knew Duncan better than anyone, and it was Isaac's reaction in that moment that had finally convinced me my 'insane' theory might actually be true.

I didn't answer Isaac because I didn't have to. We'd come out of the cover of trees, and the moonlit lake lay in front of us like a vast mirror. And in the centre of the lake was the small, rotting boat I'd seen resting in the reeds next to the jetty, the first time I'd swum here. And standing on the boat, a single oar clenched in his hand, looking down at something in the hull, was Duncan. The sky above was clear and a full white moon shone down, casting the lake and the boat in silver. It was like looking at a black-and-white photo.

'Duncan?' called Sarah from the foot of the jetty.

Duncan's head snapped up. The boat was perhaps thirty metres from the end of the jetty, but even from that distance I could see a look of horror flash across his face. 'What are you doing here?' His voice was unlike I'd ever heard it – hard and cold.

'What the fuck are you doing, Duncan?' Isaac's words were tinged with panic. 'Why are you in the middle of the lake?' He stepped in front of Sarah as he spoke, walking slowly down the jetty.

Duncan sighed, his shoulders slumping as he looked down. He rubbed a palm up and down over his face, then through his hair. 'You're not supposed to be here.'

I walked forwards until I was shoulder to shoulder with Isaac. 'Where's Cam, Duncan?'

There was a soft moaning sound, and my stomach lurched as, from the hull of the boat, the fingers of a hand slid into view, their grip tightening on the side of the boat.

'Cam!' Sarah's cry pierced the cold air, sending birds flapping up from the black trees surrounding us. She ran to the end of the jetty, but Isaac ran after her, grabbing her dress and pulling her back.

'Duncan, what the fuck?' I'd never heard Isaac's voice like that before, a panicked falsetto breaking through.

'Cam!' Sarah struggled against Isaac's chest.

'Will you just shut up! Both of you!' Duncan shouted. The boat rocked under him with the force of his words. 'It . . . it was just an accident. We were in the boat and Cam fell and hit her head. Isn't that right, Cam? Do you remember that happening?' He crouched down and pulled her into view. Her shoulders slouched and her hair fell across her face.

Sarah whimpered, reaching out her arms towards the boat.

'Duncan, mate . . .' Isaac had changed tack. His words were slow and clear. 'Maybe just row the boat back here and we can all head back to the house and get Cam's head looked at . . . and it'll all be OK. Yeah?'

Duncan didn't respond. He remained crouched in front of Cam, and appeared to be whispering something to her. I knew what he would be saying. He was bargaining. He was trying to get her to agree not to say anything to Sarah.

Cam shook her head. 'Fuck you!' she shouted, and made to stand up, but Duncan grabbed her by the shoulders and pushed her back. She stumbled on the bench seat and fell with a smack into the bow.

Sarah screamed, and I rushed forwards, joining her and Isaac at the end of the jetty.

'Duncan!' I called. 'Sarah knows everything! She knows about Isaac and Vangie. And it's all OK.'

Duncan stood, gaping at us, his hands raised to his head, a look of despair on his round, white face.

Keeping my eyes on Duncan, I reached a hand towards Sarah and found hers, squeezing it tightly in my fist. *Go along with this.*

'Duncan—' I tried to keep my voice level '—Acanthus is safe. Sarah's not going to tell her parents, and she's not going to do anything that will endanger the company. Isn't that right, Sarah?'

I looked at Sarah, her distraught face angled towards her daughter, her breath coming in jagged gasps.

Isaac looked at me, then at his wife. 'Sarah,' he said. She turned to him as if she'd only just noticed him standing there. 'Tell Duncan that everything's going to be OK with Acanthus.'

She nodded, turning back to face the boat. 'Yes. Yes, Duncan, you don't have to worry about Acanthus.' Her voice was a desperate whimper. 'We can all work this out amicably. So you can bring Cam back now.' The last words descended into sobs.

'Theoretically that sounds great, Sarah, but unfortunately I don't think your upstart of a daughter is going to be that keen on keeping this secret from her grandparents.'

He leaned forwards and pulled Cam to her feet like she was a rag doll. She writhed against him and the boat rocked, drifting to the right.

'Cam, *please*!' I shouted. 'Tell him you're not going to say anything to your grandparents. Tell him everything will stay just as it is.'

'OK!' she shrieked, hunching her shoulders as Duncan gripped the back of her neck. 'I'm not going to say anything to Nan and Grandpa. I just . . .' It was the first time her voice had held a quiver. 'I just needed Mum to know, that's all.' She tried to move her head to the side so she could look at Duncan, and he peered back, his face pressed close to hers. 'I promise I won't say anything.'

Duncan pushed her and she collapsed back onto the bench, the boat spinning around in a circle, sending silver ripples into the rushes.

He raised his hands to his head again, a demented stare on his face as he looked down at the black water. He shook his head, eyes darting manically from side to side. 'No, no. You see, I don't believe you . . . just like I didn't believe Jamie.'

There was a moment of silence, the words suspended in the silvery air. Then a sound splintered the darkness. A ferocious roar erupted from Cam, and she propelled herself from the end of the boat, Duncan turned just in time to grab her shoulders before she could push him over. Her arms flailed, her fingers clawing at his face as she screamed. But he was too strong for her. He gave a shove, sending her back into the bow of the boat. She gripped the sides, heaving herself up again, but Duncan had already seized the oar. And as Cam launched herself towards him again, he brought it up in a swift arc through the air, the end of it catching her full in the side of the face with a loud crack, her head jerking sideways before she collapsed, sprawled over the bench, unmoving.

'No!' Sarah's feral scream tore at every nerve in my body. It was jagged and desperate, and like nothing I'd ever heard before. She made to run off the end of the jetty, towards her motionless daughter, but Isaac grabbed her again, pinning her arms to her sides.

Duncan bent down and pulled at Cam, manoeuvring her towards the side of the boat. He heaved her shoulders up so her head dangled over the side.

'Duncan!' Isaac shouted, his voice bordering on the hysterical now. 'Don't do anything stupid—'

'I need to *think*, Isaac!' He sounded mad. His gaze darted about again, as if trying to work out an impossible puzzle. But he couldn't do it. He'd completely lost the ability to reason.

I looked at the expanse of water between the jetty and the boat, trying to calculate how quickly someone could swim that distance. Not quickly enough. If Cam went under there was no way even the fastest swimmer would get to her before she drowned.

Duncan slumped next to Cam. His arm rested on her back as her head lolled like a puppet over the side of the boat, the fingers of her left hand trailing in the water. 'Fuck you, Isaac! You've made this so difficult for me, haven't you?'

'I . . . I have, and I'm sorry.' He sounded like he was about to cry, his voice weak and pleading. 'But come back to the jetty and we can talk about it.'

'No! You see, I don't have anything to bargain with if I come back. It's simple boardroom power tactics, you know that, Isaac. Here . . .' He nodded his head towards Cam's lifeless figure, '. . . I have power. Because if I slung her over the side right now, she'd sink like a stone, wouldn't she?'

Sarah wailed. 'Please, Duncan, please . . . Please don't hurt Cam. Don't hurt my baby . . .' Her words descended once again into sobs and she crumpled to the floor.

'We had the perfect opportunity to build an empire . . . Have a life most people can only dream of.'

'We do, Dunc. We *do* have that life . . . and that's because of you, and how brilliant you are.' Isaac's tone was that of a father reassuring a hysterical child.

I realised this might be my only chance. Duncan was busy with Isaac, and Sarah was sobbing on the floor. Duncan had no interest in me or what I had to say, so I seized the moment. I kept Isaac and Sarah's figures in front of me as I crept backwards towards the start of the jetty.

'Why do you make this extra work for me? Even when I found Sarah for you, you had to make things hard. *Oh, she's married. Oh, we're just friends.* You're so bloody good at the shmoozing . . . Why could you never see the big picture, and what was really important?'

As I slunk sideways towards a thicket of trees, I watched Isaac's distraught face. 'I don't know, mate.' He gave a pathetic shrug. 'I guess I'm just not as ambitious as you. I just . . . I don't take things as seriously as you, and I'm sorry.'

'Yes! Yes, that's it. You don't take things seriously. You're too busy joking and partying. You leave me to do all the heavy-lifting, completely oblivious – not only to the big stuff, like making sure you and Sarah got together, but to the havoc you're creating in your wake. I mean . . . Shagging my wife?'

'Listen, I'm so sorry. Vangie and I aren't—'

'Oh, for fuck's sake,' he shouted, impatiently. 'You don't get it, do you? I don't give a shit about you and Vangie. Whether you're in love, or just shagging, or any of that bullshit. Why does no one seem to understand that the only thing that has ever been important is that *Sarah* is happy? Why is it only Cam who gets that? It's as she explained in France – the only reason either of us have what we have . . . the only reason Acanthus exists . . . is because of Sarah. Don't you understand that?'

Once I was hidden by the darkness of the trees, I crept along the curve of the lake. I was now observing the conversation in profile, and their words were more distant and muffled.

'I guess I just never felt that Acanthus was the most impor—' Isaac stopped himself and shrugged.

Duncan started laughing then, but it wasn't the jolly belly laugh I was used to. It was a manic high-pitched laugh. 'Oh my God! You didn't realise Acanthus was *important*?' The last word came out as more of a screech.

'No! That's not what I meant! I just . . . I suppose there were other things I was focused on back at the beginning, and I hadn't really—'

'What, your pathetic little cocktail business you were going to start up with Sarah's husband?' The frenzied laughter was back. 'Archie and his wanky whiskey? You were going to completely cut me out of that, weren't you? After it had been the two of us all through uni, you and Archie were just going to set that crappy little bar up together and leave me to rot.'

'Mate, it wasn't like that. It wasn't your thing. We weren't trying to leave you out of anything, it's just—' Isaac ran his hands through his hair, eyes scouring the surface of the lake as if the right thing to say might be there.

'Don't worry, *mate*. I understand. That was just another moment when good old Duncan had to swoop in and make sure his clueless mate was set along the right path.'

I was almost alongside the boat now, as I watched Isaac sink to the floor and wrap his arms around Sarah. 'Duncan, how's Cam doing?' he said. 'Can you check she's OK? Please?'

Duncan shook his head, placing his fingers to Cam's neck as her head still lolled over the edge of the boat. 'I mean, she's out cold. Bit of a pulse going on there, but not sure how much longer that's going to last.'

Sarah cried out and stood up. Isaac stood too and pulled her back again.

'Duncan, she needs an ambulance.'

'Either of you reach for your phones and I'll chuck her over the edge, and when I say something like that, I mean it, OK?'

'Can I come and get her?' Isaac said. He began unbuttoning his shirt. 'I'll just swim over and get her, and you can stay on the boat – no one will touch you.'

'Not going to work, sorry.' With a sigh, Duncan pulled Cam back into the boat. I felt a surge of relief, but then, with disturbing calmness, he took hold of her legs and heaved them over the side, into the water, her upper body dragged quickly after her by the weight. Sarah screamed. Just before Cam's head went under, Duncan grabbed the shoulders of her jumper, leaning over the side himself to keep her face just above the surface.

'I think I need some assurances before we proceed.' He spoke with the calm confidence of someone in a business meeting.

'Anything, please, Duncan! Please!' Sarah wailed.

I unbuckled the straps of my shoes before kicking them off. Then I walked a few metres further, making sure the boat was in front of me, and that Duncan wouldn't spot me in his peripheral vision.

The mud was thicker at the edge of the bank. Here, the earth gave way to long rushes that pushed up through the surface of the lake. I lowered myself onto the slick ground, feeling my dress stick to my legs. I slid my feet, then my calves into the freezing water, my skin screaming as the cold enveloped me. The lake bed oozed between my toes and my skirt floated up around me as I waded deeper. Cold cut through me like a knife. It bit into every pore and cell. I willed myself to stay silent, not to gasp or cry out.

Reeds tangled around my legs and I ducked down, submerging my shoulders so I could wrench myself free. I needed to get further out, so I could swim. Tearing the rope-like strands from my skin, I kicked away from the bank. I felt my muscles twitch and shudder in the icy water as I tried to keep my strokes submerged, desperate not to make a sound.

'You don't need to hurt Cam, Duncan. She's got nothing to do with Acanthus.'

'She's got everything to do with Acanthus! One word to her grandparents and we're through, Isaac! Don't you get it?'

I slipped through the water, towards the boat, all the time trying to focus on what I needed to do, and not let my thoughts be drowned out by the blood-numbing cold that swamped my senses, causing my pulse to throb against my skull. If Isaac and Sarah could see me approaching the boat, they didn't give any sign of it.

'No, no, no.' I could hear Duncan's voice, but I couldn't see him as the rotting wooden hull loomed in front of me, its flaking paint glowing white in the moonlight.

I trod water with my face close to the hull, the water lapping against the wood. I made my way around the boat, trying not to touch it in case I gave myself away. If I could reach Cam without Duncan noticing, perhaps I could grab her. But would he launch himself after us? Would we all drown? Edging around the back of the boat, I peered around the side. Duncan's white fists held onto the shoulders of Cam's black jumper, and her head lolled forwards. Her hair fell in straggles like a weeping willow, and her nose and mouth dipped in and out of the water as Duncan adjusted his position.

Isaac called out again. 'If you hurt Cam, nothing will get sorted out, Duncan. Sarah will never forgive you.'

'I hear what you're saying . . . maybe you're right.' His voice vibrated through the wooden slats of the boat as my cheek brushed against its rough surface. 'Maybe Sarah's a problem too.' This last sentence was quieter, as if he was talking to himself, but Isaac still heard it.

'No, no. That's not what I was saying!'

'Sorry, mate. I think they've both got to go.'

Before my brain could process these words, the boat gave a violent lurch. I heard Sarah scream as Duncan plunged his fists down, Cam's shoulders then her head disappearing under the water.

'No!' I shouted. Duncan started, Cam's face bobbing back up as he twisted to glare at me. I pulled on the side of the hull, the muscles in my arms burning with the exertion. Once my upper body was high enough, I grabbed at the bench, dragging myself into the boat and collapsing in a heavy heap next to Duncan's legs.

He let go of Cam and sprang to his feet. I watched, horror-struck, as she slipped silently under the water. I turned to Duncan, watched his fury-filled eyes as he raised his arms towards me. Then I saw it. The oar he'd used to hit Cam was lying across the bench. I stooped to grab it, Duncan stumbling towards me. I raised it over my shoulder and, as he lurched forwards, brought it down with a sickening crunch on the top of his head. I watched his stunned eyes grow wide and his legs buckle, but didn't wait any longer. I hurled myself head first over the side of the boat, right next to the spot where I'd seen Cam disappear, the cold and the darkness enveloping me in a freezing, silent world.

I opened my eyes and they burned against the frigid water, the full moon a blurry silver disc, warped and distorted above. I looked down, and there it was. A dusting of silver light sprinkled on golden hair. I pushed down through the water, muscles screaming as I reached out, stretching as far as I could. My fingertips found the strands of gold and I twisted and pulled. I reached again, fists closing around the sodden fabric of her jumper, feeling the weight of her body lifting as my legs thrashed against the icy water, dragging her up and up until we broke the surface.

Her eyes were closed, her eyelids blue-veined. Lying back, I put my arms under her arms and kicked and kicked, vaguely aware now that the screaming sound wasn't the blood rushing in my ears, or the pain in my head from the cold, but Sarah from the end of the jetty. She seemed so far away. I had to keep going, keep kicking.

Then someone else was there, someone taking her from me. I screamed, grabbing her tighter.

'It's me! Let me take her!' Isaac was in the water next to me. He scooped her from me and swam with her towards the jetty, holding her with one arm and slicing through the water with the other. Sarah leaned over, grasping for Cam as Isaac pushed her up.

Then there were people running through the trees, two people with a stretcher, someone with a big green bag. At last I arrived, numb, at the jetty and looked up, not knowing if I had enough strength to pull myself out. Feeling my muscles like frozen lead under the water. I felt hands tugging on my arms, gripping me, hauling me out of the water. A blanket wrapped around me. An arm around my shoulder. A light shining in my eyes.

I looked back towards the lake and it was as still as glass again, except for the moonlit boat making silent spirals towards the distant trees.

Chapter Twenty-Five

They found the body the next day. I'd killed him. Or at least, I was certain the way I'd struck him had caused him to fall into the water and drown. The police, who'd released me the night before, called me in for further questioning, but I couldn't offer anything other than what I'd originally told them . . . The truth. So I waited and waited, knowing they would be looking at my police record . . . the stalking of Christopher Thorpe, the criminal damage, the restraining order . . . And that they'd soon begin the refrain I was now so used to. *She's a liar. She's unhinged. She's dangerous.*

After several hours then, imagine my surprise when a crumpled-looking detective with greying stubble entered the room and announced I was to be released immediately. When I asked why, he told me mobile phone footage had been handed over, showing the events at the lake. The detective and his superiors had reviewed my actions, which they said showed clear *self-defence*, and *defence of another*. The video apparently also showed a stunned but conscious Duncan hauling himself up and launching himself off the boat several seconds after I'd jumped in to save Cam, in an apparent attempt to come after us. He just hadn't resurfaced. The detective said these events were highly unlikely to result in criminal charges being brought against me, and although the footage would have to be reviewed for the coroner's inquest, they saw no reason to detain me. I asked who had supplied the footage, and they told me it was the same person who'd called the police and ambulance services – a Mrs Evangeline Slade.

Vangie had been in the middle of the living room trying to discreetly identify someone who could eject me from the party, when Isaac, Sarah and I had pushed through and headed for the front door. She'd followed us around the side of the house and to the lake. Unlike us, she'd stayed hidden amongst the trees, and filmed the whole thing. I have to admit that despite my internal scoffing when she'd waxed lyrical about her *law training* and her *instincts kicking in*, she really had played the evidence card incredibly well this time. However, should it come to that, I still stopped short of wanting to ask her to be my defence lawyer.

Cam remained in a medically induced coma for two days before being transferred to a trauma ward. A few days later, I googled the ward and visiting hours. I gave my name to a round woman in green scrubs at the nurses' station, where the smell was overpowering. Antiseptic and chrysanthemums. I asked where Camellia was being treated and she pointed to a private room. Peering through the gaps in the frosted glass strips on the window, I could see the room was dark but for a glowing green monitor next to the bed. I felt my stomach squirm as I gazed at Cam, her skin dull and her golden hair lying limp and greasy on the pillow. A thin tube came from her nose, and IV lines snaked into her arms. Sarah sat watching her sleep. She turned around just as I was wondering whether to knock. Her eyes grew round when she saw me, making my heart beat hard in my ears.

I couldn't just stand there, so I went inside. The door clicked shut and Sarah and I stood facing each other in the muffled darkness, the only sound the soft beep of machinery. Her face was worn and her hair lank and unwashed. But she was still so beautiful. When she sniffed, I noticed her amber eyes were full of tears, but I was unprepared for her to step forward and wrap her arms around me, squeezing me so close I could feel her heart beating against mine. I felt her hair on my face and smelt her floral perfume as I tried to hug her back, my own arms constricted by the ferocity of her embrace.

'Thank you,' she whispered into my ear.

We didn't talk about that night. We sat and watched Cam, and made occasional comments about the changing weather, the hospital vending machine, and my work at the café. The doctors had told her Cam's oxygen levels were good, and the swelling in her head had reduced sufficiently for them to offer an optimistic prognosis. She couldn't wait for Cam to wake up so she could take her home. They had a lot to talk about, she said. They needed to *work out how to move forward*. I didn't ask about Isaac.

Before I left, I squeezed Cam's hand. It was cold and clammy.

'I'm sure she'll want to get in touch with you when she's recovered,' said Sarah.

I nodded, not sure if that was true, but happy to leave it up to Cam to reach out if she wanted to. After being so intent on carving a place for myself in their lives, it felt strange to look at Sarah now and be unable to see how I would fit any more. And as we hugged goodbye, I knew she felt the same. I knew we wouldn't see each other again. Just as I knew I'd never go back to Riverdean.

Misha looked at me like she wished the café had a panic button installed when I gave her a brief outline of what had happened at the lake. She didn't believe me for one second. And neither did Kate, based on the text she sent Hen, which read: *I'm sorry to bother you, but you need to know that Dinah is having another episode. I'm no psychologist, but the story she's telling points to pathological or compulsive lying, possibly combined with some sort of narcissistic personality disorder. That's just my opinion. Just thought you should know. Kxx*

It's a strange feeling when you eventually decide to start telling the truth, and no one believes a word you say.

I decided to afford myself the satisfaction of replying to Kate's message as Hen, sending a link to a *Broadsham Chronicle* newspaper article. The item gave a vague account of the events at the party, and included a banal quote about *giving everyone space to process what's happened* from *family friend, Dinah Marshall*. I texted: *Dinny isn't lying. Perhaps you should check your facts before making assumptions.*

After that, Misha and Kate couldn't get enough of me. They wanted all the details. *What exactly happened? Who died? Did you actually see it?* I told them that, with a potential court case looming, I was duty-bound not to give away details, and had the further satisfaction of repeatedly saying, *I'm sorry, I can't answer that question,* and watching their hungry eyes glitter and their mouths twitch with frustration.

I told Hen everything too, which prompted innumerable phone calls and texts over the next few weeks. I had contemplated not telling her anything, but, as I explained to Dad when I went to visit him, there had been so many lies, I felt a new and almost compulsive urge to tell the truth.

Sometimes I worried about the inquest, and whether somehow, something would turn my innocence into guilt. But the police informed me they were now conducting a more weighty investigation into the deaths of Jamie Kerr and Archie Trent, given the comments made by Duncan in the boat. When it transpired I hadn't known either of these men, I knew there were others who would be subjected to far more lengthy spells of questioning than me.

I thought about Duncan too, and his loss of control at the lake. I wondered what could possibly have been going through his mind to believe that killing Cam was the only way forward in that moment. After all, that third drowning would inevitably have been linked to the deaths of Jamie Kerr and Archie Trent, even if it hadn't been committed in front of witnesses. But I supposed all logic had evaporated at that moment. I wondered if Vangie ever mused upon the sick irony of the accusations she'd levelled at me – that I was an unhinged fantasist who'd latched on to the group for my own obsessive motives. I wondered if she'd now truly come to terms with the fact that she'd been married to the most unhinged of us all: someone who was content to murder in order to achieve and maintain his status within their group.

I couldn't bring myself to roam around the crooked back streets of Covent Garden any more. The sight of the designer boutiques sent a sickening ache through my core. So much had happened since I'd bought that first dress for my trip to Eden House, and sat on the Tube, clutching the bag, anticipation fizzing inside me. Who would ever have imagined it would come to this?

One lunchtime in November, I found myself wandering further afield, across a bustling Leicester Square. The early Christmas baubles and lights glowed in the damp air as I forged on towards the sweet and spicy smells of Chinatown. Turning onto Wardour Street, it was only a couple of minutes before I was standing outside the glossy, black door of Eden House.

I stayed on the opposite side of the road, and thought of the world behind the door. A world I'd yearned for with my whole heart. A world I'd never truly belonged to. I knew then that I'd never have the courage to approach that door again, and felt a surge of grief that lodged in my throat and stung my eyes.

My phone pinged in my hand. It was Hen.

Hi Dinah, just checking in on you. Shall we chat this evening? Been thinking about our conversation – I love that you're seeing this as a fresh start. Can I come and stay with you soon? Like we said on the phone, we can toast to 'new beginnings and good decisions'! Hxxx

Bless Hen. She'd been floored by what had happened at Riverdean, and was on a frenzied mission to make sure I didn't spiral into the depths of despair again. This involved constantly bombarding me with hippy articles entitled things like *A Thousand Reasons to Smile* and *The Hardest Times Lead to the Greatest Moments*. For the first time, though, I allowed myself to feel touched rather than insulted by my sister's concern.

I was trying to think of a reply when the door to Eden House swung open, so I turned and strode away, desperate not to be caught lurking. Desperate not to be made to feel like an outsider all over again.

'Diana.' The voice pulsed through me like the bass from a loud speaker.

I turned and looked across the road, into the pale, sea-green eyes I'd looked into for the first time on the other side of that glossy, black door.

'Isaac.' I tried to sound strong, but a whisper was all I could manage.

We stared at each other across the street as a black cab rolled between us. He wore a smart navy jacket over a white shirt, and brown chinos.

As he crossed to where I stood, his expression fell into a frown. 'I mean . . . Dinah. How are you?'

'I'm OK.' I shrugged, not knowing what else to say.

'That was . . . pretty spectacular, what you did at the lake. I still can't believe you did that.' He stared at me in that way he did. That way that made me feel like my soul was transparent. 'I didn't know whether I should get in touch . . . it's just, with everything that happened, I thought—'

'It's OK. I really didn't expect you to get in touch.' I cleared my throat, trying to get my voice to sound normal and not tight and strained. 'How are you?'

He nodded, his lock of hair falling down over his forehead. 'I'm not too bad. Someone's buying Acanthus so that'll be out of our hair soon. I think Sarah will be relieved not to have anything left to talk to me about.'

'What about the house?'

'I think she's going to stay. We've got lawyers sorting all that stuff out. I'm going to collect the last of my stuff this weekend and I've told Sarah she can chuck the rest.' He shrugged as if he was telling me about a boring Sunday afternoon, and not the collapse of his business empire and the death of his marriage.

'How are you feeling about . . .' I didn't know how to finish the sentence.

'Duncan? Um . . . still not really managed to get my head around that one, if I'm honest.' He tousled his hair and gave me a sad smile, and I felt something clench around my heart. 'Think that's going to take some time.'

'And Vangie?'

He blew out air and shook his head. 'Harriet next door told Sarah that Vangie's selling Blackworth House and moving away with Freddie. But that's as much as I know.'

I took a deep breath, thinking about Vangie and how she'd laid my secrets bare. 'Look . . . I'm sorry about everything that—'

'Oh God, you don't need to apologise. You were the hero of the hour.' He smiled.

'But I told so many lies.'

He gave a soft laugh. 'Didn't we all?'

Those words were like a balm, sending a gentle pulse of warmth through me. *Didn't we all.*

He shifted on his feet and ran a hand through his hair again. 'Listen, I don't know your story, or why you came into our lives, but amongst the mess of everything that's happened, right now I don't have the energy to ask. I'm sorry.'

'Wow. Someone who doesn't want to ask me a million questions. That's . . . refreshing.'

A smile flickered on his lips. 'OK, one question I *will* ask you – can you guess where I'm working?'

'I have no idea.'

He gestured with his thumb over his shoulder towards Eden House.

'What? What do you mean?'

'I spoke to James, the cocktail guy, and he spoke to the manager, and hey presto – mixologist in training.'

He grinned, and I felt myself gawping at him. He looked like a schoolboy who'd just found a fifty pound note. At the age of forty-five, he'd just witnessed the death of his best friend, broken up with his wife and watched his multi-million-pound business crumble . . . And he could not look happier that he'd secured a job working behind a bar.

'I thought I knew about cocktails, but James is the business. He really knows his stuff. So he's sort of training me up. Maybe it'll lead to something. We'll see.'

'That's great.' I nodded my approval. 'You look . . . happy.'

He gave a deep sigh then, and something like guilt seeped into his features. 'I suppose . . . life has just got a lot simpler.'

I nodded. I'd been thinking a lot about Isaac and how I'd misunderstood him from the beginning. Because of his lifestyle, I'd always thought of him as a hot-shot businessman with charisma to match. Now I realised it was Duncan who was the hot-shot, and Isaac and his charisma were just along for the ride. Of course, Duncan couldn't have built Acanthus without Isaac, but Isaac really had just gone along with it when, ultimately, he would rather have been making cocktails. A simpler life did sound much more fitting for this new version of Isaac I was seeing for the first time.

But among my changed perceptions, I realised some things were the same as they'd ever been, as I saw his eyes widen and give their familiar twinkle. 'Why don't you come in and I'll show you the cocktail I've been working on today?'

There it was. I hadn't felt it for weeks, but there was the heat filling me up, pulsing through my veins and tingling my skin. I also had an image in my head. An image of me walking back into Eden House, but this time being smiled at and waved through because I was with Isaac. Because I belonged. Then I remembered Hen's text, and my promise to her about new beginnings and good decisions. 'I . . . I'm not sure that's a good idea. Sorry.'

He raised an eyebrow. 'But it's that incredibly expensive speciality cocktail you almost ordered when I met you for the first time . . . and it's free. *Forbidden Fruit.*'

'How the hell can you remember which cocktail I *almost* ordered the first time we met?'

He flashed me a coy smile and shrugged.

351

I sighed and looked down at my phone. I needed to be back at work in fifteen minutes. I quickly typed a reply to Hen's message: *Absolutely. New beginnings and good decisions. Dxxx*

I glanced up at Isaac and he twinkled down at me. 'What do you think?'

I smiled back. 'When have you ever known me to turn down a cocktail?'

Acknowledgements

I can't believe I'm actually writing an acknowledgements section to my debut novel. This is the stuff of dreams. But dreams need help and encouragement to turn into reality, and for that I have some special people to thank.

Thank you to my wonderful agent, Jo Williamson. I will be forever grateful for how positive you've been about my work, and for your continuing belief in my writing throughout our journey to get here. Your support, patience, and enthusiasm have meant the world to me.

Thank you to Sam Humphreys, not only for believing in me and my book, but for being so knowledgeable and approachable. I couldn't have wished for a better editor. Thank you to Lucy and Flora, and the rest of the Black & White team for all their enthusiasm and expertise.

Thank you to my Curtis Brown Creative friends, CBC Novelists, for the unstinting support and banter via our international WhatsApp group. It's so wonderful to be part of a group of writers who champion each other, and check in with each other through the ups and downs of this crazy world of writing we've landed ourselves in.

Thank you to Becs for being my first writing partner, and such a supportive friend. Our Fiction Fridays started this whole thing off – one of our weekly prompts leading to the novel that secured me my agent. Who knows how many hundreds of stories, articles, books, competitions, and flash fictions we've shared since the beginning!

Thank you to Laura for being such a great beta reader, saying yes to reading everything I write and giving brilliant feedback however manically busy you are. Thank you Liz and Paul for the endless chats about writers and books and all things theatrical, the drinks and the laughs, and for your endless words of encouragement and belief.

Thank you to Jericho Writers, Curtis Brown Creative, The Writers Bureau and Faber Academy. Thank you to Fraser for taking the time to create such beautiful animations of the book.

Thank you to my parents, Thirza and Rick, for always believing I could, and should, do anything I wanted to, whether that was being a musician, singer, actor or writer. You've always let me know you were proud of me as I've galivanted off down these unpredictable, rejection-strewn career paths, and your pride and support have given me the confidence to believe in myself.

Heidi and Maeve, I love you to the moon and back (and all around the stars and the planets a million times). Maeve, you make us laugh so much, and, although you don't understand all this book stuff yet, your hilarious energy has cheered me up so many times on this roller-coaster of a journey. Heidi, you are such a gorgeous, sunny, positive person, and have been such a huge cheerleader for me, always asking questions so you can learn about writing and publishing, and always striving to understand what news we're waiting for and why it's important. I will always remember us holding hands on the kitchen floor whilst I had the phone call telling me my book was going to be published.

Thank you to my wonderful husband, Ollie. I love you, and I love how enthusiastic a champion you've been for me. From the day I first showed you a story I'd written, you've raved about my writing to anyone who'll listen, never once making me feel I was being silly or over-indulgent for wanting to pursue this. I know you are as excited as I am about the whole thing. I could not wish for a more supportive husband. Thank you for just being brilliant.